welcome to paradise

welcome to paradise

paradise

the kincaids, book one

ROSALIND JAMES

author's note

This is a work of fiction. Names, characters, places, and incidents are products of the author's imagination or are used fictitiously and are not to be construed as real. Any resemblance to actual events or persons, living or dead, is entirely coincidental.

table of contents

america alive 1885:
the contestants

♡

*M*ira *(Almira Grace) Walker,* 28, management consultant, Seattle, Washington. Enjoys "getting to see my friends when I'm home. Walking, bike riding, and just being outdoors in beautiful places."

Scott Mitchell, 29, corporate attorney, Seattle, Washington. Enjoys "basketball, Muay Thai...anything that's competitive. The tougher, the better."

Alec Kincaid, 32, software engineer, Los Gatos, California. Enjoys "working. Oh, you mean hobbies?"

Gabe Kincaid, 32, sports medicine doctor, Fremont, California. Enjoys "strength training, rock climbing, trail running, skiing. I don't have time for any of it, but I do it anyway."

Arlene Filippi, 43, textile designer, Boston, Massachusetts. Enjoys "weaving, sewing, baking from scratch."

Martin Deveraux, 41, professor of cultural anthropology, Boston, Massachusetts. Enjoys "genealogy, hiking, and research in my field."

Lupe Garcia, 45, home health aide, Minneapolis, Minnesota. Enjoys "cooking and spending time with my children and grandchildren."

Maria-Elena Garcia, 18, student, Minneapolis, Minnesota. Enjoys "hanging out with my friends, beauty, and fashion."

Chelsea Santangelo, 23, model/actress, Los Angeles, California. Enjoys "Bikram yoga, Pilates, beach volleyball, singing and dancing."

Melody Foster, 23, model/actress, Los Angeles, California. Enjoys "living in California, going out dancing."

Stanley Douglas, 65, assistant principal (retired), USMC (retired), Mount Airy, North Carolina. Enjoys "my kids, my church family, fishing, watching sports."

Calvin Douglas, 28, PE teacher, Raleigh, North Carolina. Enjoys "basketball, everything about it: playing it, coaching it, watching it."

Zara Carrington, 66, singer/songwriter, La Jolla, California. Enjoys "music history, hearing music in my head, and hanging around with my husband."

Hank Carrington, 65, singer/songwriter, La Jolla, California. Enjoys "getting paid to sing with my wife. Best job in the world."

Kevin Holtzman, 36, bartender, Portland, Oregon. Enjoys "the gym, music, and, OK, I admit it, the occasional club."

Rachel Holtzman, 39, river raft guide/ski instructor, Bend, Oregon. Enjoys "river rafting and skiing, obviously. Kayaking, backcountry skiing, rock climbing…if it's outdoors, I'll do it."

alpenglow

♡

"We are in the middle of friggin' nowhere."

Gabe Kincaid looked across at his brother in amusement. Alec had one hand on the steering wheel, the fingers of the other drumming on the leg of his Levi's as he gazed disgustedly through the windshield at the rolling hills that extended into the distance, the long stalks of green—grass?—wheat?—Well, some kind of crops, anyway, undulating in the wind like waves across a limitless sea.

"That's the idea," Gabe said mildly. "It's the Palouse. It's not supposed to be Silicon Valley."

His twin grabbed for the water bottle in the cupholder between them and took a long swig. "At least find another radio station," he complained. "I swear, this is the same song we just heard."

"The trouble with you," Gabe said with a grin, "is that you aren't sufficiently open to new experiences. And that you don't pay attention. This guy is leaving his tears on the jukebox. The last guy was falling in love."

"Well, it all sounds the same to me," Alec grumbled. "And I thought there were supposed to be cows in the country. I haven't seen another living thing for an hour."

"The change is going to do you good," Gabe promised. "And pay attention. We're about to get into Pullman."

"Thanks for warning me. I might have gotten all flustered by the traffic lights. We could have ended up in Canada."

Gabe laughed. "You need to learn to focus on one thing at a time. This is a perfect chance to start."

"I focus just fine." Alec slowed as they entered the small university town, took the turns that led him past Washington State University and onto the highway that led to the neighboring town of Moscow. "Nobody who's spent as many hours in front of a computer screen and drunk as much Dr. Pepper as I have in my life can be accused of not being able to focus."

"You need to focus on what matters," Gabe said quietly, serious now. "Your inner life."

"Thank you, Deepak Chopra," Alec said tersely. "I don't have a whole lot of desire right now to look at my inner life."

"Which is why you need to do it." Gabe knew that, for all his brother's protests, on some level he recognized the truth of what Gabe was saying. In fact, they both needed a break, a chance to take the deep breath they'd been unable to find time for amidst the hectic pace of their lives.

"Stop it," Alec said now.

"What?"

"Your Spidey Sense. Knock it off. Quit looking inside me. I'm fine. I said I'd do this with you, and I'm doing it. And we just crossed the state line. Welcome to Idaho."

♡

"That's it ahead," Gabe pointed out a few minutes later, as Alec pulled to a stop at yet another red light in the sparse evening traffic. "The University Inn."

"Right across from the field full of cows. The booming metropolis."

Gabe smiled, then ran his tongue across his teeth. "Well, I'll be glad to get there, myself. This bonding road trip has got me stiff. And I need to brush my teeth."

"Damn."

"What?" Gabe asked in alarm.

"I left my toothbrush back at the motel."

"Well, you're not borrowing mine."

"Right. We're going to the mall." Alec belatedly put on his left blinker, waited for the two oncoming cars to proceed through the intersection. Heard a loud blast on the horn from the car behind him before the driver swerved around and passed on the right with a screech of tires and a parting one-fingered salute out the driver's window.

"Asshole," Alec muttered as he turned into the lot. "So much for country values."

Ten minutes later, toothbrush duly purchased, they pulled into the University Inn parking lot and gratefully emerged from the car. Driving all day was never going to feel good, not even in a Mercedes. Alec went inside for the keycard, while Gabe began to haul out suitcases, then stopped in his tracks.

A couple spaces beyond, a young woman stood next to a glossy black BMW with its door open, her gaze turned up to the eastern skyline. Gabe could see why. The view was tinted a rose pink that lay softly over the mountains, giving them an almost ethereal glow.

She sensed his presence behind him, turned with a warm smile that was a perfect complement to the light bathing the landscape behind her. Her soft pink mouth curving, a sudden image of his teeth sinking into that plump lower lip flashing straight through him, waking his body up fast. Her smile rising all the way to the wide-set eyes that shone with happiness beneath dark winged brows.

"Alpenglow," she told him.

"What?" he asked stupidly.

"That's what they call that pink thing. Alpenglow. Isn't it beautiful?"

"Yeah," he smiled slowly. "It sure is."

She nodded, looked back at the mountains with a sigh, leaving Gabe free to take in the view that interested him most. She wasn't especially slim—in fact, she was downright...rounded. Arms, breasts, hips, it was all there, all the good stuff. A nicely defined waist, too, in a slightly crumpled short-sleeved summer dress that flared out at the hem, fluttered a little in the breeze. Long, shiny brown hair caught on the side of her head in a simple braid that reached nearly to her hips, ended in a curly tail.

All right, she was attractive. A pretty face, nice hair, a beautiful smile. But she wasn't gorgeous. Why was he staring at her?

"Cute," Alec said quietly beside him.

"Yeah." Gabe gave himself a shake and began to turn away.

"Hey." The man was striding quickly across the parking lot. Light brown hair, parted neatly. Slim and tall, somewhere between Gabe's six foot and Alec's six-two. And, Gabe realized, the same asshole who'd flipped them off earlier, at the light. Frowning, now, as he came to join the woman. "What are you doing? I've been waiting for you."

"Sorry," she said. "I was just looking at the view."

"Did you get the car cleaned out?"

"Not yet."

He sighed impatiently. "I've got all our stuff inside already, *and* unpacked, while you've been standing here. Could you get a move on, please? I want to go to dinner."

"Sorry," she said again. "It's just so beautiful."

The man smiled tightly, still not acknowledging Gabe or Alec, who had come up to stand beside his brother and watch the pair. "All I'm asking for is a bit of focus here, sweetie. Eyes on the prize, remember? Can you do that for me?"

"Of course," she said. Gabe could see the flush spreading up her cheeks, her embarrassment at the reproof in front of strangers.

Not his business, he reminded himself. None of his business at all.

♡

"Love her, hate him," Alec said a few minutes later as they watched the young woman head into the motel, loaded down with a trash bag and various odds and ends.

"Yeah."

Alec shot a look at him. "You OK?"

"Anger management issues." Gabe looked at his brother wryly. "I was ready to take him out for a minute there. Haven't felt like that in a long time."

"You probably just need to get laid," Alec said practically, pulling his bag across the lot. "How long has it been?"

Gabe smiled. "Too long."

"Anyone since Crystal?"

"Nope." Gabe stood back as Alec used the keycard on the motel door, then humped his suitcase and pack inside. "Too busy."

"Bro, you're never too busy for sex."

"All right. Not in the mood, then. Tired of all the drama. I don't have the energy for it anymore."

"That's why I don't do the drama." Alec lifted his suitcase onto the bed, eyeing the dark green quilted synthetic spread with distaste. "Keep it light. You don't have to get involved, you know. As long as you're upfront about what you want, where's the harm?"

"Maybe I'm just not a damn rabbit, like some people. And by the way," Gabe said seriously, pulling a luggage rack from the closet and lifting his own suitcase onto it before unzipping it. "Be careful, while we're here. These are close quarters we're going to be in. Strings are most definitely going to be attached. You do your player stuff, and we're going to find ourselves out on our asses."

Alec laid a hand over his heart. His mouth was solemn, but his dark blue eyes, the only feature identical to Gabe's, laughed at his twin. "I solemnly swear that I will keep it in my pants for the duration. Now all we have to worry about is your Sir Galahad impulses."

"No problem. I'm tired of rescuing," Gabe assured him. "I've lost the desire to solve anybody else's problems. I'm not even all that confident anymore that I have the solutions. I just want someone...happy, I guess. Happy and fun, to hang out with. Are there any women like that?"

"Not for an ugly bastard like you," Alec said cheerfully.

a double dose of hot

♡

"Aren't you ready yet?"

Mira started at the demand, uttered so abruptly from behind her, almost burned herself with the iron she'd borrowed from the front desk.

"Just getting the wrinkles out," she promised, setting the iron down on the bedside table and picking the dress up from the bed. "Five minutes."

Scott looked at his watch. "You know I hate being rushed. We have to be in the ballroom to meet everyone at ten. Why couldn't you have done it last night when we got in?"

"Sorry. Five minutes, I promise." He was in a bad mood because he was nervous, she knew. Once they got through the initial orientation and he knew what to expect, he'd do better. Until then, she'd just keep from annoying him further. She'd had plenty of practice at that after years of bouncing between her parents' various households. If there was one thing she was good at, it was not making waves.

Ten minutes later, Scott was shifting impatiently from foot to foot at the hostess stand of the motel restaurant. A busy waitress glanced across at him as she filled coffee mugs. "Be right with you folks," she called, then bustled over and grabbed menus.

"Good morning," she said cheerfully, leading them to a table by the window, with its uninspiring view of the parking lot and the field of cattle across the highway. "Coffee?"

"Please," Mira said.

"A cappuccino for me," Scott corrected.

"Sorry," the waitress said. "We don't serve espresso drinks."

"Coffee, then," he sighed.

When the waitress came back with their coffee, she brought something else too. The two men from the evening before, whom she was clearly planning to seat next to Mira and Scott. They both smiled at her in recognition as they approached, and she found herself smiling right back. It wasn't hard to do. Both men were dressed in worn Levi's that clung in all the right places, and T-shirts that stretched across broad chests. Both had dark brown hair, though the shorter one's was darker, almost black, and wavier than his—brother's? It must be, she decided. They looked too much alike to be anything else, though the taller one was leaner, not as deep through the chest or as wide across the shoulders. More handsome, too, his features a little more finely hewn, brow ridge and cheekbones a little less harsh, and a straight, strong nose instead of something that looked as if it had been broken, once upon a time. She wouldn't kick either of them out of bed for eating crackers, though. There was so much warmth, too, in both sets of dark blue eyes, the generous, well-formed mouths. They were a double dose of hot, that was for sure. Was this what Idaho men looked like?

"Grace." Scott's voice broke in on her thoughts as the waitress came to their table, order pad in hand. "What do you want?" He hadn't seen the men, she realized, from his position with his back to them.

"Oh! Just eggs. The two-egg breakfast, I guess. Whatever," Mira said, looking belatedly at the menu.

He nodded. "This show's going to be good for both of us. More exercise, less to eat. But I guess you might as well have one last big meal before we start."

Was that about her weight? She knew he was disappointed that she hadn't been able to follow the gym routine he'd set up for her in preparation for the show. She smoothed her dress over the slight rounding of her stomach, wishing it were flatter. Those last ten or fifteen pounds never seemed to come off. Too many breakfast meetings, too many restaurant meals, too many late nights in strange offices.

Not for the first time, she wondered if agreeing to do this with Scott had been a good idea or the biggest mistake she'd ever made. It was one thing to date someone during her breaks between assignments, she'd begun to realize. And another thing entirely to be with him twenty-four hours a day, especially the way he'd been acting lately. He'd started out being so nice to her. Had flattered her, sent her flowers, taken her out to the best restaurants. But that was a good year ago. Lately, it seemed like nothing she did pleased him, no matter how hard she tried. The drive from Seattle the day before, with Scott anxious, jumpy, and snapping at her at every opportunity, had been a long six hours.

He was frowning again now as the waitress seated another party at a big interior table next to theirs. A couple with three young children, the eldest of whom, a boy of about ten, walked and seated himself with difficulty. Cerebral palsy, maybe.

"Great," Scott muttered. "Kids."

"They have a right to eat too," she said, keeping her voice low.

Scott averted his eyes from the family as the waitress bustled up with their food. He buttered his toast and took dubious bites of egg, picked at the well-fried hash browns.

"It does feel daunting," Mira told him, working her way through her own meal with guilty pleasure. She loved English muffins, no matter what Scott said about the virtues of whole-grain toast. And who knew what they'd be eating tomorrow, or how hard it would be to make it? "But everyone will be in the same boat, surely," she went on. "I can't imagine they'd have chosen any survivalists or experts for the show. That has to be the appeal—to watch regular twenty-first-century people trying to live in 1885. Everyone else will be nervous too, and struggling as much as we are."

"I'm not going to be struggling," he retorted sharply. "I've done my homework, and I'm in great shape." His critical gaze swept down her torso. "I'm just worried about whether you're going to be able to handle it."

So if they were voted off, it was going to be her fault? "I'll do my best," she said, a rare flash of anger giving an edge to her voice. "That's all I can promise. But I'll be doing that."

Why did everyone doubt that she could do this? She was a hard worker, she got along with people, and she was pretty good at observing and evaluating their interactions. Surely all those things would help her. But her father, too, had thought little enough of her chances. And had been downright appalled at her choice to do the show in the first place.

"*What?* Why?" Dr. Steve Walker, plastic surgeon to Seattle's finest, had demanded when she'd paid him a duty visit at his Mercer Island home to say goodbye. "What about your job?"

"I took a leave." She could feel herself starting to get flustered already. So much for the self-assured announcement she'd practiced aloud on the drive across the bridge. "It's only two months.

"And what did Jeff say about that?" he pressed, referring to the partner who was her direct supervisor. And, unfortunately, Steve's former patient and current golf buddy.

"Well, he wasn't too happy," she admitted. "But there'll probably still be a spot for me afterwards, he said."

"Probably? Probably doesn't cut it," he snapped. "I pulled strings to get you that job. And you're going to throw it away in order to be on some trashy reality show that you probably won't last a week on anyway? How is that going to make me look?"

"I've been at that job for five years, though," she said, hating how defensive she sounded. Her father might have got her the job, but she wouldn't have kept it if she hadn't been good, she reminded herself for the hundredth time. "It seemed like time to reevaluate. And the show isn't trashy. It's on the History Channel! I thought it might be fun, and a good challenge." She'd dared to hope that he might admire her for trying it. Clearly, though, she'd been wrong.

"It sounds fun to me too," Becky, her father's third wife and barely ten years Mira's senior, said from her spot on the couch beside her husband. "Too bad you're doing it with Scott, or I might just have decided to join you."

"Like hell you would," Steve growled.

"Oh, quit being so grumpy," Becky laughed. "I didn't do it, did I? And Mira's right, it'll be good for her. She'll be putting herself to the test. I've seen that show, and so have you. It doesn't look easy. The physical aspect, or the strategizing and maneuvering either. It's a great challenge."

Maybe it was the softening of age, or just Becky's confident personality, but Mira still marveled at the way her husband's frequent impatience seemed to bounce off his latest wife's armor without making a dent. And at his obvious affection for her, the attention he paid to her in spite of, or maybe because of, the fact that she defied him so often. An affection and attention he had certainly never showed his first two wives, or Mira herself for that matter.

"I have seen it," Steve said grudgingly. "You and I could have done it. But that's because we're tough enough to handle it. Whereas Mira...Well, Scott will figure out how to come out ahead, if anyone can. She can listen to him."

Becky looked unconvinced. "Listen to your own instincts," she counseled a few minutes later, hugging Mira goodbye at the door. "You'll do great. And I really *am* envious. It sounds like a wonderful adventure. Go for it. Give 'em hell."

♡

Movement in the corner of her eye, a sudden clatter, wrenched Mira from her thoughts, had her turning toward the next table. The oldest boy, who'd been struggling with his meal, had knocked the corner of the plate with a clumsy hand, sent it tipping over the edge of the table and falling to the floor, knocking over his glass of orange juice along the way. Juice and scrambled egg flew, a fair amount landing on Scott's pant leg. He reached down with a look of disgust on his face to wipe the light material with his napkin, and glared across at the family.

The brothers had turned as well at the noise. Now, the shorter one got up, came over and picked the plate up off the floor, set it on a nearby table together with the overturned glass. He smiled at the boy, who was scarlet with embarrassment and attempting a flustered apology.

"Could happen to anyone," the man said cheerfully as the waitress hurried over to clean up. "Here." He reached for the plate of toast at his own place. "I'm not eating this. Something for you to work on while they bring you another egg or two." He winked at the boy, sent a reassuring smile to his parents before sitting down again.

"Sorry," the boy's mother said to Scott, seeing him osten-tatiously dipping his napkin into his water glass to clean the spots that remained on his pants. He nodded curtly, but didn't respond.

"It's all right," Mira told her hastily, her embarrassment rising at Scott's ungracious response. "No harm done."

"Let's go," Scott told her. He shoved his chair back, knocking into the chair of the darker-haired man sitting directly behind him, causing his own eggs to fly off the fork he had begun to lift to his mouth.

The man reached for his napkin as Mira watched, wiped egg from his shirt, then grinned across at the boy, who smiled happily back at him. "See? What did I tell you?" the man said. "Could happen to anybody. And yes, you're excused," he said pointedly to Scott, who, Mira realized with chagrin, still hadn't apologized. Well, no chance he was going to now.

♡

Back in the room, she set quietly about brushing her teeth, checking her hair. Scott came up behind her as she straightened up after rinsing her mouth, wrapped his arms around her from behind and reached around to kiss her cheek.

"Sorry. I'm just really stressed about all this," he said. "You still in it with me?"

She smiled reluctantly back at him. "Of course. And I do understand. I'm nervous too. But...I was embarrassed back there, for that boy. I wish you'd told him it was OK." She didn't mention the man. She had the feeling he could fight his own battles.

"I can't help it. I don't see why people have the right to take kids like that out in public and make everyone else uncomfortable. They should get a babysitter or something, don't you think?"

"No," she said, stepping out from the circle of his arms. "I don't. Maybe you just shouldn't look, if it bothers you."

"Well," he said with his best smile, "I guess I'll just look at you. You look pretty good." He took her hand, turned her to face him, then bent down and kissed her. "Still got that focus?" he asked. "I need you at a hundred percent. You can do that for me, can't you?"

"Yes. I said I would, and actually, I'm looking forward to it. The chance to take a real break, think about what I want to do next."

"Recharge your batteries, get a better attitude so you can go back and grab that promotion," he suggested.

"Yeah," she said. "I guess."

introductions

♡

Mira gave a final tug to her dress, checked that all her buttons were fastened one last time before following Scott into the hotel ballroom twenty minutes later. Two rows of chairs sat unoccupied save for one middle-aged couple, talking intently together. Several other people were standing around, looking at the cameramen, the twisting cables attached to huge light setups. Somehow, it made it all seem real. They hadn't even started yet, and they were already being filmed.

Mira smiled at a tall, broad, older African-American man who moved forward, his kind expression a contrast to his powerful body. "Hi," he said. "Another brave soul taking the plunge, I see. Stanley Douglas."

"Mira Walker." She offered a hand that he accepted, pressing it gently and quickly before releasing it. Clearly a man who knew his own strength, and was used to harnessing it. "And Scott Mitchell," she added.

"My son Calvin," Stanley said, gesturing to a smaller, much leaner version of himself standing nearby, his expression less amiable than his father's.

"The token Black men," Calvin said. "It's just us and the Latinas, I guess." He nodded to two women talking to an older couple nearby. "Minority Number Two."

"You think the four of us are the only people of color who applied?" his father asked. "And yet they selected us, us four individuals. Nobody's asking you to represent your race, just like nobody's asking Mira here to represent hers."

"Pop," Calvin sighed. "You don't really believe that."

"That's how I choose to look at my time here," his father corrected him. "I can't be fussing about what anyone else thinks."

"Have you met the others?" Mira asked, uncomfortable with the topic.

"Yeah." Calvin raised his voice a bit, caught the eye of the woman and girl to his left. "Lupe and Maria-Elena Garcia, do I have it right? I'm trying to remember names."

"That's right," the woman said, coming forward to meet Mira and Scott. "I'm Lupe, and this is Maria-Elena, my daughter. I'm so excited," she said, patting her considerable chest with her hand and laughing a bit at herself. "I can't believe they chose us. I didn't think we had a shot."

"Demographics," Calvin began, then subsided at a warning glance from his father.

"You have got to be kidding me," Mira heard Scott mutter. Turned to see what had incurred his displeasure now, and felt her breath catch.

It was the two men from the coffee shop. She could see the moment when they caught sight of Scott, clearly surprised and not any more pleased than he was. Her own sudden shortness of breath had nothing to do with the potential awkwardness of the situation. Something about the dark, slightly tough look of them seemed to go straight to her...heart.

"Who are they, do you know? Because they are, like, totally smokin'," Maria-Elena said, sounding a bit breathless herself, brown eyes wide in her plump, pretty face.

"And way too old for you," her mother said.

"*Mommm,*" Maria-Elena protested. "They are *not.*"

"They've got to be thirty, at least. Too old," her mother repeated, to the accompaniment of an exasperated sigh and an eye-roll from her daughter.

A door at the front of the room opened, interrupting whatever would have come next. Mira recognized the man who came through it instantly. Cliff Talmadge, the show's host. Just as blond and surfer-handsome as she recalled him, and with a magnetism about him that drew the eye, but smaller than he appeared on television.

"Hi, everyone," Cliff said to the faces that quickly turned his way. "If you'll take a seat, we'll get started."

Scott steered Mira to the opposite side of the rows of chairs from the dark-haired men, next to the middle-aged couple who'd remained firmly planted there as the others had mingled.

"Looks like we're mostly here," Cliff said, looking around. "Go see if you can round up the last two, would you?" he asked a young man hovering nearby who seemed to be some sort of production assistant. "Never mind. Here they come now."

Everyone turned to look behind them. The two young women certainly made an entrance. Blonde, tanned, and thin, they immediately made Mira feel frumpy. No question why these two had been chosen. They looked around, seeming not in the least discomfited at being the last to arrive, and immediately made a beeline toward the two dark-haired men, giving an almost identical flick to their hair as they took their seats.

"So, now that we're all here," Cliff went on smoothly, "Welcome to *America Alive: 1885.*" A smattering of applause greeted his pronouncement. "We're here to take you back into the nineteenth century. With a couple small differences. Because of course, they didn't have these guys around then." He gestured to the two cameramen, one of whom was filming him, the other with his lens pointed towards the group on the chairs. "Let me introduce Mike and Danny, our lead cameramen. They're going to be your shadows, together with some other guys you'll meet as we go along. I know it feels strange now, but trust me, within a few days you'll have forgotten all about them. That's their job, to be invisible. But anything you don't want them to see…Well, you'd better not do it."

A nervous laugh or two, a murmured burst of conversation at that one. Cliff began to speak again, broke off at a hand raised in the audience by the man sitting next to Scott. "Yes?"

"I'm sure I speak for all of us," the man said, "when I ask why we were selected in groups of two. That's never happened on *America Alive* before, as you know. I believe we're all curious. Perhaps you wouldn't mind enlightening us now."

"Ah," Cliff answered good-humoredly. "That'd be telling, wouldn't it? We've got to keep you guessing a little, and the audience too, now that we're into our fifth season."

"When will we find out?" Scott asked abruptly, almost interrupting Cliff. "How we're going to be divided, or whatever it is that you're not telling us? How the game is going to be set up?"

"We'll get into all that later," Cliff promised. "Right now, let's have you get to know each other a bit. Maybe you two would like to start," he said to the man who'd spoken first. "Just tell us your names, a few words about where you're from and what you do, why you came on the show. Besides the million dollars, of course," he added to another laugh.

"Martin Deveraux," the man, thin and fortyish, said.

"And Arlene Filippi," the heavier dark-haired woman next to him cut in. "We're from Boston," she went on. "We're keenly interested in the negative impact that modern technology has on personal relationships and family dynamics. In fact, we've set up our own home as a technology-free zone, and we try to keep our children's life simple too. No TV, no video games, no iPods," she said proudly. "When we heard about this show, we felt it was the perfect chance to truly experience life as our great-grandparents lived it, and to model that simpler lifestyle for the rest of the country."

Mira heard a snort, and turned to her right to catch the devilishly dancing eye of the man sitting beside her. He raised his eyebrows comically, and she had to fight the urge to giggle. But it was their turn now, and Scott was speaking.

"I'm Scott Mitchell," he said. "And this is my girlfriend, Grace Walker."

"Mira, actually," she broke in. "I prefer Mira."

"I'm an attorney in Seattle," Scott went on, "and...*Mira*," he added after a pregnant pause, "works for a management consulting firm. I came on the show because I enjoy a challenge. And by that, I mean I enjoy winning. I'll just warn everyone now," he went on with a jocularity that, Mira thought with an inward squirm, probably didn't deceive anybody, "that I'm a pretty fierce competitor, in *and* out of the courtroom. I'm in it to win it."

The introductions went on. The couple next to them were brother and sister, it turned out, Rachel and Kevin. Lupe and Maria-Elena, Stanley and Calvin, she'd already met. The blondes, Chelsea and Melody, were former college roommates ("sorority sisters, betcha anything," Kevin murmured beside her, forcing her to suppress another giggle), and were currently "breaking into acting" in Los Angeles. And then the two dark-haired men. Mira leaned forward to get a better look as the taller one spoke.

"Alec and Gabe Kincaid," he said easily. "Brothers. Twin brothers, actually. San Francisco Bay Area, these days. I'm a computer geek. And Dr. McDreamy here," he said, slapping his brother on the shoulder, "is the real deal. A real live doctor. Anybody want to break a leg or have a baby out here, Gabe's your boy."

That had her sitting back in her seat with a thump. And the blondes leaning in a little closer as Gabe put up a hand in protest.

"I'm not here as a doctor," he said. "Let's get that clear right up front. My malpractice insurer would kill me if I started doing anything medical out there. I'm sure there's help standing by." He gave Cliff a quick glance that was answered with a nod. "You get a blister, I'll take a look. Anything worse, call for help."

Mira was still readjusting when the final couple began to introduce themselves, but looked up in surprise as she heard the woman give their names. Hank and Zara. Hank and Zara Carrington, to be exact.

Wow. Her mouth formed the word as she exchanged a wide-eyed glance with her friendly neighbor.

Although she hadn't yet been born during their heyday, Mira had grown up listening to the sound of Hank and Zara's smoothly intertwined voices on the folk rock albums her mother loved. She hadn't recognized them by sight, of course. The photos on her mother's CDs must have been taken thirty-five or forty years earlier. Zara's trademark long hair shone silver now, pulled back from her thin face in a braid nearly as long as Mira's own. Beaded silver earrings drew attention to a long, graceful neck, and her body still looked lean and strong. Her face might be more weathered than it had been in her heyday, but her dark eyes shone with the same luminous glow, the nose and chin still faced the world with determination, and the laugh lines at the corners of her mouth gave mute evidence of her habitual outlook.

Hank's face was equally lived-in. No plastic surgery for either of those two, Mira thought, and liked them the better for it. He was lean and gray as well, his features large and not handsome, but he shared the same sharpness of eye and quirk to the corners of his mouth as his wife and longtime partner. Mira hoped that, however this show was going to be arranged, she'd get to spend some time with the two of them. Because that looked like it would be a lot of fun. And who knows, they might even sing.

"And now that we've done the hard part," Cliff said after the introductions were complete, "we're going to take a fifteen-minute break to sort out some logistics here, and give you all a little more opportunity to chat. Coffee's over on the side wall, and I strongly advise you to take advantage of it while you can. Because your life is about to get a whole lot tougher."

He disappeared through his door again, and the group stood, headed in the general direction of the coffeepot, broke into little groups.

"Hank and Zara. Well, *that's* pretty thrilling," Mira's neighbor Kevin said as they stood and waited for their turn at the coffee. Scott, she saw, was chatting to their other neighbors, the Zero Technology People, as she'd privately dubbed them. "I do love me my celebrities."

"I'm so excited," Mira confessed, "I'll probably do something embarrassing like ask them for their autograph. I grew up on their songs."

"Probably best not to say that," Kevin's sister Rachel laughed behind him. "That wouldn't be too diplomatic. But by the way, what's the deal on the name thing?"

"What name thing?"

"Yours. You renamed yourself, and your boyfriend doesn't like it? Or what?"

"Oh. No big deal. My name's Almira," she said, looking around to make sure Scott wasn't watching before adding a generous dollop of half & half to the coffee she had just poured. She turned, discovering with a start that Alec and Gabe were standing directly behind her. Only realized she was tilting her coffee cup when she felt the fiery touch of the hot liquid hitting her hand, running down her dress. She exclaimed in distress, hastily transferred her cup to the other hand and shook her right hand in the air to rid it of the scalding liquid. What an idiot. What was she, sixteen? And her dress was pale yellow. Pale yellow with brown splotches, now. *That* was attractive.

"You OK?" Alec asked her with concern. "Burn yourself?" He handed his own cup to his brother and took her hand in his, patted it dry with a napkin.

"I'm fine," she said, fully embarrassed now. "Just clumsy. I'm all right."

"Sure?" he persisted, still holding her hand.

"Positive," she said with a nervous laugh. "It just startled me."

"You were explaining your name," Alec said. "Or should I say, your dual personality." His brother stood by, his dark gaze intent on her, and she felt more awkward than ever.

"Your name," Alec prompted, finally letting go of her hand.

"Oh." She shrugged. "They're both my names. Almira Grace. I go by Mira, normally."

"Almira. Princess," Alec said. "In Arabic. Perfect."

"How do you know that?" she asked in surprise. "It's not exactly a common name. It was my great-grandmother's. Old-fashioned, I know."

"I know many things," he said portentously. "Many use-less things," he added with a charmingly sweet smile that, Mira thought, he'd used before, and often. "But they come in handy sometimes."

"Well, Scott doesn't like Mira much. And he doesn't like Almira at all. So he calls me Grace instead."

"He refuses to call you by your *name?*" Rachel said in disbe-lief. "That's not good, huh, Kevin?"

"I'd call that a major relationship red flag," Kevin agreed. "Mr. Wrong—Here's Your Sign. And I should know. Because, honey, I'm the world's expert at dating Mr. Wrong." He struck a camp attitude, hand on hip, that had Mira laughing guiltily despite his cataloging of Scott.

24

"And there he goes, flinging himself out of the 1885 closet," Rachel said, putting a muscular arm around her brother and giving him a squeeze. "Ready or not, here he comes. Can't keep a good man down."

"I can't imagine that's going to be a problem here, though," Mira said. "Not in this day and age." She looked at Alec and Gabe, who gave almost identical shrugs. Wow. They really *were* twins.

Kevin looked at her in amusement. "You haven't been around the block too many times, have you? I'm pretty sure it's going to be a problem for somebody. But it's *their* problem."

The brothers turned away as the women Mira was already thinking of as "the blondes" approached. Rachel looked after them, then turned to Mira with a grin on her friendly face, surrounded by a riot of curly brown hair as exuberant as her personality. "They've covered all the bases, haven't they?" she asked. "You've got your hot girls, your hot boys—" She nodded at the Kincaid brothers. "They outdid themselves there. Twins. Yum. Imagine the possibilities." She sighed with satisfaction. "Fun times. Anyway. Your gay guy, your African-American and Hispanic contestants, your minor celebrities, your obnoxious know-it-all couple…"

"And the couple you're hoping will break up onscreen," Kevin added.

"Who's that?" Mira asked suspiciously.

"That would be you," he answered. "That's why you're on the show. Because he is *such* a tool. There has to be somebody we all love to hate, and honey, I can already tell you're with him. That body language. Like he just can't wait to step up and show us all how it's done. And 'I'm in it to win it?' Classic."

"Come on. He isn't always like that," she said defensively. "OK, that was kind of…"

"Arrogant?" Kevin asked. "Indicative of jerkitude?"

"Kevin," Rachel scolded. "Stop it. You trying to make enemies already? That's her *boyfriend.*"

"He's nervous, that's all," Mira said. "Most of the time, he's
a really nice guy."

"We'll all see soon enough," Kevin said, clearly unconvinced.
"Reality shows are all about those stress points. That's what I
love about them."

"What do you mean?"

"Theory time," Rachel said with a grin at Mira. "Don't worry.
You get used to it."

"How much reality TV have you watched?" Kevin asked
Mira, ignoring his sister.

"Not that much," Mira admitted. "An episode here and
there. *Survivor, The Amazing Race,* this one. In the hotel room at
night, when there isn't much on."

"Why did you come on the show, if you're not a fan? Never
mind, I can already guess. Boyfriend's idea, and you went along
with it."

"It may have been his idea initially, but I wanted to do it
too." She'd surprised herself, in fact. It hadn't been the money.
She'd just wanted to know if she could do it, if she could make
it through something so tough. She'd never been camping, never
participated in team sports. But somehow, she'd thought she
might be able to do this.

"Kevin," Rachel chided, "quit being bitchy."

"Right, reality TV," Kevin said. "If you'd watched as much as
I have, you'd know that people come on the show with all these
strategies of how they're going to behave, how they'll appear to
the other contestants. And lo and behold, a week in, their true
self has come out. Because no matter how hard you try, you can't
hide who you are when you're with people 24/7. That's what
makes these shows so addictive. Especially the self-delusion part.

Bet your boyfriend thinks he's smarter than the average bear, doesn't he? Stronger, smarter, shrewder, am I right?"

"Maybe," Mira conceded. *Absolutely,* she thought. But Scott *was* strong and smart, and determined too. Was it so bad to have confidence in yourself? She'd always wished she felt as sure of herself as he did.

"One week," Kevin predicted. "And everyone on the show is going to have formed their own opinion."

Mira was grateful when Cliff called them together again after the break. She liked sharp, incisive Kevin and ebullient Rachel, but their blunt honesty had rubbed against more than a few raw nerves. Scott really wasn't coming across well, she thought in despair. Maybe there was some way to suggest—tactfully, of course—that he dial it down. He could be charming when he tried. That was how he'd attracted her, after all.

"Now," Cliff went on when they were assembled again, "time for a little history. The people who actually settled this area came from all over, just like all of you. Some from even farther— Scandinavia, Germany. And, like you, they came from all different backgrounds. Some knew how to farm, how to care for animals, and some didn't have a clue. If we were really being authentic about this, we'd just dump you out there on the bare ground with some animals and a few tools and supplies and let you fend for yourselves, sink or swim. Most of you would fail, and some of you would die. Which would be good TV, but unfortunately, these days, there are these little things we call lawyers."

He paused with the true showman's instinct for another laugh from his audience. "So we're going to do this in stages. And if you'll go back to your rooms and get packed up, we'll get to that first stage in..." He looked theatrically at his watch. "Exactly half an hour. Out front. Those of you who drove in, leave your keys with Jay here, and he'll see that your cars are stored. Otherwise, see you in thirty minutes."

"Will our arrangements there, at this first stage, be period?" Martin asked as Cliff turned to leave. "I'd like to start acclimating myself as soon as possible."

"Don't worry," Cliff answered with amusement. "You're going to get all the authenticity you can handle soon enough. Believe me, I've never had anyone say, 'I wish this was harder.'"

"We can handle hard," Scott said confidently. "We're ready."

♡

"He'd better not be on our team," Alec muttered to Gabe as they left the room after handing their car key in to Jay as they went. "I'll accidentally chop something off within a week, I guarantee it."

"Which one?" Gabe asked wryly.

"Either of them," Alec said.

"Threat analysis," he added as soon as their motel room door swung shut behind Gabe.

"Damn. I lose," Gabe said, glancing at his watch.

"Huh? Lose what?"

"I thought it'd take you ten seconds to start planning strategy once we were back here." Gabe began folding clothes and placing them into his suitcase, watching with amusement as his brother flung items willy-nilly into his own bag, tossed onto the middle of his unmade bed.

"Come on," Alec said impatiently. "You're at least as competitive as I am. You can't con me with that saintly act. We're here anyway, thanks to you. We might as well win. Biggest threats— Hank and Zara, definitely."

"Older," Gabe pointed out. "Presumably not as strong on the physical parts. Though they both look tough enough."

"And the celebrity factor," Alec said. "Don't underestimate that. Other than them...maybe Stanley and Calvin. Stanley's older too, but I'll bet he can work. Rachel and Kevin...wild card. Depends how seriously they take it, especially him. She's freaky-strong, and tough too, I'll bet. A river raft guide? Wouldn't want to arm-wrestle her. Yeah, they could do it."

"You don't think Chelsea and Melody are going to go all the way?" Gabe grinned.

"Not in the game, that's for damn sure. With you and me? I'd bet on that. Maybe together, even," Alec went on, holding a dirty shirt in his hand, a faraway look on his face. "You ever do it with two girls? Back before you became such an upstanding citizen, of course. In the football days?"

"I did a lot of stupid things back then," Gabe said dismissively. "And I don't want to hear your sordid stories either. Back to the game. Maria-Elena's too young—for anything," he added with a warning glance at his brother.

Alec held his hands out in a gesture of surrender. "No argument. I don't do teenagers. And game-wise, you're right. Not exactly a ruthless competitor—well, either of them, for that matter. Mr. and Mrs. Granola, now..."

"Mr. Granola and Ms. Hemp, *please*," Gabe corrected. "Way too annoying. They're already pissing people off. And you haven't mentioned Mira and Scott," he pointed out before ducking into the bathroom to retrieve toiletries.

"No threat," Alec said positively, reaching a quick hand out to grab the bottle of shampoo Gabe tossed him.

"He looks as strong as you," Gabe needled. "Same gym muscles. Not as strong as me, but then," he said with a mock-satisfied sigh, "so few people are. And he already told us all how seriously *he's* taking it."

"He's the guy fidgeting in line ahead of you at Starbucks, checking his iPhone and snapping at the barista for taking too long with his half-caf nonfat extra-hot latte with no foam," Alec said. "Never going to make it out here. Not a chance. Either we'll all kill him, or he'll implode."

"Bet she'll do all right, though," Gabe said. "A little quiet, but really sweet. And there's something solid there."

"Yeah, but she's with him, for some bizarre reason. That's her weak spot. What would you call that color of eyes?"

"Hazel," Gabe answered shortly.

"Almost gold. Really pretty. One hell of a kissable mouth. And the way she looks up at you, a little shy...that's nice. That cuddly body, too...She's even got freckles on her nose. I'm a sucker for freckles. She's really growing on me. Yeah, it'd be good to take her away from him," Alec decided. "For all kinds of delicious reasons."

"You're not doing that." Gabe was dead serious now as he looked at his brother.

"Quit trying to be my freaking conscience," Alec said with annoyance. "I have one of my own, you know. There's no ring on her finger. He's not treating her right, and he doesn't deserve her. It wouldn't be a sin, it'd be a public service."

"All points granted. But you're still not doing it. You're not pulling that stuff on her. She deserves something more than that."

"Whoa, boy. Going after somebody who's in a relationship? Not really up to your high moral standards, is it? And I thought you weren't rescuing anymore."

"She doesn't need rescuing," Gabe said with conviction. "She's just with the wrong guy."

"And I suppose you're the right guy?"

"You never know."

welcome to 1885

♡

"Whew." Alec fell across the narrow iron bed in the rustic cabin less than eight hours later. "Not sure how I even ate dinner. I about did a faceplant into the beans at one point there. I'm too tired to take off my boots."

"Well, you'd better do it anyway, and get your butt in the shower," Gabe told him, sitting on his own bed to untie his bootlaces. "Because I'm not sleeping next to anybody who stinks that bad."

Alec turned his head far enough to look at his twin out of one blue eye. "Don't think there'll be showers where we're going. Might as well get used to it."

Gabe pulled his T-shirt over his head and slapped his brother across the chest with the sweat-stained thing. "Up."

Shedding his filthy jeans while he listened to the water running in the tiny, metal-walled shower that took up half the space in the Spartan bathroom, Gabe permitted himself a wince or two of his own. He'd thought he was in pretty good shape, but he was going to be feeling his shoulders tomorrow. And this had only been the afternoon.

It had started out mildly enough, with a forty-five-minute trip through rolling fields of yellow and green, a few tiny towns barely more than a couple streets wide, getting ever closer to the blue mountains beyond, until they reached an area beyond the farmland, where evergreen trees were interspersed with the occasional open space. And pulled into a gravel parking lot with a long, low log building directly ahead of them, and a number of tiny log cabins scattered around. As the vans rolled to a stop, two huge, furry animals lumbered forward to greet them.

"Well, hi," Gabe said, jumping down and putting out a hand to one of the big dogs. "Who are you?"

"That's Duke." A lean man in faded Wranglers and well-worn boots had come to join the dogs. Gray hair and leathery brown skin spoke of a lifetime outdoors. "And I'm John. I'm here to show you the ins and outs of this homestead business, and Duke and Daisy are here to keep the critters away while you're out there."

Gabe gave the big head a scratch as he introduced himself. "Bernese Mountain Dogs, huh?"

"Yep. Need something of a good size where you'll be. Nothing like a good dog when a bear comes sniffin' around."

Both men turned at the shriek. Maria-Elena was pressed back against the van as far as she could get, her hands up beside her head, while Daisy nosed her pocket.

"Daisy. Come!" John ordered. The big dog turned immediately, trotting over obediently to sit at John's feet.

"She won't hurt you," he assured Maria-Elena. The others were gathering around now, grabbing the suitcases and bags the drivers unloaded from the backs of the vans.

"I don't like dogs," Maria-Elena said tremblingly, still pressed against the back of the van. "Nobody said there'd be *dogs.*"

John looked at her a bit incredulously. "You'll be mighty glad to have a dog around when the deer come to get your garden."

"I *like* deer," the girl protested. "They're pretty."

"Not when they eat your garden down to a nub, they're not," John said prosaically. "But you're going to need to get used to these guys. Come on over and meet her."

"It's OK." Gabe smiled down at the girl as she made her hesitant approach. "They're well trained. I'll stand right here by you. Put the back of your hand out for her to sniff." He took Maria-Elena's hand in his own, let the dog sniff both of them, feeling the young girl trembling at his side. "See? Now she knows you. Now just rub her head a little. That's it. All right?"

She nodded, leaned into him a bit. "Thanks," she breathed, her brown eyes full of something he recognized all too well. Oh, boy. He could have thought *that* one out better.

After that inauspicious start, they were fed a quick lunch, then separated by gender. And that was when the fun had really begun.

"We'll just do the basics today," John announced. "A little sawing, chop a little wood, get you familiar with your animals."

John's version of a "little" hadn't been Gabe's, he thought as Alec finally emerged from the shower, a thin, skimpy white towel inadequately covering his lower body. First couple days were bound to be the hardest, Gabe reminded himself, stripping down the rest of the way for his own shower.

"About time," he grumbled. "Man, I'm ready to hit the sack. A few hours of physical labor and I'm already wiped. Eight more weeks of this."

"If we're lucky," Alec corrected. He pulled on a pair of boxer briefs and lay across the bed again. "Or unlucky. Can't decide."

He grinned at the enraged yell from the bathroom, the string of curses, got up and poked his head through the bathroom door. "Meant to tell you," he told a furious, shivering Gabe. "I got you started on your acclimatization, since this whole stupid thing was your idea. Used up all that decadent hot water for you. Welcome to 1885, bro."

wood and water

♡

" I t's *dark*," Chelsea complained the next morning, shivering theatrically beside Mira. "And *cold*. Can't we have the heat on?"

Alma, their guide to women's work, 1885 style, looked at her in amused disgust. "It's almost July. You don't turn the heat on in July. Put on a sweater if you're cold. Or at least something with sleeves. Those pretty arms are going to get mighty scratched up by the end of the day, otherwise. And five is when you start, if you're going to have breakfast on the table when the men come in from their chores at seven."

"I want to look nice, though," Chelsea said, giving a tweak to the tight white tank top that barely concealed her generous cleavage. "If we're going to be on camera." She cast a glance at Stu, filming from the corner, angled her assets a bit more his way, tossed the blonde hair she'd left loose this morning in contrast to Alma's instructions. "Why can't they make their own breakfast, anyway? How hard is it?"

"Because that's not the way it works," Alma said. "Not for what you're doing, it sure isn't. Men do their part, you do yours, it all gets done. Not as easy as you think, either. Just be glad you're not pregnant, with a couple of kids hanging on your skirts."

She looked around, hands on her bony hips. "Now. Nine women in a kitchen's about six too many. Anyone here know how to collect eggs?"

"I do," Lupe said quietly. "We had chickens growing up," she explained to the others, a bit flustered at being the focus of attention, especially with Stu turning the camera on her.

"Good," Alma said. She nodded toward a basket hanging on the wall. "Take a couple of the others with you and show 'em how it's done."

"How what's done?" Arlene asked with a frown. "Don't you just go in there and pick the eggs up?"

"You have to reach under the chicken," Lupe explained. "Come on with me, and I'll show you."

"I'm coming too," Zara decided. "I've suddenly realized that my life's been sorely lacking in time spent reaching under chickens."

"Good," Alma said with satisfaction as the women left. "Not so many of us falling all over each other now. We can get something done. You," she nodded at Rachel and Maria-Elena. "I'll show you how to get the stove going. And we'll need some more wood for it." She handed Chelsea a big piece of canvas with leather handles on either end. "Here. Woodbox is about empty. You can fill it. That'll get you warm."

"Where? How?"

Alma looked at her in exasperation. "From the woodpile," she said slowly, as if she were speaking to a slightly dim child. "Fill up the carrier, bring it in here, dump it in the woodbox, go back out and get some more. Think you can handle that?"

"Yes," Chelsea said haughtily. "I just needed to know. What about gloves?"

"Gloves?" Alma asked blankly. "What kind of gloves?"

"For my hands. My nails."

Genuine amusement lightened Alma's expression. "Did you get mixed up, get on the wrong bus? This is the country, not the Miss America pageant. Your nails are the least of your worries. And you two," she said to Mira and Melody, dismissing Chelsea with one more shake of her gray head, "you can take these buckets and go get more water out of the well. Fill up both these big kettles on the stove, then bring in another bucket each. That'll do, for a start."

"There's a sink here," Melody pointed out. "Why should we carry water?"

"Because you're learning. Gol darn it, am I going to have to explain every little thing? You got a lot to learn about living in the country. Somebody tells you what to do, you just do it. You don't sit around and ask a hundred questions before you decide whether you want to or not."

"I just *asked*," Melody muttered as she left the kitchen with Mira. "God, she's a bitch."

"Well, we do have a lot to learn," Mira pointed out as they headed toward the well that stood in the space behind the big kitchen/dining hall building that formed the center of the hunting camp. "She's right about that. And it's her job to teach us."

She caught sight of Chelsea, then. No wonder she hadn't come back with any wood. She was at the woodpile, right enough. In fact, she was sitting on it, watching Gabe and Alec as they chopped wood. They were wearing plaid flannel shirts this morning against the dawn chill. How could a man look that good just by putting on a flannel shirt, tucking it into some tight jeans, and adding a pair of work boots? It really wasn't fair.

"Morning, Almira," Alec said, setting down his axe with a grin just as Gabe brought his own tool down, blunt edge first, onto a wedge set against the top of a huge log cross-section, neatly splitting it in two.

"And Melody," Alec added. Gabe looked up and nodded at the two women with a smile, causing Melody to veer off and head over to say her own good-mornings closer up.

"Morning," Mira said with a wave of her hand, crossing quickly to the well and setting down her bucket on the stone rim, then laboring to turn the handle just to pull up a single bucket-ful of water, the way Alma had shown them the day before. She kept an eye on the brothers as she worked the handle, watched as Alec gestured Melody back before splitting his own chunk of log. In the meantime, Gabe had reduced the piece he'd been working on to several chunks of firewood in a few efficient motions. She looked down to pour the water from the well bucket into her own galvanized pail, then sneaked another peek before lifting her bucket from the well again and starting back to the kitchen.

She wouldn't have minded sticking around to watch herself, but Danny was filming the scene, and her pride kicked in. It wasn't hard to figure out what the storyline would be there, and the idea of appearing on TV as one of a gaggle of girls vying for the brothers' attention like teenagers at a boy band concert made her cringe. Instead, she focused on trying not to spill any of the precious fluid from the heavy bucket. *This* was going to get old pretty quickly, especially if she had to do it alone.

She met Alma on her way through the kitchen door. The older woman stepped back to allow Mira to come through with her heavy load, an expression of displeasure on her face.

"She's headed out there to tell them what's what," Rachel guessed. "Drama on Day Two. That's what I call great television."

Mira laughed. "Yeah, I think I'll settle for being that quiet girl in the background." She dumped her bucket into the kettle on top of the stove, which was warming up nicely as Rachel fed more wood into it, and headed out for another bucketful of water. And had to step aside this time for Alma, driving a laden Melody and Chelsea ahead of her like a rather cross sheepdog with a pair of stragglers.

"Plenty of time to flirt with good-lookin' men when you're out there on the beach in LA," the other woman was scolding. "Right now, you're here to work."

"When are we *supposed* to talk to them?" Melody complained. "They're always out there, and we're always in here!"

"You see 'em when you feed 'em," Alma said. "That's the deal."

♡

"So," Zara said to the men when they were all seated at the huge wooden table more than an hour later, eating a laboriously prepared breakfast that featured only slightly burned eggs and bacon, slightly underdone biscuits, and slightly gummy oatmeal, "what did you learn in school today, kids?"

"I learned why they call cowboy boots shitkickers," Calvin grimaced, prompting a rueful laugh from every man but his father.

"Language," he growled in his deep rumble. "Ladies."

"We've heard the word," Arlene protested. "It won't burn our tender ears."

"Calvin would never have said that word in front of his mama," Stanley countered, "and you wouldn't want her to hear you say it now, would you, son?"

"No," he muttered. "Sorry."

"You don't feel that kind of double standard is really another way of infantilizing women, part of the patriarchal belief system that's kept them from full participation in society?" Martin asked, seeming genuinely interested.

Stanley looked at him in amusement. "No, I surely don't. I'd like to have heard you call Calvin's mama infantile, or try to keep her from participating. Where I'm from, you don't use that kind of language in mixed company, that's all."

"Not around here, either," Alma put in. She and John were joining the group for breakfast before the next segment of their training. "At least not with the older folks like me. And sure as heck not in 1885, would you say, John?"

"That's for darn sure," he agreed. "You all might have to learn some new vocabulary to use when you whack your thumb with the hammer. Who knows, maybe when you get back to the big city they'll think you invented some brand-new cuss words. Might start a whole new trend."

giving mira her lesson

♡

Several grueling days of training later, Mira was walking with Maria-Elena behind Alma through the woods, toward a ripping sound that cut through the quiet air. She finally spotted the source: Stanley and Martin, engaged in cutting through the trunk of a medium-sized pine with a two-man saw under John's careful eye and Mike's ever-vigilant camera.

"Wait," Alma commanded. The women stood where they were, behind the semicircle of watching men, as the tree gave way, falling to the ground with a groan and a crash of branches. "OK, come on."

She waited until the tree had finished bouncing. "Hey, John. You got a couple guys with time to show these girls how to chop wood? Be easier to learn before they're into all those skirts."

"I could do that," John said, shoving his hat back on his forehead and giving his head a scratch. "Be a relief, tell you the truth. Only one of me and eight of them, and there's a couple of 'em I don't trust a bit with that saw." He jerked a head toward where Martin and Stanley stood waiting for him. "That one, I have to babysit him every minute."

"Stanley?" Alma asked with surprise.

"No," John chuckled. "He's a good man. No, it's the other one. He's a menace."

"Better not have him do it, then," Alma said.

"Nope," John agreed. "Chop somebody's finger right off. Pret' near done it himself already. Take those brothers back with you. They look good on camera. I thought they'd be useless, being from California and all, but they know how to work, especially Gabe. I don't mind giving them a break."

He turned back to the tree and hollered. "Gabe! Alec! Come over here a minute, will ya?"

"I need somebody to teach these two to split wood for kindling," Alma announced when the brothers joined them. "I've seen you out there," she said to Gabe. "You're pretty good with your hands."

"Why, thank you, ma'am," Gabe said, clearly fighting a laugh, Alec frankly grinning beside him.

"Then take them back, show 'em how it's done," Alma said. "Because I don't have the time to spare. You won't believe this, but I'm still trying to teach a couple of those girls to peel a darn potato. I'll say one thing for you," she told Mira grudgingly, "you can peel a potato."

She turned back to John again. "You're supposed to get 'em all tomorrow, right?"

"Yep," he agreed. "Shooting lesson."

"That should be a sight to see," she muttered. "I'd buy tickets to that. Hope nobody dies. So," she glared at Gabe, "you got it? You and your brother there?"

"Yes, ma'am."

She grunted. "Your mama taught you manners. Good for her."

She stalked away, and Gabe looked at Mira, eyebrow quirked, as the four of them turned back toward the house in her wake, another cameraman having materialized to film this latest adventure.

"Somebody's got her in a bad mood," Gabe commented.

"She's getting a little frustrated," Mira said, glancing quickly at him, then away again. "The milking last night didn't go too well. Somebody screamed. Who was that?" she asked Maria-Elena.

"Melody," the girl answered immediately. "Gross!" she mimicked, jumping up and down and beating her hands against her legs. "She was all like, 'Eww! *Disgusting!*' As soon as she touched the...the..."

"Teats," Gabe finished with a smile, making her blush.

"We've got our work cut out for us, then," Alec said, stepping forward where the path narrowed, neatly edging his brother out and forcing him back with Maria-Elena. "If we're not going to get on Alma's bad side."

Mira snorted a little at that. "You're not going to do that, and you know it. She has such a crush on the two of you. I saw the size of those pieces of pie she gave you last night."

"She told me she likes a man who can swing an axe," Alec sighed in mock satisfaction. "We get you swinging a hatchet, Maria-Elena," he said, turning back to her as they entered the camp area, "maybe she'll give you a piece of pie too."

Gabe maneuvered neatly. "How about if you show her that, then," he said, "and I'll give Mira here her wood-splitting lesson."

"Oh." Mira looked around at Alec.

"Hey," Gabe said quietly, pulling the big axe out of the block and setting it carefully aside before picking up a split log. "I know I offended Scott that first day in the coffee shop. And that he doesn't like me any better now. But can you and I get past that? I'm not such a bad guy."

"What? I didn't...I'm not upset about that! I thought you were nice that morning. Well, not nice to Scott," she added honestly, "but I liked what you said to that boy. You made him feel better, I'm sure."

"What, then?" he asked. "What is it? Why don't you like me?"

"I don't dislike you," she protested, looking down and wiping her hands on the legs of her jeans.

"Come on. You hardly talk to me. You don't even seem to want to look at me. What is it?"

Her nervousness was growing by the moment. She hated being put on the spot like this. "Aren't you supposed to be teaching me to chop wood?"

"In a minute," he said, his expression hardening. "After you tell me what I've done to offend you."

"It's not you. It's...It's the doctor thing, all right?" she said in a rush. "I was surprised, that's all."

"You don't like me because I'm a doctor?" he asked, looking confused. "Believe me, it doesn't exactly turn most women off when they find out what I do for a living."

"Yeah," she muttered. "I can believe that."

"So what?" he persisted. "Oh," he realized. "I get it. You went out with a doctor. Engaged, living with him, something big like that. And he cheated on you. Notorious cheaters, doctors," he said with a rueful smile.

"No! Nothing like that. But yeah, I've known a lot of doctors, and they've tended to think they were pretty special. Pretty entitled. I always said, that was the one man..." She broke off in embarrassment.

"The one man you wouldn't marry," he guessed.

"Sorry," she said, her face crimson. "You aren't asking me to marry you. All right, you're a nice guy. Now could you please show me how to use a hatchet?"

"I'm not always a nice guy," he corrected. "But I'm a reasonably decent man, I hope. And yeah, I'll show you. Now that we've established that your father's a doctor, and a cheater, and probably not a very good guy."

"Have we established that?" she asked, startled.

"Haven't we?" She grew even more flustered beneath the intensity of his gaze as he looked down at her, seeming unaware that he was still holding the piece of wood.

"Judge me for who I am," he said quietly. "And I'll do the same for you."

She nodded in confusion. "OK." Her voice sounded far too uncertain. She cleared her throat. "OK. Sure."

"Friends?" he asked, setting down the wood at last and holding out a hand.

"Friends." She took the hand he offered, and felt her own swallowed up in it. The warm touch of him, his broad palm against hers, combined with the look on his face, sent a delicious thrill up her spine.

"Hey," Alec complained from behind them. "Do we have to change partners for Mira to get her lesson?"

"No," Gabe said, his eyes still on Mira's. "I'm going to give her her lesson."

♡

She didn't know how she managed to avoid chopping her fingers off after all. Gabe's hand over hers on the hatchet handle, his smile of approval as she got the knack of sinking the hatchet into the top of the wood, then lifting the entire assembly and bringing it back down on the block to split the thing in two. The look of him as he bent to pick up the split kindling, plaid shirt straining over those shoulders, Levi's hugging one of the best butts she had ever seen, on screen or off.

You're involved with somebody else, she reminded herself sternly. *And he's a doctor. He could still be a jerk, for all you know.* Tried to bring her temperature back down, and failed miserably.

"You all!" Alma came out and called to them, giving a welcome interruption to her wayward thoughts. "When you finish with the kindling, come on in here and get these cookies and lemonade to take back to the men."

"Thanks for the lesson," Mira said, bending down herself to pick up the last pieces of kindling with Maria-Elena's help.

"Anytime," Gabe said, hefting the box of wood. "I'm happy to teach you. Anytime at all."

"OK if we have the girls walk us back?" Alec asked Alma when they had delivered the kindling and collected the pitcher of lemonade, the basket full of cups and cookies. "They could bring this stuff back to you afterwards."

Alma nodded grudgingly. "As long as you don't dilly-dally," she told Mira. "I need you both in the garden after this."

"How's your training going?" Alec asked Mira, somehow beside her again as they began the hike back to the woods.

"Harder than I expected," she admitted. "There's so much to do. And we haven't even got there. When do you think it'll happen?"

"Soon, I'm betting. The shooting's the last big thing I can think of. Could be tomorrow, even. You excited?"

"I really am. Nervous, but excited too. We all are, I think. Well, except maybe Chelsea and Melody," she corrected. "Even Maria-Elena's got into it a bit." She heard the girl laugh from behind her, and glanced back to see Gabe helping her over a fallen log.

Alec followed the direction of her gaze and smiled. "The young ones always go for him. Every time. He's so safe."

"Safe?" Mira asked, startled. "Gabe?"

"Yeah," he said in surprise. "What, you don't think so?"

"No," she said, then stopped short. No, he didn't feel safe to her. The way he'd touched her, the meaning she'd seen in his eyes...It was heat she was sensing, not safety.

"Don't tell me my brother's muscling in on my territory," Alec complained.

"I'm not your territory," Mira said with alarm. "Or your brother's, either. I have a boyfriend, remember?"

"Yes, you do. But I'm supposed to be sweeping you off your feet here, making you forget about ol' Scott. I'm the one with the bad-boy cred that says I can do it."

"I don't believe you're a bad boy," she smiled. "You're too nice."

"Worse and worse,' he groaned. "I guess this means we're not going to be having a hot affair out here."

She laughed out loud. Outrageous as he was, he was so disarming. "I guess it does," she said, still laughing as they approached the men again. "Too bad."

♡

Gabe heard the delighted laugh and scowled. Alec, putting on the charm again. What gave him the right to pull that with Mira? He glanced at the group of men, working under John's guidance to trim branches off the big pine, and was taken aback by the look of naked hatred on Scott's face as the four of them approached. He, too, had heard that laugh, it seemed, the easy way Alec and Mira were walking and talking together, and had drawn his own conclusions. Well, Scott hadn't liked either of them, not since Day One. Nothing new there.

When the women had delivered their cookies and drinks and taken away the remains, and John had set Gabe and Alec to sawing branches along with Scott, Gabe was forced to revise his opinion. This was something new. Scott was working furiously, his expression grim, thin lips set in a hard line. He was always competitive, but now he seemed determined to outdo Alec, constantly sneaking glances at his progress across from him.

"Whoa," John said as Scott threw a large branch behind him with savage abandon. "Hang on there, son. The tree's not going anywhere. It's not a race. Slow and steady."

Scott looked up at him furiously from under his wide-brimmed hat. "I'm fast," he snapped. "Is that a crime?"

"It is if you're too wore out to finish the day," John said pragmatically. "From what I understand, you'll be seeing enough contests to satisfy even you, soon enough. No point starting them now. The tree didn't do anything to you, and these two boys didn't either. So you can just slow right on down."

Scott muttered under his breath. He backed off his furious pace a little, but the dark looks he sent Alec's way throughout the afternoon didn't bode well for the future. Gabe wasn't feeling too warmly toward his brother himself, but he made sure he stayed nearby, closed ranks in the way that was as familiar to him as breathing. Whatever else happened, he'd always have Alec's back.

"You should stop sniffing around Mira," he said abruptly when they were back in their cabin again after dinner, pulling off their sweat-soaked shirts and dirt-encrusted jeans. Gabe hung the jeans on a hook in the rough wall with a grimace. He still wasn't used to putting on dirty clothes, but he'd have to get there fast. Surely it was about time for the show to begin in earnest.

Alec laughed, and Gabe felt his blood beginning to boil. Why did women always go for his brother? Couldn't they see how little he was offering? Didn't they want more? Alec wouldn't mean any harm, but that wouldn't stop Mira from getting hurt. And Gabe was more than done with consoling Alec's broken-hearted exes. He'd had a lifetime's worth of that during high school. "I mean it," he insisted. "Quit messing with her life. You aren't serious, and it's not right."

"Calm down, Galahad." Alec hung his jeans next to Gabe's and stripped his T-shirt over his head with a groan. "Damn, I'm sore. And hard as it is to believe, she isn't falling for my devastating charm."

"She sure sounded like she was."

"She likes me. I'm *nice*," Alec said with disgust, tossing the shirt onto the floor, then picking it up with a sigh at his brother's frown and stuffing it into the laundry bag. "And you know what that means. Kiss of death."

♡

"You made kind of a fool of yourself flirting with Alec today, don't you think?" Scott was asking Mira at the same moment. She had just come out of the bathroom after a quick shower and was wrapped in one of the thin towels, her hair inadequately turbaned in another.

"What?" she asked in confusion, hitching her towel a little higher.

"Sweetie, you need to realize, guys like that are used to women wanting to get with them. You don't think he's really interested, do you? You just made yourself look ridiculous."

"I wasn't flirting with him," she protested, feeling the humiliation start to burn. Had it really looked like she was throwing herself at Alec? Had he thought so? "I like him as a friend, that's all. And I'm sure that's how he feels about me too."

"I explained this, remember? We're not here to make friends. We're here to win."

"But wouldn't it be easier to win if we *did* make friends?" She was sure she was right. Pretty sure, anyway.

"If we made alliances," he corrected. "And I've been working on that. Cultivating Martin, for one. I'm working on Calvin, too. You need to be cozying up to Arlene, like I told you. And it wouldn't hurt to get to know the blondes. They don't seem to have any alliances yet, and I know I can manipulate them to do what I want. They shouldn't feel threatened by you," he mused, "so you can probably get on their good side."

She caught his meaning perfectly. She knew she couldn't stack up against the blondes' slim, long-legged perfection, but she wasn't actually unattractive, was she? Scott hadn't used to think so, anyway. She didn't know how to pursue the topic, though, without sounding insecure and needy.

"I know I haven't watched that many of these shows," she said, pushing the uncomfortable thoughts aside with an effort, "but I do think it takes more than alliances to win. They don't always work anyway, do they? Especially if you don't have a real bond. It seems to me that developing friendships, real ones, could be as important as strategizing. And don't you think a lot of it is just about getting along with people and being helpful to your team, so they'd rather get rid of somebody else?"

"Sweetie," he sighed. "You must know how naïve that sounds. Don't you think it's time you grew up and learned how the world works? This isn't a party, full of nice people all being nice to each other. It's a *game,* and we're trying to win. We can only win if everybody else loses. That's the real world. And I'm doing all the heavy lifting. I'll take care of the planning, and any manipulating that has to be done too. The only thing, the one single little tiny thing I'm asking you to do is to follow my lead. I know you can do that."

A stubborn streak had her digging in her heels. "I think my approach could win just as well."

"That's ridiculous," he snapped, losing the patient tone. Then made a visible effort and continued. "Look, sweetheart. You may think you can charm them and get ahead that way, but let's be realistic here. You know I love you, but take a look at yourself in the mirror, and then look at Melody and Chelsea. Now ask yourself, in all honesty, do you think Alec, or any other man here, is going to be looking at you with the two of them around?"

"I never said he was looking at me," she said, trying to rally her defenses. "I know he isn't interested. *You're* the one who said I was flirting, not me." The treacherous tears had shown up, right on schedule.

"Aw. Come here," he said, pulling her to him. "Don't be so sensitive. I'm just trying to help. You don't know how guys think, that's all. They can be pretty cruel about girls who throw themselves at them. You stay away from him, and work harder to make friends with Arlene and the blondes. I'll do the rest." He tugged the towels away so she was standing naked before him, wrapped his hands in her hair, and pulled her in to kiss her.

"Scott," she protested, "my hair's all wet. You should go take your shower."

He pulled her to the bed, pushed her down onto it and came down on top of her. "Not yet. I want to do it right now."

It should be exciting, she thought in dismay, being desired like this. But she kept getting distracted by the dirty, sweaty clothes he pulled off, not to mention the dirty, sweaty body underneath them. His words had made her feel frumpy and unattractive, too, with her wet hair and her skin mottled from the evening chill in the unheated cabin.

And, as so often happened, it was too much, too fast. He'd made even less concession to foreplay than usual, hadn't kissed her, or talked to her, or even looked at her much. Just straight into the main attraction.

Relax, she told herself. She closed her eyes and tried to enjoy the sensation, but she hadn't had enough chance to get going, and it wasn't even that comfortable, let alone stimulating. Her mind began to drift as Scott continued on. And on. Driving hard, as if he were making some kind of statement.

She found herself thinking about Gabe again, the way he'd smiled down at her. *I'm going to give her her lesson.* He hadn't meant anything sexual by it. But imagine if he had. She let herself explore the possibilities of that, and began to warm at the thought. And then, as abruptly as he'd started, Scott was done.

"Was it good for you too?" he asked as always, still breathing heavily.

You are responsible for your own orgasm. If she didn't tell him what she needed, how would he know? And she was tired of mediocre sex. Or downright bad sex, nights like this. "Could you touch me some more? I need a little more to get there."

He sighed and obliged. But after ten minutes, his lack of enthusiasm, not to mention the fact that she kept having to gently nudge his hand back to the right spot, broke through the fantasy she'd been determinedly working on. She thought about faking it, but she was sick of pretending.

"That's OK," she said. "You can stop. I'm not going to get there. It's been a long day, and I'm tired, I guess."

"Yeah," he agreed, getting up and heading to the bathroom. "I'm going to grab a shower and go to sleep. I'm beat."

But when she was alone, there Gabe was, right back in her head, moving into her fantasy and taking control. Those hands, moving over her, taking their time. The dark blue eyes looking into hers as he talked to her, said all the things she wanted to hear. That mouth, chiseled but so generous, moving slowly down her body as his hands parted her legs.

Luckily, it was a long shower. And by the time Scott came out of the bathroom, she was feeling much better.

hitting the target

♡

"Right," John said the following morning. They had got into the vans again for the first time since their arrival and been taken to an outdoor shooting range, a simple affair of a few targets nailed to the face of a grassy bank about fifty yards away. "Who's shot before?" He looked at Stanley. "Bet you have."

"Me and my boy both," Stanley agreed.

"Did you serve?" John asked. "I've been wondering."

"Yeah. Marines."

John nodded. "Thought so. You've got the look."

"You were a Marine?" Mira asked.

"He *is* a Marine," Gabe put in. "That's the deal, right? You never quit?"

Stanley laughed, a pleasant rumble in the morning air. "You got it. Sounds like you've been around a few."

"Yeah," Gabe agreed. "I practice sports medicine, and I've worked with some of the amputees, once they're back in business. And when they get competitive, they mean it. Even on one leg. Especially," he grinned at Stanley, "the Marines."

"Anyone else?" John looked at Hank. "You?"

"Nope. Never in the service, and haven't shot a gun in years. It's not too dangerous out there on the folk rock circuit. Plus all that singing about peace and love, doesn't really fit the image, you know. When I was a boy in Texas, though, back before the earth cooled, I handled a firearm a time or two."

"I have too," Lupe said in her usual quiet tone. "Rough neighborhoods," she explained when the others looked at her in surprise.

"Gabe and I've done a little bit," Alec put in. "Scout camp. At least, that's the last time I shot."

"Yeah, me too," Gabe agreed.

Mira could feel Scott's restlessness beside her. He didn't like to be second-best at anything, and she knew it was rankling that he didn't know guns.

"All right, then," John said. "First thing I want to say today is, I don't care if this is the hundredth time you've heard all this, or the first. You need to listen, and listen good. Gun safety's no joke. Any time you're holding a firearm, you take it seriously. Always assume it's loaded. Always assume you could kill someone, if you get it wrong. So don't get it wrong."

"Can I just say something?" Arlene interjected.

"Go right ahead," John said resignedly.

"Martin and I would prefer to sit this out. We're pacifists, and we're not comfortable handling a weapon. We wouldn't shoot anything anyway, so there's no point in our learning."

"You planning on telling ol' Mama Grizz you're a pacifist, when she comes for you?" John asked. "Or when a pack of wolves shows up? You can call yourself anything you like. They'll just be calling you dinner."

"Bear attacks are extremely rare," Martin snapped. "And there's never been a documented case of a wolf attacking a human in the United States. I read up on it before we came."

"Have the bears and wolves signed your mutual nonaggression treaty?" Kevin asked innocently. "And what about livestock? Have wolves been given a bad rap on that too? Or do your rules of interspecies harmony require us to share our cattle with them?"

"You got a point there," John said. "A nice calf, that'd be a mighty tasty dinner for a hungry wolf pack. You aren't required to kill anything, just scare them off. Wouldn't manage it anyway, not unless you got lucky, not with the birdshot we'll be giving you. But with a 12-gauge and a good dog, you'll make 'em think twice."

"But why do the women have to learn?" Arlene objected. "If we're going to be stuck in the house all the time? There isn't likely to be a wolf in the kitchen."

"Just in case," John said. "You need to learn how to handle this thing safely, at the very least. I don't want anyone getting shot on my watch. Now, first rule: never point your gun at anything you're not intending to shoot."

Scott shifted restlessly beside Mira as the safety lecture continued. "Come on, come on," he muttered. "We get it. Don't keep it loaded, don't point it at anyone, blah blah blah."

"You said we aren't going to be able to kill anything," he said more loudly, interrupting John. "Why not? Wouldn't they have been shooting deer anyway, back then? We're going to get pretty tired of eating beans, otherwise. I'm tired of it already."

"Fish and Game might have something to say about that," John said. "Hunting season's not till October. And having you all out there with axes and saws is bad enough. Add buckshot to the mix, somebody gettin' excited and making a mistake, and we could have a corpse on our hands. I'm sure that'd be real good TV, but you probably don't want to be providing that kind of entertainment."

"Unless it was somebody *really* unpopular," Kevin murmured, his mischievous gaze darting to Scott. "I smell ratings bonanza."

One by one, after the safety lecture was concluded, the sixteen of them took turns handling, loading, and firing the old-fashioned double-barrelled shotgun. Mira waited nervously for her chance, watching Melody exclaim at the recoil, turn to Gabe to ask a question that John answered. And then Zara, handling the gun as easily and competently as she did everything else, no fuss whatsoever. And hitting the target, too.

Then John calling Scott forward, Scott taking the gun from him, going through the steps, nodding impatiently at John's reminders. Pulling the trigger...and nothing happening.

"What the hell?" he asked, beginning to turn the gun in his hands.

"Whoa!" John said sharply, knocking the barrel up to the sky. "You trying to shoot yourself?"

"It's jammed," Scott complained.

"That'd be you not pulling the hammer back. You want to check something, you break it open, like I said. We're not playing games here, and I haven't been talking just to hear the beautiful sound of my voice. When you're holding a loaded gun, you take your time, and you think about what you're doing."

Scott was red with anger and embarrassment by the time John finished. He stalked back to the group, his face thunderous, Mike's camera tracking him the entire way, glared at Kevin, who was frankly grinning at him. Mira had the uncomfortable feeling that this footage was bound to appear in the show's first episode, and that Scott knew it.

"Come on, then, Miss Mira," John called to her. "Come give this a try."

She stepped forward cautiously and took the heavy shotgun in her hands, recited John's instructions back to herself as she went through them, step by careful step, loaded, pulled the hammer back, and finally pulled the trigger, feeling the recoil hard against her shoulder.

"Good one," Alec said approvingly from beside her.

She smiled back at him, aimed again and pulled the second trigger, located behind the first, and laughed out loud when she saw that her shot had actually hit the target.

"You got a good eye," John said. "And you know how to listen. You'll do. Next," he said to Alec. "See if you can do as good as the little lady here."

"That wasn't too bad," Mira said happily to Kevin and Rachel. Scott had wandered away, still looking disgruntled, and she knew from experience that it would be a waste of time to talk to him now.

"Watching macho guys shoot guns isn't usually my recreation of choice," Kevin mused in reply. "On the other hand, watching those Kincaids do anything works for me."

Mira looked at Alec, taking his own careful second shot now before handing the gun to Gabe, and had to agree.

"I sure hope they put us with the brothers," Kevin sighed. "Even though they don't bat for my team, I could look."

"Mmm, me too," Rachel said. "Too young for me, but I'd relax my standards and go cougar for that. But you know they're going to be matching us up with Martin and Arlene, thanks to you, Bozo. You just can't resist, can you?"

"Not when he makes it so easy," Kevin grinned, unrepentant.

"I wish I did know how they're going to team us up," Mira said. "Who would you choose?"

"Besides the brothers?" Kevin gave it some thought. "Stanley and Calvin, for two. I wouldn't have to do much at all then, would I? And…mmm, probably Hank and Zara. She can cook, and they get on my nerves less than anyone else."

"I don't care much for your team selection," Rachel complained. "One other woman? Too much work."

"You wouldn't choose me?" Mira asked, hurt in spite of herself.

"Honey, I'd choose *you* in a heartbeat," Kevin corrected her. "Because you can cook too. But Boyfriend? No, thanks. Unfortunately, that's exactly why I'll end up with him. You know they'll put me on a team with everyone I already hate."

"You think that's how it'll work?" Mira asked, guiltily glossing over the insult to Scott. She knew she should be offended, but she liked the way Kevin and Rachel both said exactly what they were thinking. She wished she could do that. She was always too worried about hurting somebody's feelings.

"Of course," he said. "I keep forgetting, you don't watch these shows. They want conflict. That's what keeps people tuning in. People who absolutely can't stand each other, living in a confined space under pressure. Reality TV at its finest. So they'll stick Rachel and me with Martin and Arlene, for sure. And the blondes with either Zara or Rachel, because they're the only ones who'll yell at them for not working. You and Lupe are too nice. No fun at all. And you and Scott will be with the brothers, because he's halfway to full testosterone poisoning already, he's so jealous."

"Yeah," Mira sighed. "It seems like they do everything just a little bit better than he does, no matter how hard he tries. Especially Gabe." She blushed a little, saying his name. She felt like everyone could see what she'd been thinking last night. Worried most of all that *he* could see it. She'd carefully avoided even looking his way today, for exactly that reason.

"Honey," Kevin corrected her, "that's not the only reason. And oh, won't that make for some delicious TV."

the game changes

♡

K evin was only partially right, Mira discovered the next morning. They were surprised after breakfast by their first visit
from Cliff since arrival at the camp.

"I know you're all getting tired of practicing," he said, "and
that you feel more than ready for your adventure to begin. I'm
happy to tell you that it's graduation day. When you go back to
your cabins, you'll find a full set of 1885 clothing waiting for
you. Get yourself into those, leave everything else behind, and
come on back in here, because we're going to be taking a little
trip."

"When will we be told how we'll be split up?" Scott wanted
to know.

"Just as soon as I tell you," came the amiable reply.

"I don't know why they have to drag it out so much," Scott
grumbled to Mira as he opened the door to the cabin, went
through ahead of her. "All right, we're in suspense. Go ahead and
tell us already."

"Wow," Mira said, hardly listening as she spotted the twin
pile of clothes on the bed, began sorting through hers. "Look
at all this stuff. Yours looks pretty simple, but mine…They've
actually had to give me a drawing, and written instructions.
Otherwise, I wouldn't have a clue."

Scott held up the long cotton drawers and long-sleeved underwear top with distaste. "Am I really supposed to wear all this? What are we, Mormons?"

"You think that's bad, look at mine," Mira said, beginning to strip off her clothes. "This is going to take a *long* time. But I'm so glad to get started, I'm not going to complain. I just wish they'd let me take my notes." She looked longingly at the notebook on her bedside table. "I'd feel a lot more comfortable."

"You've probably got a pocket somewhere. Why don't you pull out the pages and stuff them in there?" Scott suggested, unbuttoning his shirt and tossing it on a chair.

"It's not allowed. I checked."

He heaved an annoyed sigh. "So you do it anyway, sneak a look when you're in the outhouse or whatever. You don't have to follow every single stupid rule people make up, you know. It wouldn't even be cheating. Just reminding yourself of what you've already learned."

"It *would* be cheating, though. How would it be any different from taking notes into a test?"

"So? You've never done that? Never written the answers on your arm, downloaded a term paper?"

"Of course I haven't." She stopped trying to figure out the new clothes to stare at him in disbelief. "Most people don't do that kind of thing."

"Most people *do*," he corrected. "Everyone cheats, one way or another. And this is for a million dollars. It's not Sunday School, it's *America Alive*. Everybody else here is going to be taking every opportunity they can. Why would you handicap us for the sake of some stupid principle that doesn't even make sense? The real homesteaders would've been doing anything they could to get ahead. It's all about survival out here. Then *and* now. It's a *game*."

"Well, I'm not doing it," she said, turning back to the Scary Underwear pile. "It's not worth it. Writing everything down helped anyway. I'll just have to rely on that to get me through."

"I sure hope you remember, then," he said in exasperation. "If you aren't even willing to help yourself. To help *us*. Lucky for us that I didn't have to write things down, at least. I have a really good memory."

She was silent as he finished dressing and left to join the others. She had a terrific memory, she fumed, continuing to struggle into the awkward clothes. *She* wasn't the one who'd taken three tries to pass the bar. She'd done better in school than he had, too. She might not be the most confident person, but she knew how to learn. She listened, she took good notes, and she worked hard. She'd never *had* to cheat, and she wasn't going to start now. Whatever she did out here, even if she struggled, she was going to know that she'd played fair.

Fifteen minutes later, she shut the door of her cabin for the last time and walked back into the dining hall, feeling horribly self-conscious and still flushed with the effort of getting into the corset. She should have asked Scott to stay and help her despite the argument, she'd realized too late. That had taken some major contortionist work.

Rachel took one look at her red face and laughed from beneath her printed sunbonnet. "You look as ridiculous as I feel," she said. "And just about as hot."

"How did you lace your corset?" Mira asked.

"Kevin," Rachel said with a grin. "He said this was a red-letter day in his life. That he'd never helped a woman with her underwear before, and he never will again."

Mira laughed. "I guess from here on, we just use these hooks at the front. I'm not messing with all these laces another time."

They were joined by Zara, looking rueful. "I never realized just how lucky I was to be born in the twentieth century," she said. "I thought girdles were bad, back in the day. That's why I became a Flower Child in the first place, just to get out of wearing them. How many things do we have on here?"

"Chemise, drawers, corset, blouse, skirt, apron," Mira counted. "Six. Not counting the bonnet thingie."

"Well, now that we're all here," Cliff said from the front, and they subsided. "I first want to say to the ladies, my, don't you look lovely." He grinned at the disgusted groans from his audience.

"Lovely as a potato sack," Zara muttered. "I looked up "unflattering" in the dictionary, and they showed me this outfit."

"The wardrobe expert asked me to tell you," Cliff continued, "that to be really authentic, we would have added a petticoat and a corset cover. But that she decided to take pity on you, especially because the weather service says that the next few weeks are going to be extra-warm. We don't want anyone fainting onto a hot stove."

"Considerate of them," Rachel agreed. "The guys look good, though. Why is it that men always seem to get off easier? They hardly even look different."

"Might take them longer to pee than us for once," Zara pointed out pragmatically, eyeing the men in their work shirts, canvas pants, and suspenders. "They've got buttons on those pants, whereas we get the convenient crotchless undergarment. Who knew the nineteenth century was so racy? It feels really drafty down there. Are we supposed to be having quickies behind the outhouse?"

Mira giggled. "No, I think we're just supposed to make it *out* of the outhouse in a reasonable period of time."

"That might be what *you're* using it for. Hank was pretty interested in the intriguing possibilities."

"And now," Cliff said, "comes the moment you've all been waiting for. Especially Scott," he said to the accompaniment of some laughter. "You've been wondering all along why we began this *America Alive* season with two-person teams. Here's the big news. You're not going to *be* in two-person teams."

He held up a hand at the murmuring and rustling in the room. "That's not quite right, though. I should say that you won't be in teams as you've been thinking of them. Instead, we'll be splitting each team between the two homesteads. But when you're voted out, both of you will be leaving."

"But how does that work?" Scott objected. He'd been standing with Martin, comparing notes. Both of them were frowning heavily now. "You mean when we're competing against each other, we'll be competing against our own teammate?"

"Exactly. You *will* be facing period-appropriate challenges every week, in true *America Alive* fashion. But your partner will be on the opposing homestead. The homestead that wins the challenge gets to decide which team goes home."

"Then what's our incentive to win?" Scott, protesting again.

"Your incentive," Cliff answered, "is to keep your homestead from wanting to get rid of you. You personally. To do that, you'll have to contribute, and you'll have to endear yourself to the other members, which may be a bigger challenge for some of you." He glanced at Scott and Martin. "The people who succeeded out here were the ones who had the skills and the fortitude to keep going, but they were also the ones who worked together well and got along with their neighbors, helped each other through the tough times, and were helped in their turn. Sometimes, you know, life really *is* a popularity contest."

He waited a moment for that to sink in before going on. "Only four of you, two teams, will make it to the end. To the final balloting, where you'll all have a hand in choosing the winning team. That's twenty-five percent, not that far from the thirty percent who actually lasted the five years and proved up their homesteads. Consider yourselves lucky. All you have to do to get there is last seven weeks, in the height of summer, and impress everyone else enough to be chosen as the winning team. But to get to that spot, you're going to have to work hard, get along, and have a little bit of luck as well. Just like the people who did this for real."

Mike's camera zoomed in on him, with Danny's panning the group, "And now," he said impressively, "here are our homesteads. In Arcadia, we have..." He paused for effect. "As I call your name, please come over and stand on my left. Arlene, Lupe, Rachel, and Chelsea, for the women. And Hank, Alec, Calvin, and Scott, for the men."

"Oh, boy," Rachel breathed, giving Mira and Zara a quick hug. "What did Kevin say. Alec and Scott. I see fireworks in my future. Wish me luck."

"And, as you've already figured out," Cliff continued, "in Paradise, on my right, we have Melody, Zara, Maria-Elena, and Mira, for the women. And Gabe, Stanley, Martin, and Kevin, for the men."

Mira followed Zara over to the spot Cliff indicated, her mind still reeling. This was nothing like she'd expected. She saw Scott's expression, and was glad not to be with him right now. All his carefully planned strategy, all his maneuvering, were for nothing. Because the game had changed before it had even started. And suddenly, they were playing by a whole new set of rules.

strategies and schemes

♡

They reassembled again out in the yard, standing together a bit awkwardly in their new homestead groups. The expectant buzz rose higher as two large wagons lumbered through the front gates, each pulled by a team of the sturdy horses the men had been working with all week, a Guernsey cow and calf tied on behind.

"Meet your worldly possessions," Cliff said as the drivers pulled the horses to a halt and Duke and Daisy came trotting out behind John and Alma. "We've even packed everything for you. Now all you have to do is get to your homesteads, and we've made that easy for you too. You're going only five miles. And I hope you've been paying attention this week, because once you get there, the drivers will be heading on back here, and it's all yours. Happy homesteading!"

"How will we all fit in that wagon, though?" Melody asked. "It's full already."

"Packed as full as it can get, and often more," Cliff agreed. "The way West was littered with all the things people threw out, as they realized they'd brought more than their livestock could haul. Which is why only babies rode. And since we don't have any babies here..." he eyed Melody speculatively, "that means you're walking."

"Five *miles?*" Chelsea asked in disbelief.

"You've been complaining about being stuck in the kitchen, haven't you?" Cliff answered cheerfully. "Here's your chance to explore the world around you. See you guys in a week. Good luck."

"I can't *believe* this," Melody complained as the wagons pulled out onto the dirt road, with Danny and Mike each hopping onto a four-wheeled ATV behind a driver, waiting to film the home-steaders as they began their hike, accompanied by the two big dogs. "Why couldn't they have dropped us off closer?"

"The historical rationale is this." It was Martin, in his usual pedantic tone. "The original settlers would have traveled for weeks, sometimes months. And when they finally did arrive, already physically and emotionally exhausted, they had to start from scratch. We're going to have already-planted gardens and fully constructed cabins, from what I understand. Frankly, I'm disappointed at that. I made a point of studying cabin-building techniques before I came, and was hoping to have a chance to put them to use. I for one am pleased that they're allowing us at least a taste of the authentic experience."

"Yeah, right, a taste of the experience," Kevin said. "More like ready-made drama. A little fatigue, a little bickering, maybe a meltdown or two...All good for the ratings."

He dropped behind with Mira as they followed the wagons out of the yard. "And I'd hate to think of living in a cabin built by Martin," he said. "There I'd be, innocently sleeping, buried under the rubble when it collapsed around me. If he didn't bring a tree crashing down on him while he was building it."

They began the long journey, staying well behind the heavy wagons to keep out of the cloud of dust raised on the dirt road. Despite the warmth of the early July day, the mercury beginning its rise now that it was after eight, Mira found herself enjoy-ing the walk. It *was* a relief to be out of the kitchen, and the countryside was so beautiful, with its rolling hills and stands of pines and firs, the tree-covered mountains looming ahead. A hawk circled in a blue sky with just a scattering of white clouds, and her heart soared right along with it. She was walking toward the adventure of a lifetime. Whatever happened in the game, she vowed, however far she got or didn't get, she was going to take everything she could from the experience.

The newly formed homesteads had been walking together, with Arcadia in the lead, but after an hour or so Scott left the group and waited at the side of the road for Mira to catch up. He pulled her back behind Zara and Kevin, with whom she'd been chatting in a desultory way, and launched into a monologue he'd clearly been mulling over for some time.

"This is a stupid ratings gimmick," he said irritably. "I've been discussing it with Arlene, and we can't see how the two-person teams can have any chemistry, how they intend to come up with a coherent storyline with us split between homesteads. I don't know what the producers were thinking."

"I guess just that it'd be something different," Mira said cautiously. "Something to get people talking about the show."

"Different because it's ridiculous," Scott snorted. "But since we can't do anything about it, we're just going to have to adjust our strategy. I've been thinking about how to do that, and I've realized that all we need to do is revise my original plan. We'll still be working with the same alliances. It's just that I won't be able to oversee your part of it as well as I was planning to."

Did he really think she was such an idiot that she couldn't figure out how to talk to people without his help? But the last thing she wanted was a televised argument. Mike had dropped back to film them, to her chagrin. She shoved the irritation down and asked instead, "What are you thinking?"

"I'll start bonding with my group," he began to plan. "Arlene and Chelsea are feeling left out and vulnerable right now. Probably Lupe, too. That's a group of four right there. I get one more with us, and we'll have a majority. Meanwhile, you should be getting friendlier with Martin. Stanley likes you too, I've noticed. Work on that, and I'll do the same with Calvin. But the main thing: cozy up to Maria-Elena and Melody. Get to be their best friend. Talk about clothes, brag about your boyfriend, all that girl talk."

"I'm not sure that's going to work. Because I'm *not* particularly friendly with Melody," Mira pointed out. "She sure isn't friendly with me. I don't think she's all that interested in women. And I'm not crazy about Martin either. I'm friends with Zara and Kevin, and I like Stanley and Maria-Elena. I'm pretty sure we could become friends, once we're living together. That's five, with me. A majority." She didn't dare mention Gabe.

"It doesn't matter who you're *friends* with," Scott said impatiently. "That's not the point. There's no way we'll win if we start out by making alliances with members of different teams. You need to be thinking strategically."

"It seems to me, though," she said carefully, "that it's going to work best if we get friendlier with the people we already like, who already like us. It's what Cliff said. The main thing is not having your group want to vote you off. And actually, you know," she couldn't help adding, "thinking strategically is my job. That's what management consultants do."

"You've never been the senior consultant on the team, though, have you?" he retorted. "You're an information gatherer, not the one who draws the conclusions. If you were, you'd see that you can't just take what Cliff tells us as gospel. That's what he *wants* you to think. Use your brain. Think it through. What's he leaving out? That when a homestead is deciding who leaves, they're also thinking about who's going to be leaving the other homestead. They'll want to leave their own homestead stronger, and the other one weaker. That's what I'm mainly worrying about, those times when your homestead wins and does the voting. And don't think for a moment that the others aren't going to be thinking about their own team. Alliances are everything out here, and we need to be on the same page with that."

"I'm not so sure you're right about that," Mira countered doggedly. She hated arguments, but his assumption that her team would want to vote her out, his dismissal of her professional experience had stung. When she'd confided her frustration in her role, she'd never imagined that he'd use what she'd said against her.

"OK," she conceded, "I'm not the senior person at work, but that doesn't mean I don't have any strategic input. And I think the homesteads might become more cohesive than you're imagining. People form tribes and cliques really easily. I've seen that a lot. It seems to me that what will matter most is who the group doesn't want to live with anymore. I think our best bet is just to work hard and get along, each of us, where we are." And she knew she had a lot better head start on that than Scott did, whatever he said.

He sighed. "Sweetheart. You know you're a little unworldly, don't you? Come on, now. You know that."

"Maybe I am," she said, struggling to maintain her belief in her opinion. "But I'm pretty sure I'm right about this."

"You're very sweet," Scott said, his tone softening now, becoming affectionate. "And that's your problem. You think everyone else is as nice as you, and that everyone plays by the rules they learned in kindergarten. Don't you think that I know just a little more about how people maneuver and scheme, how to get them to do what I want, than you do? You don't exactly have your dad wrapped around your finger, do you?"

"No," she said, the familiar hurt slashing at her self-confidence. "But that's different. And I still think..."

"Don't think," he coaxed. "You're a nice, nonthreatening person, and people like you. That's what you bring to the table. All I'm asking is, use a little more of that niceness on Martin and Melody. Because I've noticed you haven't gone out of your way with them, or with Arlene either. You've been pretty cold and distant, in fact, and they've noticed. That's not the way to get along out here. Don't you think you ought to have been a little more friendly?"

"I thought I *was* being nice," she said with dismay. "Have I really seemed unfriendly?" Had Martin said something about her to Scott? "I didn't mean to be. But..."

"No buts," he said, reaching out with his index finger to tap her on the nose. "You just work on that, and we'll be all set. Now you go on over there and get started, and I'll start charming my ladies."

He set off to join his homestead again, catching up with Arlene and Lupe and leaving Mira struggling with the logical argument she knew she should have made. Could have made, if she'd had a little more time and space to think it up.

Kevin dropped back to walk with her, watching Scott with a speculative look on his face. "Let me guess," he said. "Boyfriend's instructing you on strategy."

"He has a name, you know," she said, trying to rally her forces again.

"He's had a name in my cabin, too," Kevin said. "And I'm not using that one, out of concern for your delicate feelings. But come on, tell. What's his brilliant strategic plan?"

"What's yours?" she countered. She wasn't *that* naïve. Kevin had come to win, she knew that.

"Eventually, to team up with you and Zara, vote the Big Strong Men out," he answered promptly. "What do you think?"

"I think I don't want to say right now," she said with a reluctant smile. "It's too early. And I'm not going to make promises I might not be able to keep. Not good for my game *or* my soul."

He sighed. "I knew it was too easy. Not as soft as you look, are you?"

"Not soft in the head, anyway," she said. "The first thing you learn in my job is not to take anything anybody says at face value, or to draw conclusions too quickly. I like you, and I'm not looking to vote you out. But I'm not making any alliances just yet."

"Well, you've got a point there," Kevin admitted. "You don't watch these things, but I can tell you, the mistake people make is playing their endgame too early. That's why I said 'eventually.' You have to keep that endgame in mind, of course, but at this stage you're really just outrunning the bear."

"What bear?" she asked, diverted in spite of her caution.

"You don't have to be the fastest guy," he explained. "You just have to be faster than the slowest guy. I've got a couple weeks here before I have to worry about the bear catching me. Not when Melody and Martin are offering themselves up as such tasty morsels. Now, *you...*"

Kevin thought she was likely to be voted out? Then why was he trying to align with her? "I'm bear meat, huh?" she asked, trying to make a joke of it as the hurt rose inside.

"Nope. I've got to plan for it to go either way, though. Because you're up there running at the head of the pack, but Scott? He's Tender Vittles."

♡

By the time they had reached the turnoff to their separate homesteads, which, the drivers informed them, were about a mile apart, most of the group were looking fairly droopy, and conversation had fallen to a minimum. Mira had become increasingly tired, the unaccustomed layers of clothing and wide cotton skirt making for heavy going in the late-morning warmth. She said goodbye to Scott, nodded briefly at his whispered "Remember what you're supposed to do," then turned wearily onto the dirt road to Paradise. There'd be a lot to do when they got there, she knew. But at least she could stop walking.

"You have got to be kidding," she heard Kevin say loudly from his position in front of the wagon when the heavy thing lumbered to a stop at last. She walked up with Zara to see what he was looking at, and stopped dead in her turn.

"Wow. I knew it'd be rustic, but..." she began.

"Noooo!" Melody wailed from behind her. "This can't be it! Where's the real house?" she demanded of the driver.

"That's it," he said with a not unsympathetic smile. "Home sweet home."

"Maybe once it's cleaned up..." Mira began, looking dubiously at the rough cabin, the bark still clinging to the logs, with its few tiny, grimy windows and leaning tin stovepipe, set in the middle of a clearing of dirt and weeds.

"It's a *shack!*" Melody cried. "I thought it'd be cute, like a log cabin at a ski area. How are we supposed to live here?"

"Well, let's not get all lathered up yet," Stanley cut in firmly. "Looks to me to be a creek over there. Let's go sit a spell, pull a little water out of the well, eat this lunch you ladies packed us, and rest up before we tackle the rest of it. If y'all will grab the lunch," he said to Zara, "the boys and I'll unhitch the horses, be over to join you as soon as we tie up the animals in the shade and get them a drink of water themselves. Don't eat all the sandwiches, now."

He winked at Zara, and she laughed in return. "We'll do that," she said. "See you in a bit. Come on, Melody. You'll feel a lot better once you've rested and cooled off."

"I have to go to the bathroom," Maria-Elena said plaintively to Mira.

"Alma said there'd be a privy," Mira said with a tired sigh. "Probably around back. Let's look."

When the men joined them again under the willows and cottonwoods lining the stream, Melody had recovered some of her spirits. All the women had their boots and socks off and were soaking their tired feet in the creek, drinking ice-cold well water from the enamelware tin cups that they'd found in the back of the wagon next to the lunch. Danny was already set up across from them, taking in the scene with his camera.

"Saved the sandwiches for you," Zara told Stanley as he sat down next to her. "We decided that getting cool came first."

"That looks like a great idea," Gabe said, taking a spot between Mira and Maria-Elena despite Melody's inviting smile. All the men began stripping off their own footwear with eager haste.

"Ah," Gabe sighed as his feet hit the water. "Cold. Beautiful." He took the cup of water Mira held out to him and took a deep swig. "At least they gave us good boots," he said.

"You're thankful for these *boots?*" Melody asked with disgust.

"I sure am," Gabe responded firmly, receiving a thick ham sandwich and an apple from Mira with a smile of thanks. "If they'd gone period with those, we'd all have had blisters by now, and I'd be busy doctoring you all up with my limited first-aid supplies instead of relaxing. And imagine trying to do everything we have to do when your feet hurt. That would've made this a whole lot harder."

"I guess," Melody said doubtfully. "They're so *ugly,* though." She looked with disgust at the clunky brown leather things with their many rows of thick laces. "And we're supposed to wear them every day? One pair of shoes? We don't even get sandals?"

"How many pairs do you have at home?" Kevin asked lazily, lying back on the grassy stream bank. "Tell the truth, now." He took a bite out of his apple and gave Melody a stern look.

"I don't know. Maybe a hundred?"

"You have a hundred pairs of shoes?" Martin asked in astonishment.

"Maybe more," Melody confessed. "Maybe two hundred. I haven't counted."

"Hey. Looking good's serious business," Kevin said at Martin's snort of disgust. "Why, how many pairs do you have, Martin? Counting boots. Don't forget those. Because I *know* you've got boots to do all your manly practicing in."

"No more than seven or eight," Martin replied proudly. "I make sure I really need something before I add to my possessions. A hundred pairs of shoes seems like excessive consumerism to me. Think of all the resources they use. Arlene doesn't have many more than that either, so you can't tell me that women need them."

"Yes, but think of all the beauty Melody adds to the landscape," Kevin pointed out. "It all balances out, surely. How about you, Mira? Got a hundred pairs of shoes?"

"No," she smiled. "Twenty, maybe."

"But here's the $64,000 question," Zara called out from her spot at the end of the line. "How many do *you* have, Glamour Boy?"

"Ah," Kevin said, waggling his eyebrows, mischievous brown eyes dancing. "That's telling. And I don't want Martin to report me to the Resource Police. More than Mira, fewer than Melody. And that's all I'm going to say."

"Do you want a sandwich, Danny?" Mira asked once she'd finished distributing the lunch. "We've got a couple more here. More apples, too."

"No, I'm good," the cameraman said, taking a swig from his water bottle. "Just ignore me."

"How are you eating, though?" she persisted.

He sighed. "I'm not supposed to talk to you. But OK, just this once. I'll be switching off with the other guys. We get our breaks and meals, don't worry about that. Union rules. We have everything we need back at the production base."

The group of mobile homes housing Cliff and the numerous production crew, Mira knew. She'd never been sure where it was located. The cameramen just appeared and disappeared, seemingly at random. The only constant was that whatever they had done at the camp, there had always been someone filming. Except when they were in their own cabins, but she guessed that was about to change.

"How many of you are assigned to us?" she asked, curious about the logistics of it. "Are you going to be in the cabin too? And what about at night?"

"Eight for each camp," Danny said. "Day and night, inside and outside, just about everyplace but the outhouse. It's what Cliff said. If you don't want us to see it, don't do it."

"Wow, all night?" Zara asked lazily, leaning back on her elbows and paddling her feet in the water. "What do you think is going to be happening? True confessions? Knife fights? Group sex?"

"You never know," Danny said with a grin. "One can only hope."

♡

They all felt better after they'd eaten. "OK," Stanley said resignedly, drying his feet off with his socks and beginning to pull things on again. "Break's over, people. Let's get this show on the road."

"Couldn't we, like, camp out tonight and start work tomorrow once we aren't so tired?" Melody asked. She was lying down on her back now, her blouse unbuttoned to the top of her chemise to reveal a generous amount of cleavage, her skirt pulled up past her knees to show off her shapely legs, and Mira could see that Danny had his camera focused on her. Well, no question she was the most photogenic woman out here. She somehow managed to look good even in these frumpy clothes. She even had pretty *feet*.

"What would we eat?" Zara asked. "We'd have to set up a whole camp. Just as much work. And what about the animals? Let's go. Up." She gave Maria-Elena a look that had the girl fumbling with her own shoes and socks. Mira was already there, and the two of them went ahead with the men to check out the homestead, which Mira had barely taken in before in her haste to find the outhouse.

"We've got a well, and a privy," Zara said practically to Mira and Gabe once they were standing in front of the cabin again. "And a cabin."

"All the necessities," Mira agreed wryly.

"Then let's bite the bullet and look inside."

cleaning ladies

♡

Gabe reached for a piece of paper tacked to the cabin door, which hung a bit drunkenly from its leather hinges. "You've been fortunate enough," he read aloud, "to find an abandoned cabin on your land, left by the last unsuccessful occupants, who failed to improve the land during their five years and forfeited their homestead."

He raised his eyebrows at the two women. "Lucky us. After you." He stepped aside for them to enter. Mira walked in behind Zara, and nearly gagged on the smell. She turned around hastily and cannoned straight into Gabe.

"Whoa," he said, taking her by the upper arms to steady her, then pulling her across the threshold again, Zara close behind them.

"All righty then," Zara said grimly. "We've got our work cut out for us. How did they manage to get it that nasty? That took some effort."

Stanley came around from the back of the cabin. "Looks like we've all got some work to do," he reported. "Lean-to back there. We fix that up, make some shakes and nail them over the holes, we'll have us a chicken coop, storage for some feed. Partition it off, we can put the tools in there too," he mused. "I'll get going on that. Because if we don't get those chickens into some good shelter by nightfall, they're going to get eaten by the coyotes, dog or no dog." He gave Daisy a quick thump on the shoulder. "Don't want to give you too much to do, girl."

Kevin came up to join the little group. "Want to give me a hand?" Stanley asked him. "We have to start unloading the wagon anyway, find the tools, at least."

"I'll do that," Gabe offered. "Find the tools, I mean. I want to get the axe, start chopping some wood so the women can get that stove going. Maybe you could help me with that, Martin. Because I think you're going to be needing plenty of hot water." He looked at Zara questioningly, and she nodded.

"If we're going to be sleeping in there tonight," she said, "we need to get to work on it. Can you pull out some cleaning stuff for us too?"

"Sure. Come show me."

"You come too, Mira," Zara ordered. "Help me figure out what we need."

They left Maria-Elena and Melody standing disconsolately near the cabin and walked around to the back of the wagon with Gabe. He grabbed the side, swung a leg up, and vaulted inside in one smooth movement.

"Be still my heart," Zara drawled. "That was pretty good. And let me just say, purely as a connoisseur, that's one mighty nice body you've got there, Dr. Gabe. If I were twenty years younger, Hank might have to worry about me being over here with you."

Gabe grinned down at her. "Maybe he still should. You're a good-looking woman yourself. And I'm a sucker for a beautiful voice."

Too bad she didn't have one, then, Mira thought wistfully. Zara was right. That *had* been an athletic move, and he'd looked so good doing it. The dark brown canvas pants and long-sleeved blue work shirt suited him. He really did look like he'd stepped out of 1885.

"Right," he said more seriously, beginning to sort through tools and hand them down to Kevin and Martin, who'd come up to join them. "What do you ladies need?"

"A shovel, first," Mira offered. "And then a broom and dustpan."

"Buckets, lye soap, rags," Zara added. "Lots of each. Give me those masks and the bleach too. I'm getting the point of those now."

He found them everything they needed after a bit of a search. "Westward ho," Zara said, picking up the buckets with soap, bleach, and rags stuffed inside, while Mira grabbed the tools.

"Yep. That is one hell of an attractive man," Zara mused as the two of them walked toward the cabin with their booty. She gave one last glance back at the wagon, where Gabe was still sorting through tools.

"Yeah," Mira agreed cautiously. "His brother's more handsome, but..."

"Maybe," Zara acknowledged. "But I've always gone more for that rugged look, myself. And the quiet, intense type, too. Mmm, all that focus. Not to mention all those anatomy classes. He knows how to do a thing or two, bet you anything. He could show a woman a *real* good time. But what, you like Alec better? Too much of a pretty boy for me."

"I have a boyfriend," Mira reminded her.

"Honey," Zara said firmly, "if God hadn't meant you to look at good-looking men, He wouldn't have made them that fine."

She stopped outside the cabin. "All right," she said resignedly. "Let's get to this. You ready?" she asked Danny, who had been following the two of them with his camera since their first entry into the ramshackle structure. "Got your mask on?"

"You're supposed to ignore me," he reminded her. "Pretend I'm not here."

"OK," Zara said. "If you pass out from the stink, we'll step over your body." She climbed the wooden steps to the cabin, untied her sunbonnet and, after looking around, laid it over the rail of the small porch, then pulled one of the masks over her head and handed one to Mira along with a rag. "Tie this over your hair too. No point getting any dirtier than we have to. Hey, Maria-Elena! Melody!" she called. "Come on over here."

She waited with obvious impatience for the two younger women to make their slow way across the dirt yard. "You two go find some kindling, some branches we can burn till Gabe gets firewood chopped," she instructed when they were finally within earshot. "We're going to want a fire first thing."

"Where?" Melody asked. "And what are we supposed to get?"

Zara sighed. "In the woods. Dry wood on the ground. Little pieces to start the fire, and bigger pieces. Come on. You've been doing this for a week."

"How do we bring them back without that carry-thingie?" Melody objected.

"We could put them in our apron," Maria-Elena decided, lifting one large white end.

"That's thinking," Zara said approvingly. "Go do that, while Mira and I get started in here." She watched them set off, gave a nod. "Ready?" she asked Mira. "Once more into the breach, then."

They propped the door open with a branch to begin to air the cabin out and add a bit more light to the dim interior, took a deep breath of outdoor air, pulled the masks over noses and mouths, and stepped inside.

Mira disengaged her mind and began to attack the piles of animal droppings, gnawed bones, and debris with bleach and shovel, dropping the trash into her bucket, then carrying each load outside and dumping it among the stand of trees at one side of the cabin. Meanwhile, Zara was sweeping cobwebs and dirt from the rough log walls. By the time the others came back with the wood and dropped it into the big box nailed into the floor by the stove, the worst of the mess was gone, the little cabin wasn't smelling quite so foul, and Mira and Zara had decided it was safe to remove the masks.

"Eww," Melody said, looking around. "Gross."

"You should have seen it before." Zara turned the handle on the large cast-iron stove and opened the door to look inside. "Full of ashes," she said resignedly. "Go see if Gabe's pulled out the stove tools, would you, Mira?"

"I'll go," Melody said brightly.

Zara laughed. "I know you would. But I want you to go up there into those lofts and sweep down the ceiling. And Mira needs some fresh air."

♡

All four of the men were standing around a pile of large felled logs that stood in one end of the clearing, Daisy sitting to one side with her big head cocked as if she were supervising. Mira watched together with the cameraman as Stanley and Gabe took their places on either end of one of the logs, then bent deeply from the knees and hefted it into place on twin stumps.

"Considerate of them to give us all this seasoned wood, and a way to set it up to start sawing it," Gabe said as Mira approached. "We would've had a job, otherwise."

"We'll still have a job," Stanley corrected. "Give me a hand with this saw, Kevin. Start taking some chunks from this thing for those shakes, and for firewood, too."

"What can I do for you?" Gabe asked Mira, taking his work gloves off and tossing them onto a log.

"Maybe she just came over to admire good-looking men doing manly things," Kevin said, picking up the other end of the big two-man saw. "No, wait. That would be Melody."

Mira couldn't help laughing, he was so dead-on. "I need a few more things from the wagon. I'm not sure what you've unloaded yet."

"I'll give you a hand," Gabe said. He smiled down at her, reached out with a thumb and wiped a smudge from her cheek. "You look like you've been playing in the dirt."

Her hands flew to her face. "I must be a mess." She picked up the edge of her apron, used the clean underside and scrubbed it over her nose and cheeks. "Better?"

"Better," he agreed. He set out for the wagon. "What do you need?"

"Umm…" She was still a little rattled, her heart beating faster from his touch. She was going to have to get over this stupid crush. It was one thing for Maria-Elena to follow him with her eyes like a lovesick puppy. Mira wasn't eighteen, and she should be past this. And if he caught on, she'd be mortified. Or if the cameraman—Steve, she thought his name was—did. That might be even worse.

She pulled the rag from her head, saw with horror that it was dark with dirt and smeared with cobwebs. Shook it out and retied it hastily. "Um, stove tools. And kettles," she realized, "to heat the water. That'll do for now, but we'll need kitchen stuff as soon as we get the cabin clean."

"We'll unpack everything and bring it in for you," he promised. "Whatever you need."

"Oh, good," Zara said when Mira returned with the stove tools, Gabe following in her wake carrying the two heavy kettles. "Put them on the floor, please, Gabe. I'm going to have to scrub this stove down before I set anything on it. Thanks for bringing them in."

"No problem," he said, setting the kettles to one side of the stove. "Anything else you need, just send Mira out to me, and I'll get it."

"Mira, huh?" she said dryly.

A scream from overhead had them all looking up. They heard the *clunk* of Melody's broom falling to the floor, her agonized yells.

"Ack! Ick! Spider!" she squealed. "Oh, my *God!* It's *on* me!"

Zara sighed. "Go up and take over from her, Maria-Elena. Unless you're scared of spiders too. We need to get them out of those logs, or they're going to be falling on all of us, all night long. And don't worry, I'll find something equally nasty for Melody to do," she added with a smirk.

Mira was already on her knees with the small shovel and brush, cleaning the ashes out of the stove and dumping them into her refuse bucket. "OK," she said. "We can start a fire now."

"Need any help?" Gabe asked.

"Nope. What we need is more firewood," Zara said pointedly.

He laughed and turned to leave. "I'll get to it, then."

"Here, Melody." Zara handed the bucket of ashes to the girl, coming down the ladder now, her face tear-streaked and as grubby as the rest of her. "Go dump this down the privy."

"Why?"

Zara sighed. "Because it keeps the smell down, remember? Just go do it."

"Why do we all have to do what you say?" Melody asked mutinously. "I don't remember electing you the boss."

Mira hadn't thought of Zara as a celebrity since that first day, but now she saw the diva coming out as the older woman stared Melody haughtily down. "Do you want to take over?" Zara challenged. "You think you know what needs to get done?"

"Well, no, but I still don't see why…" Melody began to argue.

"You choose, then," Zara ordered. "Want to dump those ashes, or go back up and sweep spiders?"

Mira picked up the clean bucket. "I'll go get some water," she said, fleeing the scene.

By the time they saw Melody again, Zara had the stove scrubbed and a fire laid, and Mira had filled both kettles and set the water to heat. Even Maria-Elena had finished with her sweeping, and Zara had set her to work on scrubbing the grimy windows. Meanwhile, the ripping sound of the saw outside had given way to the *thunk* of the axe.

"That's so disgusting," Melody said, coming back with the empty bucket and a shudder.

"You must have taken the scenic route," Zara said. "That was the longest privy visit ever. And it'd get a lot more disgusting without the ashes. Or going in the woods. Now *that* would start to get disgusting. Just be thankful they gave us a privy."

"What about toilet paper, though?" Melody asked. "Shouldn't we get that out of the wagon? I used some Kleenex I had in my pocket, but…"

Zara laughed. "I didn't think you were listening much back there. You weren't supposed to bring anything with you. And there's no toilet paper."

"*What?*" Melody looked even more horrified.

"That's what that Montgomery Ward catalog is hanging there for," Mira pointed out.

"I thought that was, like, reading material!" Melody shuddered. "I'm supposed to use that to wipe…to wipe with? Pages from a *catalog?*"

"Better than leaves," Zara pointed out.

"Leaves," Melody moaned. "Catalog pages. Oh, yuck. Oh, gross."

"Let me just ask you," Zara began, opening the stove door cautiously to create a draft, then wider to add more of the dead-fall wood. "It's going to take forever to heat this water," she muttered, then looked at Melody again. "Let me ask you," she repeated, "what exactly did you think it was going to be like out here? Had you ever seen one of these shows?"

"They don't show them going to the *bathroom*. Not being able to wear any makeup is bad enough. Anyway, I didn't think it was going to be this...this..."

"Authentic?" Mira asked with a smile. "Yeah. That's kind of the worst, isn't it? Look at it this way, they gave us tampons. Now, you want to talk about gross...What would they have used, back in those days?"

"Rags," Maria-Elena said with a shudder, turning from her task. "My mom told me, when I..." She blushed. "When I needed them."

"That's one I don't have to worry about, anyway," Zara said with satisfaction. "Age has its privileges."

♡

"Whew." Mira joined Zara on the front porch, plopping herself down with a weary thump. They'd swept the twin sleeping lofts and the floor of the cabin thoroughly, then had sloshed bucketful after bucketful of water, pulled laboriously out of the well, over all the floors before sweeping the water and the dirt it washed up out the door in their turn. They'd scrubbed the kitchen table, work table, washstand, and benches, the rough shelves, until the wood shone white, to the accompaniment of a rhythmic pounding behind them. Stanley and Kevin, nailing the shakes they'd produced to the lean-to that was to become the chicken coop and storage shed.

"I guess I'll go ask the guys to start bringing stuff in," Mira said with a sigh, beginning to get up. "It's probably close to two already," she decided, looking at the sun. "Still so much to do." Maria-Elena and Melody hadn't even made it out of the cabin. Mira had left them sprawled on the bench, backs against the wall, eyes closed.

"No," Zara decided. "Let's go look at the garden first. Give ourselves a little break. Go get those girls. I don't want them to fall asleep in there."

fences and fatigue

♡

Gabe put down his axe at the approach of the women. He made a mental note to unpack the mirror last. Melody was going to be completely useless as soon as she saw how she looked. They were all dirty and disheveled, once-white aprons now blackened, faces and postures showing the fatigue of the seemingly endless day.

"How're you all doing?" he asked as Martin set down his own axe and came over to join them.

"Well, the cabin's clean," Zara said wearily. "We thought we'd go check out the garden before we start setting things up in the house. See what we're going to be eating tonight, besides beans and cornbread. Good thing Alma had us soak some beans last night, or we wouldn't even be having that. Want to come?"

"Sure." He drove the axe into the chopping block, put the leather cover onto the hatchet, and stripped off his work gloves. "Come on, Martin. Time for a break. We've got enough wood here for some days, anyway," he mused. "Cut some grass earlier too, spread it out to dry so you can stuff those mattresses in another few days. After this, we should get that springbox out of the wagon, find a good spot in the creek for it before we milk tonight. Too hot out here to do without refrigeration."

Martin nodded glumly. His enthusiasm for "period" living seemed to have taken a bit of a beating today, Gabe saw with amusement. "You'll want to put the cover on the hatchet," he reminded the older man. Martin shot him a look, but obeyed.

"How're you holding up?" Gabe asked Mira quietly. She'd caught the brunt of it, he suspected. Zara had surprised him—hell, she'd astonished him—but she had to be sixty-five. And the two younger women...well, Maria-Elena wasn't too bad.

"I'm OK," she sighed. "But...there's a lot." He saw her blink back a tear or two.

"Tomorrow will be easier," he said gently. He was pretty tired too, truth be told. They all were. "The hike in, all this work... it'd wear anyone out. You've done great."

She nodded briefly, took a deep, uneven breath. "Thanks."

The little band stopped in front of the neatly laid-out garden. "Close to the creek," Gabe remarked. "That'll make watering easier, anyway."

"Spinach, lettuce, chard, coming up already," Zara said, pacing the length of the plot. "Peas and radishes ready now too. Beans and cherry tomatoes pretty soon. Baby carrots now, I'll bet, and beets. And other stuff to come later. All right. Lots here. This must be, what? Seventy-five by fifty feet?"

"About that," Gabe agreed.

"Lots of weeding and watering," Mira said a little bleakly.

"Oh, great," Melody said. "I suppose that's our job?"

"You said you hated being in the house all the time," Zara pointed out. "Here you go. All kinds of fresh air. You can work on your tan."

Gabe didn't realize that Stanley and Kevin had come to join them until Stanley spoke from behind him. "A lot to fence, too," the older man said, "if we don't want the deer to get it all."

"But the deer haven't eaten it so far," Melody objected. "Why would they come now?"

"Look here." Stanley pointed to regular indentations in the ground, running along the garden's perimeter. "They've had a deer fence here that they've pulled down, just to make sure we've got something to do. If we want to eat anything besides beans over the next few weeks, we're going to have to get this fence built, and right quick too. And until we do that, and get a corral up, it's like John said. The men are going to have to be sleeping out here in pairs with the shotgun. Between the garden and the livestock, we're going to be looking like one big supermarket to the animal population. We'll have 'em lining up to take a whack at us if we're not careful. And Daisy can't patrol all this by herself, can you, girl?" he asked the big dog, who was, as usual, by his side.

"Do you think there are really bears?" Maria-Elana asked nervously. "And wolves?"

"More likely to be coyotes," Gabe said with a reassuring smile for her. "Nothing for you to worry about. But the animals can't defend themselves well enough when they're tied up. Oh, well. It won't be much less comfortable out here than in the cabin anyway, since we don't have those mattresses yet."

"All right, then," Stanley said with a sigh. "Let's get the wagon unloaded and everything put away. Then we've got the animals, dinner...Kevin and I've got that chicken coop fixed up, and the chickens and tools in it too. Got enough wood. Everyone's done real good so far. Just a couple more hours, and we'll be all set."

♡

"We've got a proposal for you ladies," Stanley said when the men had hauled in the final box of clothing and humped it up the ladder to their loft, and the women had put away the food supplies as best they could on the rough cabin shelves, started the beans simmering for their supper. "There's a good swimming hole in that creek, just a bit farther downstream. This has been one tough day for y'all. Why don't you take that nice white soap, go on down there while there's still a little bit of warmth to the sun? Get cleaned up, rinse some of the dust out of those clothes. I know you'll feel better after you've done that."

"Don't you want to get clean too?" Mira asked.

"We've still got the animals to see to," Stanley reminded her. "We'll put up the clothesline while you're gone, too, give you a place to hang your wet things. We'll clean up after you do, while you're making dinner. Least, I hope you're fixin' to do that. I'm as hungry as one of those bears John kept warning us about."

"You'll get your dinner," Zara told him. "As long as some-body gives a couple stirs to these beans, keeps them from burn-ing. Because you sure know the way to a woman's heart."

"Well trained," he said with a smile that had some sadness to it. "We'll leave you to it, then. Take your time."

"Got that clothesline?" he asked Gabe a few minutes later, stand-ing near the cabin doorway, hands on hips, surveying the yard. Martin and Kevin were with the animals. Kevin had turned out to be a surprisingly good milker for someone who, as he put it, "wasn't used to touching this part of the female anatomy."

"Yeah," Gabe said, digging in the wooden utility crate. "Here it is. We'll probably want to drive some nails in here, hang some of this stuff on the wall. Save us rummaging for it. And up in the lofts too, for clothes, all that."

"Good idea," Stanley nodded. "Do that tomorrow." He picked up the hammer and the can of nails, walked outside, around to the side of the cabin away from the creek. "Start here," he decided, "then run the line on over to that tree? Out of the way, but they wouldn't have to carry the clothes too far, come laundry day."

"I'm sure they're all looking forward to laundry day," Gabe said with a grin.

"Yep. We got the same thing on both sides of the loft here," Stanley said. "Two good workers, one maybe, and one also-ran. Hope Zara can keep those young ones going. Otherwise it's all going to fall on her and Mira, especially Mira. That Melody's about useless."

"For decorative purposes only," Gabe agreed.

"Got her eye on you, though," Stanley warned. "Woman like that, she came on the show thinking she'd get by on her feminine wiles. Then wouldn't you know, she winds up here. An old man, somebody who couldn't care less—well, probably *two* of 'em who couldn't care less—"

Gabe laughed. "Yeah, I think Martin's immune on philosophical grounds alone. All those shoes."

"Which leaves you. You just watch yourself."

"Don't worry. I'm a young, single doctor. I'm not Alec, but still. I'm all clued up on that."

"You've probably had a few patients who wanted to hang around after office hours," Stanley guessed.

"A few."

"Alec said you played some ball, too."

"Yeah, some. High school and college, that's it. Blew out my knee, junior year. Wouldn't have made it to the NFL anyway. Worked out all right in the end."

"Football player and a doctor," Stanley mused. "Yeah, I'd guess you probably know how to turn a woman down gracefully by now. And that your brother does, too. Not that he does as much turning down as you do." He chuckled at Gabe's rueful smile, then strung out the line to the distant tree, tied it around the trunk.

"How's that?" he asked when he came back.

"Good to go," Gabe said, tying the sack of clothespins to the line.

"Of course, only one woman out here worth your while," Stanley said. "On either homestead. And she's the one who *won't* be making a play for you."

"Thanks for supper," Gabe said, pushing back from the table a couple hours later. The bath in the icy stream had done as much to refresh the men as the women, and dinner had helped even more. He hadn't realized how hungry he was until he'd discovered how good cornbread could taste. No question, though, it had been a long, exhausting day.

"Five o'clock's going to come pretty early," he said, standing and stretching. "Guess I'll grab a couple of those blankets and head outside. I'll take first shot at guard duty, if somebody wants to volunteer along with me."

"I'll do it," Stanley offered, swinging his legs around the crate that had served him as a seat and standing up as well. "Been a while since I've slept under the stars. Kinda looking forward to it."

Gabe looked at him thoughtfully, jerked his chin and walked outside, where Stanley joined him a moment later. "You sure?" Gabe asked him quietly. "That leaves Martin and Kevin with the shotgun tomorrow night. Kevin's not too bad, but he's never shot—*or* slept outside, I'd be willing to bet."

"You're right," Stanley decided. "Take Martin instead."

"I was afraid you'd say that," Gabe sighed. "Well, if anything especially nasty does come around, I'll shoot, and he can open negotiations. This ought to be a fun night."

By the time Gabe and Martin had taken themselves off and she and Maria-Elena had finished washing and drying the last enamelware plate and cup, Mira knew she had never been more tired, although the dim light coming through the cabin windows told her it was probably no later than eight-thirty. The sun hadn't even begun to set, the summer days lingering this far north, but it felt to her aching body like the middle of the night. Her steps literally dragged as she washed her face and brushed her teeth using a carefully tipped-out smidgen from the precious jar of tooth powder, then made a final visit to the outhouse.

She climbed the ladder behind Maria-Elena to the women's sleeping loft, then stripped down to her chemise by the light of the oil lamp Zara and Melody had carried up with them earlier. Folding her clothes and placing them next to the wall, she spared a brief thought for modesty. A week ago, dressing and undressing next to these women might have given her pause. Now, she barely cared about the sheet they'd hung across the end of the loft to screen it from the men's sleeping area. As long as she wasn't filmed while she undressed, that was enough for her. She lay down next to Zara on the empty mattress ticking and folded quilt that covered the bare floorboards, pulled her half of their sheet and blanket over herself, and was asleep as soon as she closed her eyes.

the preacher's kid

♡

Mira sat up with a jerk at the sudden clanging in the dark. Where was she? Her groping hand encountered Zara, stirring awake beside her.

"What is it?" the other woman asked groggily, pulling herself up to sit as well, then reaching for the blanket again with a shiver.

The clanging stopped, to the accompaniment of a rumbled exclamation from across the way. Stanley, Mira realized, the world coming back into focus. Turning off the alarm clock. They were in the cabin, and it was...morning?

"Tell me it isn't five," Zara moaned.

The window above Mira's spot on the floor shone pale gray, a clearly visible rectangle against the pitch-black of the rest of the loft. She could hear Kevin voicing his own complaint, the rustling sound of the men moving around, and, a moment later, saw the faint glow of a lantern through the sheet. "It's five," she decided with a sigh. Every muscle in her torso protested as she reached for their own lantern, set carefully beneath the window the night before. She scrabbled for the box of matches and lit the wick, revealing Zara shaking a reluctant Maria-Elena awake. She got to her feet and located her pile of clothes, fumbled to find the waistband of the unfamiliar drawers and hopped from one cold foot to the other as she pulled them on. Zara, moving more slowly, began to do the same beside her.

"Which way's the top?" Zara mumbled, turning her corset over in her hands, moving closer to the lantern to check before she pulled it around herself and began fastening hooks. "If it's upside down, too bad. This is way too much work. Where's a fuzzy bathrobe and slippers when you need them?"

Mira laughed, oddly exhilarated despite, or maybe because of the early hour and the cold. The overwhelming first day was behind them, and she'd made it through pretty well, she thought with some pride. Today they would start their adventure in earnest. A groggy Maria-Elena was finally up, too, but Melody had merely turned away from them and gone back to sleep.

Zara reached out with one bare foot and poked firmly at the young woman's back. "Rise and shine. Lots to do."

Low voices were coming from downstairs now, the sound of the front door opening and closing, feet up and down the ladder. Gabe and Martin, Mira realized, coming in from outside, returning blankets to their loft before heading out again to care for the animals.

"Too tired," Melody mumbled, pulling the blanket more closely around her. "Couldn't sleep. Floor's too hard."

Zara snorted unsympathetically. "Get up and get to work, and I guarantee you'll be sleeping tonight. Come on. Let's go. Everyone else is up."

Melody rolled over and opened her eyes with obvious reluctance. "We could take turns," she suggested sleepily. "If you and Mira did it today, you could sleep in tomorrow." Maria-Elena looked hopeful at the suggestion.

"Yeah, right," Zara scoffed as Mira finished tying her bootlaces and searched her cloth bag of belongings for her brush and comb. "Tomorrow morning, you're going to draw all the water, empty the ashes, light the stove, gather the eggs, fetch the wood, and cook breakfast. Uh-huh. Nobody forced you to come out here. You volunteered for this game, and you'd better start playing it. This is what you signed up for."

"But if I don't sleep some more, I won't be able to do anything at all," Melody pleaded. "Because I think I'm getting sick. I have a really sore throat."

"That's wood smoke," Mira heard Zara saying impatiently behind her as she and Maria-Elena climbed down the ladder and into camera view. She guessed that the microphone was picking up the entire conversation. "You go ahead and do what you want," Zara continued. "But when you do get up, you can just walk right over to Arcadia and tell Chelsea you want to quit. Save us voting you out."

"All right, all right," came Melody's sulky voice. "I'm getting up."

Kevin looked up from the washstand, where he'd been splashing water over his face, and met Mira's rueful gaze. "The Beverly Hillbillies, she's not," he pronounced, reaching for the single thin towel and rubbing it briskly over his bewhiskered cheeks, then heading out to catch up with the others.

By the time Melody came cautiously down the ladder, streaked blonde hair rumpled wildly around her head, Mira and Maria-Elena had finished their woefully inadequate morning toilette: a quick wash of their faces in the ice-cold water, a brush through their hair before pinning it up with the inadequate aid of the shaving mirror perched on top of the washstand, and, of course, the requisite visit to the already less-than-salubrious outhouse.

"I am never, ever going camping," Maria-Elena declared, coming back into the cabin.

Mira laughed. "You never know. It might grow on you."

After a horrified glance in the mirror and a quick session with her hairbrush, Melody peered out one of the small windows in disappointment. "Where did the guys go?"

"Chores," Zara said economically.

"Is there coffee?" Melody shivered and pulled her wool shawl more tightly around her.

"Not till the stove gets hot, and we boil water," Mira reminded her.

"I forgot," Melody said miserably.

"Here." Zara handed Melody the bucket with the ashes Mira had just swept from the stove. "Take this with you to the outhouse. The cold air out there should wake you up. And come back right away this time. I mean it. No messing around."

"Why are you picking on me?" Melody complained. "Nobody else has to do a chore when they haven't even gone to the bathroom yet!"

"It's such a tough chore, too," Zara snapped. "Want to go get water or wood instead? You aren't actually a princess, no matter what your daddy told you, and we aren't your servants. Get busy."

"Bitch," Mira heard Melody mutter as they headed out the door together. Melody stomped down the path to the outhouse while Mira carried her own bucket to the well in the dim light of sunrise to begin the laborious process of drawing the morning's water.

♡

"Well, that's Day Four down," Stanley said a few days later, when the men were walking back from their evening bath at the swimming hole. "Not too bad."

"Except that little garden incident." Kevin said with a grin.

Gabe laughed. "That's making it into an episode for sure."

"Yep," Kevin agreed happily. "That's entertainment."

"What happened?" Stanley asked. "Martin and I missed out, huh?"

It was Kevin who answered, his tone gleeful. "So Gabe and I are digging irrigation ditches in the garden. And Melody and

Maria-Elena are supposedly weeding. Except they aren't. They're taking a "break" over in that tall grass instead. And when they don't come back with the vegetables for lunch like they're supposed to, Zara comes out to see what they're doing. And if you had any doubt that Zara's a tough customer, just lay that right to rest."

"Sounds like a sight to see," Stanley said with a chuckle.

"Yeah," Gabe agreed. "Danny was just lapping it up. Give her credit, Maria-Elena apologized. I think she did feel ashamed. She's a nice girl, really. Easily influenced, that's all."

"Whereas Melody..." Kevin said. "She just got snippy. And oh boy, the fur *really* flew then. But that wasn't the best part, was it, Gabe?"

"I shouldn't laugh," Gabe said as a chuckle escaped him. "I know it was painful. I performed the first aid duties, after all."

"What was painful?" Martin asked, sounding more cheerful than he had all day. Well, Gabe supposed, he was probably happy that somebody else had been in the injury spotlight for once. Gabe had been kept busy with him since they'd arrived, bandaging cuts and taking out splinters. How he'd managed to hurt himself so many times was a mystery.

"She got a few...ants," he said, trying manfully to stop the laughter. "In her drawers. And they bit her."

"Ouch," Stanley said sympathetically.

"Yep. Sat right on an anthill," Kevin said with satisfaction. "The wages of sin might not be death out here, but they aren't a whole lot of fun either."

♡

"If I carried a chair outside for you," Stanley asked Zara after dinner, "think I could talk you into playing that guitar for us, and singing us a song or two? I'd dearly love to hear you sing."

Mira perked up at the idea, and Zara didn't disappoint. "Only if you'll sing with me," the older woman said. "I have a feeling you know how."

"I've sung a song or two," Stanley admitted. "But I wouldn't stack up against a professional like you."

"Church choir, am I right?" she asked, as she went for her guitar case in the corner of the cabin.

"You got me pegged," he chuckled. "Y'all coming too?" he asked the others.

"Wouldn't miss it," Gabe said. "Give me a hand with this bench, Kevin. Give the women something to sit on."

"Do I have to?" Maria-Elena asked plaintively. "A sing-along is kinda lame, isn't it?"

"You don't *have* to do a single thing," Zara answered cheerfully. "I'm going to sit outside, watch the sun set, and sing a couple songs. Please yourself, though."

The girl came along, because, Mira thought with amusement, there really *was* nothing else to do. Even thinking about entertainment was progress, though. The first few nights, they'd been so tired that they'd gone to bed as soon as the dishes were done.

Outside, the air was cool enough to be glad of the layers of clothes she wore, a welcome relief after the heat of the day and the dark stuffiness of the little cabin. Alpenglow was beginning to touch the mountains to the north, and she could hear frogs in the creek begin their own nightly song.

Mira took a seat on the bench the men had carried out, Maria-Elena sinking down beside her with ill grace after seeing the quicker Melody nab the spot on the log next to where Gabe sat with his long legs outstretched, booted ankles crossed. Gabe barely glanced at her, his attention focused on Zara as she settled herself on the chair and fastened the strap of her guitar, strummed a few chords.

"Gotta be period-appropriate," Zara said. "I'll see what I can come up with." As she began the intro, Mira recognized the tune to "Michael, Row the Boat Ashore" even before the older woman's beautiful alto filled the evening air. After a line or two, Stanley added his nearly bass voice, and to Mira's surprise, Gabe almost immediately contributed his own surprisingly strong baritone.

The second time the simple chorus came around, Zara urged, "Come on, join in," and Mira obliged along with the others, shy at first, but finding that her voice blended easily, leaving her free to feel the joy of creating music, the song filling her body, resonating inside as well as in the air around her, mingling with the sound of the river as the pink-tinged mountains and sky added their own magic. By the time Zara had taken them through "Swing Low, Sweet Chariot," with Stanley providing a soulful harmony that brought tears to her eyes, everyone but Martin was singing along, some softly like her, others with less inhibition. Maria-Elena's voice turned out to be a sweet and true soprano, rising above the others like birdsong, the girl eventually closing her eyes and swaying a little as she sang. Her reluctance and teenage cool, as Mira had suspected, clearly went only skin-deep.

"We've got some gorgeous voices here," Zara declared after they'd sung every spiritual from "Go Down, Moses" to "Wayfaring Stranger," Stanley and Gabe continuing to accompany Zara throughout, while the others chimed in on the choruses. "What do you think, Stu?" she asked the cameraman. "Think we can get a recording contract?"

"You're supposed to be ignoring me," he complained from behind the lens. "You know that. Quit talking to us."

Zara just laughed. "Stanley, you didn't surprise me one bit. But Gabe, how come you know all the lyrics? You a secret churchgoer?"

"Not so secret," he smiled back. "PK."

"Preacher's kid," Stanley enlightened the others. "You and Alec," he said with his rumbling chuckle. "Well, well, well."

"Yep," Gabe grinned. "Way too many years of Vacation Bible School. When I'm a hundred and two and have forgotten my name, I'm still going to be able to sing 'Jesus Loves Me.'"

Zara began to strum the guitar, and Gabe laughed out loud. He and Stanley sang the simple verses, Zara quickly reduced to humming along after the initial chorus.

"No other takers, I guess," Gabe said as they finished. "Nobody else with my sordid past."

"That's one they don't teach you in Hebrew School," Kevin said dryly.

"I can play the Dreidel Song, if you like," Zara offered. "Or Hava Nagila. That's about as far as I go."

"That's OK. Other than the 'Jesus Loves Me' thing, this has all been pretty Old Testament-friendly. But you're not enjoying this, huh, Martin?" Kevin went on, with the devilish smile that Mira recognized as the prelude to another Martin-Tease. "Or are you providing an audience?"

"I don't approve of organized religion," he said stiffly.

"Too bad. I'm pretty sure Stanley was getting ready to announce an Altar Call, weren't you?" Kevin turned to the older man with mock seriousness. "I was just about to become a Jew for Jesus, myself. Because singing along with some traditional American music has *that* much power over me."

"I'd prefer something without religious overtones next time," Martin said to Zara, pointedly ignoring Kevin. Mira saw Stanley shaking his head slowly, and looked down to hide her own smile. "If you don't mind."

"I'll work on that," she said, then lifted the strap of her guitar from around her neck and stood up. The sun was setting now, and the air was getting chillier. "Well, that was fun, religious overtones and all," she said briskly. "Not to mention giving me the chance to introduce a whole new generation to the beautiful sound of me singing. All part of the scheme, you know. Although I *was* thinking Hank and I'd be doing it together, give 'em the full Hank and Zara Show. Still, I'll take what I can get. And since I provided the musical accompaniment," she added, "I figure that gives me first shot at the outhouse before bed. Yippee."

"This place brings you back to a lot of simpler things," Mira mused as she leaned against the wall of the house next to Gabe, who'd come to join her after the men had taken the furniture back inside. She wrapped her shawl around herself against the evening chill. "It may be on camera, but it still feels real, doesn't it? I keep finding myself forgetting it's a show, and that we're competing. I suppose it's because you can't help but be inside the life you're living, the moment you're in." She looked up at him, wondering if he understood her. "And right now that's singing for entertainment, and waiting for the outhouse."

"No distractions, no labor-saving devices. No time out, no time off. And not much to hide behind," he agreed.

"You do get what I'm saying," she said with pleasure.

"Of course I do." He looked surprised at the question. "You always only have the moment you're in, but we tend to forget that. It's too intense here to forget, though. You can't live in the past or think about tomorrow if what you're doing now requires your complete attention. And as far as competing...until our first challenge, at least, it's what Cliff said. Working hard and getting along, just like the original homesteaders."

"Neither of which seems like much of a stretch for you." She cast a sidelong look at him. "Maybe because your dad was a minister, huh? That does make sense—for you. If I'd only met Alec, though, I'd have been surprised."

"We both did some rebelling back in the day, but he's pretty much grabbed that role now. He's the oldest, so he got first pick."

"You're twins, though," she objected.

"Twenty minutes older is still older," he said wryly. "Believe me."

"Your dad must be more like you," she guessed. "More quiet and serious. More…steady. Does Alec get that…that spirit from your mom?"

Gabe smiled a bit at that. "Yeah, I'm more like my dad. But he's not like you're thinking, some kind of mild-mannered minister type. Disabuse yourself of that notion. My dad's taller than me, broader than Alec. Smart as a whip and twice as tough. And you don't want to see him mad."

He nodded towards the path where Melody's apron showed white against the gloom of twilight as she came towards them. "And it's your turn. Ladies first."

She shoved herself away from the wall, feeling the effort after another full day of physical labor. Time for bed. "You outside tonight?" she turned to ask Gabe.

"Yep. Me and Martin again."

"Ouch," she winced.

"Yeah." His teeth flashed white in the dim light as he grinned. "Hope nothing comes along to scare him. Get him excited, and I'm a lot more likely to get shot than any coyote."

dangerous curves ahead

♡

"Last one," Mira said breathlessly the next morning, coming up from the creek with yet another bucketful of water.

"Thank goodness," Maria-Elena sighed, carefully pouring the water from her own bucket down the last of the trenches Gabe and Kevin had dug.

Mira set her empty bucket down, went to grab her hoe from its spot near the garden's border, and set in on the row of beans. The plot was so big, by the time they got to the other end, they'd have to start again at the beginning, even working for several hours every morning before the day got too hot.

She was finding, though, that she enjoyed the physical work. She'd quickly got the hang of working neatly around the plants, digging up the weeds and avoiding the vegetables. In marked contrast to Melody, whom Mira had secretly dubbed the Assassin for her merciless ways with their produce. Zara was the best cook out here, but Mira was doing her share there too, as well as nearly half of the remainder of the chores. It was all strangely satisfying, the simple, physical tasks making such a complete contrast to the meetings, spreadsheets, and reports that made up her normal workload.

At the beginning, her body had protested every day. She'd never known she had so many muscles until she found out how sore each and every one could get. But although she was still bone-weary every night, she didn't wake up aching all over anymore. In any case, hoeing was a whole lot easier than digging postholes, the way Stanley and Kevin were doing right now. The garden surround was barely started, the men having decided it was more important to get the animals into a corral before tackling the eight-foot deer fence. Now Gabe had Martin helping him fell young trees, and, Mira thought with a secret grin, pulling him out of the way when they fell, while the other two were working on getting the first posts into the ground.

She almost dropped her hoe at the scream from the direction of the house. Then she was running, together with all the others, including Danny.

"Help! Oh, my God! Help!" It was Melody, pelting up the path from the outhouse as if a bear really *were* after her.

"What is it?" Kevin got out, meeting Zara, who'd come bursting out from the house at the sound of the screams. "Are you hurt? What happened?"

"My phone!" Melody sobbed. "It fell down the hole! We have to get it!"

"Your *phone?*" Kevin stared in disbelief as Mira and Maria-Elena pulled to a stop, red-faced and panting after running in the tight corsets. "What do you mean, your phone? What phone?"

"What's happened?" Gabe asked urgently, arriving ahead of Martin and the cameraman who'd been filming the tree-felling operation. "Snake? Somebody hurt? What?"

"My iPhone!" Melody was still crying. "A spider came down on a string, and it landed in my *hair!* And I *dropped* it!"

"Your iPhone," Zara said slowly. "Which you brought in, what? A pocket?"

Melody nodded, turned a pleading face to them. "I only turn it on once a day. Just one call."

"Who are you calling?" Kevin drawled. "Your no doubt over-worked agent?"

"My mother," Melody sniffed. "I just call her and talk for a minute. If I don't get my phone back, I can't call her at all." Her eyes filled with tears again at the thought.

Mira found her heart softening at Melody's admission. There was no question that the girl had suffered more out here than any of them. Kevin had appeared just as urban in the beginning, but, to his own evident surprise, seemed to enjoy using his decorative muscles in the rigorous chores that fell to the men's lot. Of course, he was also focused on that million-dollar prize, whereas the harshness of their life here seemed to have completely over-whelmed Melody. And Melody, unlike Kevin, didn't have any friends on the homestead, unless you counted Maria-Elena.

"You aren't going to get your phone back," Zara said firmly. "That phone is *gone*. It'll be wrecked anyway. And who do you imagine would be fishing down that hole to get it for you? Do you want to do it?"

"The guys will!" Melody insisted. "Won't you, Stanley?" she pleaded, looking up at him with a little-girl pout that, Mira suspected, had probably been effective on her own father. Stanley just shook his head, smiling at her in rueful amusement.

"Honey, if you can find the man who'd do that for you," Zara said, "better snap him up fast. Because that'd be true devotion. But I think I'm pretty safe in saying that nobody here's likely to take it on."

"Why do you all hate me so much?" Melody asked plaintively. "It's all backwards! Everyone likes Mira best, and I don't get it! I'm *popular!* I'm *pretty!*"

"Pretty is as pretty does," Stanley said, not unkindly. "Like my grandma used to say."

"Huh?" Melody looked at him blankly, rubbed her nose woefully on the corner of her apron.

It was Zara who answered. "This isn't LA," she said. "We have to live with you, remember. And the way you act isn't all that pretty."

"Hey," Stanley said, his voice softening at the confusion on Melody's face. He reached out for her, gave her a hug. "I'm right sorry about your phone, but it's gone. You'll just have to write your mama a letter, like the rest of us are doing. Go on back to work, now. This is the red-letter day, right? Aren't you supposed to be stuffing those mattresses?"

Melody nodded and sniffed again.

"Then go on back there, get to work on that," Stanley urged. "Because I'm real excited about sleeping on some padding tonight, and I bet you are too."

"You're a better man than I am, Gunga Din," Kevin said wryly to Stanley as everyone but Zara and Melody walked back toward the garden again.

Stanley shrugged. "We've all got our weak sides. And it's tough on her. Used to being the belle of the ball, and she can't understand why it isn't happening. Who knows, maybe she'll do a little growing up out here, go back a better woman. This is the place for it."

♡

The growth wasn't evident as the following day began. "Laundry day today, I figure," Zara said crisply, straightening up from the stove she had just lit.

Mira exchanged a rueful glance with Maria-Elena, just returned from the outhouse after dumping the previous day's accumulation of ash, then turned her focus back to pouring water carefully into the stovetop kettle from the two buckets she'd brought back from the well. She'd graduated already, she thought proudly, from carrying one bucket to two.

Melody, as always, was last down the ladder, arriving just in time to hear Zara's announcement. "Something *else?* Do we *have* to?" she moaned.

"First challenge tomorrow," Zara reminded her. "And our first chance to see the others, too. I for one would like to wear clean clothes. And otherwise," she added practically, "it'll be three more days before we can do it. Not till after the vote. We'll *really* stink by then."

"I guess," Melody sighed, reluctantly picking up the egg basket. "Well, at least there's not that much to wash. Only one set of clothes and a couple pairs of underwear."

"And the towels, and the sheets, and the men's clothes," Mira reminded her.

Melody stared at her in disbelief. "We don't have to wash their stuff, do we?"

"Of course we do," Zara snapped. "How do you imagine it'd get clean otherwise?"

"Their *underwear?* By *hand?* That's *gross!*"

"It won't be so bad," Mira encouraged her, reaching to pull down the side of bacon hanging on a hook from the ceiling and setting it on the table to begin slicing off the morning's rations. "Not really any worse than doing each other's. And it'll be nice to have clean things to wear."

Cleanliness, she realized a few hours later, was going to be relative. She was standing over the stove, stirring the undelicious contents of their largest kettle. Maria-Elena and Melody were watering the garden, and Mira was already looking forward to somebody else taking a turn over the hot stove. The day was warming by the hour, which would be good for getting things dry, but wasn't helping at all with boiling them.

After some deliberation, she and Zara had settled on boiling the women's underthings first, then the men's, and finally the women's and the men's outer garments, before starting in on the sheets and towels.

"Because we aren't going to be able to change the water," Mira had realized once they'd sorted all the dirty laundry into distressingly large heaps on the floor. "It would take forever for the stove and the water to cool off enough for the guys to lift this thing down and dump it. And then we'd have to heat it up again...We'd be washing for days."

"Yep. Underwear first," Zara agreed. "The water's going to be nasty, but once we scrub everything, and rinse them..." They looked at each other in rueful agreement.

"Yeah," Mira said. "Once we do that, we'll be wiped."

♡

"Why, honey," Kevin said, entering the hot, steamy cabin at lunchtime, followed closely by the other three men. "You never told me we were getting a sauna."

"Ha ha," Mira said grimly, using her big stirring stick to pull out the sodden skirts and dump them onto the canvas tarp she'd laid on the floor.

"Here," Gabe said, when she bent down to gather the ends, preparing to carry the heavy thing outside. "I'll do it."

"And I'll let you," she sighed, wiping her face with the crook of her arm. She'd ended up over the stove most of the morning after all. As soon as Melody had realized that the cameramen couldn't film inside the steamy cabin, she'd decided that she was more suited to the outdoor portion of today's enterprise. Maria-Elena and Mira had done some trading off, but it had been a long, sweaty morning.

"Just sandwiches today, sorry, guys," Mira said now. "Ham on biscuits. And unless you really *do* want a sauna, we'd better eat them outside."

"This is some operation y'all got going here," Stanley said, looking at the piles of clothing in the yard, the garments already hanging on the line, as he took a grateful bite of sandwich. He reached for another baby carrot, the result of yesterday's thinning operation in the garden.

"Yeah." Zara pushed a stray silver lock behind her ear and settled wearily down on the log next to him to take a carrot of her own. "I'm going to go home when I'm done with this and give my Maytag a big, wet kiss. Every single thing we've worn has to be boiled in lye soap, scrubbed on the washboard, rinsed, wrung out, put through the mangle, and *then,*" she paused for breath, "hung on the line. And every bit of water to do it with has to be hauled out of the well first. If any of you guys wants anything ironed, well, I'll just say, do it your own damn self. Because the only thing I'm going to be using that flatiron for is a doorstop."

Melody pulled her blouse, unbuttoned halfway down as usual, from the waistband of her skirt and used the hem to fan herself. "If we didn't have to wear so many clothes," she complained, casting a glance at Danny behind his camera, "it wouldn't be so bad. Bending over that washboard in this corset almost cut me in half. I don't see why we have to wear it anyway. We could wear this, you know, nightgown thingie by itself and be way more covered than I ever am in LA. And I could at least show what I *look* like, which was the whole point."

"Don't let us stop you," Gabe grinned. "Go ahead and strip down."

Zara snorted. "Trust me, nobody wants to look at me without some underpinning. I'll just stay dressed, thank you very much. Besides, remember that agreement you signed? The one that said you'd wear period dress?"

"I thought, corsets," Melody complained. "When I've worn them at home," she said, casting a glance at Gabe from beneath her lashes, "they look good."

"Bet they do," he agreed with another appreciative smile.

"But here," she complained, "first off, they're ugly. And they do push you up, but you're all hidden anyway, under these... *sacks.*" She looked down at herself with disgust.

"Oh, it isn't that bad," Gabe said. "We can still see your shape under there, trust me."

"You can?" she asked, perking up visibly. "You think other people will be able to, when the show's on?"

"Yep," Kevin confirmed. "And honey, you look *good*. Doesn't she, Martin?" he added teasingly.

"No comment," he replied stiffly.

"You've lost weight," Kevin said, ignoring him. "Hey, I've just decided on my new business venture. I'm going to be taking groups out and doing this for a couple weeks. The women get in shape, and the men..." He grinned cheekily at Gabe, who looked back at him with amusement, "get in shape."

"It'd probably work, too," Mira sighed, stretching her legs out in front of her and taking another big drink of water. "Because I don't even feel like eating."

"I know," Maria-Elena agreed. "Me too." The young woman had lost a little of the roundness in her cheeks already, Mira realized. She had no idea how she looked herself, other than bedraggled. She barely had time in the morning to check her hair in the small shaving mirror as she braided it or put it up in a rough bun. And that was the last time she looked at herself all day. But she'd probably lost some weight too, if Maria-Elena had.

Too bad that no matter how much work she did, or how little she ate, she'd never look like Melody. She felt a stab of jealousy that had her shaking her head at herself. Gabe could flirt with anyone he wanted, she reminded herself sternly. He wasn't her property. And she wasn't his.

♡

Their evening bath in the creek had never felt better, not even the first day.

"The problem out here," Mira decided, sitting on the creek bank and twisting her wet hair into a rope to wring it out, wishing for the hundredth time that she'd cut it short before she came, "is that there are no shortcuts. Boy, what I wouldn't give for a Pizza Hut right now."

Zara laughed, finished soaping up and dipped herself into the deep swimming hole with a gasp at the frigid touch of the water, scrubbing vigorously to rinse off before joining Mira on the bank again. "You've got it. I don't even need a restaurant. I'd settle for a refrigerator with some meat in it that I didn't know personally."

"Rabbit sounds good, though, after all that ham and beans," Maria-Elena objected. She was sitting on a large boulder in her chemise, combing her hair.

"I about *died*," Melody complained as she toweled off. "I don't want to go to the garden first anymore. Not if there are going to be, like, dead bunnies hanging up!"

"I'll go first tomorrow, if they've set more snares," Mira volunteered. "And it's not like we had to do the skinning and cleaning, thank goodness. I'll admit that that's one skill I'm happy to leave here without learning." She exchanged a quick look with Zara, and knew the other woman was having the same thought she was, that Melody's days of dead-bunny panic were probably limited.

"Dr. Gabe's a mean dissector," Zara said lazily, wringing out her own hair. "And I'm sure those rabbits didn't give him one moment's pause. You know he's cut up worse."

"Eww," Melody shuddered. "Don't."

"Shoot," Mira realized, pulling on her clean chemise and sorting through the rest of her things. "I left my comb at the cabin."

"You can use mine," Zara offered.

"No," Mira sighed. "Nobody else's works on my hair. Not big enough." She wouldn't bother getting dressed, she decided. Her wet hair would just soak her dress. Anyway, the men were fishing upstream, hoping for some trout to augment their pre-challenge dinner after the skimpy lunch. One evening cameraman was with them, she knew, and the other wouldn't show up until the women returned from the swimming hole. For once, she could count on being unobserved.

♡

Gabe closed the cabin door behind him. Kevin had volunteered to come back to see to the animals, but Gabe wasn't having any luck with the trout anyway. Truth be told, he didn't mind at all. He wasn't actually hating any of this, but he wasn't used to living in such close quarters. He wouldn't mind a bit of solitude, even if he were sharing it with a cow. Well, as much solitude as you could get when your every movement was being recorded.

He walked through the yard toward the corral, trailed by Steve with his camera. And stopped dead.

Mira didn't see them at first. She had her long fall of hair spread out over both hands, holding it out from her chemise.

Her *wet* chemise, Gabe realized. The afternoon sun shone through the thin, transparent material from hips to shins, revealing her legs clearly to the tops of her unlaced boots. The upper part of her didn't need any help, the wet material clinging to her skin from the low scoop neck to well below her waist. It was, somehow, more erotic than seeing her naked, and his blood was heating alarmingly at the sight. He was used to seeing her covered up, that was all, he told himself dumbly. But he'd forgotten that she was quite so…curvy.

"Oh," she faltered, catching sight of him. She stopped, continued to hold the hair away from her body, and then let it fall around her, took a step back. "I was just…"

"I was…" he began at the same time, wrenching his gaze up from her breasts, the erect nipples clearly outlined against the wet fabric. He smiled ruefully and held up the bucket. "Coming back to do the milking."

"I forgot my comb," she said, the red creeping all the way up from the beautiful breasts that swelled from the top of the chemise. She looked down at herself, blushed even more brightly, hastily pulled her hair around to cover herself, her gaze darting between him and Steve. "I'll...I'll go get it."

"Yeah," he said, unsticking his tongue from the roof of his mouth. "I'll go milk."

She nodded once, smiled awkwardly, and moved past him. He turned to watch her go. And saw that her hair had wet the back of the chemise too. And that those curves looked just as good as the ones in front, outlined against the translucent material, the pink of her skin shining through.

He called himself ten kinds of fool as he walked quickly to the corral, picked up the milking stool that sat outside, and lifted the latch on the gate. He hadn't got laid in way too long if the sight of a woman—and not even a *naked* woman—had this much effect on him. If he needed to see a woman's body that badly, he could probably make it happen with Melody. She'd be more than willing to fool around a little out here, if he could figure out a way to sneak away from the cameras. And why was he so eager anyway? Hell, he saw women more undressed than that every single day.

But none of them looked like Mira. None of them *was* Mira. She was the only woman he was aching—literally aching, he thought in dismay, shifting uncomfortably on the little stool— to see naked. That was the truth. The overwhelming, ridiculous, disastrously inconvenient truth.

double-buck saws

♡

" There they are!"

Mira heard Maria-Elena's exclamation, but couldn't see anything yet from her position farther back in the line of homesteaders walking down the trail through the woods. Within a few more steps, though, she had come out into the large clearing and could see the Arcadia team, together with Cliff and an entire production crew, standing near two big logs set off the ground in crude V-shaped stands.

"My clairvoyant powers tell me that we're going to be sawing," Kevin drawled from behind her. "And that the men get to go first. Oh, goody."

"Not like you guys haven't had some practice," Mira pointed out. Felling trees was practically all the men had done this week, between constructing the corral and beginning work on the garden fence.

"I guess it's too much to hope that Arcadia hasn't," Kevin replied. "Wow. Do *we* look like that? I really need to get a better mirror."

The group opposite did look startlingly different from when she'd last seen them, Mira agreed privately. She'd become used to the Paradise men's beard stubble, all of them having quickly abandoned close shaves with the straight razors they'd been issued. But seeing Alec's regular, fine-hewn features roughened by the whiskers was a pleasant shock. He was better-looking than any man really had a right to be, she thought as he flashed a gleaming smile at the Paradise group before exchanging a complicated, obviously special handshake with his brother.

Scott, she thought disloyally, hadn't improved as much. Maybe it was the straggly brown beard that wasn't sending her. Or maybe it was just that Scott didn't have the athletic build of the twins. She'd always admired his slim good looks, but now he just looked...skinny.

"How have you been doing?" he asked, looking her over critically in his turn as she approached.

"Good," she answered lamely, returning his quick hug and kiss.

"I'm thinking Arcadia's going to win today," he started in immediately, his tone urgent. "And I'm working a pretty good alliance. I've got all the women but Rachel, and I'm pretty sure I can swing Calvin. As long as my team has the vote tomorrow, I've got it wrapped up. So don't worry if you mess up on your part. I know you're not that good at competition."

"I'm pretty good at this, though," she began to protest. "The stuff we've been doing." But there was no time for more, to her frustration. She took the spot Cliff indicated with the rest of Paradise and listened to the plan for the day.

"Welcome to your first *America Alive* challenge," Cliff began. "Well, maybe it's been a bit of a challenge already, from the looks of you." A ragged laugh greeted that. "Call it your first competition, then. And this one's for the men. Don't worry, ladies," he assured them, "we'll be getting to you soon enough."

He indicated the double-buck saws lying near each end of the two huge logs, set about fifteen feet apart in the big clearing. "Each homestead will divide itself up into pairs, one on either end of your log. The contest is simple. Five minutes. I know you'll wish it were longer," he said, prompting some smiles. "The homestead with the most sections at the end of that time wins. I'll give you a few minutes to sort out your pairs, and we'll get started."

The Paradise men immediately gathered into a knot as the women moved back out of the way to watch. Stanley had taken clear charge, gesticulating to nods of agreement from the others before he and Martin moved to one end of the log, Gabe and Kevin taking up stations at the other.

The same couldn't be said for the other homestead. Three of the men were talking at once, Hank standing back from the fray with a bemused expression until Cliff called out, "Two minutes!" Then the older man stepped in, speaking urgently, and the men paired off, Hank staying with Scott while Alec and Calvin walked quickly to the other end of their log and picked up the big saw.

"Wait a minute," Kevin announced when everyone was set. "Time out. This shirt is clean. And it was a whole lot of effort to get it that way. I'm not sweating through it. And you *know* my fan club wants to see the results of my stint at boot camp." He quickly pulled the suspenders off his shoulders, unbuttoned his work shirt, pulled it off together with the undershirt beneath, and tossed both garments to Rachel.

"Well, if it's a contest," Calvin said with a grin over on his side, "I'll represent." Off came both his shirts as well, revealing an athletic, lean torso of gleaming brown. "Come on, Alec. Can't let the team down."

"Oh, boy," Zara breathed as she watched Alec unbutton, and the rest of the men, reluctantly or otherwise, follow suit. "This is getting good." She sighed. "I should be looking at my own husband, I know, but, mmm, I've got to say, Stanley's got one *hell* of a fine chest. There's so much of that man. He could wrap you right up. What do you think, girls? Who's your pick? That's a whole lot of male beauty on display right there."

"Alec," Melody said decidedly, taking in the broad shoulders and narrow waist, the perfectly cut hair, dark and sleek as an otter's pelt, the black stubble. He was taller than any man out here but Stanley, and without a doubt the most handsome. Tanned, too. This wasn't the first time he'd taken off his shirt on this show, Mira could tell.

"Gabe," Maria-Elena breathed, the color rising in her cheeks as his muscular torso emerged from the white undershirt.

Mira silently agreed. Scott, always wiry rather than built, looked positively thin now. But she could barely spare him a glance. No question, Alec looked good. He was much more chiseled than she'd realized. But Gabe was so much more. So strong. So...beautiful. Standing facing her, shoulders broad and heavy, chest deep and powerful atop the trim waist, the defined ridges of his abdomen. His arms as he lifted the saw...The slabs of his shoulders giving way to the bulge of biceps in front, triceps behind, the thick ropes of muscle on his forearms capping it all off.

And, she realized, he had a tattoo. Some kind of American Indian design, she thought, A band about an inch wide, zigzags above and below, an arrow pattern in the center, circling his left bicep. She didn't normally go much for tattoos, but on him...It looked *good*. As if he needed something else to make him look hotter.

"Don't stop now, boys," Zara called out from beside her. "We washed your pants too, you know."

Most of the men chuckled at that, then grew serious again, their expressions focused and intent as they picked up the heavy saws at Cliff's cue.

"Teams ready...set..." Cliff announced dramatically. The men tensed, their hands gripping the handles. "And...GO!"

The contest was on. The saws ripped through the two-foot-diameter logs at an astounding rate. In what couldn't have been more than fifteen seconds, the Paradise team had two rounds lying on the ground and were moving their saws over for the next.

"We're winning!" Zara exclaimed, her hands gripping together. Then laughed distractedly. "Wait! Am I glad or sorry?"

"Glad!" Maria-Elena shouted. "Go! Go!" She was jumping up and down in her excitement as the Paradise men kicked it up another notch. Stanley was practically pulling Martin along, while Gabe and Kevin were blazing through each segment in a frenzy of straining muscle.

Things weren't so rosy on the Arcadia side, Mira saw with a glance. Alec and Calvin were working together smoothly, although their pile of slices didn't seem to be growing quite as fast as Gabe and Kevin's. But Hank and Scott were out of rhythm, and she could clearly see the frustration on Scott's face. When Cliff rang the big bell mounted in the middle of the clearing to signal that time was up, Scott practically threw his end of the saw on the ground and stalked off, the fury evident in every line of his body.

"Well, that was a disaster," Hank said, joining Mira and Zara after Cliff had finished counting segments and had declared Paradise the winner, to nobody's surprise. The older man pulled his handkerchief from a pocket to mop his streaming face and swallowed another huge mouthful from the jar of water handed to him by one of the omnipresent production assistants, then took his discarded clothes from his wife and began to pull on his undershirt. "Holy cow. Think they could've picked a hotter day for it?"

"We kicked your butt," Zara said with a laugh.

"And you enjoyed it, didn't you?" he grinned back at her, slipping on the heavy work shirt.

Mira decided she'd never get over her surprise at the down-to-earth quality he shared with his wife and costar, or her envy at their bond. "What happened?" she asked. "Did something go wrong?"

Hank looked at her, one corner of his mouth turned up quizzically as he did up buttons. "Let's just say that your boyfriend knows all about competition, and not so much about cooperation.

Got to be the big dog, or he won't play. Should have paired off the way your team did, instead of putting the strongest performers together. Trouble is, Alec and Scott can't stand each other, and Calvin's getting there himself."

"About…" Mira faltered.

"Yep," he agreed. "About Scott. Sorry, but that's how it's going over at our place. Guess he never read that book about how to make friends and influence people."

And here was the man himself, finally approaching Mira after standing for several minutes with hands on hips, back to the group, then pulling on his clothes with savage jerks that spoke clearly of his anger and frustration.

"Don't worry," he cut off her expression of sympathy. "The Arcadia women can still win. If it's by enough points, we've still got it."

"We've got it even if Paradise wins," Mira countered. "If we vote, it won't be you and me leaving."

"That's not the point. It's our alliances that matter. Have you been doing what I asked?"

"Not exactly."

"What do you mean, not exactly?" he asked in alarm.

"Well, Maria-Elena, yes. But not Martin and Melody. It's obvious they're going first. It'd be stupid of me to align with them. I'd just put a target on my back to go next, don't you see? Because that would be an alliance with the losers."

"It's stupid if you haven't," he rapped out. "I told you what our strategy was! All you had to do was follow it! I can't believe this!"

"Never mind," he recovered himself quickly as Cliff began announcing the next event. "There's still time to fix it. We'll talk after."

cherries and brown eggs

♡

"Let's get to our women's challenge," Cliff said, standing in front of the two knots of women, who had moved at his direction into a long covered area set up as an outdoor kitchen. Two separate wood stoves were pouring smoke into the cloudless blue sky, with two pine tables standing ready for whatever was going to happen here.

At least they'd have shade for their part, Mira thought, grateful for the structure's simple tin roof. Because the temperature had to be over 85, and those hot stoves weren't looking too promising.

"Cooking challenge," Zara said at her ear. "Well, that's all right. You and I are pretty good, and Maria-Elena's not half bad."

"None of us is as good as Lupe," Mira said, "but we stack up pretty well overall. We can do it." She hoped she was right. No matter what Scott said, she wanted to win. The men had put on a real performance, and she wanted to do the same for them. And if Arcadia won...If what she'd seen had been any indication of Scott's overall performance or his popularity with his homestead, her stay here could be awfully short.

"I'm happy to announce," Cliff said as the eight men settled themselves on two rows of benches at one end of the shelter to observe and the cameramen took their places. "that it's a special season in the Pacific Northwest. It's sour cherry time!"

Two production assistants came in from a room built into one end of the kitchen structure, each ceremoniously carrying a giant earthenware bowl of red fruit, and set their heavy burdens carefully on the work tables.

"There must be two gallons in there," Zara said with dismay. "I have a really bad feeling about this."

Mira could only nod in agreement as the assistants added seven quart-sized canning jars to each table, along with a pile of lids and rings, a huge canning kettle and smaller pot, a ladle and wooden spoon, and a container of sugar.

"I know Alma taught you all how to can," Cliff began again, "and luckily, she's here today to do the judging." He gave a flourish with his hand, and Alma stepped out of the room in her turn.

"Let's see if they remember anything," Alma said pessimistically. "Those jars don't seal, they're going to be eating a lot of cherries these next few days."

"Well, with that vote of confidence," Cliff said, "here's your equipment. Hairpins." He held up eight of the small U-shaped implements. "Which Alma assures me you know how to use. If you'll just distribute these," he handed them to the waiting assistant, "we'll be all set. Just like the men's challenge, it's pretty simple. You've each been given exactly eighteen pounds of fruit. Alma tells me your jars and lids are already sterilized, just to make it that much easier. The homestead that ends up with the most quarts of properly canned cherries in the shortest time is the winner. We'll give you a minute to strategize, and then we'll get to it."

"Strategize what?" Mira asked blankly. "We wash, we pit, we cook them in sugar syrup, we fill the jars, we boil. Right?" She and Maria-Elena looked at each other and shrugged.

"The guys get great big saws and five minutes, and we get teeny pieces of wire and, what, an hour and a half?" Zara picked up her single black hairpin with disgust. "Can I trade challenges?"

"Wow," Maria-Elena breathed. "Look."

It was Chelsea, over on the Arcadia side. She'd flipped down the top of her apron and unbuttoned her blouse, and was now unhooking her corset and throwing both garments into the corner. "If we're going to be out here doing this in the boiling heat," she told Cliff with a defiant toss of her ponytail, "I'm going to be comfortable, just like the guys."

Maria-Elena stared enviously. Her mother was already catching her eye, though, and shaking her head. "That'd be, like, so much cooler," Maria-Elena sighed. "And hot," she giggled. "Look at the guys staring."

It was true. Chelsea's torso, revealed in nearly all its glory in the skimpy garment, was definitely attracting some attention.

"Well, *I'm* doing it," Melody decided. "Because Chelsea's right. It's too hot out here to wear all these clothes."

♡

"Aaaand here we go," Kevin announced from his spot in the spectators' section. "Ladies and gentlemen, we have a contest on our hands. In this corner, the champion, Chelsea, rocking those 34Ds. And here's the challenger, giving her a run for her money."

"Whoa," Gabe grinned as Melody pulled off her blouse, unhooked the corset, and tossed both garments aside in her turn. "A little extra eye candy for the folks at home. And here I thought this challenge was going to be boring. Funny how exciting a little bit of flesh can be when the girls are so covered up all the time."

"Not so much of the candy," Alec said, eyeing Melody and Chelsea in the thin, low-cut, sleeveless chemises. "The tech guys are going to be busy blurring out those puppies."

"Well, at least they don't move much," Gabe said wryly. "That'll make it easier."

"Yep," Kevin agreed. "Two fine examples of modern surgical technique, LA style."

"That kind always look so much better than they feel," Alec murmured. "One of life's little ironies."

"And you're speaking from experience, I take it," Gabe sighed, turning to his brother. "We *talked* about this."

"Relax. No hearts broken, I promise. She's bored out here, that's all. And you know how chivalrous I am about helping a lady in need."

"We weren't issued condoms," Gabe reminded him, keeping his voice low, mindful of Mike's ever-present camera.

"I paid attention in Health class, Doctor. A little messing around, that's all. Passing the time. And ensuring a vote for you and me at the end."

"Bro, that's some ego you've got there. What if she winds up hating you?"

"But they never do. Leave 'em smiling, that's my motto."

"Yeah, I have to say, that seems to be the way it works out for you," Gabe conceded. "Somehow or other."

"Because I only get involved with the ones who don't want to get...involved, these days. You know that."

"And you didn't confide any autobiographical details?" Gabe pressed. "Because she doesn't strike me as the reserved type."

"I am but a simple programmer," Alec assured him. "What about you? Making beautiful music with the lovely Melody? She's no slouch herself in the looks department."

"Not my type. And unlike some people, I have to feel a connection."

"Uh-oh." Alec followed the direction of his brother's gaze. To Mira, concentrating fiercely on the cherries she was pitting, sweat beading her forehead and her thick braid falling over her shoulder as her fingers flew. "I have a really bad feeling all of a sudden. Like I'm not going to be the one getting us in trouble for once. That's not going to go over well at all, you know. Vote-wise or any other way."

"What?" Gabe asked, but knew it was a losing battle. It was no use keeping anything from Alec. He wasn't quite as astute at homing in on his twin's feelings as Gabe, but he did his fair share.

"Hands off, bro," Alec said firmly. "That's just way too much complication. And nobody can tell me that she's up for a little messing around. She's not in it for a good time. That'd be serious business."

"I'm not doing a thing," Gabe said irritably. "F—Lay off. She's a really nice person."

"Yeah. And so is Zara. I bet Maria-Elena's a nice person too. Go charm them. Charm *him,* for that matter," Alec said, nodding around Gabe at Kevin. "Anybody but her. Because that's going to lead us both straight to disaster."

On and on the challenge went, the tedious business of pitting the fruit proceeding slowly despite the women's haste. Their hands worked the curved hairpins with varying degrees of dexterity. Lupe was good, Gabe saw with some trepidation, but nobody else on the Arcadia team came close to matching her speed. Chelsea was frankly useless, stopping frequently to wipe her stained hands on her increasingly sticky apron, rubbing them together and grimacing as the acidic fruit shriveled her fingers, exclaiming with disgust as she accidentally dropped her pits into the bowl of fruit and had to go digging for them. Meanwhile, Zara, Maria-Elena, and Mira worked doggedly and efficiently, Melody was putting forth a surprisingly game effort, and the Paradise women made steady inroads on their pile.

Mira stopped to take a drink of water. "Eyes on the prize, sweetie," Gabe heard Scott calling from the row behind him. "You're falling behind. Come on! Try harder!"

Mira immediately set down her water jar and looked in alarm at the other team. She picked up her hairpin and started in again, but fumbled in her haste, cherry and hairpin slipping out of her hands onto the floor. She bent to search for them, came up a minute later, red-faced and breathing hard, quickly pulling the hairpin out of the fruit and splashing water over it before starting in again.

"Come *on,*" Scott exhorted again. "You can do better than that! Concentrate!"

"What the hell are you doing?" Alec demanded, turning to glare at Scott. "She's on the other homestead! We want to win, remember?"

"Don't worry," Scott answered smugly. "We'll win. Trust me."

"You're messing with her head," Gabe realized, swiveling in his turn to look back at the other man. "You're *trying* to throw her off."

"Hey," Scott said, with a wink for Calvin, sitting beside him on the rough bench. "Whatever it takes."

"Man, you'd mess with your own teammate?" Calvin asked in disbelief. "With your *girlfriend?*"

"Right now, she's not my girlfriend," Scott said. "She's the opposition. And the point is to beat the opposition, so we get to do the choosing. So we can figure out how to stay strong and weaken them."

"No," Alec corrected him, exchanging a disgusted glance with Gabe. "The point *right now* is not to be a dickhead who gets voted off by his homestead. And gets his teammate voted off too."

♡

For all Scott's continuing efforts and Lupe's skill, the Paradise women finished their pitting first, and soon had the fruit boiling in its syrup. When Arlene began to argue with Lupe on the correct extent to which they should screw on the lids before putting the jars into the boiling water, causing the older woman to throw up her hands in resignation, the result was a foregone conclusion. At the end of the challenge, the Paradise team's jars had all come through the canning bath with seals firmly set and were sitting proudly on the table, having passed Alma's inspection.

"Well, good news is," Alma said judiciously, testing Arcadia's seals with a poke at each lid, "you can take these cherries on back tonight, bake a couple pies with 'em. Bad news is, you've only got five of them sealed, and you did it slower, too. Looks like Paradise wins this one."

Gabe joined the rest of the Paradise men in applause as the women laughed in delighted, exhausted relief and hugged each other with stained, sticky hands. Then he rose with the other men to congratulate or console their homesteads.

Melody flung herself into his arms. "We both won!" she enthused. "Isn't it *great?*"

She pressed herself against him, and Gabe thought wryly that if he'd been in any doubt as to the source of that spectacular chest, it was now entirely removed. He extricated himself gently. "Great," he agreed.

"I was worried," she confessed, "but I did it! Even though my hands got all icky."

"You did real good," Stanley agreed, coming up to give her a hug that was warmer than Gabe's version. "You stepped right up to the plate today. Good job."

Gabe congratulated a beaming, flushed Maria-Elena, then turned to Mira, standing a little apart and scrubbing at her hands, a frown on her face. "You were terrific," he told her.

"I got flustered," she admitted without looking him in the eye. "I'm just glad the others kept it together."

"You got distracted for a little while," he corrected. "By somebody trying to distract you. And then you got yourself back on track. Congratulations." He reached out and pulled her close, felt her melt against him for just a moment before she pulled back again.

"Thanks." She smiled a little shakily, lifted her apron to wipe her eyes on a clean corner. "Well, nobody could say *you* got flustered. Good to know that if the doctor thing doesn't work out, you can always get a job logging."

"OK, homesteads." They both turned at Cliff's voice, rising above the hubbub. "Get on out of here, all of you. You've got a date with me tomorrow night."

"What?" Martin asked in surprise. "You mean we do. Paradise does."

"Nope," Cliff responded. "That's not how it's going to work. Both homesteads will have a team member sent home, remember. So it seems only fair that all of you hear how the discussion goes, even though only Paradise will be allowed to participate. And Paradise, you'll have some talking to do amongst yourselves. Because you've got your first tough decision coming up."

By unspoken agreement, nobody mentioned the subject on the walk home, everyone seeming content to relish their homestead's undisputed triumph.

"I'm declaring another fishing trip," Stanley announced. "Soon as we get the animals set. We all deserve a good dinner, and the ladies deserve a break. We might even be real daring, bust loose and wash the dishes for 'em. Fishing first, though. Who's coming with me?"

"I will," Gabe volunteered. "Fishing sounds terrific." Standing beside the creek, he thought with pleasure, in the long shade of late afternoon. That would feel good. Casting into that spot at the base of the rocks with the technique he'd begun to pick up from Stanley. He was feeling lucky today.

"Me too," Kevin decided. "Not saying I'll catch anything, but I'll give it a shot."

"I'm going to pass," Martin declared. "I brought Thoreau's *Walden* with me, and I haven't had a single moment to read it. This seems like the perfect time."

"You do that," Stanley agreed cordially. "Commune with nature. We'll work on bringing a mess of nature back with us."

"Thank God. You know he'd have hooked one of us instead," Kevin murmured to Gabe, who couldn't suppress a grin. "He already got my shirt yesterday. Going for my pretty face, but as always, he missed."

"What are you ladies going to do?" Stanley asked. "You could use a little indulgence after all that hard work."

"What do you think?" Zara smiled wearily, holding out her still-stained and shriveled hands. "We're going to have a nice, soapy, *cool* Paradise Creek bath. Our very favorite thing."

♡

"You're looking forward to that, I'll bet," Gabe said to Mira, dropping back to walk with her. "That was a tough challenge."

"It was," she agreed. "On both sides. But you did great. And a tattoo, huh?" she added impulsively. "I was pretty surprised."

He smiled. "Secret's out. Relic of the football days, and my youthful infatuation with my bit of Cherokee heritage. It seemed like a good idea at the time. Famous last words. What about you? Got any body art hidden away there, someplace I haven't seen?"

She felt the blush creeping up her throat at the look in his eyes. He was thinking about the evening before, she could tell, when he'd seen…quite a bit of her. And he was flirting with her. Wasn't he?

"No," she said lamely, wishing she were better at flirting. It just made her nervous. "No tattoos."

"Good," he said with satisfaction. "Your skin's too pretty to mark up. It always reminds me of one of those brown eggs."

"My skin reminds you of an *egg?*" Wow. He wasn't that much better at flirting than she was.

He laughed. "I guess that wasn't too smooth, huh? But it does. You know, that pretty light brown, a few freckles. A *nice* egg. A farmer's market egg."

She lifted the sunbonnet she'd been swinging along beside her. "I'm probably getting too many of those. I should put this back on."

"Not on my account," he said. "I prefer my eggs with some freckles. Just like you."

caveman tendencies

♡

They were back in the Clearing again less than twenty-four hours later, and Mira found that she was experiencing a different kind of trepidation this time. She'd known all along that people would be voted out, she reminded herself. She was glad she wasn't the one leaving, but knowing that she was going to have a hand in making two other people so unhappy…It wasn't pleasant. And she wasn't sure what to expect today.

She'd just listen and learn, she vowed. There were plenty of others willing to do all the talking required.

This time, they ended up at the opposite end of the clearing from the big outdoor kitchen, at a covered U-shaped arrangement of benches. The homesteads took their seats facing each other, glancing out of the corners of their eyes at the third set of benches, making up the bottom leg of the U.

"Wondering who's going to be sitting there?" Cliff asked them, coming to take his spot at the top of the layout. "That's for the jury. Two of you will be sitting there next Sunday afternoon, listening to us talk. Just like Arcadia is listening tonight. But, Martin," he went on, "start us off. You did a lot of research beforehand. Has the experience met your expectations?"

"Yes, in large part," Martin said judiciously. "It's certainly been authentic. I feel I have a much more accurate picture now of the challenges the original homesteaders faced."

"Harder than you anticipated?" Cliff asked innocently.

Mira shot a glance at Kevin, sitting to her right. "He's been watching the footage," Kevin whispered. "Storyline time."

"I believe it's been difficult for everyone," Martin said stiffly.

"Gabe, what's been the hardest thing for you?" was Cliff's next question.

"I'm not saying the physical work is easy," Gabe answered slowly from his spot at the end of the bottom bench, "or that I'm not more wiped than I've ever been. Except maybe that first year of residency," he added with a reminiscent smile. "But the hardest thing? I'd have to say it's seeing the women get so exhausted, how tough it is on them."

Stanley nodded beside him in thoughtful agreement as Gabe went on. "I can see how, if you really *had* brought your family out here in 1885, you'd feel driven every minute of every day. I'll bet a lot of them didn't realize beforehand how much work it'd be. Just like none of us really did, and we've had it a whole lot easier than they would have. As a man, you'd feel so responsible for putting your wife in that position, seeing her get that worn down. And the thought that most of them did fail—I'm getting a sense for how crushing that would have been, after all that effort. Even after only a week here. It's a whole lot more real, living it."

"You're shaking your head, Martin," Cliff said. Martin was, in fact, trading a disapproving glance with Arlene, who was frowning heavily opposite him and looked on the verge of bursting out with a rebuttal, clearly frustrated by the no-talking rule on her side of the shelter.

"I must say I disagree," Martin said. "Frankly, that sounds incredibly patronizing. Why should the men have been responsible for their wives' happiness or unhappiness? If a couple, a family, set up a homestead, why would we assume that was the man's decision? Why wouldn't it have been something they decided to do together, and worked toward together? Women aren't fragile clinging vines who can't handle hard work—then *or* now. Yes, I'm sure it was disappointing not to make it, but Gabe's attitude…Well, I'm afraid his macho inclinations may be getting the better of him, and that he has his head even further back than the nineteenth century."

"That Gabe," Kevin drawled. "What a caveman. *So* unattractive."

"I don't see how that's patronizing, what Gabe said," Mira objected as Martin scowled at Kevin's back. "Why *wouldn't* a man who loved his wife feel bad to see her working so hard, and getting so tired? Because it *is* really hard. Much harder, physically, than I anticipated," she admitted. "And it just never, ever ends."

"Nothing to show for it, either," Zara put in. "The men—at the end of the day, they've built a corral, chopped down trees, whatever. They've *done* something. And we've just…maintained. Cooked and cleaned, weeded and watered. Over and over. And at least we have each other. When I think about a woman, alone in her cabin except for her children, the nearest neighbor miles away, no support, nobody to talk to…" She shuddered. "And as for what Martin said—I did a little reading myself," she added, "when I knew I was coming on the show. It was almost *always* the man's decision to come out here. Women didn't have any rights then, remember. Different times, different roles. You can't judge them by today's standards. And for a woman with kids…No, I can't imagine they were excited about taking this on. It doesn't mean they weren't strong and tough once they got here. You'd have to be, to survive it."

"So how do you think a woman would have felt, Mira?" Cliff pressed. "If she'd come out here with her husband, kids, maybe pregnant, and was faced with all this? What do you think her emotional state would have been?"

"I think it would depend," Mira mused, caught up in the imagined scenario, one she, like Gabe, had given so much thought to during this past week. "On what kind of person she was, and on her husband, how she felt about him. I think everyone's right, in some respects. Probably some marriages *were* partnerships, just like they are now. And if your husband appreciated how grueling it was, how lonely you were, that would make all the difference. The first day here, when the guys arranged for us to have a break and get clean, that meant a lot." She saw the expressions on the faces of the women opposite, and guessed that the men on their homestead hadn't been so considerate.

"So, yes," she continued. "If you were married to someone who loved you and cared about you, if the dream was something you shared, and you saw him working hard for you, trying to make things better and easier for you like Gabe was saying, like the guys have done for us, I believe you'd do anything to help him in return." She recognized the annoyed look on Scott's face, felt the reassuring presence of Stanley beside her, his contemplative gaze on her, and went on. "But if your husband took you for granted, or worse, if he was unkind or even cruel to you, you'd just want to run away. How could it be worth it? But you couldn't, I guess. You'd be stuck in that marriage, in that life. That's pretty horrible to think about."

"Not necessarily. Divorce was actually more common than you'd think," Cliff said, "especially out here, in the West. Women initiated most of those divorces, too. And just as not everyone made it back then," he segued smoothly, "two of you homesteaders are going to be leaving tonight. Kevin. What will you be basing your vote on?"

"On who's productive," Kevin said promptly. "And who isn't."

"So will it be a difficult vote, or is that pretty easy to figure out?"

"Oh, this is the easy one," Kevin assured him with a smile.

"Agree with that, Stanley?" Cliff asked.

"Yeah," Stanley answered economically.

"Melody, how about you? Basis for your vote?" Cliff asked.

"Well," she began judiciously, tapping her lips with one finger, "I'd say there are different ways of being productive. The most important thing is winning the challenges, keeping our fate in our own hands. If you get all worn out during the week, where's your energy at challenge time? And then, too, it's who contributes toward a positive mood. Who makes things more attractive and is, you know, bubbly and fun. And who's just, like, snarky and sarcastic all the time." She, too, sent a poisonous look at Kevin's back. If looks could kill, Mira thought with amusement, Kevin would be stone-dead by now.

"And with that," Cliff announced, "it's time to vote. One last-minute thought: you're voting for a team. You may want to consider who'll be leaving the other homestead as well as your own."

Mira saw that Scott was nodding significantly at her. But she and Kevin were right about this one, she was sure of it. At this point, it was all about who was at the back of the pack. And there was no question who the bear was going be eating this week.

♡

"Well, at least she'll be able to call her mom," Kevin said as the seven remaining Paradise homesteaders began the walk home in the lengthening afternoon shadows. "I can hear her now, crying about how mean we all were. 'I'm *popular!*'" he mimicked. "I'm *pretty!*"

"I can't say that was a painful decision," Zara agreed, "although it was harder than I thought it'd be a couple days ago.

And I did feel a little pang of remorse when I saw the look on Chelsea's face. I'll bet Melody's in for a few harsh words before Mommy makes it all better."

Kevin snorted. "From what Rachel told me yesterday, things wouldn't have been any different if Arcadia had won. Chelsea might have a more forceful personality, but let's just say she isn't a workaholic. They might have had a little more discussion than we did, though. Opinion was divided, I hear."

Zara shot him a warning glance.

"Who else?" Mira asked, the hollow feeling inside telling her that she already knew the answer.

Kevin cast a quick look behind him, saw that Stanley and Gabe were following, with Martin bringing up the rear in earnest lecture mode with Maria-Elena as his unfortunate victim. "Arlene's ruffled some major feathers among the women," he said. "There's nothing that she hasn't read up on. Or even worse, she's done it before, and she can kindly point out how you're doing it all wrong. It's getting on Rachel's last nerve, and I think even Lupe's had it. She's a harder worker than Chelsea, though, which saved her this time."

"Oh," Mira said with relief.

"But don't fool yourself," Zara told her bluntly. "Scott's not winning any popularity contests with the men—*or* the women. He doesn't exactly fall all over himself with gratitude for what they do, Hank says. Saying 'thanks for dinner' now and then goes a long way, you know."

"Why are you telling Mira that?" Kevin protested. "It's just going to upset her. I thought *I* was the resident bitch."

"She's already heard some of it. And she needs to know what's happening," Zara argued. "Maybe she can persuade Scott to lighten up next time she sees him. Unless he does, and swings the tide back to Arlene, Mira's going to be gone the next time Arcadia wins. And I don't want to be left here with four guys and

Maria-Elena. She's done better than I thought she would, but she's no Mira."

"Right," Kevin scoffed. "Mira's going to tell Scott to shape his nasty ass up, and he's going to say, 'You're right, sweetheart. I've been a real tool. Thank you so much for pointing that out, so I can change.' Wanna bet?"

Mira dropped back a pace, not wanting to hear any more, her emotions in turmoil. She'd warmed at Zara's praise, but her heart sank at the thought of having to leave just when she was getting the hang of this. Her steps slowed, and she found Gabe coming up beside her.

"That wasn't too fun," he began. "The voting, I mean."

"No," she agreed. She was still casting about for what to say next when he went on.

"Thanks for coming to my defense back there. My caveman tendencies, I mean. I should tell you," he confessed, "I still open doors too. Pure reflex by this point. Blame my regressive upbringing."

"Well, Arlene might not like it," Mira said with a little smile, "but I suspect most women would. We want to be taken seriously, but a little consideration never hurts either."

"I've been meaning to ask you," he said, "why did you apply for the show in the first place? Besides the money, I mean. Not to further your show-business career, unless I'm dead wrong. And you aren't a reality-show fan. So why? Was it Scott?"

"Partly," she admitted. "He wanted to win the million dollars, of course—and just to win. You've probably guessed that. But I wanted to do it too. I'd have to, to have taken the risk. I'm not even positive that my job will be waiting for me when I go back. That's pretty scary."

"Is this where you tell me your grandmother needs life-saving surgery that costs, let's see, half a million dollars?" he asked in alarm.

She laughed. Despite the ridiculous response he stirred in her, he was so easy to talk to. "Nothing like that, thank goodness. I just wanted a…a break. A change. I've been in the same field more than five years now. And it's a job a lot of people would kill to have," she felt compelled to point out. "It pays well, and it's got a great career track."

"Management consulting," he remembered. "What does that mean, exactly?"

"For one thing, it means you're never home. We're mostly onsite, at the client's office. Living in hotels. And nobody likes you. It's like being a dentist. When the management consultants show up, people are going to lose their jobs, and everyone knows it. That part's hard."

Gabe's mouth twisted in rueful agreement. "Yeah. That's why I'm *not* a dentist. Or a gynecologist. Talk about being an unwelcome visitor."

She was startled into a giggle. "Yeah, even worse. 'Hi, I'm Dr. Gabe. Meet my freezing cold speculum.'"

He let out a surprised bark of laughter. "You've got a spunky side in there after all, don't you? You should let it out more often."

"Not everyone likes it," she smiled back at him.

"I do," he assured her. "You can show me that side anytime."

She warmed at the appreciative look in his eyes. Maybe she didn't hate flirting so much after all. "Maybe I will. Anyway, I'm loving the chance to have some weeks—a couple weeks anyway," she amended as she remembered what Zara had said, "of being in one place, and things being so…so simple. Having such a completely different experience. Challenging myself. I don't really care for the competition aspect," she admitted, "but we haven't had to deal much with that yet, have we? I'm just trying to enjoy it." She laughed a little. "When I'm not hating it because I'm dirty and tired and there's still so much to do, that is. Because it's nothing like I expected. I thought I'd be spending a lot of time sitting outside, or going for long walks. Ha."

"It's hard," he agreed, "but that's the good thing. The focus. No multitasking possible. If you're cutting down a tree, you can't be checking your messages. And there's time to think."

"Is that why you came too? Not because you want a career as a glamorous TV doctor? I bet you could get one."

He chuckled. "Not hardly. We'd like to win, of course," he acknowledged. "For its own sake, just like Scott. But it'd sure be nice to get all my student loans paid off too. That's my rehearsal for my why-I-deserve-a-million-dollars speech. How does it grab you?"

"Bad." She couldn't seem to stop smiling. "I'd go with the sick grandmother option."

"I'll take it under advisement. But maybe I should save that one for you."

"I doubt I'll need it. Pretty obvious that second place is the most I can possibly hope for, and even that's looking like a major stretch goal. So I'd better be getting all I can out of the experience, for as long as I've got. And that's what I intend to do."

"That's the other part for me too," he said. "I came here to enjoy it, if you can use that word for something this hard. And I thought it'd be good for Alec, though I pretty much had to drag him along kicking and screaming. He doesn't do downtime too well. Pretty much lives his life at full tilt. Not that my own life has been much different. Seems like I'm running hard just to stay in place, a lot of the time. College, med school, establishing my practice, all that. Not that it's wrong to set goals," he went on hastily as she looked intently up at him, "and that's what life is anyway. It's about working, you and I both know that. But I've started to wonder, out here, if there's any way to make things not quite so...complicated. Because this is hard, but it's not complicated, is it? So, yeah. Besides the money, I'm here for the same reason as you. A break, a chance to think about what I could do differently. Alec needed it too, I was right about that. It's been good for him already."

"Did you get to talk to him, then, yesterday?"

"A bit," he shrugged. "Not much. But I can tell."

"The twin thing," she guessed.

"Yeah." He smiled down at her, the deep blue eyes warm, and she felt the little hitch in her breath that that smile always aroused. "The twin thing."

too much excitement

♡

"OK," Mira said, taking a final sip of her coffee before getting up from the breakfast table the next morning. "Garden time. You done, Maria-Elena?"

"Yeah." The girl finished a last bite of biscuit and stood up herself without too much of a sigh.

"That's the downside of voting somebody out," Stanley said sympathetically. "More work for everybody else."

"Well, not as much as it might've been. Considering it was Melody," Zara said tartly. "More for Mira, mostly, having to pick up her share of garden duty."

"I don't mind," Mira said. It was almost true. She liked being outside, at least until the day got too hot. Zara was doing enough in the cabin. She was the best baker, and it only made sense for her to do the breakfast dishes and then get started on the day's bread while the younger women tackled the heavier work of weeding and watering.

"I'll churn the butter later," Mira promised Zara. "In time for lunch."

"Mmm, buttermilk," Stanley said with satisfaction. "I'd forgotten how good a glass of cold buttermilk could taste."

Mira made a face. "It's obviously an acquired taste. I like it in the biscuits, but…"

Stanley laughed. "Good thing we don't all like it as much as I do, or there wouldn't *be* any for the biscuits."

Mira pulled her sunbonnet off the nail near the door, picked up a bucket, and stepped outside. There was still a bit of morning chill in the air, always a help when she was hauling water from the creek.

She saw the movement behind the rails of the half-completed fence while she and Maria-Elena were still thirty yards away. Something brown. Something...big.

"It's a bear!" Maria-Elena shrieked, turning to run.

"It's not a bear," Mira snapped back at her, picking up her skirts and running in the opposite direction, toward the fence. "It's a cow! Run get the guys!"

It *was* a cow, she confirmed when she'd made it around the edge of the half-built fence. And a calf. *Their* cow and calf. Eating her carefully tended lettuce!

She slowed her steps, feeling the annoyingly tight boning of the corset, digging into her ribs as always and making deep breaths difficult. She didn't want to spook the cow, make her run and trample the vegetables any more than, she saw with dismay, she already had. Half their chard bore the marks of hoofprints, and, worst of all, a fresh cow pie.

She walked closer, talking softly to the big animal until she got close enough to grab the rope hanging from her halter, then led her to the edge of the planted area, wincing as the huge hooves landed on spinach leaves the entire way.

Gabe and Kevin were running toward her now on the opposite side of the fence. The calf, seeing all the activity, decided that this was a delightful game and began frisking around the garden, each playful bounce flattening another tender plant.

"Take her back to the corral, Mira," Gabe called to her, closing in with Kevin on the calf from either side. "The calf will want to follow."

All the same, she'd had the cow back in the corral, with the gate carefully secured, for five minutes before the men appeared leading the calf.

"Good job getting hold of her so fast," Gabe said, "and keeping her calm, too. If *she'd* started running around, we'd really have been in trouble. We were able to herd this guy mostly over by the potatoes," he went on, tying the little animal securely to the fence, "so he wouldn't trample anything we wanted to eat, at least. And I don't think they did all that much damage. They can't have been in there that long. Just during breakfast."

"How did it happen?" Mira asked. "How did they get out?"

"I have a sneaking suspicion I know," Kevin volunteered. He pointed to Stanley and Martin in the distance, leading the two horses back by their halter ropes. "And that we're about to find out for sure."

"I'll go back to the garden. See what's destroyed, and what we can salvage," Mira decided. She didn't need to be part of this.

♡

"There must be something wrong with the latch," Martin was still protesting ten minutes later. "Or they must have opened it."

"Cows aren't that smart," Stanley replied. "They haven't figured out how to lift a rope over a post just yet."

"Yeah, I don't think they teach that at Cow University," Kevin agreed. "Now, if we had a chimpanzee in here..."

"One of the horses could have nudged it over, maybe," Martin persisted. "Horses are smart, right? I'm sure I fastened the rope on."

"Just say you must have forgotten," Gabe said in exasperation. "It's not a crime to screw up. But it sure as hell is one not to admit it."

"I didn't screw up, though." Martin dug in his heels, flushed and flustered with defensive anger. "I fastened it! I'm sure of it!"

"This is getting us nowhere fast," Stanley said with finality. "What's done is done. We'd better get that garden fence finished, that's the bottom line. How bad is it?" he asked Gabe.

Gabe shrugged. "We're going to be a little low on salad greens, but could've been worse. If you're OK working without me for a while, I'll go see what I can do to help clean things up over there."

"What do you think?" he asked Stanley three days later, reaching out to shake a fence post, testing its set in the ground. "Another day?"

"Yeah," the older man answered, tipping back his hat and wiping his brow with a red bandana he pulled from a pocket. "Finish it tomorrow, while the women are doing the laundry. We'll have it done before the challenge. All of us sleeping in the loft...that'll be a novelty."

"Might not be crowded in there, all the same, for more than a night," Gabe said with meaning. "If we win on Saturday."

"Yeah. That's really the only choice, isn't it? He's tried hard enough, give him credit for that. But he's like John said, a menace out here. Now, Kevin...I thought at the beginning that he'd be the dead weight, but he's shaped up right nicely."

"You ever worked with a gay man before?" Gabe asked with a smile. "New experience?"

"Not that I know of, I haven't. And I wouldn't have said I was prejudiced. We're all God's children, that's the idea, isn't it? But I never had one for a friend either. I guess I had some bias after all, because I didn't expect much, going in."

"Well, to be fair," Gabe acknowledged, "I wouldn't say Kevin came across as much of a he-man at the beginning. I think he's surprised himself."

"And among the women..." Stanley went on. "Maria-Elena would be first there, you ask me. She's a real sweet girl, and working harder than I would've expected, but the other two are better. But all that's down the road. Martin first."

"If we win," Gabe corrected.

"Yeah," Stanley said heavily. "If we lose, I'm pretty worried about our Miss Mira. Hoping it'll be Arlene on the other side, but..."

"He's not popular," Gabe agreed. "Alec knows I don't want Mira leaving, but there's no love lost between him and Scott."

"Well, then." Stanley shot him a penetrating glance. "If it's important to you, I guess we'd better win."

♡

Mira crouched by the creek, dipped her bucket into the cold, clear water, then straightened and turned. For some reason that made perfect sense at the moment, she was barefoot, wearing only her chemise, fully transparent in the strong sunlight. Showing all those beautiful curves, the luscious peach of her skin glowing through the thin fabric.

She saw him standing there, and her face lit up with her slow, sweet smile. As he watched, she set her bucket down, reached for the hem of the garment, pulled it slowly over her head, and tossed it aside, her eyes on him all the while, pulled out the pins holding her hair in a knot at the back of her head, then shook her head so it fell around her shoulders, down her back. And then she stood there, naked and glorious, and looked at him, that smile warming him, beckoning him. Inviting him.

"WOOF!" The deep, sharp sound of Daisy's warning bark shot Gabe straight out of the dream. He sat up with a start, fumbled to disentangle himself from the twisted blankets as the barking frenzy began in earnest.

"Shit!" He threw the blankets aside at last, searched in vain for his boots, heard the vicious snarling amongst the barks. "Coyotes!"

"I've got it!" Martin said, breathing hard with excitement.

Gabe finally located his boots and pulled them on. Heard, to his instant alarm, the sound of the shotgun being broken open, then slammed closed again. Struggled to see Martin in the inadequate starlight, caught sight of him running toward the chicken coop. Toward the noise of the continuing struggle. Toward the cabin.

"Wait!" he shouted urgently. "Hold on! Martin! Stop!"

The blast of the big gun, then, splitting the night like a blow from an axe. The snarling ceasing, the barking continuing, fading now. Daisy, chasing the pack of coyotes as they fled.

"Got 'em!" Martin laughed triumphantly as Gabe ran up to him, a cameraman close behind. The gun was still aimed at the cabin, and Gabe knocked the barrels skyward before snatching the heavy thing from the other man's hands.

"You *idiot!*" he snarled, rage and fear fighting for ascendancy. "Are you trying to kill somebody?"

"What do you mean?" Martin fired angrily back. "They were trying to get our chickens, and I chased them off!"

"You shot at the *house!*" Pure fear, now. "Oh, God. What did you hit?" He saw the glow of light, the door opening as the others began to pour out of the little structure. Stanley in the lead, the lantern in his hand.

"You guys OK?" Stanley asked. "What happened?"

"Is everyone here? Everyone all right?" Gabe strained to see past the pool of light, his night vision destroyed now. "Count heads."

"All here," Stanley said with relief as Kevin appeared, still buttoning his pants. "What happened?"

"Martin took a shot at the cabin, is what happened," Gabe answered grimly, shaking with anger and the residue of adrenaline.

"OK, I'm sorry. Sorry," Martin gabbled. "I misjudged, that's all. No big deal. Everyone's OK. No harm done. Just an accident."

"What the *hell* were you thinking?" Gabe demanded.

"I was scaring them off!" Martin protested. "Like John told us to do!"

"He also told us," Stanley pointed out, his voice uncharacteristically cold, "that you never aim a gun at anything you're not intending to kill. No thanks to you that you *didn't* kill anyone. Because that hit the cabin. There was one heck of a thud. Didn't hear any glass breaking, so I don't think it hit any windows, thank the good Lord."

"It was below our window, I think," Mira said, her voice a little shaky. "The one in our loft. I felt it...hit."

Gabe looked at her in alarm. "It didn't hit the window?"

"No. No. I was standing right there. I heard it, and felt it. But it didn't break the glass."

"You were *standing* there?"

"I heard all the noise. The dog, and then the shouting," Mira said, her explanation coming out in choppy bursts. "And I got up to see. But Martin's right. Nothing hit the window."

Gabe looked at her as closely as the inadequate light allowed realized she was trembling. The night air, the shock. "Let's go inside, out of the cold," he said abruptly. "No reason for us all to be standing around out here."

He didn't breathe easily until more lanterns had been lit and he'd seen for himself that Mira truly wasn't hurt, merely shaken. "Time to break out that medicinal whiskey," he decided. "Kevin and Maria-Elena, go grab some blankets from the lofts. We all need to get warm and calm down."

Once all the others had their allotment of whiskey and were beginning to laugh and joke in a release of tension, he and Stanley climbed the ladder to the women's loft, examined the window.

"Nothing. Not even a crack. That was damn lucky," Stanley said soberly, measuring the bottom of the frame against his body. "I don't know how close it did come, of course. Guess we'll see in the morning. But this was Martin's last piece of guard duty. I'll stay out with you the rest of tonight."

"He's got to go," Gabe said with finality. "We'd better win this next challenge, because enough's enough. He's got to go."

He was even more sure of it the next morning when they were all standing beneath the loft window under Danny's watchful lens, looking at the wall of the cabin just below the sill. Looking at the hundreds of tiny black pellets embedded in the logs, forming a circular pattern almost two feet in diameter.

"That's what you did," Stanley told Martin grimly. "If you'd aimed just a foot or so higher, Mira standing at that window…"

Martin shifted uncomfortably. "But I wasn't higher," he pointed out weakly. "And it's ammunition to kill birds, right? So it wouldn't really have hurt her badly, would it?"

"At that range?" Stanley said. "You bet it would've, huh, Gabe?"

Gabe swallowed as his vivid imagination painted the picture. Birdshot and glass shards. "Yeah," he said shortly, mindful of Mira standing silently nearby. "Yeah, it wouldn't have been good."

"Excitement's over," Zara said briskly. "Back to work. We've got a challenge this afternoon, and plenty to do before it."

She put an arm around Mira. "You OK, hon?" Gabe heard her ask as the women turned back. "Want me to do the garden?"

"No." Mira shook her head decisively. "Of course not. I'm fine. It was close, that's all. And close doesn't count, except in horseshoes. Like they say."

But Gabe was watching Danny pan slowly over those damning black holes in the cabin wall, just below the window where Mira had been standing.

Sometimes, close counted. And this was going to be one of those times.

♥

"Well, since we're done with fencing," Stanley decided when the men were alone again, "guess we'd better get started on that haying. We're low on feed, and I've got a suspicion that something like that's going to come up in a challenge at some point. Might as well get working on it, get some practice. But, Martin," he said, as if struck by a sudden thought, "if you wouldn't mind, it'd be good to get some more wood chopped before we head out. Running low there too, and nobody's going to feel like doing that tonight."

"Right," Martin said, clearly relieved that the discussion of his actions of the night before was over. "I'll do that."

"Don't want him out there with a scythe," Stanley said to the others as they walked out toward the tall grass. "Chop someone's leg right off."

♥

Mira was returning from the creek with yet another bucket of water when she heard the scream. Nothing like Melody dropping her iPhone down the hole. This was louder, truly agonized. Before she had fully registered the blood-chilling sound, she had dropped her bucket with a splash and was running toward it, Maria-Elena following belatedly behind.

Mira got there first. Martin was on the ground, on his back behind the chopping block. The first thing Mira saw was his contorted face. And the second was the axe handle, sticking straight up into the air above the hands desperately clasping his leg. Because the axe was in his foot.

She turned back to Maria-Elena, running up behind her. "Run get Gabe!" she ordered. "Right now!"

"Oh, my God." Maria-Elena stood stock-still and stared at Martin, her face going white.

Mira turned her bodily. *"Run!"* she demanded fiercely, shoved her hard. *"Run!"*

She turned back to Martin. Registered Zara running along the path from the outhouse, and that Martin was still screaming. She scrambled around to his feet just as Zara came up.

Should she pull the axe out? she wondered desperately. Or would that make it bleed more? The dilemma was solved for her as Martin jerked his leg skyward and the axe clattered to earth, narrowly missing her.

"What?" It was Zara, panting to a stop.

"The axe was in his foot," Mira shouted over Martin's screams. She picked up the foot in question by the ankle. Elevate it to slow the bleeding. She knew that. *Hurry, Gabe,* she prayed.

Zara dropped to the ground next to Martin, held his arms, began talking to him urgently. "Help's coming. We've got you. You're going to be all right." Over and over, as Mira held Martin's booted foot in the air.

Mira wondered for a brief moment if she should try to get the boot off. But it was all she could do to hold his leg up, the blood flowing down, running red over his leg, her hands. At least his screams had subsided to a steady, anguished moaning under Zara's calming influence.

It seemed she'd been holding on forever, her arms aching, her mind whirling, but it couldn't have been more than five minutes before Gabe was running toward them, the rest of the men, and Danny with his camera, close behind.

"Good," Gabe said sharply, coming up next to her. "Come around the side, hold his calf from underneath." He began unlacing the heavy boot, his fingers fast and sure, loosened the laces and pulled the boot off, revealing the once-green wool sock, dark and wet with blood. He pulled the sock quickly off in its turn, revealing the long gash, the flesh split cleanly open almost all the way through, the edges of bone showing white. And all the blood. Mira swallowed and looked away quickly.

"Apron," Gabe snapped, taking over holding Martin's foot in the air. "Get it off and give it to me."

She hastily untied it and pulled it off, fleetingly grateful that she'd put it on clean this morning in preparation for the challenge, handed it to Gabe and then, without his prompting, grabbed Martin's calf again, allowing Gabe to fold the cotton into a pad and set it against the wound.

He pressed both hands to it. "How long did they say?" he asked Danny.

"Less than ten minutes." Danny looked a little pale himself, but kept his camera trained steadily on the scene.

"A few minutes ago," Gabe calculated. "OK. Kevin, get over here and help me elevate this leg, give Mira a break." He glanced at Maria-Elena, sobbing in Stanley's arms, and seemed to dismiss her. "Mira," he said. "Go get me kitchen towels. As many clean ones as we have. And a blanket to cover him."

She nodded and ran. Came back with them, realizing belatedly that her hands were wet and red with Martin's blood. Gave the blanket to Zara, who covered Martin with it. Then went back to stand by Gabe, handing the towels to him one at a time as he continued to apply firm pressure to the wound.

Zara continued to talk reassuringly to Martin. A string of words, always the same meaning. "We've got you. You're going to be all right. Help's coming."

And at last, the welcome sight of the ambulance, jolting over the track into the yard. The doctor and paramedic running to them with the gurney, loading Martin onto it and into the back of the vehicle.

"OK," Gabe said with a sigh of obvious relief as they watched the ambulance disappear again. "That was a little more excitement than we were expecting today."

Mira laughed, heard the edge of hysteria in her voice, stopped herself abruptly. Looked down at her hands and swallowed hard.

"Let's get you sitting down," Gabe said, his attention shifting abruptly back to her. "All of you. Let's go."

He put a steadying arm around Mira, walked her into the cabin and sat her down on a chair.

"Feeling faint?" he asked her.

"No. Just a little shaken," she assured him. She was trembling, and her hands, her dress were covered in blood.

"Zara. You OK?" Gabe asked.

"Yeah," she said soberly. "I'm good."

"Then take Mira, get her cleaned up. She'll feel better once she gets that blood off her. Maria-Elena," he snapped at the still-sniffling girl, "make some coffee." She nodded and moved automatically to obey.

"And Kevin," he decided, "get everyone some water in the meantime. Everyone sit a bit. I'm going to go clean up too."

"You're as bloody as me," Mira said, trying to rally.

"Yeah," he said. "The difference is, I'm used to it."

working the alliances

♡

"It's been quite the week, hasn't it?"

Cliff's wry comment prompted some subdued laughter. The Paradise homestead had been surprised to get the summons to the Clearing after the previous day's challenge had been canceled.

"We're not going to have to get rid of somebody after all, are we?" Maria-Elena had asked nervously over breakfast. "Which homestead would even, like, vote?"

"No," Kevin said positively. "It's not that. They don't want to get rid of more than one team a week. That'd mess their season right up. They just want to talk to us, get some reaction shots across the aisle. Have us see what's going on over in Arcadia, them see what's happening here. Let everyone at home analyze the homestead bonding versus the original team connections, how those stack up after a couple weeks of this."

"Good to know we've got you to explain it to us," Zara said. "It's like we've got a spy in the production camp."

"My talents may be meager," Kevin proclaimed, "but the lessons learned from a life wasted watching reality TV cannot be denied."

"What do you think *has* been going on over there? At Arcadia?" Mira asked him, getting up for the coffeepot where

152

it was keeping warm on the stove and pouring second cups all around.

"Well," he began judiciously, "based on what we saw last week, and what Rachel said then, we're a whole lot more functional than they are. Who did we have who wasn't really meshing with the group? Melody and Martin, and they're both gone."

"And they've lost Chelsea and Arlene now," Zara pointed out. "So there may only be two women left, which would be a whole lot of work, but I'll bet there's zero conflict in that kitchen now."

"But on the men's side..." Kevin pointed out, with a meaningful glance at Gabe.

"Yeah," he said. "That'll be interesting to see, won't it?"

And it was, he thought now with yet another stab of worry for Mira. Scott was seated next to Lupe at the end of the front row of benches opposite. Rachel rounded out the row, with the rest of the men on the bench behind them. Scott was still on the outside, obviously. Literally. Well, Gabe hadn't expected anything else. Alec had hated the man from the first moment, and Hank and Calvin were no fools. Stripped of his lawyer clothes and the black BMW, what was Scott? Not anyone Gabe would have wanted on any kind of team. Out for himself, first and last.

"Most importantly," Cliff began, "let me assure all of you that Martin's going to be all right. His Olympic sprinting career is probably a thing of the past, but the doctors tell me that everything should heal up just fine, and he's already doing much better. Thanks to some pretty good first aid, they say," he added with a nod at Gabe. "Which kept him from losing any more blood than he did."

"I just took over from Mira," Gabe said. "She was the hero of the hour. Kept her head and did exactly the right things." He looked across at her and smiled, saw her glow at his praise, even as she looked a bit flustered at the scrutiny from the opposite homestead, the knowledge that the camera was on her.

He saw Scott's obvious discomfiture and felt even better, looked the challenge straight across at him. *Going to take her away from you.* And saw that the message was received, loud and clear.

"I hear it wasn't the only adventure you had yesterday, Mira," Cliff said. "Talk about what happened earlier."

"Gabe can really say more," Mira demurred. "He was there. I guess it was a close call, but that's all."

"Take us through it, then, Gabe," Cliff suggested.

"We've had a little bit of everything," Gabe said wryly. "Comedy to tragedy. Though it could've been a whole lot worse, in all cases." As he described their garden fiasco, then the episode with the shotgun, he watched Scott's expression grow ever darker, and his satisfaction changed to something a little less comfortable.

"There's been some excitement with the shotgun at Arcadia too, hasn't there?" Cliff asked innocently as Gabe finished his recital. "Scott, what happened over there?"

"Nothing," Scott said shortly. "I chased off some deer, that's all. Trying to get in the garden."

"Which isn't fenced yet, I hear," Cliff persisted. "Hank?"

"Well…" Hank shot a glance at Alec, then down at Scott on the bench below him. "No. We haven't got it fenced yet. We had a little…difference of opinion on a couple matters, ended up with some variation in the depth of our post holes. Turns out that they weren't dug quite deep enough after all."

"So what happened?" Cliff asked.

"The fence fell down, that's what," Calvin said bluntly. "Had to pull every…blessed post out of the ground and dig the holes deeper, and now we're going to have to put the whole thing up again."

He glared across at Scott, who looked back at him defiantly.

"It should have worked," Scott snapped. "I was just trying to get the job done as efficiently as possible."

"Well, yeah," Hank drawled. "Except it didn't work, did it? So needless to say, we're still sleeping out there, guarding our vegetables. And some of us guard more…enthusiastically than others."

"I was scaring the deer off," Scott argued, his face flushing. "That's why we have the gun."

"Duke was doing a pretty good job already," Hank pointed out.

"But I'm sure you've frightened them into the next county now," Alec added with patently false sincerity. "Letting off both barrels at once like that. Good job." He looked across at his brother and grinned, and Gabe got the message. *Double team.*

"How did that happen?" Cliff pressed.

Scott gave a quick, angry shrug of his shoulders. "I pulled both triggers. Which is way too easy to do. If you'd given us a modern shotgun like you should have, instead of some antique model, that couldn't have happened."

"And what did that do?" Cliff asked.

"Knocked him on his ass, is what it did," Alec responded promptly. "And gave him the mother of all bruises too. You should see his shoulder. Want to have Gabe take a look, Scott? He's a pretty good doctor, you know. Ask Mira. Sounds like she knows."

The look Scott shot him was pure poison. "We've all faced challenges out here," he snarled. "Nobody's been all that impressed with your performance either."

"You think I should be worried?" Alec asked in mock alarm. "I'd better do some quick scrambling this week, I guess. Work on my *alliances.*"

"I understand you practiced a little gender role reversal over there too, since the last time we were here, when we had our discussion about that," Cliff said after a moment.

"Yeah, we tried that too," Alec agreed. "Since everything else was going so great. It didn't work too well either. Surprise."

Gabe saw Chelsea and Melody look at each other on the jury bench. Arlene wasn't with them. Staying with Martin, he guessed. But the blondes seemed to know what Alec was talking about.

"I thought she had a point," Rachel put in. "I mean," she went on, "Arlene was right that in 1885, single women, widows, they homesteaded too. And they would have had to do everything themselves. We've already all figured out," she said with a wry glance at Lupe, who nodded agreement, "that they had to be pretty tough in the first place. So when Arlene wanted to see what that was like, I kind of admired that."

"But you didn't want to join her," Cliff suggested.

Rachel laughed. "Well, no. Pulling up all that water, taking care of the garden is bad enough. Not to mention the horror of the laundry. Isn't that the worst?" She looked across at the other homestead, received nods and smiles of recognition. "I don't need to be digging holes too. And I'm pretty sure that cooking breakfast is more fun than shoveling...manure."

"How long did that last?" Cliff asked.

"One day," Alec grinned. "Give her credit, she worked hard, but by dinner...What was it she said?" he asked Calvin.

"Said, 'I think we've all learned a lot from this experiment,'" Calvin said, clearly keeping his face straight with an effort, "'but I'm satisfied that I've proved my point.' I'm not saying a woman couldn't do the physical work out here," he added with a hasty glance at his father, "and props to Arlene for trying it. But I think you'd have to be in shape, 1885 style. Growing up doing all that, you'd be talking some upper-body strength. But Arlene—not so much."

♡

After the session, they were given a bit of time to talk to their teammates on the other side. With the cameras still trained on them, of course. Kevin had been right, clearly. This get-together was all about furthering the storyline: the strength of the original teams, the pull of the new homesteads.

"Coming on a little strong, aren't you, with Scott?" Gabe asked Alec after performing their ritual handshake and giving his brother a quick hug. Damn, it was good to see him.

Alec shrugged. "Why not? Not like he's got any friends out here. Lupe's the only one who's even civil to him at this point. Well, Hank. But he just says he's known so many assholes after forty years in the music business, one more doesn't even register."

"What you said at the beginning, though," Gabe persisted. "About him imploding. He looks on the verge right now."

"So? What's he going to do? And who are you to talk? You did everything but lay a big wet one on Mira right in front of him."

"That was before I saw how far he was down the road," Gabe said slowly. "You need to back off. His ego can't take much more."

"His ego got supersized a long time ago. He's got plenty to spare."

"It's big," Gabe agreed. "But it's fragile as hell. Quit baiting him so much. I mean it. I don't have a good feeling."

Alec sighed. "If you say so. You're the one with the X-ray vision. You sure, though? I keep pushing him, he's bound to do something outrageous enough to make even the lovely Mira give him the boot. And you can't tell me that isn't what you're aiming for."

"I'll take care of things with Mira," Gabe said. "You just take care of yourself. And that means backing off."

Alec sighed, but he didn't argue. "What else is happening over there?" Gabe asked after a minute. "You doing all right with Hank and Calvin?"

"Yeah. They're both cool."

"Close, though?" Gabe pressed.

Alec sighed again. "Yes. Close. And yes, we have a plan."

"How about Rachel and Lupe? Where do they fit into it?"

"A little tougher," Alec acknowledged. "I've been working on Rachel. And no," he put up a hand to forestall the next question, "I'm not going to be the poster boy for *America Alive* sluttiness this season. We've talked about adventure sports. She's really into them, and so is Calvin. That's all the bonding I'm doing with her. I'd be scared anyway. That woman knows a *lot* of knots."

"And Lupe?"

"Surprisingly tricky. She likes Hank a lot, but she likes the rest of us too."

"So how is that tricky?"

"She's probably the swing vote, if Rachel gets sneaky and pulls Hank in. Hank's a great guy, but a big threat to win. He's been singing over there. That's just way too endearing. And Lupe's close to Rachel too. Scott's a non-factor, but if the other three get together, and as popular as Hank is..."

"The celebrity factor's a tough one to beat," Gabe agreed. "Same story over here on the allies. I'm tight with Stanley, pretty good with Zara and Kevin, though he's a tricky bastard. He and Rachel have the best shot at making it further in the game, but we can win against them—if they don't maneuver us out first, like you say. And all that's important," he finished, "but don't forget what we started out with. Don't push Scott to breaking point. He's way too close already."

♡

Mira watched Scott approach, dreading the coming minutes. He was still looking thunderous after the needling remarks from the other homesteaders. She knew how important appearances were to him, and nobody could say that he'd made a good impression just now. The knowledge that whatever he was about to say would be recorded made her cringe a bit inside.

"Sorry to hear about your shoulder," she said as he joined her. "Is it all right?"

He brushed her question aside. "I'm fine. We don't have much time, so listen. I'm having to rework alliances now that Arlene and Chelsea are gone. Why did Martin have to go and chop his foot? That's screwed things up royally."

"He was badly hurt," Mira protested. "He was so lucky it wasn't worse, and it was serious enough as it was. He could even have died, Gabe said, if he'd hit an artery or something. I was so glad when Gabe told me I did the right thing. It seemed like forever until he got there. The whole thing was terrifying," she said with a shudder of remembered horror. "And it made me realize that there are things a whole lot more important than a million dollars. Or winning a game."

Surely Scott would say something about what she'd done. She didn't think she'd been a hero, but she *had* kept her head. And it hadn't been easy.

"You hadn't worked the alliance with Martin anyway, though, had you?" he accused instead.

"No." She refused to feel bad about that. "He almost *shot* me, for heaven's sake! Nobody was going to keep him after that, even if he hadn't left the gate open."

"He *didn't* shoot you, though, did he?" Scott pressed. "I don't want to hurt your feelings, because I know you're doing your best, but I need to tell you that it isn't coming across well, the way you've presented all this. It's looking like you have to be the center of every story. Because what I was hearing back there was: *I* was almost shot. *I* had to save the day when Martin got hurt. When actually, nothing at all happened when Martin let off the shotgun, did it?"

"No," she agreed, "but..."

"Sweetie. Nothing *happened*," he said patiently. "No more than it did when I shot at the deer. Both Martin and I did what we were trained to do out here, scare off some animals. And Gabe's the one who did the important stuff for Martin when he got hurt, not you, isn't he?"

"Yes, but he said what I did was really helpful," she argued.

"I'm glad he made you feel good, but I'm sure you could have left it to him and everything would have been fine. I'm telling you this for your own good, sweetie. We'll do a lot better out here if you aren't trying so hard to be the Queen Bee. Everyone can see what you're doing, and it's not attractive."

He talked right over her instinctive protest. "Anyway, we've got our work cut out for us. It looks like you're doing all right with Maria-Elena and Zara, and it's obvious Stanley likes you. I'll work Hank and Lupe. I don't think I can get Rachel," he conceded, "but I may be able to turn Calvin against Alec. I've got a couple ideas there. Alec and Gabe are an obvious threat to win. That's where I'm going, and I need you to plant that same seed on your side."

"I'm not going to do that!" Mira protested, glancing over at Mike, wishing he weren't recording this. "It wouldn't work anyway. Gabe gets along with everyone. The women love him, and he's friends with both the guys. And he's the strongest one out here."

"If he's strong," Scott explained, with the air of someone holding onto his patience by a thread, "that just makes him more of a threat. Try to think strategically. Anybody with any sense has to be thinking about voting him out at this point. You just need to work that. Be subtle. Ask them first, who do they think is the biggest threat to win? And if they say Gabe, you can say, 'I wonder if we should consider voting him out? What do you think?' Like that."

"But if we voted him off," she argued, "our homestead would be weaker for sure. Nobody's going to go for that."

He shrugged. "Two men left over there, and Stanley and Kevin are both strong. The challenges are all that really matter."

"Gabe's a lot stronger than Kevin," she felt compelled to point out. "Stronger than Stanley too. That's obvious. There's nothing I can say that's going to change people's minds on that."

"Exactly why he needs to go," Scott snapped. "You just have to make the others see that. And try harder to fly under the radar yourself."

She wasn't going to do it, Mira thought rebelliously a few minutes later, as Paradise began the walk home. It wouldn't work anyway, and she wasn't going to try. If she and Scott were voted out, they were voted out. There was no chance they would win anyway, so what did it matter?

"Doing all right?" Zara asked, coming up to walk beside her.

"Yeah," Mira said slowly.

"Good to see Scott?"

"Um…" *No.* "Can I ask you something?" she asked hesitantly.

"Sure."

"When I was talking back there…Did I seem…stuck on myself? Like I was trying to make it all about me?"

Zara looked at her sharply. "Kevin," she called back, "come up here."

"No, wait," Mira protested.

Zara ignored her. "Now, Kevin, my darling," she began when he joined them. "Mira would like to know whether she seemed stuck on herself, back in our little assembly. Whoever do you think could have put that idea into her head?"

"*That's* what he had to say to you after today?" Kevin asked in astonishment. "What's he going to do next, try to convince you that up is down? Day is night?"

"I didn't think I did," Mira said boldly. "And neither of you thought so either. Be honest."

Kevin sighed. "Honey. He's screwed the pooch over there, and he knows it. He's scrambling like mad to somehow make it your fault when you guys get voted off. If he doesn't end up 'accidentally' shot first himself."

He paused as second, then called, "Hey, Stanley!"

"Hmm?" Stanley rumbled, turning on the path ahead of them.

"What's that thing they had in Vietnam, when some unpopular second lieutenant would end up an unfortunate casualty of war?" Kevin demanded.

"Fragging," Stanley replied instantly, then looked at Mira with a twinkle of speculation.

"That's right," Kevin said with satisfaction. "I think Boyfriend's about due to get himself fragged. And I for one wouldn't prosecute."

a walk down memory lane

♡

Back at the cabin again, Kevin and Stanley took themselves off to see to the animals.

"You ladies need anything?" Gabe asked the women as Maria-Elena relit the stove. "We're about done outside for today. Put me to use."

"Chop some wood," Zara decided. "Getting low. Martin was supposed to do more yesterday, and needless to say, that didn't happen. And if you wouldn't mind pulling up a few more buckets of water for us, too, that'd help."

"Got it," he said, and headed outside again.

"I was thinking that we could stew the rabbits this time," Mira suggested to the others. "I could get some carrots and onions to go in with them, some green beans to add near the end. And I saw a recipe for dumplings in our recipe box. They look easy, and they'd cook right on top of the stew. That'd be almost the whole meal, and less to wash."

"I like your thinking," Zara decided.

"I could maybe bake a pie with some of those cherries, once we get the stew started," Maria-Elena offered. "I'll stay in here and do that."

And have a chance to talk to Gabe, Mira thought with a bit of amusement. She couldn't really feel jealous, despite her own growing attraction. Gabe couldn't have treated Maria-Elena any more like a little sister. And Maria-Elena was clearly enjoying her crush so very much.

"We're getting pretty competent, aren't we?" she said with a smile for the girl. "It's only been a couple weeks. Zara already knew how to cook, of course. But aren't you kind of amazed that you and I can do all this?"

Maria-Elena laughed happily. "My friends at home are going to be *totally* shocked when I get back. And my mom—she'll be thrilled. Because she's always wanting to teach me, you know, how to make things, and I'm, like, 'Mom, *lame.*' But now I wish I'd done it."

"Maybe you can ask her for lessons when you get back," Mira suggested.

"Yeah, maybe. I want to learn *mole.* We don't have what you need for it here, but eating this bland food makes me crave chiles and spices, you know? I bet rabbit *mole* would be good."

"Well, I'll go get what we do have," Mira decided. "Extra onions, at least. Spice it up as much as we can."

Twenty minutes later, vegetables gathered, she'd set herself up with a chair under the shade of the big pine at the edge of the cabin clearing to snap green beans and look at her favorite mountain view. She turned, though, at the sight of Zara emerging from the cabin, Gabe following behind her like an acolyte with a second chair, which he set down across from Mira.

"I got a huge rip in my shirt," he told Mira. "I backed up against the wall, caught it on a nail, and there it went. Luckily, I softened Zara up with my help in there, and she said she'd mend it for me."

Mira smiled up at him. "Good thing she did. I couldn't have. But I thought doctors knew how to sew."

"Shh," he said in mock alarm. "Don't tell."

Zara laughed. "Go on, go chop some more wood. And if you want to offer us a little entertainment out here, you can take off your shirt while you do it. Better than TV."

He grinned. "Always happy to oblige a beautiful woman."

"He's really doing it," Mira said, sneaking a glance across the yard, her hands stilling on her beans. "Wow." She sighed as Gabe lifted the axe, his broad back to them, then brought it down with a powerful swing, splitting the heavy section neatly in two.

Zara took her own long look, a satisfied smile settling over her lean face, tanned now despite the sunbonnet, before she pulled needle and thread out of the little sewing basket. "I was right," she said. "Better than TV. Ah, the simple pleasures."

She turned her attention to the three-inch rip in the back yoke of Gabe's shirt "Never thought I'd be sewing by hand again either," she added wryly. "I have this lovely dry cleaner I take everything to, and it magically comes back perfect again. She's another one I'm going to kiss when I'm done with this. A whole lot of people are going to be surprised by how affectionate I've become."

"It must have been nice to be with Hank today," Mira offered after a minute, continuing to snap off bean ends, pulling the strings and dropping the waste into her apron before tossing the beans into the bowl at her feet. "You guys always look so thrilled to see each other, even after all this time."

"It's true," Zara agreed. "We've got so used to each other, working together, living together all these years, sometimes I forget how much I just plain like him. Kinda good for us to have this time. Apart from anything else, being reminded that we're together because we want to be. Honestly, I can't wait to be done with this, so I can hear everything he has to say about how it was over there. Sit on the couch with him and watch the show, see what the producers make of it."

Mira sighed wistfully. "That's great. You're lucky."

"Yep. I've spent a fair amount of time out here thinking about my first marriage, one way or another. That reminds me in a hot minute just how lucky I am."

"Your first marriage?" Mira asked in surprise. "I didn't know you were married before. You must have been awfully young."

"Twenty. And it isn't a secret. You clearly haven't followed my fascinating life story nearly closely enough."

"Sorry," Mira said hastily. "I'm sure I've read it somewhere."

Zara laughed. "Way before your time. And yeah, I was married before. To the absolute wrong guy. The wrongest guy you could ever hope to meet. Started out great, of course. That kind always do. Mr. Charm. But pretty soon," she went on thoughtfully, her head bent over the shirt, "all his compliments started to have that little sting in the tail. He'd tell me I looked good, much better than yesterday. Clue me in that nobody really wanted to hear me sing, that I was making a fool of myself. That was a great party, but hadn't I been a little loud with his boss? Like that."

"So you left?" Mira prompted.

Zara laughed ruefully, cut a thread. "Thread this needle for me, will you?" she asked, handing it across together with the spool of thread. "I do hate that part about getting older. You can't see a thing, close up."

Mira obliged, and Zara took the needle and spool back again. "And no," she went on. "Oh, no. That would've been way too easy. It took a lot more than that. Because by then, of course, I thought I *was* loud at that party. That nobody *did* want to hear me sing. He'd got me pretty beaten down. No, I left when he started beating me down for real. I had that much self-preservation left, at least."

"He hit you?" Mira asked in shock.

"That started slowly too. Grabbing me, shoving me. My fault, of course, for making him that mad. Then being all lovey-dovey afterwards. Give a little, take it right back again the next

166

time. Got to keep me off-balance. But the night he cracked two ribs, that was it. That woke me right up."

"What did you do?"

"Called my dad. This was before the days of battered women's shelters, when nobody had ever heard of domestic violence. It was called a 'family matter' then." Zara grimaced in remembrance. "The good old days. After he stormed out of the house, I called a friend. Out the door with nothing but my purse and what I had on my back, terrified I wouldn't be in time, that he'd come back. It hurt so bad, I thought I was dying. I called my dad from my friend's house. He drove through the night to get me. Took one look at me, put me into the car, and that was it. I was out of there."

She held up the shirt to examine her handiwork. "Of course, now," she said, "I can see I should have called him about a year earlier. But I felt stupid, you see, for the longest time, for getting myself into a situation like that. Didn't want to admit, even to myself, how bad it was. But after I'd been out of it a while, I realized...guys like that, they've been practicing forever. They're experts at taking the weakest part of you and picking away at it, dragging you under. And I finally forgave myself for being dragged."

A reminiscent smile, then. "And then I met Hank. Found out what it was like to be with somebody who appreciated what was best about me. Who wanted to build on our strong sides, so we could be even stronger together. What a concept."

She folded the shirt, gave it a little slap. "Well. That's about it for the walk down memory lane. I'll just go see how Maria-Elena's getting on in there. Those beans about done?"

"Yeah," Mira said, lifting her apron carefully to take the bean ends to the chickens, then picking up her bowl. "Done."

hazardous duty

♡

"Another pie?" Stanley asked with pleasure the next evening, when Mira brought it to the table after a supper of trout, cornbread, beet greens cooked with the last of the chard in a little bacon grease, and the inevitable beans.

"That's Maria-Elena," Mira said. "My crust always falls apart. I've given up on pies. But Maria-Elena's a whiz."

"You really are," Gabe said as he took a bite. "This is plum, right? Delicious."

Maria-Elena blushed right on cue at his compliment. "My mom taught me to make empanadas a long time ago. The pastry isn't that different. And Mira picked the plums."

"I did," Mira laughed. "Try climbing a tree in a long skirt sometime. It's a real feat."

"You were careful, right?" Gabe asked in some alarm. "Next time, come get me before you do something like that."

"You were busy haying," she protested. "And that's a whole lot more dangerous than climbing a tree."

"Only if you're Martin," Kevin said.

"I shouldn't laugh," Mira said ruefully after she'd done just that. "But he *was* accident-prone."

"Easy to have accidents out here, though," Stanley said thoughtfully. "Farming's still a mighty dangerous occupation, and even more back then, for women and men both. And if something *did* happen, miles from a doctor, no way to get help…" He shrugged. "Wouldn't have been good. Still plenty of ways to get hurt even now. So Gabe's right. Be careful out there, Miss Mira."

"I will," she promised, with the glow that the men's protective concern always aroused in her. Especially, she had to admit, Gabe's. "But we're making plum jam tomorrow, and you're going to be glad I climbed that tree, Stanley, when you get some of that on your biscuits."

"That'll be right nice," he said. "I'll look forward to that."

"This sounded like a good idea at the time," Maria-Elena sighed late the next morning. "We'll just barely be done with this, and it'll be time to fix lunch." She wiped her glistening face with her sleeve as she continued to stir the fruit and sugar on the hot stove, the water boiling in the big canning kettle adding its measure of steam to the climbing temperatures in the little cabin.

"Extra time in the creek this afternoon," Zara promised. "And if we have a jam challenge, we'll be all set. Step aside for a minute." She reached into the kettle with her tongs, pulled out the jars and lids one by one and set them carefully on the clean dishtowels she'd spread ready on the table. "Ready to fill," she declared. "Bring the fruit on over here, Maria-Elena."

Maria-Elena obliged, using potholders and lifting the heavy pot with the muscles they'd all developed these past weeks. Mira bent down and opened the door to the firebox to add the extra wood they'd need for the processing time. And to cook lunch, she thought with a sigh of her own. She shoved the sticks of wood in, gave them a jab with the poker to settle them. Saw the glob of pitch catch fire, and jumped back from the resulting gout of flame a moment too late.

It took her precious seconds to work out what had happened. That the bottom of her hair, braided as usual at the side of her head, had swung into contact with the flame. Her hair was actually on fire, she realized with shock. It was shriveling up her braid, spreading to her blouse now.

Smother it, she thought as the room filled with a terrible stench and Zara and Maria-Elena turned alarmed faces her way, began to rush forward. Mira dropped the poker she realized she was still holding and grabbed for the bottom of her apron, frantically pushing the wadded fabric against her braid. Zara, with commendable presence of mind, picked up the bucket of water sitting by the stove and dashed it over Mira's head, then reached for the hot pads Maria-Elena had dropped and pressed them into the shriveled hair to make sure the fire was out.

They stood for a moment, staring at each other, all three pairs of eyes wide with shock, before Zara pulled the woefully scorched hair aside, exposed the long, charred patch of clothing beneath.

"Go get Gabe," she snapped at Maria-Elena. "Run."

Poor Maria-Elena, Mira thought, a bubble of hilarity rising within her, having to run for help yet again. And poor Gabe. "He didn't think he was going to have to do so much doctoring on this show," she said with a laugh that came out too shaky, and much higher than she'd intended.

"Sit down," Zara ordered, pushing her into a chair by her unburned left shoulder, then hastily untying Mira's apron and pulling it over her head. She'd just begun unbuttoning Mira's blouse when Gabe came bursting in through the door.

"You're fast," Mira said to him with another giddy laugh. Why did all this seem so funny? "The jam," she remembered with a start. "We need to get it in the jars."

Nobody paid any attention to her. "He was on his way back with the hay," Maria-Elena got out, puffing inside in her turn.

Gabe had already taken over from Zara and was pulling Mira's blouse gently off, exposing the corset and chemise beneath. "Looks like that corset's done some good for once," he muttered. "How do you unfasten it?"

Zara reached for the hooks. Removing the corset, however, caused the burned section at the top of the chemise to separate from the intact area below, which immediately dropped below Mira's right breast, causing her to grab at it in embarrassment.

"What's going on?" Stanley said in alarm, he and Kevin entering the little cabin and, Mira thought with another burst of inward laughter, turning the scene into a French bedroom farce, especially with Danny filming the whole thing. She struggled to pull the remnants of her chemise up higher and sent Gabe a wild glance.

"You two and Maria-Elena," Gabe ordered, "get out till I'm done here. You too, Danny."

"But—" Danny protested. "I'm supposed to film everything."

"You're not filming this," Gabe said, the set of his jaw leaving no doubt of his seriousness. "Get out or I'll throw you out."

"Thanks," Mira said shakily when Danny had closed the door behind him. "I don't..." The tears were coming now, the sense of hilarity vanishing. "I'm sorry. That was so stupid. I don't know how I even did that."

Gabe put his hands over her own where they were clutching her clothes. "I need to see what's burned," he told her gently. "I'm being a doctor here. Trust me."

She swallowed and nodded, releasing the fabric and allowing him to pull the chemise off. When she'd imagined him taking off her clothes, she'd never thought of this. This was just...humiliating. And her skin was burning.

"Get me a wet towel," Gabe ordered Zara. "Nothing too bad here," he said with relief, his fingers moving over Mira gently, "but we'll cool it down some more. Who poured water on her?"

"Me," Zara said, coming back with the dripping towel.

"Good job with that. And you're going to be just fine," he told Mira reassuringly as he laid the cold, wet cloth against her heated skin. "A patch of first-degree burn, a few small blisters, nothing too much worse than a bad sunburn. And it's only in this one area, on your shoulder and upper chest above your corset. That protected you from anything worse. Though I'm afraid your pretty hair's done for," he said with a rueful smile before he turned to the washstand, began to lather his hands.

"I don't care about that," Mira said, holding her left elbow awkwardly across her uncovered breast. "I've wanted to cut it for a long time. I guess I'll get my wish."

"I think you will." He reached for the first-aid kit they'd been given, then came back to her. He removed the wet towels and dabbed the area dry before gently applying a thin film of antibiotic ointment to the burned area, then covered it with gauze pads that he fixed to her skin with adhesive tape.

"The beautician part of this is going to be a lot harder than the doctor part," he promised. "Because you're all set." He shook out two Ibuprofen and handed them to her. "Got a glass of water, Zara?"

"Here you go," Zara said, pouring it out. "You take those, Mira, and I'll go get you something to wear."

"No corset for the next few days, until it isn't hurting anymore," Gabe declared. "I don't want that rubbing up against the burn."

"That's going to be kind of…natural," Mira said doubtfully, the embarrassment returning as she put both forearms up to cover her bare breasts.

He laughed. "Stanley will avert his eyes, and Kevin doesn't care."

"And you won't be looking either, right?" Zara said dryly, coming down from the loft with an armful of clothes, helping Mira off with her skirt as she stood, then pulling the chemise over her head, dressing her as if she were a child. A gesture that felt strangely comforting.

"Well…" Gabe said, closing the first-aid kit and putting it neatly back in its place. "I'll do my best."

♡

Which wasn't going to be very good, he thought as he left the cabin. When he'd been worried about what he'd see, it was true, he'd been all doctor. But now that he knew she was all right…It might not have been the way he'd envisioned seeing her naked, but it had worked pretty well all the same. And those memories were going to be sticking around, he knew, making his life even more difficult.

"You can go in now," he told the others. "Coast is clear."

"How's Mira doing?" Stanley asked, concern clearly visible on his kindly face.

"She's going to be fine," Gabe assured him. "A little shaken up, as you'd expect. But she'll be good as new, with a new haircut and a few days."

"And how are you?"

"Me?" Gabe shrugged. "I'm good. Like I said, she's fine."

"And that didn't shake *you* up," Stanley said flatly. "When Maria-Elena came flying out like that, and you heard Mira was burned. When you took off like a bat out of the hot spot."

Gabe read the understanding in the older man's face, the same look he'd seen a hundred times from his own dad, and caved. "Yeah," he admitted on a sigh. "Yeah. That was a rough one."

"About time to make your move, then, don't you think?" Stanley asked.

Gabe looked at him, startled.

"There's a time and a place for nobility," Stanley advised. "And boy, this isn't the time or the place."

worse things than macaroni

♡

"Do you think you can make it cute?" Mira asked, sitting down on the kitchen chair Gabe had carried out to the shade.

"I've cut lots of people's hair," Maria-Elena assured her. "You're going to look, like, so much hotter when I'm done. That super long hair was kinda lame."

Mira laughed, feeling more cheerful than she should have with a burned chest and shoulder and a head full of scorched hair. Maybe it was the rest Gabe had made her take while Zara and Maria-Elena had belatedly finished the jam and made lunch.

"You need it more than you realize," he'd insisted.

To her surprise, he'd been right. It must have been the shock and fright, added to the pain of the actual burn, because she'd fallen asleep almost immediately, lulled by the sound of the women working and chatting in low tones downstairs, and had only woken up when they'd called her to eat.

"That's two close calls for you, Mira," Kevin had said over their hastily prepared lunch of corned beef hash, fried eggs, and biscuits. "You're getting to be as bad as Martin."

"Well, to be fair, she couldn't help the gunshot thing," Zara said. "And I've come close to catching my hair on fire myself. It just swings right in there."

"Well, it won't any more." Mira fingered a crispy end. "My fire danger's over, I think. So I can get back to work, once Maria-Elena cuts off the burned part. Because phew, this stinks. How can you all stand it?"

"You forget, I'm Mr. Animal Husbandry," Kevin said. "You smell better than the corral. But it's close."

"And as far as work," Gabe put in, "you're still taking it easy this afternoon. Simple things, all right. Chopping vegetables or whatever. But that's it. Anything harder, that she'd usually do," he said to Zara, "tell me, and I'll do it."

♡

Now, he was sitting with them on a chair of his own, churning butter and keeping them company. And keeping an eye on his patient, he'd insisted. He'd known it sounded stupid, and he'd said it anyway.

"Thanks for doing that," Mira said lazily as his arms worked the dasher. "But you know that's only Part One."

"Then you'll have to direct me on Part Two after this," he said. "Give me a tutorial. I'm pretty open to instruction. Anyway, it beats haying."

"That's all the burned stuff," Maria-Elena declared, snipping off the last wet, frizzled lock. "It smells better already. You can wash it again in the creek after I cut it, get all the burned smell and little ends out."

"Am I allowed to go in the creek?" Mira asked Gabe.

"Sure. Take the dressing off first. The cold water should feel good on the burn. I'll dress it again after your bath," he promised. Despite himself, his eyes went momentarily to her breasts before he brought them hastily back to her face again. He caught an expression there, saw a shiver that, he hoped, wasn't just about her wet hair.

"How short do you want this?" Maria-Elena asked.

"Umm…" Mira considered. "Long enough to put up, still? What do you think?" she asked Gabe. "You have an opinion? Got a preference in women's hair?"

She was flirting with him, he realized with delight. He looked across at her, hair parted in the middle, a single length chopped off above the shoulder. *Eyes up here,* he reminded himself. "Yeah, I'd leave some of that," he decided. "You have beautiful hair. Maybe you could make it more…curly, Maria-Elena?"

"Layered," she corrected. "So her curl comes out." She lifted a piece of hair with the comb to consider it. "I can do that."

"How did you learn this?" Mira asked her.

"I wanted to be a beautician," Maria-Elena confided, beginning to comb and snip. "When I was younger. I still kinda want to. But my mom really wanted me to go to college. So I'm starting at the state college this fall. Living at home, though," she added with a disgruntled sigh. "I can't afford to live on campus, even with, like, a scholarship and loans and things. God, I hate being poor."

"It's not great," Gabe agreed, still methodically churning. "But there are worse things than starting out broke. Like not knowing how to be poor. People can get into some real trouble that way. It's a lot easier to go up than down that ladder."

"Huh?" Maria-Elena asked.

"Trust me, learning how to live cheap, if you don't start out having to do it, is the hard part. Learning how *not* to be poor—that's easy. Just ask Alec."

"But you guys can't know about being poor," Maria-Elena objected. "You're a doctor. And you have a really nice car. I saw it, at the beginning. At the motel."

"Alec's," Gabe explained. "We're not poor now, no. But my dad's a Presbyterian minister, and my mom's a part-time school secretary. Not what you'd call your lucrative professions. Lots of macaroni and cheese, moving around, living in some kind of cheap housing provided by the congregation. A single-wide in Winnemucca...that was middle school. High school, it was Chico. Our first actual house. We thought we'd arrived, let me tell you."

"So how did you go to college, and to medical school?" Mira asked. "And Alec? He's got a degree too, doesn't he?"

"Just like Maria-Elena. Loans and scholarships. Football, for me."

"You were a football player?" Maria-Elena asked, clearly more impressed than ever. "A pro one? Like the NFL?"

He laughed. "No. They tend to be a lot bigger than me. And better. College, that's all."

"What about Alec?" Mira asked.

"Ah. Alec. Full scholarship to Stanford. But we both had to work, still. Me, it was the landscaping crew. Alec wasn't into getting his hands dirty. Which is going to have made this show pretty interesting for him."

"You were a *landscaper?*" Maria-Elena asked. "Like, cutting the grass?"

"Yep. And a whole lot more. Good for football, actually. Built as much muscle as the gym. Carrying stone for patios, digging, putting in plants. Just like here. That's why I don't mind it. And hey, I had to do something to earn some money, and I didn't have that many skills, not like Alec. A scholarship doesn't pay for everything. Clothes, pizza. Going out," he added with a smile. "Not all girls think a walk and a picnic's romantic, unfortunately."

"I would," Mira said quietly. "I'd rather do that than look across a restaurant table at a guy all night, try to think of conversation."

"Not me," Maria-Elena put in firmly. "I want to go to nice places. Don't you just want to buy and buy stuff?" she demanded of Gabe. "Now that you're rich?"

He laughed. "I'm not rich. There are these things called medical school loans. I've about got them paid off now, but it's put a big crimp in the old lifestyle."

"But Alec has that car, you said," Maria-Elena pressed. "What about him?"

"He's a bit better off," Gabe admitted. "He's the catch, I'm afraid." And that was enough about that, he decided.

"What about you, Mira?" he asked. "How are your poverty skills? They as good as Maria-Elena's and mine?"

She smiled a little, the snippets of russet-brown hair falling around her. Gabe couldn't tell how her hair was going to end up. But even if it wasn't perfect, he knew, she wouldn't be making a fuss. She seemed strangely calm, in fact, for somebody who'd just had her hair burned off, and was now having it cut by an eighteen-year-old wannabe beautician. Not many women he'd known would have been able to roll with this one. Hell, probably *no* woman he'd known. Certainly none he'd dated.

"No," she said now. "No poverty skills."

This churning was getting old. Gabe opened the lid and peeked inside. "Is this butter yet?" he asked Maria-Elena.

She leaned over and took a look. "Nope. It takes longer than that. Keep churning."

"Slave driver," he muttered, making her laugh.

"So you were a princess, huh? Did you have one of those fancy bedrooms?" Gabe asked Mira, starting to work the dasher again. "My sister always wanted one of those, with one of those things over the bed. What do they call those?"

"Canopies," she said, her face closing. "No. Two bedrooms, always. But no princess thing."

"Your parents are divorced?" Maria-Elena asked. "Mine too. I can't wait for my dad to see the show. He was really excited about me being on it. Is yours too?"

"No," Mira said again. "He didn't think it was…a good idea. A good use of my time."

"What about your mom?" Maria-Elena asked, snipping the hair around Mira's face now.

"She's on a cruise with her new husband. I emailed her. She'll have got it by now, I guess. I'm sure she'll enjoy watching it."

"Second marriage, huh?" Gabe asked. Mira's normal transparency was completely missing. Something was wrong here.

"Fourth," she said.

"Wow," Maria-Elena said. "She's been married four times? What about your dad?"

"Three," Mira said shortly. "You aren't doing bangs, are you? I'm not sure what I want, but I don't think I want bangs."

"No bangs," Maria-Elena assured her. "We'll part it on the side, and it'll fall in waves. It's going to be really gorgeous, I promise."

Gabe dropped the subject. The older he got, the more he realized that there were worse things than macaroni and cheese for dinner, clothes handed down from older boys in the congregation, however much they'd rankled at the time. And one of those things was growing up without love.

when it's right

♡

"Everything's healing up nicely. Looking good down low here," Gabe pronounced after Mira's late-afternoon dip in the creek two days later. His fingers were gentle against her skin as he began to fasten the new, smaller dressing. "How's it feeling?"

"Fine," she said, her breath quickening a little at his touch, the sight of his head bent so close over her breast, where her hand was holding the chemise. "It's only a little sore now up where the blisters are."

"You can go back to wearing the corset tomorrow," he decided. "If you really have to," he added with a grin, pulling the strap of her chemise back up onto her shoulder and sitting back on the chair he'd pulled out to face her.

"I'll admit, it's more comfortable without it." She picked up her blouse where it lay beside her on the bench and shrugged into it again. "Not much support, though, bending over in the garden. And I can't run at all. Though the corset doesn't make for the most comfortable running either. It'd be nice to have a bra." She looked down at herself ruefully as she fastened her sleeve buttons. "I'm not a big fan of 1885 underwear, I've decided."

She looked up, and became even more flustered at the heat in his gaze. Why was she talking about her underwear? It must be the doctor thing.

"Oh, I don't know." His smile started slow, began to spread. "I'm getting pretty fond of this—what do you call it?" he asked, giving a last rub to a bit of insecure tape, then lightly touching the strap he'd just pulled up.

"Chemise," she said, her hands arrested on the bottom button of her blouse.

"Yeah. Chemise. Seen you in it a few times now, under a few different circumstances. I have to say, I like the wet version best. But all of them work for me."

♡

"I'm not going to be feeling like singing tomorrow night," Zara said as Mira and Maria-Elena finished the nightly ritual of washing dishes and grinding coffee beans in preparation for the next day, the men lingering over their final evening cup of coffee. "Not after laundry day, I'm not. And we've got the dance on Friday, the challenge on Saturday...We'd better make it a good one tonight."

"I thought I'd miss music the most out here," Maria-Elena said to Mira, watching the men get up obligingly to begin the almost-nightly task of carrying the bench and Zara's chair outside. Zara was already removing the guitar from its case with the tender care she always demonstrated. "Besides my phone, I mean. Like Melody."

They grinned at each other as Maria-Elena went on. "At home, I always have my iPod in. But this has been even better. At first I thought the songs were kind of, like, lame. But now...I don't know, I sort of love them."

"Yeah," Mira agreed, giving one last wipe to the cast-iron skillet and hanging it on its hook on the log wall. "Maybe it's just the lack of other entertainment, but I don't think so. There's a reason those songs have hung around so long, I guess. And you have such a gorgeous voice. It's been one of the best things out here for me too, the singing at night. And listening to you in the garden. I'll bet you'll be doing a lot more singing once you're home again."

"You have a nice voice too," Maria-Elena said loyally.

Mira laughed. "I've enjoyed accompanying you, let's just leave it at that." She left the dark, stuffy cabin gratefully and stepped out into the late evening light. The days weren't quite as long now, but the sun still wasn't setting until after eight-thirty, allowing the group plenty of time for their almost-nightly music sessions. She was in time, though, she saw with delight, for her favorite view of the day. She should be used to the Alpenglow by now, but the pink light on the mountains still gave her the same lift of the heart it had that first night, in the motel parking lot.

And just like that night, there was Gabe, standing by the bench, watching her drink in the beloved sight.

"I will lift mine eyes unto the hills," he quoted.

"From whence cometh my help," Stanley added, seating himself with Kevin on the log that made up the third section of their little music circle.

"I thought for the longest time, as a kid," Gabe confessed, seating himself between Mira and Maria-Elena on the bench, "that that meant the help came from the hills themselves. Because my dad always said it just like that, didn't add the rest of the psalm."

"Maybe because he felt that way," Mira guessed, "the same way I do. When you look at them, they're like that, aren't they? Reminding you of what's good, and strong, and...and permanent in the world. The things that matter, the ones that last."

She cut herself off. "I'm sorry. That was really sappy."

"No," Gabe said forcefully as Stanley smiled his agreement, his gaze warm and approving. "Why shouldn't you say what you think? Why shouldn't we be honest out here?"

"Maybe because we're playing a game, and it's not necessarily a good idea to expose yourself," Kevin said quietly, serious for once. "Not always wise to show your vulnerability, Mira."

It was Zara who answered. "Mira doesn't care that much about the game. No more than I do. She knows she's not going to win it, not with Scott. She's getting what she came for. And maybe even more."

Her gaze rested a moment on Gabe before she began to strum the guitar. "Going to break the rules a little here tonight," she declared. "Do some songs I love, period-appropriate or not."

"Some of yours?" Mira asked hopefully, still feeling softened and moved by the sight of the mountains, the acceptance she'd felt from the others.

"If you want," Zara agreed. "And if you'll help me sing them."

She sang of love and loss, heartbreak and longing. Traditional songs, and more recent ones too, each one winching Mira's heart just a little bit further open. And then switched to a more upbeat note, the folk songs popular in her heyday. They all joined in on "If I Had a Hammer," but only Maria-Elena could manage the Spanish lyrics of "Guantanamera."

Mira sang softly, as always, listening to Gabe's strong baritone beside her, the words and melodies familiar and so moving. The bench wasn't large, and she felt the thrill of his thigh, warm and hard against hers, of his shoulder pressed to her own, as surely as if she'd been in his arms. She didn't dare look at him, afraid he'd see the truth in her face. She'd already revealed so much tonight.

"Got one last song to do for you," Zara announced as the fading light told them all that it was time to start wrapping it up. "I can't sing it in Judy Collins's angel voice, of course. But maybe you'll help me out on it, Maria-Elena. You've got a bit of that yourself. 'Someday Soon.' You know that one?"

"No," Maria-Elena admitted. "Sorry."

"Well," Zara smiled, "it's not that hard to pick up, once I sing the chorus once. This one's all about the way love can sweep you off your feet. About the terror and the certainty of it. About knowing when it's right. So I thought I should sing it for you tonight."

She began, the sound of the guitar, then her lovely alto, rising to fill the evening air. Mira sat back and listened, her skin prickling, the chill running down her neck, her arms at the lyrics, the plaintive melody. Gabe shifted beside her, and then his hand was closing around her own where it rested in her lap. She felt him lift it, set it between them on the bench, lace his fingers through hers. Felt the warmth of his broad palm against hers, the solidity of his thigh against the back of her hand.

She cast a quick glance at him, saw his eyes fixed on Zara even as his thumb began stroking the sensitive skin of her forefinger. The music filled her, while every bit of physical awareness focused on where he was holding her, the places his body touched hers. She saw Zara's eyes on her as she sang, and realized that she meant the song for her. For her and Gabe.

"Take a walk with me," Gabe said when the song was over and Zara had pulled the guitar strap from around her neck, signaling the end of the concert.

"The camera..." she murmured.

"Screw the camera. I have a pretty good idea what the storyline of this show's going to be, and so do you. And the next scene happens right the hell now. Let's walk."

She got up with him, her heart beating fast, saw that Stu was indeed following them at a discreet distance, and found she didn't care.

Gabe walked fast, seeming almost angry. He waited until they were on the path into the woods, out of earshot of the others.

"Are you still in love with Scott?" he asked abruptly, still walking, not looking at her.

"No," she said softly. Then, more strongly, "No." Not for a long time now, she realized. Certainly not since she'd come on the show with him.

"You going to break up with him, then?"

"Yes." She couldn't think, suddenly, why she hadn't done it sooner. She didn't even want to see him again, let alone talk to him. Or, more correctly, listen to him talk to her. She'd done a whole lot better than he had out here. If anyone had the right to berate their partner, it was her.

"Good." He stopped on the path so abruptly that she nearly bumped into him, turned to face her. "When?"

"Next time we see them, if I can. Friday at the dance, I'm thinking. But having it happen on camera would be so humiliating for him. Maybe I should wait till we're voted off after all. It can't be that long." Sadness filled her at the thought of leaving this place. Of leaving with Scott.

"If he's humiliated, that's his problem," Gabe said. "You need to get yourself free. For yourself, and for me. Because I need to kiss you. I can't wait much longer. Hell," he groaned as she looked up at him in the twilight, those eyes shining almost gold, "I can't wait at all."

He did kiss her, then. Pulled her into him, the way he'd wanted to do since the first time he'd seen her. He wrapped his hands around her head, fingers tunneling into the new waves that she'd left loose tonight, tilted her face up to his, and settled his mouth over hers.

The heat of it was like a shock. Her soft lips opening under his, her gasp into his mouth. One hand left her head, moved down to pull her lower back into him. He felt the press of her uncorseted softness, her entire body held against his now, and almost groaned aloud with it. Her own hands were on his shoulders, holding on, and she was kissing him back with a passion that told him she'd imagined this almost as many times as he had.

They stood like that for long minutes, lips and tongues chasing, exploring, the soft sounds of her desire taken into his mouth, her body, with all its beautiful curves, straining against his own. Then Gabe pulled his mouth from hers, raw need pounding through him, urging him on. Resisting it took every bit of his strength.

"That's all," he said, his voice rough. "That's all we're doing until he's gone. And until we have some privacy."

She nodded, looking as shaken as he was feeling. "OK," she whispered. Her body swayed against his, though, and those eyes, looking up at him with so much yearning, urging him to abandon every principle, nearly undid him.

"Don't look at me like that," he ordered harshly. "I'm trying to do the right thing here. And it's hard as hell." He turned back to the cabin, but took her hand in his again. He wouldn't do anything else if he could help it. But he was damned if he wasn't going to hold her hand.

"Friday," he reminded her when they were in sight of the clearing once more. It was full dusk now, and everyone else was already inside. Except, of course, the ever-present Stu, still patiently recording.

"Friday," she agreed. "I'll do it then. Even if it's on camera," she said, with a return of worry in her voice. "But I'd hate to do that."

"He's humiliated you on camera enough times, I'll bet. All you'd be doing is turning the tables for once."

people who speak
to your heart

♡

The little cabin was still steamy the next evening as they sat down to one of their less ambitious dinners. Beans with salt pork, cornbread, and greens.

"Sorry it's not more exciting, guys," Mira sighed. "Laundry day's a tough one." Kissing Gabe in the cool twilight felt like something that had happened a week ago.

"What you've got here is just good Southern cooking," Stanley objected. "This is what I was raised on. No apologies necessary." He lifted the glass of buttermilk Mira had, as always, set out for him. "Here's to another good meal."

"Think they'll have alcohol tomorrow?" Kevin asked. "At the dance?"

"Wow. Alcohol," Zara said, pushing beans around her plate with her fork. "There's a concept. I could use a cold beer right about now."

"Didn't the laundry feel easier to you today than the first time, though?" Mira asked her.

"Hmm." Zara considered. "It did, I suppose. Not quite as bad."

"Isn't that interesting?" Mira asked, the chance to sit, the food beginning to revive her. "We've got twenty-five percent fewer people here now, and twenty-five percent less laundry too.

And, of course, twenty-five percent fewer women to do it. So technically, it's the same amount of work per person, right?"

"Right," Zara said slowly.

"But our perceived effort is less," Mira went on, caught up in her analysis. "Because we know what to expect, and how long it'll take. And we had to boil fewer loads, which I always think is the toughest part. We spent more of our time working outside, which feels easier. And," she added, "we actually *were* more efficient. First, we know what we're doing. And second, we didn't get rid of twenty-five percent of our productivity when Melody left. More like..."

"Ten percent," Zara said dryly. "Or eight."

"She wasn't that bad," Maria-Elena protested.

"No, she wasn't," Mira agreed. "At least at the end there. But it does make you wonder how much more efficient we could get over time. Whether we'd find some shortcuts, as laborious as the process is. It's interesting to think about, isn't it?"

"Absolutely fascinating," Kevin said with a straight face. "There's nothing I personally love more, after a day spent slaving over a hot stove, than a bit of process engineering. Maybe you could create some bar graphs, Mira, and do a PowerPoint presentation for us next week."

Gabe laughed. "She can't help it if she's good at her job. You can take the girl out of the conference room, but you can't take the conference room out of the girl."

"You're right," Mira said with a smile of her own. "And I haven't got to practice my skills as much as you have out here."

"Yeah, well," he said, "I could've done with practicing my skills quite a bit less myself. I wasn't counting on Martin."

"Well," Mira got up from the table. "I guess it's time to get efficient with the dishes."

Zara got up to help, but Mira waved her back down. "You take it easy. Maria-Elena and I've got it."

"I'll wash tonight," Gabe decided, getting up in Zara's place. "Give you two a hand."

"Whoa," Mira said. "Pretty daring, isn't it?" She nodded toward Stu, filming from his corner as usual. "What's Alec going to say about your role reversal when you're found out?"

"That I obviously had an ulterior motive." He lifted the heavy kettle from the stove, poured hot water into the washpans on the high work counter, added a bit of cool water from the bucket, a dash of the harsh lye soap into one of the pans, and began scrubbing the plates Mira had already wiped out. "He'll say that I was trying to make points before the dance. And making sure my partners had some energy left to dance with me."

"I wonder what kind of dancing it'll be," Maria-Elena said, picking up the plates as Gabe dropped them into the rinse pan and wiping them dry before setting them on the shelf above.

"Square dancing," Zara said. "That's got to be it."

"What's that?" Maria-Elena asked doubtfully. "It sounds kinda lame."

"You're going to think it's *completely* lame," Kevin predicted. "We had to do it in P.E. in middle school, and *I* thought it was lame. And I'm gay. We *like* dancing."

"Guess we'll all learn how to do it tomorrow night," Gabe said. "Personally, I'm up for any kind of dancing. Are you and Hank going to sing for us?" he turned to ask Zara. "That would really be something. I'd dance to that. Especially one of those slow ones." He looked at Mira as she dumped silverware into the washpan, reached for her hand under the soapy water, wrapped his own around it and held it fast. She stood stock-still, her gaze caught by his own.

"They waltzed in those days, right?" he went on, his eyes not leaving Mira's. "I'd love a waltz. In fact, I'm asking for it right now."

"If they ask us to sing, we'll sing for you," Zara promised. "And if we do, it'll be my pleasure to help you get your waltz."

"All right, then," he said, his slow smile growing. "I know what I'll be looking forward to."

♡

"I'm going to take the chance while it's still light," Gabe announced once the last dish was washed and he'd dumped the pans of water outside, "to check the corral fence. That top rail was looking a little wobbly. And we won't have much time tomorrow."

Maria-Elena watched him go, a wistful look in her eyes. "And no singing tonight," she said with a sigh. "I think I'll go up to bed early. I'm tired anyway." Not much to stay up for, Mira thought with some sympathy, without Gabe around.

"Hard being young out here, nothing to do," Stanley said with a smile of understanding.

"Yeah," Maria-Elena agreed. "I mean, there's lots to *do*. But nothing *fun*. I miss going to the mall. I miss my friends. But I don't mean it's, like, bad," she went on with a hasty glance at Zara. "I like the singing and stuff."

"That's OK," Zara said. "I was young once too, about a hundred years ago. I do vaguely remember."

"How about you, Miss Mira?" Stanley asked, leaning back against the wall of the cabin and taking a contemplative sip of coffee as Maria-Elena set about getting ready for bed and Mira took a seat at the table again. "You're young too. Miss the mall?"

Mira laughed. "Nope." She paused, struck by the thought. "Partly, I suppose, because I *am* more than ten years older than Maria-Elena. I don't shop much for entertainment."

"You astonish me," Kevin drawled.

"Yeah," Mira smiled. "I guess that was obvious. I mostly just have a work wardrobe. And that's the other thing. I've spent so much time traveling, living out of a suitcase, staying home is what's exotic to me."

"I'm with you there," Zara said. "Airports, hotels...Seen one, seen 'em all."

"It's weird," Mira went on impulsively. "But being here, this place, even this funky little cabin. It feels more like home than anyplace I've ever lived."

She caught herself, looked down at the tabletop in pained embarrassment. What was it about being here? She kept over-sharing. It was a *game,* she reminded herself miserably, rubbing at a smudge with her finger, pretending to be busy, trying not to show the tears. These weren't really her friends. They certainly weren't her family. She might very well be voted out in a few days, even if Paradise won.

She got up, pasted on a smile that felt a little wobbly despite her best efforts. "Since we're not singing, I'm going to take a walk. See my favorite view."

Stanley got up himself. "If you don't mind a little company," he decided, "I'll go with you. Better not to walk alone at dusk anyway, animals and such."

Mira fetched her shawl, and they walked without speaking for a few minutes on the open path that led through the hayfields toward the Clearing, Daisy trotting along behind.

"I know how you feel," Stanley finally said, breaking the silence. "About this place feeling like home. Even though you felt foolish saying it because you're supposed to be playing a game, competing with all these folks."

Mira glanced up at him, startled, then hastily away again.

"But I've felt that too," Stanley said. "Seems you just can't help but get close when you're living together, working together every day. You get to know a person, doing that. And if you've been lonely..." He stopped, walked on a few more yards before continuing. "Well, it's natural, then, to form some bonds.

Natural, and human too, no matter what other people might say about strategy and competition. Plenty of things more important than a million dollars. Can't help realizing that out here, if you've got a lick of sense."

Mira nodded, a lump forming in her throat at his understanding. "I think you may have been lonely too," she said softly. "I'm sorry if I'm trespassing. But I think maybe so."

"Yeah," he said, his deep voice gruff with emotion. "Yeah, I sure have been, ever since my wife passed. That's probably why I agreed to do this with Calvin. It's not about the money, not for me. I'm all right there. Never been rich yet. Wouldn't even know how to be. I thought it'd be something good to do with my boy. And even though we're not doing it together after all, we're still sharing it."

They kept walking for another minute before he went on. "And there's been the bonus, too, the part I didn't expect. Making real friends out here. You think, at my time of life, you've made all the friends you're going to get. You forget that friends can come in all ages, all shapes and sizes and colors, anytime at all. That they're the people who speak to your heart." He looked down at her. "People like you."

She took his arm and squeezed it, then held on. It felt so good, so solid and comforting. She could tell he didn't mind, because he brought his other hand around to press hers.

"That's right nice," he said, "having a woman on my arm like that. It's been a long time."

"How long?" she asked. "Since your wife passed away? What was her name?"

"Althea," he said with a sigh. "Almost two years now. She didn't last long, once they found it. The cancer just moved too fast, took her right away from me."

He stared into the distance, his gaze on the mountains, as they continued to walk. "I always thought we'd get old together.

Rock away into the sunset, on the front porch. When she got sick..." He broke off, looked up at the sky, took a deep breath before he resumed. "She was so brave. When she asked me to shave her head, during the chemo. Made a joke of it, a little party. Wore those scarves, those hats, like they were some kind of fashion statement. We'd go to church, and she'd be hugging everyone else, asking after their kids, their grandkids. She broke my heart. And I couldn't do it. I couldn't be as strong as she was. She was the one dying, and she was comforting *me.*"

He took the handkerchief out of his back pocket, wiped the corners of his eyes, gave a little laugh. "Sorry. It's knowing you, thinking how much you remind me of her, when we were young."

"I suspect," Mira said slowly, squeezing his arm a little tighter, "that it could be harder to be the one who's left behind than the one who...leaves. She'd had a good life, I'm guessing. She'd made her peace. I'm sure the hardest thing, the very hardest thing for her, was leaving you alone."

"That's what she said," he agreed with a sigh. "You got it. Leaving our kids, and leaving me. The last thing she said," he said, his eyes tearing up again, "was, 'I'll see you soon. I'll wait for you.' She's in a better place, I know that. Maybe she had to go on ahead of me, because she knew how hard it'd be for me to get there. That I'd need some help from up there, a reminder to do right so I can join her someday. That's what I hold on to."

Mira lifted the corner of her apron to wipe her own eyes. "I think," she said softly, "that your wife was a lucky woman. And I think she knew it."

He shook his head. "I was the lucky one. Even though I lost her. Because at least I had her. I got to love somebody that much, to have my angel love me with her whole beautiful heart, for almost thirty years. I had her to show me the way."

He pulled out his handkerchief again, gave his nose a good blow. "That wasn't what I meant to talk to you about at all.

You're too good a listener, is what it is. You've got a beautiful soul, Miss Mira. A heart full of love. Don't you ever let anyone tell you that's a bad thing, or a weak thing."

She was the one who had to look away now. "I won't," she promised at last, her throat tight with emotion. "Not any more."

"And now I'm going to ask you what Althea would, if she were here," he went on more briskly. "How are you using your precious, God-given, one and only life? Would you say you're doing what you were meant to do?"

"No," she said with a sigh. "No. I'm not sure what I was meant to do. But I'm sure I'm not doing it."

"And why is that?" he pressed.

"I don't know. Trying to please my dad, I guess. He wanted me to go into business, since I didn't like medicine. And then he got me hired at my firm, originally. A favor from a patient. He's a surgeon," she explained. "He wanted me to be one too, or at least a doctor, but I just couldn't. I'm not tough enough. Too soft, just like he said."

"Does he like you better now, since you did the business thing? That all work out good for you?"

"No," she admitted. "I don't think anything I did would make him..." She trailed off. "Approve of me, I guess."

"Say you just pleased yourself, then," he suggested. "What would that look like?"

"I'm not sure," she said slowly. "I'd have a different job, I know that. One that...mattered to somebody. And where I could stay home instead of traveling all the time. Where I'd be able to spend time with my friends, and get to know my neighbors. Where I could say hi to the checker at the grocery store, know that she had kids. Maybe even know their names."

"And what about your heart?" he asked gently.

"I want what you had," she said soberly. "I want it more than anything. I thought I had it with Scott, at first. I thought this could be it. But it's not even close. I've figured that out. I'm a lousy picker, that's the problem. I choose the wrong guy, over and over. Or I let him choose me, I suppose. That's probably more like it."

"Sometimes," he said, "the first step is just recognizing what you've been doing wrong. That you deserve better, that you can set your sights higher. You're a good woman, and you deserve a good man."

She glanced across at him, a little smile hovering at the corner of her mouth. "And Scott isn't it?"

He chuckled. "You know he isn't. Not even close. None of us knows what's in someone else's heart, or can tell anyone else what they ought to do. I'm finally old enough to have learned that. But I'll do it anyway, just because I've been around a few years longer than you. If you were my daughter, I'd be telling you to kick that bum to the curb."

"I just feel so…stupid," she said, wiping away the stubborn tears again. "I'm going to be on TV, looking like a fool."

"Nope. You're going to be on TV, looking like the smart, strong woman you are. Believe me, when you dump his sorry hind end, people are going to be standing up and cheering. And rooting for you to get with the good man who's been carrying that torch for you ever since we got here."

"Gabe? You think he…he means it?"

"I know he does. And in case you haven't figured it out yet, that's what a good man looks like. A man who deserves a woman as good as you."

"I think," she said, her voice catching, "I think I know what a good man looks like. Because I think a good man looks an awful lot like you." She stopped and turned to him, put her arms around him as he held her close, the powerful arms cradling her gently, his warmth and strength bringing tears to her eyes again.

She pulled back at last. "Thank you. Thank you for opening your heart to me, sharing something so special. And for everything you said."

"We'd better get on back," he said, turning around. "It'll be dark soon. But you remember what I said, you hear? It's time to let that spirit of yours shine out. Time to show it to the world."

square dance

♡

"So what's it like, being a twin?"

Gabe looked down at Mira, walking beside him towards their unknown barn dance destination. "You need some distraction, take your mind off tonight?" he asked. "Not sure my fascinating life story will do it."

"It's about all I've got, though," she smiled back. "So tell me, if you don't mind. I'm sure you've been asked that question a lot, but I'd really like to know."

"It's good," he began lamely. "Well, good and bad, I suppose. It just...is. Alec was always there. That's what it's like. My mom says we reached for each other in our crib as soon as we could reach for anything. That we were each other's toy and comfort object all in one. And when we got older, every time we moved, it didn't matter so much, because I was never walking into that new classroom alone."

"That sounds wonderful," Mira said with obvious envy. "What could be bad about that?"

"If you're the follower twin," Gabe said wryly, "that's a lot of following."

He paused, thinking about it. Being five or six, and Alec directing their make-believe adventures, his fertile imagination always providing something fascinating to do. Following Alec onto the swings, the slide at the park. Alec the one who talked in class, his lightning mind and stubborn self-assurance sometimes getting him in trouble, but always getting him noticed. Gabe sitting back, watching, listening, taking everything in from his spot in his more outgoing brother's shadow. Always shorter, too, not as good-looking, never the one the girls whispered about, the one whose name they wrote in their notebooks. Never scoring quite as high on the tests. He'd been bright, but Alec had been brilliant.

And then the wonder of starting to fill out, once he'd turned fifteen. Going out for JV football and making the team. Finally having something Alec couldn't do. Football had given him a separate identity at last, a separate life, and he'd thrown himself into it body and soul. And when Alec had been a National Merit Scholar and Gabe had been only a Commended Student, it hadn't hurt as much. Because there was that football scholarship to make it up.

He didn't know how to explain all that to Mira, though. This walk wasn't nearly long enough to bare his soul. Instead he just said, "It changed some in high school, once I went out for football. Alec doesn't like organized sports much. He'd rather make up his own game, play by his own rules. And he doesn't go much for the whole team thing. Never been big on anybody telling him what to do."

"That would make this experience a little challenging," Mira suggested.

Gabe laughed. "Yeah. Bet it has. Luckily, Hank's enough older that Alec will listen to him. You couldn't grow up in our house and not have respect for your elders. That will have kept him in line some. But Alec and Scott...major Antler Lock."

He could feel her stiffen beside him, was sorry he'd mentioned Scott's name. But she merely paused a moment, then went on. "I thought you said you stopped playing football, though.

That you were injured in college. That must have been hard, because it sounds like it was awfully important to you."

Had he told her that? Or had she just figured it out? "It was horrible," he said bluntly. "When they said my knee would keep me out for a year, towards the end of my junior season. That was my whole football career gone right there, wasn't it? Of course, what was I thinking? I had to know I wouldn't make it to the NFL, but I must have had some pipe dream about it anyway, because I thought my life was over."

"So what happened?" she prompted.

"The trainer talked to me. I'd got to know him pretty well, had always asked him a bunch of questions. I was a Bio major, but that was mostly because I liked animals. I had some vague idea about becoming a vet. But he said I could be a doctor, encouraged me to try. I'd never considered it."

"Why not?" she asked.

"Being a doctor was for smart people, I thought. People like Alec."

She looked up at him, startled. "I guess I've just seen the downside of the twin thing," she said slowly. "I never thought of that. It was my major fantasy, growing up. Almost like an imaginary friend, except I had it for a long, long time. A twin sister who'd be with me everywhere we went. Move into my new bedroom with me, go into that classroom like you said. A friend I would always have, no matter where I was. I'd love her best of all, and she'd love me the same way."

She broke off. "And that sounds like some kind of sappy commercial," she said with a little laugh. "Sorry. I thought about this a *lot,* in case you can't tell. I spent a lot of time alone as a kid."

Why did she always pull back as soon as she revealed anything personal? Was she so afraid that he'd judge her? "I guess you moved a few times too," he said.

"When your mother gets married and divorced as often as mine does, you move. And she didn't always marry them, either."

"I'm surprised you didn't live with your dad, then."

"Ah. Well. He had a new wife too, you see, and she wasn't all that maternal. You could hardly expect it. She wasn't even twenty-five, I don't think, when they got married. Surgeons tend to go through wives, you probably know that. And my dad's had a few. He's got a pretty new one now." She laughed a bit at her choice of words. "Pretty, *and* pretty new. I like her, though."

Gabe smiled, but pressed a little more all the same. "Even if she wasn't excited about the idea, though, didn't your dad want you with him?"

"Not so much. I'm not..." She paused, then seemed to force herself to go on. "I'm not really his type. Too shy, not confident enough. He'd have liked Alec better. He'd have liked *Scott* better. He loves Scott."

"Wow. That's some bad taste he's got there. And what do you mean, his type? You don't have a type when it comes to your kids."

"Maybe *your* parents don't," she said shortly.

Gabe wanted to say more, though he wasn't sure how you even responded to something like that. But he couldn't anyway, because here they were.

♡

"Well, I'd say my chances of hooking up at this dance are right about nil," Kevin said resignedly as they walked through the big rolling door into the brightly lit space.

"What?" he protested as Zara looked at him in amusement. "It could happen. You saw *Brokeback Mountain.*"

"Well, I know better than to judge by appearances," Zara said. "But I'd agree that nobody here looks too promising."

Wrenching her mind back from the unexpectedly intense conversation to take in the old barn that had been transformed for tonight's dance, Mira was forced to agree with Zara. The huge space was scattered with groups of hay bales for seating, some stacked two-high. A fiddler stood on a raised wooden platform that formed a small stage, tuning his instrument, and another man with an accordion now jumped up to join him. A third man, middle-aged like the others, and dressed like them in jeans, white button-down shirt, and string tie, with cowboy boots and hat completing the Western regalia, was leaning down to talk to a member of the production crew, who already had their lights and camera equipment set up around the dance floor. A dozen or more strangers in period costume milled about near the stage, chatting with their neighbors and eyeing the Paradise homestead in clear speculation.

"Locals," Kevin said. "Making it festive, making some numbers for the dancing. They could at least have got some young ones."

"Nobody younger than forty-five out there, I'd say," Mira decided.

"They wouldn't have known how to square dance," Stanley said. "And looks like that's what we'll be doing tonight."

"To accordion music," Kevin said glumly. "Whoopee."

"How can you tell?" Maria-Elena asked. "That we'll be... square dancing?"

"The instruments," Zara said. "And that guy," she motioned with her chin at the obvious leader of the musicians, "he'll be the caller."

"Did you used to do this?" Maria-Elena asked.

Zara laughed. "I'm not *that* old. No, but I've seen it done. How about you, Stanley?"

"Even done it a time or two myself," he admitted. "My wife loved to dance."

"Althea," Mira said. "And you loved to make her happy."

"That's right," he said, putting his arm around her and giving her a quick squeeze. "Thanks for using her name. People don't do that too often."

The Arcadia homestead entered the wide doorway, the big door rolled back to admit the low rays of evening sunlight. "You OK?" Stanley asked more quietly.

"Yeah," she said, as firmly as she could manage, even though her heart sank at the sight of Scott.

"I'm right here with you," Stanley promised. "You need me, you just holler."

She nodded briefly, grateful for his support as Scott approached. Her gaze kept wanting to skitter away from him, and she willed herself into resolution. She was breaking up with him tonight, no matter what. She'd ask him to walk outside with her, she decided, once the dancing was in full swing and the focus was off the two of them. Hopefully, the cameramen would be busy enough filming the festivities that they wouldn't notice.

Right now, though, Danny's camera *was* trained on her as the two groups converged, the original teams pairing off as always.

"What happened to *you?*" Scott asked, after giving her a kiss that actually repelled her. His light brown beard, even longer and wispier than the week before, felt foreign, and his lips felt… wrong. If she'd needed proof that she needed to break up with him, that was it.

"What?" Could he tell what she was thinking?

"Your hair," he gestured impatiently. "Why in the world would you cut your hair out here? And why didn't you ask me first? I like it long. You know that."

Her new hairstyle had garnered a little attention from the rest of Arcadia as well, others turning to check it out.

"I burned it off," she explained. "I had an accident with the stove. And Maria-Elena cut it for me. I think she did a really good job. And I love it," she added boldly. She'd left it down tonight to show off her new waves. Zara had prepared a vinegar rinse to add shine, about the only beauty treatment they could manage out here, and Maria-Elena had twisted and pulled it back at the sides so it wouldn't fall in her face while she danced. All three of the Paradise men had complimented her on her new look when she'd appeared downstairs tonight, dressed in her meager best.

"You look modern now, not so old-fashioned," Maria-Elena had said.

"You look hot," Kevin had corrected. "Doesn't she, Gabe? Oh, wait. She always looks hot to you."

Gabe had just laughed. "Yep. She does. But Kevin's right. You look especially hot tonight." His warm smile and the look in his eyes had convinced Mira of his sincerity even as they flustered her.

"And ready to take on the world," he'd added, giving her hand a quick, secret squeeze.

♡

"Well," Scott said begrudgingly now, "I guess you can always grow it out again."

"I'm not going to grow it out again," she retorted. "I like it like this. It feels light, and young, and...fun. Maybe I'll go all the way, cut it all off when I get home," she said recklessly. "Who knows? Whatever I want."

"That's the spirit," Zara murmured beside her. "You go, girl."

"Aren't you even going to ask if she was hurt?" Stanley demanded of Scott. "She just told you she burned her hair off, that she had an accident. Doesn't that concern you?"

"It's obvious she isn't hurt," Scott snapped. "Just another dramatic *near miss,* I take it."

"She was lucky," Stanley countered, outrage evident in every line of his broad face. "She *was* hurt, not that you care, and she's lucky it wasn't worse. You sound like you're sorry about that. What kind of a man are you? Never mind," he finished in disgust. "I already know the answer to that."

Whatever Scott would have said in response was lost to posterity, to Mira's immense relief. A loud note from the accordion drew their attention to the stage, where the leader of the group of musicians was beginning to speak. There was obviously some sort of microphone hidden somewhere, because his voice was clearly audible through the huge space.

"Welcome, folks," he began. "I'm Gus Brickman, and the boys and I are going to be helping you out with a little entertainment tonight. I understand you've all been working pretty hard, could use a break. Well, we've got some good old-fashioned dancing for you here. Let's have some of our local experts show you how it's done, then you can have a try."

Eight members of the little crowd came forward to form a square, one couple on each side, as the fiddle player launched into an upbeat tune.

"I knew it," Kevin groaned. "Square dancing."

"Well, you've gotta bow to your partner, bow to the left," Gus began in a singsong chant as the fiddle continued its lively accompaniment. "Circle to the left, go round. Everybody run on up in the middle and back."

Mira watched the couples perform the movements seamlessly as Gus called them out. "I hope I can do it," she murmured to Zara, standing beside her.

"Don't worry," Zara assured her. "Just have a good time. That's what I'm planning to do."

Mira looked around, saw that Scott had walked off, was standing apart from the others, and turned her attention back to the dancers. Zara and Gus were both right. She'd earned a break, and this was her chance to have fun. It didn't matter what Scott was doing, or that Maria-Elena was already muttering "laaaame" and rolling her eyes. It didn't look lame to her, it looked fun. And maybe, she thought hopefully, Gabe would ask her to dance.

Seven or eight lively dances later, she was flushed and laughing, finishing up yet another outing, this time with Kevin next to her. Scott still hadn't joined any of the squares, even though there were plenty of partners to go around, but she hadn't let that bother her. Instead, she'd swung, turned, twirled with the others. Had gone the wrong way more than once, been turned back again by a friendly hand. And, whether she'd started out that dance with him or not, had always encountered Gabe at some point. Always in her square, always looking out for her. And giving her the same little thrill every time his hand touched hers, his arm swung her around.

"We're going to take a break now," Gus announced at last, mopping his brow. "Give all of you a chance to catch your breath. But we'll be back again to do a few more numbers before we call it a night."

And here was Gabe again, turning her from Kevin with a light hand on her arm.

"Well, it may be lame," he said with a grin, "but I'm enjoying myself. How about you?"

"Big-time. I guess it's all about the available alternatives," she smiled back. She nodded in Maria-Elena's direction. The girl was laughing up at Alec, tossing her head as he said something that was clearly flirtatious. "I'd say everybody's having a pretty good time."

"They've even got some beer," Gabe said. "Want to get real daring with me?"

"I'd love a beer." She was thirsty, and a cold beer sounded terrific. A number of other people had had the same idea, she saw as Gabe took himself toward a barrel in the corner of the barn, where much of the crowd was now congregating. He came back with two opened bottles, and she took a cautious sip, then a larger swallow.

"Wow," she decided. "That is just absolutely fantastic. Square dancing and beer."

"Pretty sophisticated," he agreed. "Well, you said you were a cheap date. A walk and a picnic," he reminded her. "My kind of girl."

"And it's going straight to my head," she smiled back, "it's been so long since I had any alcohol. You may have to carry me home."

"I'd do that," he promised, the look in his eyes sending a shiver of desire through her. "I'd do that in a heartbeat."

She'd almost forgotten Scott in the fun and excitement of the evening. But she spotted him now, catching her eye, then getting up from the out-of-the-way hay bale where he'd been perched. The three empty bottles next to him gave evidence of how he'd spent his time while she'd been dancing, and the look on his face told her that whatever he was coming over to say, she wasn't going to enjoy hearing it.

But three beers weren't enough to make a man drunk, she assured herself. And in any case, it wasn't her problem. *He* wasn't her problem, not anymore. She handed her bottle to Gabe and prepared herself to take Scott outside and tell him so. This was it, what she'd come to do. Showtime.

Scott made his way across the sawdust-covered floor to where she stood, walking a little too deliberately, each step hitting the ground a little too hard. Mira stepped away from Gabe's side, went to meet him.

"You've danced with everybody but me tonight," he began, his tone belligerent. "What do you think you're trying to prove?"

"It's square dancing," she said, trying to sound more powerful than she felt. "All you had to do was join in. If you didn't want to, that's not my fault."

"Well, I want to now," he said, his hand closing around her upper arm. "And I don't care what kind of dancing it is, you'd damn well better stay with me from now on. Quit making a fool of yourself, like you're the fucking Homecoming Queen."

"I don't want to dance with you," she said, keeping her voice down in what she knew was a vain hope that Danny's camera boom, inevitably tracking toward her, wouldn't pick it up. "You're drunk, and I don't like you grabbing me. But I do want to talk to you. Let's go outside." She began to turn toward the door.

"Forget outside. We'll talk right now." He swung her around a little too hard, making her stumble a bit. "What do you think you're doing, hanging on him like that?" He jerked his head contemptuously in Gabe's direction, and Mira glanced around, saw him starting forward, a look on his face she'd never seen before.

"Don't you see what he's doing, throwing it in my face that he's living in that cabin with you, and I'm not?" Scott went on furiously. "He's trying to get to me, trying to push me, get me off balance. Because I'm the threat, and he knows it. And you're falling for his act. You look like a tramp, snuggling up to him when everyone knows you're with me. You're making a fool of yourself, and you're making a fool of me. You're supposed to be my girlfriend. You're supposed to be my *teammate.* It's time you started acting like it!"

"I'm not your girlfriend anymore." She wrenched her arm out of his grasp and took a step back, her heart beating hard. "As of right now. This isn't how I was planning to do this, but you want to do it now, OK, we'll do it now. I'm breaking up with you."

"What?" He stared at her, mouth hanging open for a moment before he shut it with an angry snap. "You can't be serious. We're on the show! You can't do this!"

"I'll do the show. I said I would, and I will. Not because you want to. Because *I* want to. And I *am* serious. I'm breaking up with you. That's it. It's over. Right now." She stopped herself, wrapped her arms around her waist, physically holding herself together to keep from rattling on any more. She was shaking, but she was glad to have it out there. Scott didn't even look like the man she'd fallen in love with, with his eyes bleary and unfocused from the drinking he'd done, his beard bristling out around lips that she realized now were too thin, too tight. Why hadn't she noticed those lips before?

"Come on, Grace," he wheedled, the alien name falling more harshly than ever now that she'd become unaccustomed to hearing it. "You don't really want to do this." He stepped closer again, reached for her shoulders.

She cried out with pain. "My burn!" she gasped. "Let go!"

He lifted both hands, took a startled step back. He didn't even know where she'd been burned, she realized. Had never even asked.

He didn't acknowledge her pain, just grabbed for her hand this time, held on. "You don't really want to do this," he began again. "We just haven't had enough time together, that's all. And it's been so stressful, being on the show. You haven't been at your best. I understand that. Plus I know you're upset that I've never asked you to marry me. But I've decided I'm ready now. We can get married as soon as we're back home again."

She'd thought she'd been embarrassed before, having this whole ugly scene caught on camera. Now, she wished the floor would swallow her up.

"Wow," Zara said dryly from behind her. "*That* was romantic. My little heart's goin' all pitter-pat."

Mira could feel the heat burning in her cheeks, her legs trembling under her. Danny was still focusing the camera on her, while Mike, seeing the disturbance, had brought his over to train it on Scott. Her first proposal, being captured for posterity in all its glory.

"No," she said, the front of her shoulder throbbing where he'd grabbed at the still-tender blisters. "I'd say 'No, thank you,' but I don't think I will. I'll just say no. I think I'll hold out for somebody who loves me. Somebody who's at least *nice* to me. Someone who calls me by my *name*. I don't know why you'd want me anyway. You don't respect me. You sure don't admire me. You don't even seem to like me, half the time. You just want somebody you can push around, and I've been that. Well, not anymore. Go find somebody else to push around. Or better yet, get some help! Because you need it."

"You're saying something's wrong with *me?*" he asked in disbelief, his color as high as hers. He seemed to realize he was still holding her hand, dropped it hastily. "Just because I'm not licking your boots like Dr. McDreamy here? He doesn't think you're any more amazing than I do, you know," he said contemptuously. "He doesn't *admire* you. He just wants to get in your pants."

He glared at Gabe, who'd moved even closer as the argument got more heated. "I'll save you the trouble," he spat viciously. "She's lousy in bed. Unless you want someone who's just going to lie there like a limp rag, don't bother. But who knows, maybe you're into that. She sure as hell didn't do it for me. I had to close my eyes and pretend I was with somebody else just to get off."

Mira gasped, the swift tide of humiliation flooding her and making her feel physically ill. This was why she didn't do confrontation. Because she always, *always* lost. All she wanted to do was run away and cry. But she couldn't stand to give Scott the satisfaction. She stood still, fought to keep her eyes from dropping. Sensed the solid bulk of Gabe as he moved to stand beside her, the tension in him, and felt her courage return.

"Did you ever think," she said through the tightness in her throat, forcing the words out through lips that trembled with anger and emotion, "that that was *you?* Maybe you just don't know how to satisfy a woman."

Scott's face flushed an even deeper red, and he opened his mouth to retort. Gabe shook his head once, twice, like a bull shaking off a pesky fly, and stepped forward to stand between the two of them, his posture rigid.

"Why the hell are you still here?" he demanded of Scott. "Are you looking for even more of a smackdown? She's going to be describing that pencil dick of yours next. Get out. Right now. Or better yet, don't. Because I am just itching to kick your ass."

Everyone had come closer to listen, Mira saw with a return of humiliation and shame. Alec put a restraining hand on his brother's arm. "Easy," he told Gabe quietly.

Stanley was coming forward now too, edging in front of Gabe, putting his big body between the two bristling men. "Time for you to go," he told Scott. "Before this boy forgets his raisin', starts something right here." He clamped a hand around Scott's elbow and began to walk him toward the door.

Scott tried unsuccessfully to yank his arm out of the bigger man's grasp. "I'll go when I'm damn good and ready," he said furiously. "Get your fucking hands off me."

Every bit of Stanley's six foot three and 225-plus pounds seemed to expand right there in front of them as he loomed over Scott. Suddenly, it wasn't hard at all to believe he'd been a Marine.

"You're ready right the hell now," he growled, his voice seeming to penetrate every corner of the huge space. "You want your butt kicked, *boy,* I'll be happy to oblige. Outside."

He nodded to his son, Calvin stepped up to take Scott's other elbow, and the two men frog-marched him out the door in true MP fashion.

"Holy *shit,*" Zara breathed happily from behind Mira. "I've been waiting a month to see that, and damn if it wasn't entertaining. And hot. If I wasn't so happily married, I'd be volunteering for some close-order drill right now. Sign me up, Sergeant. Yow."

"We've been on this show too long," Hank said with a grin at his wife. "Way too long. Time for you to make some music, and remember whose job it is to take you home."

Zara laughed. "You're right. You okay, hon?" she asked Mira, coming up and putting an arm around her.

Mira leaned into her. "Yeah," she said, her voice trembling now that it was all over. "I think so. That was horrible."

"Oh, I don't know. I think, looking back, you're going to find that this was one of your better days."

Zara caught Gabe's eye as he came back from closing the big barn door behind the three men, his expression still grim. "I'm going to turn this girl over to you," she told him. "I have a sneaking suspicion that you'll do a better job of comforting her than I can. And I think Hank's right. A little music would do us all good right now."

The group around Mira and Gabe began to drift away as the musicians picked up their instruments again and begin an upbeat tune, Zara and Hank jumping up onto the raised platform to join them, beginning to sing.

"Thanks," Mira said to Gabe under cover of the music, trying to smile even as she felt her knees quivering under the full skirt. "I know that was a long time coming, and it's good it happened, but it was no fun at all. Thanks for your help."

"No problem," he said, taking her hand, then threading his fingers through hers, holding it openly now. "Just wish I *had* kicked his ass."

He sounded almost as shaky as she did, she realized. The hand holding hers wasn't entirely steady. "Hey. Are you OK?"

He looked down at her, eyes troubled. "When he grabbed you like that, hurt you, I wanted to deck him. Only stopped myself because I figured you still had something to say. But I'm wishing now I hadn't held back."

"You were right, though. I needed to tell him. And if you'd hit him, they'd have made you leave the show, wouldn't they?"

"I didn't even think of that," he admitted. "But you're probably right. And that would've left you here with him without me. So yeah, probably best I didn't. I'm pretty sure Stanley can control himself too, though I'm also sure he's holding onto Scott harder than is strictly necessary right now."

"Who knew he could get that tough?" Mira asked wonderingly. "Look that...scary? He's always seemed so gentle. That was impressive." It was easier to talk about Stanley than to think about what Scott had said. The humiliation of it still burned more fiercely than her shoulder, but she shoved it aside. Because the song was coming to an end, and Gus was addressing the crowd.

"Well, folks, we've had some real excitement here tonight, one way or another, and it's about time to pack it in," he announced. "But before we go, we'd like to end the evening off right. Here's a song you may recognize, one that goes way back to the nineteenth century with you people. And we have two of the best musicians you'll ever hope to hear to sing it with us. You'll want to get hold of the lady of your choice for this one, gents, because this is when you get to hold her tight and do some waltzin'."

"Sounds to me like they're playing our song," Gabe said. "Come on. Let's dance."

"Hope I don't step on your feet. I'm not feeling too coordinated right now," she admitted. The musicians had launched into the opening chords of a song she did indeed recognize, she found with a rush of gratitude. "Goodnight Irene." One of the earliest Hank and Zara hits.

"As long as you let me lead, we'll be OK," he promised, leading her out and turning her to face him as Zara and Hank began to sing the familiar chorus, their voices falling into an effortless harmony.

"I've got no problem with you leading. Not while we're dancing, anyway." She moved into his arms, accepted his broad hand over her own, his other hand firm at her waist, guiding her in the direction he wanted her to go.

"Only for the physical stuff, I promise." He began to waltz her backwards across the wooden plank floor, their feet gliding easily over its coating of sawdust. "How are you doing? How are you feeling?" he asked abruptly.

She laughed, surprised that she could. "How long is this song? I'm feeling a lot of things, I think."

"I have all night to listen," he promised, seeming to relax a bit, lose a little of the tension that had been gripping him.

"You must be a really good doctor. Because you have one heck of a bedside manner."

"Depends entirely on the bed," he said, pulling her in closer as the fiddle launched into the refrain yet again, the musicians seeming as reluctant as the two of them to end the song, and the evening. His body was warm against hers, his back solid under her palm. She could feel herself relaxing as well, moving as if her body were part of his own, and was at once comforted and aroused.

"Feelings," he prompted as the song went on.

"Hmm? Oh," she sighed. "Umm, shaken up, obviously. And relieved that it's finally over. Kinda proud of myself, actually. I've never told somebody off like that. That was new. And embarrassed at the same time, for the same reason. Sad, too," she went on, "that it ended so ugly. And," she admitted, "scared about what these next weeks are going to be like."

"Scared how?"

"You saw how furious he was. He doesn't like to lose. And losing in front of everyone, on camera, what I said, what you said…he's going to be pretty unbearable. I'm not sure just how nasty it's going to be, but it could be bad. And we're all stuck here. At least he's not going to be on our homestead, not right away anyway. But once he is…that scares me. And it'll be rough over there. I hope Alec's going to be OK, being your brother and all."

Gabe laughed softly, and she felt the rumble of it vibrating in his chest, into her own body. "Alec can take care of himself," he promised. "And I can take care of you."

She felt the decidedly un-PC thrill of that all the way through her. She'd been living in the nineteenth century way too long, for that to make her feel so good. And was aware, as he pulled her even closer, that he was as aroused as she was. And that, as she'd noticed the other evening, his version was…impressive.

"Do you still want to know how I'm feeling?" she asked him breathlessly.

"Dying to hear. I think you can tell how I'm feeling. I'm just hoping you're somewhere in the ballpark."

"I'm in the ballpark. I'm all the way around the bases."

And he, Gabe thought, still somehow managing to dance, was wondering what it was going to feel like to slide into home.

tough challenges

♡

Five o'clock had never come so early, Gabe thought with a sigh the next morning at the sound of the alarm, the slap of Stanley's big hand shutting it off. Especially after exactly one beer, and staying out until all of nine-thirty.

"Right," he said in resignation. "The price of high living." He stood up, grabbed his clothes off their nail, shrugged into his shirt, buttoned his pants, pulled up the suspenders. He'd got over his squeamishness about putting on dirty clothes, anyway. He wondered how his more finicky brother was doing with that. Well, everything was bound to get good and filthy today. Challenge day.

"Bet they'll have a good one for us this time," Kevin mused a few minutes later, picking up the milking stool and opening the corral gate in the gray light of dawn, Gabe following behind with the shovel and wheelbarrow.

"In particular, you mean?" Gabe asked.

"Yeah. Because we missed it last week." Kevin seated himself on the milking stool while Gabe began to shovel. "And because of that nice bit of extra tension you provided last night. Bet they're sorry now that they don't have a cage fight planned. At least I hope they don't. That wouldn't be too period."

"A regular fight would be, though," Gabe decided. "And that would suit me just fine. I'd win, too."

"Oh, I'd have no problem nominating you to defend our homestead's honor," Kevin agreed. "Or Mira's, more like. Though I think you might have to duke it out with Stanley for the privilege. He sounded sorry that Scott didn't give him any excuse when he walked his drunk ass back to Arcadia last night."

Gabe snorted, scooped one last shovelful of manure, and turned the wheelbarrow to head out with it. "Bullies don't mess with anybody bigger than them. I'm sure you've found that out yourself by now."

Fight or challenge, he vowed as he trundled the heavy wheelbarrow over to the manure pile, winning was going to be the best revenge. Because they needed to win, or it was pretty clear Mira would be leaving with Scott. And that wasn't going to happen. Not if he could help it.

♡

"Ready for this?" he asked her as they neared the Clearing a little after noon. She'd been quiet all morning, subdued after the late night, all the emotion. He'd held her hand on the walk, just as he had on the way home last night, and it felt ridiculously good just to be able to touch her.

Now he gave that hand a little extra squeeze, looked down at her, wishing he could see her face, hidden from him by the sunbonnet.

"Yeah," she said firmly. "I'll do my best. My very best."

"I know you'll do that," he assured her. "But I meant, ready to see Scott."

"Oh." He felt her hand tighten for a moment in his. "No choice. And he can't do anything today. Not with everybody around."

♡

Nothing but look like he wanted to kill her, her and Gabe both, she realized as they stepped forward to meet Arcadia, coming from their own path onto the Challenge field. Both homesteads moved toward the spot where two big stacks of skinny logs, some shorter posts, and a double pile of tools were laid out. The spot where Cliff and John were standing already.

She averted her eyes from Scott's thunderous face, let go of Gabe's hand and moved with Zara and Maria-Elena to the spot indicated by the ever-present Jay, a single long bench where the Arcadia women were already seating themselves.

"Welcome to our men's challenge," Cliff announced. "We've had to get you here a little earlier today, because this one's going to take some time. I know you were disappointed that the log-sawing went so fast," he went on to a few rueful grins, "so today you get a much tougher assignment. You're going to be building something special."

"Oh, boy," Zara said with satisfaction. "We're going to kick butt on this. Arcadia's only just got their garden fence up, Hank told me last night."

"You're not secretly rooting for him?" Mira asked.

"I should be, I suppose," Zara said, sounding surprised at herself. "Because if they win, I know I'm not going to be the one going home this time. But I can't help it. This is my team."

"Since you've got an extra man, Arcadia," Cliff was saying now, "you're going to need to sit somebody out. I'll give you a minute to decide who that's going to be."

"Only one choice," Zara muttered. But to Mira's surprise, the decision wasn't happening easily. She could see Scott's furious face, his vehement refusals, Alec's posture eloquent of disgust as he rapped out a few choice words. Calvin merely stood, arms crossed, while Hank looked back and forth between the two angry men, his expression bemused. After several minutes of argument, he shrugged, said something to the others, and turned toward the bench.

"Looks like I'm taking a break," he said, sitting down beside his wife as Mira shifted to make room for him.

"Now that you all have got that sorted out," John said, taking over from Cliff to address the remaining men, "you've probably figured out that you're going to be building fence today. Building a pigpen, to be exact. Got everything you need for a ten by twelve pen, just enough for a sow and some piglets. Guess we'll see what you've learned out here, because I'm not going to tell you any more than that. Points for how fast you do it, points for how good you do it. That's about it."

"Challenge is on," Cliff announced.

As the two little groups huddled over their materials, Zara reached for Hank, gave him a quick kiss, rubbed her hand down the grizzled stubble on the side of his face. "What happened just then?" she asked him. "Not that I'm not glad to have your company, but I would've said that was a no-brainer, unless he actually *wants* to leave."

Hank shot a glance at Mira.

"Don't worry about me," she assured him. "There's not much you can say at this point that would surprise me."

"Well." He took off his hat and scratched his head, then set it firmly in place again against the midday sun, stretched his lean legs out in front of him, and considered. "Can't tell that man a thing, is what. Thinks he knows it all. And he sure can't take criticism. Sets his back right up. He can't be sat out, because that'd mean he was the worst. And he can't be the worst. Wasn't much we could do, short of hog-tying him and dragging him off. Which a couple of 'em would have done, quick enough," he added with a grin.

"Trouble already," he added with a sigh, eyeing his team's progress. "Unless Paradise finds some way to mess up bad, you all are gonna win this one."

It was true. The Paradise men had seemed to decide quickly on a strategy. Stanley had paced off the dimensions of the pen, and Kevin had searched through the supplies for a piece of string and was laying it out along Stanley's hypothetical fenceline. As soon as he was done, each of the men picked up a posthole digger and started in.

Meanwhile, Arcadia was still talking, Scott and Alec again in vehement disagreement, Calvin wandering over to the pile of supplies, seemingly deciding to get started on his own.

"Yep. I smell another crash and burn," Zara pronounced.

"We'll see," Hank said with a grin. "We may have a late surge. You never know."

"Now that we've got that going," Cliff said, having made his way over to the women's bench, where a camera crew had been filming all along, "time to get you ladies started. Don't worry, we haven't forgotten you."

"We don't mind being the decorative audience," Rachel assured him. "Or the cheerleaders. We've lost Melody and Chelsea, but I'm sure I could scare up some pom-poms somehow. And Mira's got a cute ponytail now and everything."

"Nice try," Cliff smiled, "but no dice. Come on over to the kitchen area, and you can take a look at what we've found for you to do."

The clucking that greeted them from a pen near the covered structure, the four chopping blocks set up, each with a hatchet and bucket set ready, told their own story.

"Oh, no," Maria-Elena groaned. "Oh, gross."

Mira felt a little sick herself as Cliff went on. "It looks like you've got the picture. Two women from each homestead are going to prepare a rooster for the pot. I know Alma taught all of you how." He nodded to the woman who came out to join him. "And she's here to judge how you do today. You've all eaten a chicken or two out here, haven't you?"

"Once," Zara said. "We decided it was too much work. Which it is." She and Mira exchanged a concerned glance. In fact, the guys had done the worst parts for them. Stanley had killed the two young roosters they'd sacrificed to the cause last week, and Gabe had cleaned them. All the women had had to do was pluck, but the whole thing had been disgusting and tedious enough that they'd made a unanimous decision to stick to corned beef, trout, and rabbit from then on.

This was one time when the Paradise men's consideration might work against them, because Mira was willing to bet that Scott hadn't cleaned anyone's chicken. And sure enough, it was obvious from Rachel and Lupe's confident nods that they had a leg up on this. She felt a surge of trepidation.

"So, Paradise. You've got the extra member this time," Cliff went on. "Who are you sitting out?"

The three women looked at each other. "I'm sorry, guys," Maria-Elena said, appearing truly ashamed. "It's just, like, so gross. I'd be puking the whole time. I don't think I can."

"That's OK," Mira said firmly. "Zara and I can do it, can't we?"

"You bet we can," the older woman agreed, her chin lifting. "Go sit down and cheer us on, Maria-Elena. Don't get distracted and wander back to look at cute guys, now."

"I won't," the girl said earnestly. "I promise."

"Ready to get to it?" Cliff asked.

"Ready," Mira called back as Maria-Elena took herself off to the spectators' bench.

"Then I'll let Alma explain what you're going to be doing," Cliff said.

"You all know," Alma said briskly. "Least you should. I'll be judging on time, and on preparation. You leave pinfeathers in, do a sloppy job of cleaning, that's points. I want to see a nice, clean bird."

"And with that," Cliff said, challenge is..." He lifted his arm in the air. "On!" he shouted as he dropped it.

All four women raced to the wire pen, Rachel getting there first. Within seconds, they had each grabbed a young rooster.

Mira wrapped her arm around the flapping wings as she ran to one of the chopping blocks, forcing her mind onto autopilot.

Upside down, she remembered, visualizing Stanley holding the thing by the feet to quiet it, then laying it on the block, holding it down for the hatchet. She did the same, then realized she didn't have the hatchet, had to lean over awkwardly again to pick it up, trying not to lose her hold on the struggling rooster in the meantime. She heard the *thunk* from the block next to hers, and saw that Lupe had already dispatched her own bird.

She lifted the hatchet. "Sorry," she whispered. She forced herself not to close her eyes, brought the blade down, severing the neck with one strong blow. And then had to close her eyes after all for a moment against the sight.

Drop the body in the bucket. She did it even as she heard the shriek, and looked up to see that Rachel had forgotten that important instruction. Her rooster was running, headless, blood spraying from its neck, and Rachel had lost her usual aplomb.

"Oh, my God. Oh, my God," the other woman moaned, until Lupe ran out from the kitchen, caught up with the still-moving body, gathered it up and stuffed it into Rachel's bucket with a quick word.

Mira raced for the kitchen herself, toward the Paradise stove with its kettle of boiling water. Reached into the bucket for the feet again, dipped the rooster's body by them into the water, careful not to burn herself again in the process.

The stench immediately rose to fill her nostrils, and she fought back the sickness, wishing she hadn't eaten lunch. She pulled the body out, made way for Zara to scald her own bird, and moved back outside, where Lupe, of course, had already begun plucking, sitting on her chopping block surrounded by feathers.

Mira took a deep breath, hustled to her block, pulled the wet, stinking body from her bucket, and began to pull out handfuls of white feathers. This, at least, she'd done before. And the smell, the feel of it were just as disgusting this time. Her gorge rose, higher and higher, until she couldn't stop it. She leaned over and lost her lunch next to her stump, wiped her mouth on her sleeve, and went grimly back to plucking.

You can do this, she told herself fiercely. She knew how hard the guys were working, and that Gabe and Stanley, at least, would be putting forth that much extra effort on her behalf. She wasn't going to let them down.

The next hour was a disgusting blur of plucking, pulling pinfeathers, and, finally, working with a sharp knife to clean the bird. By the time she'd finished, Mira had vomited twice more. On the other hand, everyone but Lupe had done the same. It was a pale, sweating group that laid their birds out on the kitchen workbenches for inspection. Lupe was first to finish, Zara barely last. And when the judging was over, Paradise had lost for the first time.

"But only by 15 points," Zara pointed out shakily as they sat in the shade, having washed up as best they could with the pitcher and bowl provided. She wiped the sweat from her face with the underside of her blood-splattered apron and took another big gulp of water from the Mason jar. "Not too bad. The guys don't have too much to make up."

"I wanted to win it for them, though," Mira said miserably, wiping her eyes on her own apron as she had so many times out here. "You know they're trying to do it for us."

"Did you do your best?" Zara demanded.

"Yes," Mira said, still a bit tearful. "I really did."

"I couldn't even do it," Maria-Elena put in. "You guys did awesome. It's just that my mom's really good at that stuff."

"And that our guys are too nice to us," Zara agreed ruefully. "Chivalry has a price. But I did my best too, and that's all any-body can do. Let's go back over there, see how they're doing.

Looks from here like they're well in the lead. I'm guessing that they're going to bring it home for us one more time."

♡

Gabe glanced up at the sight of the five women coming wearily back across the Clearing to join Hank on the bench. His eyes flew, as always, to Mira. He saw the blood staining her apron and was alarmed for a moment, until he realized that the rest of the women, except Maria-Elena, looked the same.

"Looks like a rough one," Stanley grunted, working with Kevin to lift a top rail into place near the spot where Gabe was digging yet another posthole. They'd dug the holes on the first twelve-foot side together, then settled that Gabe, the strongest of them, would dig the remainder, while Stanley and Kevin worked to set and tamp the posts, fasten the rails in place.

"Yeah," Gabe agreed, reaching down for his jar of water and taking a swig. "We know who won?"

"Arcadia," Stanley said grimly. "Cliff just told us. But only by 15 points. And judging by the looks of them," he nodded in the direction of the other homestead's pigpen, "we've got this. Long as we keep it up. You want me to spell you some on that?"

"Nope. I'm good." Gabe looked at Stanley's shirt, the huge sweat-soaked patches on the back, under the arms, and knew his own looked the same. But Stanley was almost thirty-five years older than he was, and the day was hot. "You're drinking enough, right?" he cautioned. "You get dehydrated, we'll lose for sure."

"Yeah, Doc," Stanley grinned back tiredly. "I'm drinking. You just keep digging. Don't worry about your girl. We'll win it for her."

♡

"All righty, then." John stood in front of the bench where the six men sprawled, dirty and exhausted, an hour and a half later.

"We've got us two pens here, all right. Let's talk about how you did."

He walked to Paradise's pen first. "Stanley," he began. "Want to tell me why you decided to put your rails on the inside of the posts, instead of the outside like Arcadia did? What made you choose to do that?"

"Thought a pig'd be less likely to push the posts over that way," Stanley answered, wiping his handkerchief over the back of his neck, wet now from the pitcher of water he'd poured over himself.

"And that was a good thought," John said approvingly. "Get a 400-pound sow shoving up against those posts, she'll push 'em right down. That's 10 points from Arcadia, putting the rails on the outside."

"What?" Scott exploded. "Nobody ever told us that!"

John looked at him coldly. "I have a pretty good recollection of talking about building fence with you all. If you weren't listening to everything I said, thought you knew it all already, guess that's your look-out."

He walked around a little more. "Now," he went on, "what about the latch on the gate here? Now that, Arcadia, you *did* put on the inside. What was your thinking on that?"

"That you'd care more about getting out fast than getting in fast," Scott said proudly. "In case there was any trouble."

"Uh-huh," John said. "Only problem with that is, pig's smarter'n a dog. She can figure out how to lift that latch in no time. Now she doesn't even have to push over the posts. She can just open that gate up, walk right on out. That's another 10 points from Arcadia. Ten more points gone for being second, and another 5 for being second by a country mile, and we've got… Paradise winning by 35 points," he finished.

"And that means," Cliff said, "since Arcadia won the women's challenge by 15 points, that Paradise wins today by 20 points.

And that I'll see all of you here tomorrow night, when Paradise will be doing the talking once again."

He went on over the sounds of celebration on the Paradise side, the glum silence from Arcadia. "And I know you're all pretty hot and tired after all that. Probably don't feel much like cooking dinner tonight, do you?"

"Nope," Rachel agreed with a sigh. "Not even chicken."

"Well, I've got good news for you," Cliff said. "You don't have to. Go home and get cleaned up, take care of your animals, and come on back here. You're going to get the best dinner you've had yet out here tonight, and a surprise too."

"What about our chickens, though?" Rachel asked practically. "After all that work, we'd better get to eat them."

"Already in the freezer," Cliff promised. "We'll give them to you last thing tonight so you can cook them for dinner tomorrow. I'm sure I don't need to tell you, though, to put them in the springbox until you're ready to do that. Nobody's died on *America Alive* yet, though you've made some pretty good attempts at it. We'd like to keep it that way."

i will fight no more forever

♡

The first thing they noticed was the smoke.

"Barbecue," Stanley said appreciatively. And sure enough, the long table set up in front of the kitchen area wasn't the only thing that had changed when they returned to the Clearing a few hours later. Two huge barbecues were now pouring smoke into the late-afternoon sky, manned by two men, while two women moved between kitchen and table. The men's jeans and long-sleeved shirts weren't much different from the homesteaders' own attire, but their coloring was impossible to mistake.

"I wondered about this," Gabe said. "If they were ever going to talk about the original inhabitants. About time, too."

He broke off then to greet Alec, nodding to the rest of the Arcadia group. Scott, he saw, stayed near Lupe as she greeted her daughter with a warm hug.

"Yeah," Alec said, following the direction of his gaze and reading his thoughts perfectly, as always. "The only one softhearted enough to give him the time of day at this point. I have to say, sorry you won. Because having him around another week is going to be a killer. And I'm guessing you aren't going to be voting Mira out tomorrow."

"Nope," Gabe confirmed as they walked toward their dinner. "Not hardly."

♡

"Welcome," Cliff said when they were all seated around the long table. "I promised a good dinner tonight, didn't I? Fresh salmon, to be exact, graciously provided by members of the Nez Perce tribe, who are your hosts tonight."

Food had never tasted so good, Gabe decided, as their hosts served the meal and settled down to eat it with them. He was always hungry enough out here to enjoy anything put before him, but the perfectly cooked salmon fillets, so fresh they must have been caught that day, took it to a new level. Add buttery, pine nut-flecked carrots, tender roasted potatoes, and tortilla-like flatbread, and he was a happy man.

He groaned aloud when dessert was set in front of him. "Maria-Elena, I think you've just been given a run for your money," he announced. "And vanilla ice cream. I think I've just died and gone to heaven. What kind of pie is this?" he asked the woman across from him, who'd introduced herself as Deborah.

"Huckleberry," she smiled. "They're ripe now. You should find some good patches up the mountain a bit from you. Have you done much exploring?"

"Not much chance," he said ruefully. "You've just given me a good reason to make time, though. These are delicious." Like blueberries, but smaller, with a tart/sweet quality all their own.

"Just watch out for the bears," she cautioned. "They'll be pretty interested too."

Finally, though, the last piece of pie was consumed—by Stanley, Gabe was amused to see. Well, that had been a pretty tough challenge today. He'd eaten two pieces himself, and was starting to wonder if undoing the top button of his pants was an option.

"Many of you probably appreciate the irony of what you've experienced tonight," Cliff said as the last plate was shoved away with a sigh of satisfaction, the last swallow of coffee drunk. "You know already, of course, that the Homestead Act was enacted to settle the open lands of the West. But of course, the land was only open because the original inhabitants had been removed. Jeff Bradford here," he indicated the man who now rose to take a spot at the head of the table, "is a professor in the American Indian Studies program at the University of Idaho, and he's going to give you some of that history tonight."

"Nice," Kevin murmured happily to Gabe's left as he eyed the muscular build, high cheekbones, and strong nose of the man who stood now to face them, the glossy black hair cut short. "More eye candy, just for meeee."

Gabe fought back a chuckle, but quickly sobered as the man began to speak.

"The spot where you're sitting tonight, the homesteads you're been working, everything you see around you," he said, gesturing around in a wide circle, "was all Nez Perce land less than ten years before your group is supposed to have settled on it. Not just by tradition, but by treaty. The 1855 Treaty of Walla Walla assured us over seven million acres, and gave us hunting and fishing rights on the rest of our ancestral lands, the lands we ceded then to the government. But less than twenty-five years later, the U.S. government decided that wasn't enough. That they wanted everything. So they broke their treaty, and told us to get out. Told us they were taking our land, and we were moving to the reservation."

"Right," Gabe heard from several seats down. "Now it starts. Of course." Scott. Who else?

He saw Deborah stiffen, felt the uncomfortable shift in Mira's posture to his right, even as Kevin murmured in his ear, "He's not sure he's nailed that Most Unpopular Contestant title. He's going for the gold."

"Excuse me?" Jeff asked, looking down the table at Scott, an expression of polite interest on his handsome face.

"I know all this is the politically correct viewpoint," Scott said. "And that we're supposed to buy into it now, no questions asked. I'm not denying that abuses took place, but I've never seen how a tribe could have claimed to own some huge swath of property, just because they'd camped on it occasionally. The whole basis for the Homestead Act was that you had to improve the land, be doing something with it, be *settled* on it, for it to become yours. That concept, in fact, is firmly established in English common law, the basis of our legal system. What would you expect any government to do, especially back then? Isn't it a social good, and simple economics, to put the land to its highest use?"

"You got a car?" Jeff asked him.

"What?" Scott stared at him. "What does that have to do with it?"

"You got a car?" Jeff asked again.

"Yes. A BMW," Scott finally answered.

Jeff's mouth twisted a little at that. "Well, I've got a higher use for your BMW. April here's a visiting nurse," he said, nodding at the woman a few seats down. "Her car just broke down, and she needs a new one. Public health nurse versus what, lawyer?" He caught the nods and grins of the others. "I'd call that a no-brainer social good, right there."

"It's not the same thing at all," Scott said stiffly.

"Nope, it's not. But if I were holding a shotgun to your head while I asked for the keys, we could get a little closer," Jeff decided.

"But back to my story," he went on calmly, leaving Gabe sure that he'd encountered this argument before. "Suddenly the Treaty was gone, and we were supposed to march ourselves off to the res. Because the U.S. government had a *higher use* for our land. But not everyone was willing to go. Eight hundred men, women, and children took off, led by Chief Joseph, to join Sitting Bull and some of the other Lakota Sioux in Canada. They traveled over a thousand miles, across four states and multiple mountain ranges, pursued the whole way by two thousand U.S. soldiers. Two hundred Nez Perce warriors held off or defeated those soldiers, ten times their number, in eighteen battles."

Another pause. "But they didn't make it, all the same. Chief Joseph was finally forced to surrender, along with the rest of the survivors. They were only forty miles short of the Canadian border. His surrender speech is remembered today by every Nez Perce. You might want to think about this, while you're settling your land."

He quoted from memory, his voice strong but not loud.

"I am tired of fighting. Our chiefs are killed. Looking Glass is dead. Toohoolhoolzote is dead. The old men are all dead. It is the young men who say, "Yes" or "No." He who led the young men is dead. It is cold, and we have no blankets. The little children are freezing to death. My people, some of them, have run away to the hills, and have no blankets, no food. No one knows where they are—perhaps freezing to death. I want to have time to look for my children, and see how many of them I can find. Maybe I shall find them among the dead. Hear me, my chiefs! I am tired. My heart is sick and sad. From where the sun now stands I will fight no more forever."

"So when I hear people say this land was uninhabited, free for the claiming..." Jeff went on into the silence around him, "I can't help but think, this land wasn't free. It was paid for with the blood and the tears and the lives of my people."

♡

The group broke up soon after that, the homesteads preparing for the walk back in the evening twilight.

"Just a moment," Gabe told Mira. He found Alec by his side as he walked over to talk to Jeff.

"Thanks for that," he told the other man after introducing himself and Alec. "Don't judge us all by that one...bad apple. The rest of us appreciated it. The story, not the food," he clarified. "Although the food was fantastic too," he added with a grin.

"You got a little Indian in you, the two of you?" Jeff asked, looking from one to the other. "I see it in you, mostly," he told Gabe. "Not so much him."

"We had a Cherokee great-grandmother," Gabe confirmed. "Oklahoma, I guess, back in the day. So we're, what, an eighth."

"Enough to be enrolled in the tribe," Jeff said with a wry smile. "If you want all the fabulous benefits."

"Enough to know the story, anyway," Alec said. "The Trail of Tears. Not so different from what you talked about tonight."

"Except that a lot more died," Jeff agreed soberly. "No shortage of sad stories, is there? All along the way."

♡

"If you guys want to vote Scott off tomorrow," Mira told the others, the day's emotional and physical toll weighing on her like a suffocating blanket as the quiet group walked back to Paradise, "I'll go."

"You're not responsible for the ignorant things he says," Zara said firmly. "You weren't before, and you sure as hell aren't now."

"How could I have gone out with him, though?" Mira asked in anguished bewilderment. "How could I not have seen what he was really like?"

"Well, why do you think?" Zara asked.

Mira thought a moment. "Because he didn't show it, I guess, early on. He just seemed confident, and strong, and self-assured.

And I admired that, at the time. I didn't see the...the mean side. Or I didn't recognize it."

"Yep," Zara said. "That would be it. Bet he was a dreamboat when you were first dating. They're different when they're trying to impress you."

"Yeah," Mira agreed with a sigh. "It still took me way too long to wake up. But at least," she went on more strongly, "I *did* wake up. And at least now I'm making more informed decisions."

"Because Gabe hasn't been trying to impress you," Kevin said dryly. "Yeah, right."

"Hey," Gabe protested. "Way to cut a man down."

"Nothing wrong with trying to be a better man for a woman's sake," Stanley put in. "If it wasn't for that, we'd all still be living in caves."

a lot of romance

♡

It was a more rested but not a happier group that seated themselves on the benches in the Clearing again the following afternoon. Martin, Mira was glad to see, was back in action and sitting on the jury, if still on crutches. She gave him a little wave that he returned with a nod from his spot next to Arlene. And there were Chelsea and Melody, looking even more groomed and glossy than the previous week. They must have brought an awful lot of beauty products with them, Mira guessed. Either that, or somebody was shopping for them, wherever they were stashed for the duration.

"So, Kevin," Cliff began, bringing her thoughts back to the present. "What's been going on over there? Got a little romance happening?"

"Nope," he answered promptly. "A *lot* of romance. But sadly," he sighed, "none of it's been mine. Well, Bessie the Cow was getting kind of a thing for me, but I had to tell her it wouldn't work out."

"Nice attempt at a diversion," Cliff said with a smile. "I guess I'll go straight to the source. It's been an eventful week for you, Mira, and I'm not just talking about your hair. You've made some pretty big changes. Done everything but quit your job."

"I'm waiting on that till I get back," she found herself saying recklessly.

"Really." He actually looked surprised.

"Yeah." She laughed, a little giddy at the thought. "Consider this my two weeks' notice. Oh, wait. By the time my employer sees this, I'll be long gone, won't I? But, yeah. I've made up my mind."

"Wow. What's happened to you out here?"

She kept her eyes on Cliff, avoided looking across at Scott. One quick glance as they'd arrived had been plenty. Instead, she took a tighter hold of Gabe's hand where it was hidden by her skirt, and decided to answer the question honestly.

"The very first day, Kevin said that you can't hide who you really are on a show like this," she began. "At the time, I didn't appreciate what he meant, but now I see it. Because it's so draining, physically and emotionally. You don't have any energy left to…present a front, I guess. At home, I'd come in from a trip, and I'd think, I've got nothing in the fridge. And that would seem really hard, to have to go to the store when I was worn out. But here, if you want milk, you have to get it from the *cow.* Even if you don't want it," she added with a little laugh. "You have to milk that cow anyway. And everything's like that. Just so much harder."

She went on, caught up in her thoughts. "So, yes, you can get close to people really fast. Because you're seeing them every day, in such close quarters, and under the very toughest circumstances. Seeing who they really are, under the surface. And the same thing's true of the person you came in with. You're going to be seeing them more clearly too."

Her hand trembled a little in Gabe's as she replayed everything she'd just revealed. She didn't have to look at him, though, to feel his support. It was there in the solid press of his shoulder and thigh against hers, the sure grip of his hand.

"I think it's more than that, though," Zara interjected. "In Mira's case, and for all of us. You also find out, out here, what *you're* made of. How much you can handle. I suspect all of us at Paradise have seen that we're stronger than we realized. You work until you can't do any more, but then there's more to do, so you just do it. And that can't help but have an impact, give you the courage to make the big changes."

"Well, as you all know, this isn't just a journey of self-discovery," Cliff said. "It's also a game, and two people are going to be leaving that game tonight. Gabe, any concerns that you've put an even bigger target on your back, or put one on hers, by having such an obvious alliance with Mira?"

"Is that what we have?" he asked. "Not what I would've called it, but OK. Not too concerned, no. You want to vote so you weaken the other homestead, and lose as little strength as possible on your own. I hope my team thinks I'm a strong contributor, and as for Mira...Well, voting her out tonight would do just the opposite of those two things, wouldn't it? It would hurt us, and help Arcadia," he said baldly. "So, no. Not too worried."

"Kevin," Cliff went on. "Same question. Are you concerned tonight?"

"I think you always have to be concerned," he answered. "But even though I'm not as strong physically as Gabe, I'm the best with the animals. And I'm guessing there could be an animal challenge coming up. That's my ace in the hole."

♡

"I do hate this part of it," Stanley said on the walk home. "And that was much harder than the last one."

"I just hope that Lupe doesn't think it was anything Maria-Elena did wrong," Mira agreed unhappily. "Because she did great. It was just..."

"That she's eighteen," Kevin finished. "And that I *am* good with animals."

giving mira another lesson

♡

They were surprised two mornings later by a visit from John.

"Going to get you started on the plowing," he announced when the five of them were gathered in the yard. "You've got some pretty good hay in, got a reasonable woodpile too," he judged. "Not near enough to make it through to spring, of course, but a good start. But all that's just maintenance. Survival. If you'd been doing this for real, you'd have had to get started on your crop. Because you had to have a good amount of land under cultivation, at least forty acres, to prove up your homestead. You had to make some cash money too, buy your supplies. And all that means planting."

"What can we plant now, though?" Kevin asked. "I'd think planting started in the spring."

"You'd be doing that too," John acknowledged. "Spring, you'd be putting in some alfalfa, better feed for your animals than that hay you've been cutting. Dried peas and lentils, too. Bet you didn't know that the Palouse is the lentil capital of the United States."

"No, I did not know that," Kevin admitted. "My lentil knowledge is sadly lacking. I barely know what one is. Little brown things? Taste like sawdust?"

"That'd be your lentil," John agreed. "But you're right, that's spring planting. Right now, what you've got is your winter wheat."

"It grows in the winter?" Kevin asked, puzzled. "I thought it snowed here."

"Sprouts before it freezes, lies dormant under the snow," John explained. "You can harvest early, that's the idea. That's your cash crop, next summer. Get you through another year out here. Unless you're unlucky with your weather, of course."

"Of course," Kevin said gloomily.

"And the first step," John said, "is the breaking plow. That's what I've got here." He indicated the heavy implement sitting in the yard now, the truck that had delivered it having moved conveniently out of camera range. "You already know how to hitch your horses to the wagon, how to use 'em to snake trees out of the woods. Now I'm going to teach you how to hitch 'em to a plow, and what to do with it once you do."

"I knew there was a reason I chose bartending instead of farming," Kevin groaned at lunch, his hair still wet from the scrubbing of head and hands that he and the other men had done in the creek before coming into the cabin to eat. "Thanks," he added to Mira as she handed him a plate filled with red flannel hash, beans, and the inevitable cornbread.

Stanley accepted a glass of cold buttermilk from Mira with a weary smile, took a long drink. "You did the best of all of us, though, keeping the furrows straight," he pointed out. "But you're right, that's a heck of a job."

"What makes it so hard?" Mira wondered, dishing up her own plate last and joining the rest of them.

"The ground, for one thing," Gabe explained. "We had that cloudburst yesterday, softened the dirt up a little bit. That's why

John's here today. But we still had to put a log on top of the plow, give it a little more bite to get through the soil."

"Well, we don't have to actually do forty acres, that's the good thing," Stanley said. "Do it for about a week, John said. Then run over the same ground with the cultivator. And only one of us can be plowing at once, somebody else up there leading the horses. Lets us trade off, and leaves someone to help you in the garden, Mira. And keep the woodbox full, draw some water for you all."

"We're not actually planting anything, though," Zara said. "Are we? Not like somebody's going to be harvesting that wheat in the spring. So why do you have to keep doing it? Just so we can have more sessions with Cliff, talking about how hard it is?"

"Nope," Kevin said promptly. "But we have to hope Arcadia looks at it that way, decides that they'll do it while John's watching, then take it easy. Because don't you figure that's going to be our next challenge?" he asked the others.

"Yep," Gabe agreed, taking a last bite of lunch, a last swig of coffee, and swinging his legs back around the bench again with a sigh. "And practice makes perfect. Let's go."

♡

Mira walked with Zara up the path from the swimming hole that afternoon, stopped suddenly as they approached the corral.

"What is it?" Zara asked. "Leave something behind?"

"I'll just go in and…tell Gabe they can take their bath," Mira said. "If that's OK with you. Since we've got the rabbit stewing already, and all."

Zara smiled at her tolerantly. "You do that. Take your time."

Mira opened the corral gate, closed it carefully, then picked her way among the piles of manure to where Gabe sat, his back to her, milking Bessie.

"Fish not biting?" he asked without looking up from his task.

"It's me," she said, suddenly feeling shy.

He looked around quickly, his hands stilling on Bessie's teats. The smile started, then. "Yeah, I see it's you. Hi, you."

"Hi." She smiled back at him foolishly. They hadn't had any time alone together since a short walk on Sunday evening after the challenge, when they'd been followed relentlessly by Stu, and had confined themselves to talking in low voices and holding hands, ducking into the cover of the trees for a few rushed kisses before admitting defeat and returning to the cabin.

"The other guys fishing?" she asked now.

"Yep. I said I'd take care of the evening chores. Virtue's more than its own reward, in this case. Because now I get to talk to you. Here." He got up and grabbed an empty feed bucket. "Come sit by me."

"Can I try milking?" she asked, settling herself on the stool, Bessie turning around to give her a curious look.

"Sure, if you want to," he said with a laugh, upturning his bucket and sitting next to her. "Got a burning desire?"

"I do. I'm out here, after all. I might as well learn. I've only done it once, with Alma. Come on," she said, looking up at him with a reckless smile, "teach me something new."

He looked down at her, arrested. "What are we talking about here?" he asked slowly.

"I'm not sure," she confessed. The freedom of it was heady. Could she really just ask for what she wanted? Was it that simple? "For right now, since we're sitting here in the manure... Teach me to milk."

She was clumsy at first, but became more confident after a few minutes, some quiet words of instruction. Gabe's hands over hers, showing her how to draw the milk out more efficiently, didn't hurt either.

"It's not so bad," she said with pleasure, as the creamy milk squirted freely into the bucket.

Gabe laughed. "That's because Bessie's a little bit of a slut, like Kevin says. She doesn't quite perform for me the way she does for Kevin, but you put your hands on her, she lets her milk right down."

"Who knew he'd have such a touch with women?" she asked. "Women of the bovine persuasion, anyway."

She gave up after fifteen minutes, her hands cramping from the unfamiliar activity, but lingered with him while he finished.

"Well," she said, getting up reluctantly as he stood with the heavy pail, moving it carefully away from Bessie's careless hooves, "I'd better get back and help Zara."

"Yeah," he agreed. "I'll walk up with you, get this milk into the separator, then come back and do the rest of the chores before I go have my own bath. You aren't going to want to sit at the dinner table with somebody who smells as bad as I do right now."

"I always want to sit with you," she said, latching the gate behind the two of them. "No matter what. Even," she began to laugh, "next to a cow."

"I'll make a deal with Kevin, then," he said, smiling down at her. "Take on the evening milking from now on, get you to myself for a few minutes. And I'll make sure," he added, "that I get the stint in the garden with you tomorrow."

♡

It wasn't as easy as that, he found the next morning.

"Why don't you go get some shots of the plowing?" Mira asked Danny as he set up in the garden that she and Gabe were laboriously watering, one bucketful at a time. At least, Gabe thought, there was less to water now. The peas had finished producing, the lettuce had bolted, the radishes were done, and the spinach was full of aphids. Two-thirds of the big space, though, was still plenty to weed and keep watered in the hot sun of August.

Danny shrugged. "Gordon's out there with them," he reminded her. "But unless somebody hurts himself, it's not all that interesting."

"Zara's making bread, and a pie," she suggested hopefully.

"Also much less interesting than this," he assured her with an understanding smile. "Face it, Mira. You get the A team, because you're the ones providing the story."

"Not if you don't leave us alone, we're not," Gabe growled. "We're not lab rats. We don't reproduce under observation."

Mira gasped, then laughed. "That's true. Pretty ironic, isn't it, Danny? You want romance, you've got to give us some space to have it."

"I just follow orders," he apologized. "And you're not supposed to talk to me. Just...do your thing."

"Right," Gabe muttered, turning back toward the creek with his bucket. "My *thing.*"

Mira reached a hand out for his, pulled him back toward her. "So what is it you want, Danny?" she challenged him. "What are you hoping to find out here? This?"

She tugged at the straps of her sunbonnet, pulled it off and tossed it aside. Then moved against Gabe, stood on tiptoes, and pulled his head down to hers.

"Kiss me," she muttered against his mouth.

"Mira," he protested, his hands coming around her all the same, as if they had a mind of their own. "He's *filming.*"

"So? Your patients going to be shocked that you kissed a girl? Come on, Dr. Gabe," she taunted. "You said you wanted to do it. Kiss me."

"Oh, man," he groaned. "I am so going to regret this." Then threw caution to the winds, pulled her against him with one hand, shoved the other one into her hair, and kissed her, long and sweet. And despite the fact that they were standing in the dirt, and she was wearing that stupid corset, and Danny was ten feet away, it felt just absolutely fantastic.

Mira dropped back to her heels, kept her hold on him as she turned toward Danny. "That enough for you?" she challenged the cameraman. "Or do you want us to have sex against the fence?" Her hand reached for Gabe's midsection and began to inch downward. He grabbed her wrist and stared at her. What the hell?

"Mira." Danny was holding the camera away from him now. "Come on. Stop it. You know I'm just doing my job."

"Well, Gabe's right," she said. "We can't have a romance if I can't even kiss him. And I *want* to kiss him. So give us a chance!"

"What do you want from me?" he asked in exasperation.

"A few minutes of privacy, that's all. Let me talk to him while he's milking. Give us a couple minutes when we're in the garden. Come on. Have a heart."

"You're going to get me fired," he grumbled.

"No. What would get you *fired* is if you *did* film us having sex against the fence," she corrected. "And I'm *this* close to going for it. Go film Zara making a pie, if you don't want to see."

♡

"I am *not* having sex with you on camera," Gabe exploded as soon as Danny had taken himself off to the cabin. "Or out here in front of whoever walks by. What are you *doing?*"

"Getting us a little privacy, like I said," she said, her earlier confidence beginning to shrivel at the storminess of his expression. "It worked, didn't it? I know we're supposed to ignore the cameras," she went on, looking up at him pleadingly. "But I *can't.* I can't talk to you if they're filming. Not the way I want to. Don't you feel that way? Don't you want to talk to me too? Don't you want to...do more?"

"You must know I do," he said, still looking upset. "I can't exactly hide how you make me feel. But *warn* me next time. I about had a heart attack. I thought you were actually going to ask me to have sex against the fence. And the worst thing about it?" He started to laugh. "I probably would've done it. That's how crazy you've got me."

She began to giggle as relief filled her. The giggles increased until she was leaning against that same fence, laughing helplessly, her hands on her knees. "I can't believe I said that," she got out. "I didn't know I was going to. I don't know what's *wrong* with me. I start by telling Scott what I really think, and it's like...I can't help myself."

He came to prop himself next to her, picked up her hand. "Never been bad before, huh?" he asked with a grin.

She shook her head, smiled up at him. "Nope. I've been a good, good girl for twenty-nine long years. Never made waves, not a single solitary one. But it's starting to look like those days are over. So look out, world."

a way with animals

♡

That *had* made things a little better, Gabe thought on Saturday as they walked along the path toward today's challenges. They'd had a few minutes in the garden another day, the half-hour they'd spent milking every night. Not exactly the most romantic spot, though. He wasn't far enough gone yet to grope a girl in the middle of the cow pies.

No, not nearly enough chances to be with her. A couple short walks, always trailed at a discreet distance, pulling her into the trees to kiss her. Lingering for a whispered goodnight, a brief embrace before climbing the ladders to their opposite lofts. And, whenever he could, holding her hand. It had felt so good when he'd first had the chance to do it, he thought, squeezing that same hand in his own now. How quickly, though, he'd wanted so much more.

He sighed in frustration and tightened his hold on her as they approached their destination. They'd been given directions to a new spot this time, not the Clearing, which had occasioned some conversation. But they'd just have to see when they got there. And if he didn't get his mind into the game, he reminded himself, and win this challenge, he wasn't going to have any more time with Mira at all, because she and Scott would be leaving.

"Oh, no," Gabe heard Zara say from behind him as Arcadia came into the challenge area from the opposite direction. Four contestants walking. And one, Hank, on crutches. "What happened? And why didn't I know?"

"Welcome," Cliff said when both teams had arrived in front of him. "We've got you in a new spot today, as you've noticed, closer to Arcadia. And that's partially because of Hank. Good news is, it's just an ankle strain. We're keeping him off it today though, Zara, just to be on the safe side."

Hank waggled a crutch at his wife with a grin. "Need to watch where I'm going better, that's all," he called out. "Stepped in a gopher hole and twisted my ankle. Good as new in a couple days."

"So that makes it pretty obvious who Arcadia will be sitting out today," Cliff went on. "Because as you can see, the men are going to be plowing today."

Sure enough, two horses were standing with their handlers, each hitched to the smaller cultivator, Gabe saw with relief, not the big breaking plow. Small mercies, anyway.

"This one is going to be man against man," Cliff told them. "Three separate races, plowing down to the end of the field here, then turning around and coming back. Easy, right? You'll be getting points for how straight your furrow is, and, of course, how fast you do it."

He stopped for effect before going on. "Here are our pairs. We've selected them for you, just to make things easier. First up, Stanley against Alec. Second, Gabe against Calvin. And for our last leg," he paused significantly, "Kevin against Scott."

Hank swung himself over to the bench, took a seat with the three women as the rest of the men gathered in their teams at their start lines.

"Good thing we practiced," Gabe muttered to Kevin and Stanley. "Let's hope they haven't."

But as Stanley moved down the field alongside Alec to start the event, it was clear that Arcadia, too, had done its share of plowing this past week. Stanley was giving it his usual strong effort, but Alec had clearly been getting into shape out here. Gabe watched in dismay as Alec made the turn ahead of Stanley, widened the gap on the return journey. At the same time, he found himself proud of his normally deskbound brother. No Dr. Pepper, no late nights now, and Alec was showing the results. He was leaner, harder. And, Gabe thought as his twin pushed with all his might for the finish, taking this completely seriously.

Stanley didn't let up despite Alec's lead, and was blowing hard, sweat standing out in huge patches on his pale blue work shirt, by the time he reached the finish line.

Gabe handed him a jar of water, clapped him on the back. "Good job," he told the older man.

Stanley shook his head tiredly, took a welcome gulp of the cold water. "Twenty years ago, I would've left your brother in the dust. I'm not the man I was then, and that's the truth. Hope I haven't given you too much to make up. Can't believe I'm saying it, but I'm betting you can beat my boy out there."

"I know what you mean," Gabe said ruefully. "Loyalty's a bitch, isn't it?"

"And that's 10 points to Arcadia," John announced after coming back from inspecting the two men's furrows. "Alec came in with a good lead, but Stanley, you plowed it straighter."

"Next pair up," Cliff called. "Gabe and Calvin," he gestured widely, "come on down."

Gabe glanced across at Calvin, frowning with concentration behind his plow. Stanley thought he had this, he reminded himself. And Stanley ought to know.

"Ready...set...GO!" Cliff shouted, and they were off. Gabe kept his eyes glued on the black soil ahead of him, concentrated on plowing a straight furrow, on walking as quickly as he could while using all his considerable strength to keep the plow firmly rooted in the ground. Began the turn around the post at the end of the field, and saw with relief that he had a bit of a lead already.

Calvin wasn't going to make it easy, though. The other man was pushing himself to the limit. Gabe wrested his gaze away again, focused with all his intensity on the task at hand. By the time he had reached the finish line, he was blowing as hard, sweating as much as Stanley had been. But had also come in ahead of Calvin.

"You both plowed it straight," John announced. "And Gabe came in a little faster. That's five points to Paradise, I'd say. So we've got..." He stopped. "Arcadia by five."

"Which means it's a cliffhanger," Cliff agreed. "It all comes down to the last leg. Kevin and Scott, come on over and get started."

Gabe felt a stab of worry as Kevin lined up behind his horse and Scott did the same. Not that Kevin couldn't win. Gabe didn't have a doubt in the world that Kevin could beat Scott if he tried. *Would* he be trying, though? Kevin and Rachel would be better off, after all, if Arcadia won today. And strategy was always uppermost, Gabe knew, in Kevin's devious mind.

"Ready...set...GO!" Cliff shouted for a final time. And the challenge was on.

Two things were clear to Gabe at once. First, that Kevin would have to practically lie down behind the horse to lose to Scott. And second, that he wasn't going to. As always, Kevin and the horse seemed to have established an immediate rapport, some magic that traveled down the reins and made the animal go exactly where the man wanted her to. And Kevin, too, had gained muscle and stamina out here.

Scott, on the other hand...Gabe supposed, watching the tall, thin figure struggling behind the horse, that Scott had got stronger. It was pretty hard not to when you were doing this much physical labor every day. But as far as rapport with animals... whatever was traveling down the reins from Scott was the opposite of encouraging. In fact, his horse seemed to be slowing down, not speeding up.

"Go! Damn it to *Hell! Go!*" A string of curses followed from the end of the field. Kevin had made the turn, was on the way back, but Scott was floundering badly, the horse seeming to decide that he would just as soon keep heading straight ahead.

In the end, Scott had to leave the plow, go around to the horse's head, and lead him by the bridle to make the turn. And by that time, Kevin was all but galloping home, to the whoops and cheers of the rest of the Paradise homestead.

John watched, his expression bemused, as Scott finally approached, red-faced, furious, and still swearing, back at the finish line, then dropped the plow handles with disgust and moved to confront the older man.

"How am I supposed to compete," he raged, "if you give me a lousy horse? This was rigged! The whole thing's a setup!"

"Wellll..." John removed his hat and scratched his head thoughtfully, then settled it carefully back on his grizzled head. He scuffed a boot in the dirt, seeming to examine the ground before looking back up at Scott, who stood clenching and unclenching his fists impatiently. "Didn't seem like anybody else had any problem," John drawled. "Alec, now, he did just fine. Calvin too."

"The horse was worn out," Scott insisted. *"Their* horse," he nodded contemptuously over at Paradise, "was still fresh. Whereas *my* horse was obviously overworked, or weak to start with. It couldn't do it!"

"Uh-huh," John said. "Couldn't do it, you're right about that. Horse isn't a machine. You gotta talk sweet to 'em. Kinda like a woman that way. You push 'em around, you aren't going to get a whole lot of cooperation. Maybe you should ask Kevin there for some lessons."

"With horses, not with women," Kevin clarified solemnly. "Or maybe ask Gabe. He might be able to help you out with both. He wins, oh, pretty much all the time, from what I've seen."

Scott's face got, if possible, even redder. His mouth opened and closed, and Cliff came forward hastily. "What are our points for this round?" he asked John.

"The full 15 points to Paradise, this time."

"Which makes it Paradise by 10," Cliff announced. "But don't worry, Arcadia," he went on, ignoring the still-furious Scott, who had gone over to stand near the other members of his homestead, none of whom looked especially welcoming. "The women's challenge is worth the same 45 points. You're not out of this yet."

The margin was too narrow, Mira thought nervously. It all depended on what the challenge was. Rachel was good, Mira had seen that since Day One. And she wanted to win this game as much as Kevin did. If Arcadia won today, Rachel and Kevin were safe for another week. But if they lost...This wasn't a must-win challenge for Rachel, but it was close.

"Guys, I know you're tired," Cliff went on, "so we're not going to make you move." The men had, in fact, settled down now onto the spectators' benches and were sitting with elbows on knees or legs sprawled in front of them, resting after their labors.

Two young men appeared from the trees, leading a cow apiece. "That's right," Cliff said. "It's going to be short and sweet. A milking race. As you know, milking might have been done by either men or women out here. And even if men did it most of the time, women had to take their turn when a man was unavailable for some reason. Which may or may not have been the case for all of you. So if you'll come forward, the three of you…" He beckoned to the women.

"Rachel," he said when they were standing before him. "As the only woman left on Arcadia, you're obviously nominated. But to make this fair, we're going to let you select your opponent. Mira or Zara. Your choice."

Mira thought fast. She schooled her face into a worried frown that was all too easy an expression to assume as Rachel looked sharply at her, then shifted her gaze to Zara.

Don't pick me, Mira attempted with all her might to project. She didn't dare look to see Zara's expression, but she was willing to bet it appeared less anxious than her own, even though Mira was the better milker. Zara hadn't done it since their one lesson with Alma, but somehow, she always appeared confident anyway.

Mira saw Rachel's face firm with decision, but wasn't sure she'd convinced her until she heard the words.

"Mira," Rachel announced. "I'm going up against Mira."

Mira bit her lip, looked across at the cows uncertainly as they were led into place, tied to stakes driven into the ground in front of the spectators' area. If she could lull Rachel into complacency, so much the better. In fact, it wasn't too hard to act concerned. She'd only been milking the past few days. What if Rachel had been doing it all along? Maybe she, like Kevin, had an affinity for animals.

Stop it, she commanded herself. She could only do what she could do. And right now, that meant milking a cow just as fast as she could.

"We've got two Guernseys for you here," Cliff announced as Zara returned to the bench, leaving Mira and Rachel to approach the big brown animals. "Same breed you're used to, and we've selected them specifically to match, to make this fair. They each give about the same amount of milk, and give it equally easily. Piece of cake, right?" he asked with a smile to which Mira responded with a nervous laugh that she didn't have to fake.

"Mira," he went on, "Since Rachel got the pick of opponents, you get the pick of cows. Which one do you want to milk?"

"This one," Mira decided. She went to the cow on the right, who had turned to look at her with what Mira chose to think was a kindly eye, and laid a hand on her flank. "This is my cow."

"All right, then." Cliff nodded at the milking stool and pail already set next to the cows. "The winner is the one with the most milk at the end of twenty minutes. Simple." He waited until they were both seated on their stools, with their buckets positioned under the udders. "And challenge is...*on!*"

Mira shut all thought of Rachel out of her head, put her head against the big, warm flank and tried to send calm and certainty into the hands that grasped the rubbery teats. To her relief, the cow was docile and good-natured, and let down her milk as easily as Gabe had joked about Bessie doing.

On and on she went, her fingers squeezing steadily, the milk squirting into the bucket. She focused on the rhythm, felt her hands tiring, and refused to slow down. When her mind began to spiral down into fear, the pain in her hands threatened to distract her, she began to sing in her head. The very first song they'd sung together, that first night. "Michael, Row the Boat Ashore." She finished the last verse she remembered, started at the beginning again, milked to the rhythm, the upbeat tune reverberating in her head, mingling with the sound of the milk hitting the bucket.

She was fully engrossed, lost in a trance of milking and singing, when she heard Cliff shout, "Time!" She came back to herself, let go of the teats, and sat back as Jay removed the bucket.

As she turned around on her stool and got to her feet, she found that her legs were trembling, her hands shaking now that the ordeal was over. She wrapped her arms around herself and watched Jay carry her bucket to a table where two large jars were set ready, volume measures clearly marked on their sides, tried to see inside Rachel's bucket, but couldn't tell how much it held.

She'd done her best, she repeated to herself. She'd kept it together, and she'd done her best.

"We'll measure Rachel's milk first," Cliff announced. "And she got...just over six quarts. Six and an eighth quarts, to be exact." He paused for the congratulations of the Arcadia homestead.

"And now, Mira's bucket." He paused portentously.

Just measure it, Mira thought desperately. She tried to think how full her bucket had seemed, how that would have translated into quarts, and for once in her life, couldn't do the math.

All too slowly, Cliff poured her bucket into the big jar. He paused dramatically before announcing, "Seven and seven-eighths quarts! Paradise wins the women's challenge, and Paradise wins again!"

Her teammates crowded around her as she laughed in exultant relief. There was Stanley, giving her an exuberant hug, telling her how proud he was of her.

"Mira," Kevin was saying sternly now, standing back with his hands on her shoulders. "Did you just play my sister?"

"When you pasted that anxious look on your face, I about died," Zara said. "'Oh please, B'rer Fox, don't throw me into that briar patch!'" She began to laugh. "Who knew you had it in you?"

Mira laughed back at her, although she still felt shaky from effort and emotion. "I wasn't sure it would work. But it did! She bought it!"

Gabe shook his head ruefully, gathered her into his arms and gave her a squeeze of his own. "I've thought from the beginning that there was a lot more to you than met the eye. Remind me not to go up against you. I'm beginning to think I've met my match out here."

"I think you may have done just that," Stanley agreed with a smile. "And that our Miss Mira has some real hidden depths."

♡

Despite their exuberance at the moment of victory, it was a sober group that walked home again after the challenge. Mira knew that everybody else's mind was turning over the same question she was. Who were they going to vote out next? If last week's decision had been hard, this was agonizing.

"When do you think they'll put us together?" she finally turned to ask Kevin, walking behind her and Gabe. She dropped back to talk to him.

"After this next vote, I'd think," Kevin said. "When there are eight of us. Which means," he went on, his normal cheeky humor resurfacing, "if you make it through till tomorrow, you and Scott should be safe."

"Because everybody wants to go to the end with us," Mira agreed. "And nobody has to worry that we'll win Safety. And meanwhile, if he's too awful, we can get the boot anytime. Because when you think about it…nobody's going to want to give Scott a hundred thousand dollars. That might even out-weigh the certainty of winning the million, for some people. Not for you, obviously," she said with a laugh.

"Hey," he grinned, "I came on here to be strategic. I came on to *win*. And I haven't had to live with Boyfriend all this time. I could put up with him for a few weeks. For a million dollars? You bet I could."

"Yeah, but can Rachel?" she pointed out. "And stop calling him Boyfriend. He's not my boyfriend anymore, remember?"

"That's the question," Kevin agreed. "If Rachel can. And I really doubt she and I are going to be winning any Safety chal-lenges. Have to get through on our looks and charm. Gabe and Alec, now…"

"My ears are burning," he said, turning around ahead of them. "What about me?"

"We're talking about the Safety challenges, once they put the two teams together," Kevin said boldly. "And who's likely to win them."

"What's that I feel on my back all of a sudden?" Gabe asked, twisting around to check himself out. "Oh, yeah. A target."

"If I'd had any sense," Kevin sighed, "I should've made sure we lost that challenge today. I'm sure Zara's had the same thought, not that Mira gave her a chance. Because then we'd both have had another guaranteed week out here. But I couldn't help it. I couldn't stand to lose to Boy—to Scott. Testosterone poisoning claims another victim."

He looked behind him to where Stanley was bringing up the rear with Zara, "But as it is," he said, "you've got Stanley and Mira, Gabe, and Mira's got the two of you. Which means that it's one of two people tomorrow. And that I'm one of them."

getting ruthless

♡

"Hey," Gabe said quietly after their music session that evening, shorter than usual after the difficult day. "Want to take a walk?"

"Sure." Mira got up with him, exchanged a quick look with Zara, and set off on the path toward the mountains. The last bars of late afternoon sunlight fell on the fields of grass, turned golden now by the August heat. They'd have a few extra minutes together tonight before it got dark. A few minutes to be alone, or as alone as they ever were.

Gabe waited until they'd entered the forest of white pine before speaking. "I wanted to talk to you about the vote. At least," he smiled down at her, "that's one reason I brought you out here. Let's get the hard part over with first, though."

"OK," she said resignedly. "Zara and I talked about Kevin already, while we were making dinner. Is that what you're thinking too?"

"No," he said bluntly. "The guys and I...we're thinking Zara."

"Oh." She swallowed. "Oh."

"Because with three of us guys," he went on, "and without Hank there as a possibility, it'll definitely be Scott, plus the other two, of course, against us in the challenges. And those are some pretty good odds."

"That's a valid point," Mira conceded.

"Because otherwise, you know," Gabe continued, "if Arcadia wins next time…"

"Yeah," she agreed. "If they win, Scott and I leave. I know that. And Zara makes sense anyway. Because if the two of them, Hank and Zara, make it to the final…they're both too popular. I can see that."

"You can?" he asked in surprise.

"Of course I can." She looked at him with a bit of exasperation. "I love Zara. But I do get that it's a game, you know."

"I know you do. But you still surprise me, all the time," he admitted. "OK. Zara. Do you want to tell her it's Kevin, or would you rather I did it?"

"I will," Mira decided. "That'll work much better. I went for a walk with you, we talked about it, and we agreed on Kevin. But I do hate this part. I hate to lie."

"It's no fun," he agreed. "Especially lying to somebody you're as close to as Zara. And I know it'll mean more work for you, even assuming they put the homesteads together right away. Six men and only two women. That'll be a lot to do, but we'll help. You'll have to tell us what to do, but we'll take turns in the garden, with the cooking, the laundry, everything. We already discussed it."

"OK," she sighed. "It's a plan. It's just that everyone is a friend now, aren't they? I wish there were still somebody here I didn't like so much."

"You're such a soft touch," Gabe said with a smile. "Tell me, when you thought about coming on the show, did you think about this part?"

"Of course I did. But I wasn't expecting to get so close to everybody. And if you think I'm not capable of thinking strategically," she went on boldly, "well, you can think again. Because I know *exactly* what I'd do if I thought I had a snowball's chance of winning. And if I *cared* about winning."

"And what's that?" he asked, still smiling.

"Talk to Zara and Kevin about voting you off, of course," she answered promptly. "Because you're the biggest threat out here by far," she went on at his bark of surprised laughter. "And you know Kevin would do it. Stanley wouldn't, but Kevin? In a heartbeat. He'll try to do it at the end, if he gets that far. There's no way he wants to go up against you in the final vote."

"Who knew you were so ruthless?" he said wonderingly. "All soft and innocent on the outside, all those cuddly curves, those freckles on your nose. Why didn't I realize that was just a front? Guess I'd better be more careful. You could just be softening me up for your sneak attack."

"I could," she said with a toss of her head. "You just watch yourself."

"You're getting pretty sassy, aren't you?" He stopped walking on the forested path, turned her towards him and laced the fingers of both hands through hers. "And you know what happens to girls like that."

"No, what?" She smiled up at him happily.

He backed her up against one of the big pines, lifted her hands above her head, turned his own so they were the ones resting against the rough bark, while keeping a tight grip on her. "They get in trouble," he promised.

"Mmm. What kind of trouble?" she asked innocently, opening her eyes wide at him. She'd never teased and played like this before. And wasn't it just the most fun ever.

"The kind of trouble I'm going to be showing you all about, just as soon as we're out of here," he assured her. He moved even closer, pressing her against the pine, then lowered his mouth to hers.

She welcomed the pressure of his hard body, the invasion of his mouth. His lips left hers, moved to her cheek, then down to her neck. He kissed her there, moved his teeth over her, biting gently, and she arched up into him, moving her head to the side and moaning aloud at the almost unbearable sensation, feeling her nipples hardening inside the constriction of the corset.

"You like that, huh?" he murmured against her skin, before he began again, biting a little harder, moving around under her ear and making her gasp even more. Each delicious movement of his mouth seemed to go straight to her center, and she squirmed against him, trying to get closer, thrilling at the feel of his erection through the layers of clothes, wishing she weren't wearing the corset, that she could feel even more of him.

"OK," he breathed, letting go of her hands at last and taking a reluctant step back. "OK. I should know better than to start something with you. You make it so hard to stop."

She stayed where she was, pressed against the tree, her hands above her head. "You don't have to stop," she said, looking up at him. "We could tell Stu to leave us alone. Or...sneak off."

He shook his head. "We do that, that's exactly when he's going to follow us. One of them's got us in some kind of long shot right now, and you know it." He reached a hand out to grab her around the waist, pulled her towards him. "But if you stand there like that, you're going to end up starring in *Mira Does Montana.* Because you're killing me here."

She felt ridiculously happy at the thought that she could affect him that much, that she was actually testing his self-control. At least, the part of her that wasn't hopelessly frustrated was happy.

"We wouldn't have to show much," she said slyly, as he began to pull her by the hand down the path again. "Maybe you haven't noticed our underwear's...unique feature."

"What?" He looked down at her, startled.

"It's crotchless," she said, amazed at her own boldness. But she had a feeling that was a piece of information he'd enjoy having.

"You're kidding."

"Nope. Just a...slit. What do you think about that? I could be up against that tree and..."

"Help," he said ruefully. "I've created a monster. You realize you've just added another fifteen wakeful minutes to my nightly frustration."

"Really?" she asked, inordinately pleased. So she wasn't the only one.

"Oh, yeah," he assured her. "Lying awake, thinking about you? Imagining how it's going to be? You'd better believe it."

regrets and plans

♡

The vote had been just as hard as she'd feared, Mira thought the next afternoon as she walked back to Paradise, her hand in Gabe's as always, Danny riding backwards on the ATV ahead of them to film.

Zara had only smiled sadly, though, when the votes were read. "I did wonder," she'd said. "Well played," she'd murmured as she gave Mira a hug goodbye. "See you soon. Love you."

Mira herself had teared up, of course, watching her walk off with Hank and the others: Chelsea and Melody, Lupe and Maria-Elena, Arlene and Martin, still on crutches, toward whatever waited on the other side of the trees. It had been the right decision, but life was going to be a lot lonelier without Zara.

"I couldn't believe it," Kevin said now, interrupting her thoughts. "I was *sure* we were going to merge. They've *always* merged at eight. When Cliff told us to go on back, I was, like, *what?* But it has to happen soon. The only question is, before or after the next challenge? Will the next one be homestead against homestead, or a Safety challenge with our original partners?"

"No telling," Stanley said philosophically. "We just go on the way we are, wait and see. Don't borrow trouble."

"It matters, though," Kevin argued. "Strategically."

"Why?" Mira asked. Kevin looked at her, startled, as she went on. "I mean, of course there's a difference in the outcome, but there's not much you'd be able to do as far as planning for it, even if you knew which way it would go."

"Oh, yeah?" Kevin asked dubiously. "Instruct me."

"Say we do merge on Saturday," she began. "That would make it a Safety challenge. Then it all depends on who wins Safety. If you and Rachel win…then it's tough. Then it's Alec and Gabe going home, or Stanley and Calvin, depending on who Rachel's tight with, who she can sway. And there's nothing you can do about that now. You can try pitting Stanley and Gabe against each other this week, but that'd probably just antagonize both of them, and you'd be worse off than you were before. And if Alec and Gabe win it," she mused as Kevin looked at Gabe in astonishment and Gabe grinned back at him, "then you and Rachel go. Because you're a much bigger threat than Scott and me, obviously. Again, nothing you can do about that now. And if Stanley and Calvin win it, it's also you and Rachel, for the same reason," she finished.

"So unless Rachel and I win, I'm screwed," Kevin said gloomily. "OK, Smartypants, what if you and Scott win?"

She laughed. "Not in the realm of possibility. But if we do? Then you go, and you know that too."

"What if we don't merge?" he asked with fascination. "And who knew I should have been coming to you for advice all this time?"

Gabe put up a hand. "I did. You think I hooked up with her just because she's hot?"

Mira laughed. "My advice is always free of charge to you," she assured Gabe. "And OK," she told Kevin seriously. "If we don't merge, then what? Then it's a homestead challenge. If Arcadia wins, I'm gone. And if Paradise wins…"

"I'm gone," Kevin agreed with a sigh. "I don't like the outcome of any of your scenarios much. Why is it that most of them end up with me leaving? Looks like my only strategic option, besides hoping that Rachel's been more effective than I have, is to try to break you and Gabe up. I'd work on Stanley's loyalties, but I have a feeling those are going to be pretty tough to shake."

"About as tough as breaking those two up," Stanley said with the grin Kevin always elicited from him. "You really are a piece of work. Can't work this angle, and you may as well admit it."

"Sadly, I fear that you are correct. And if I throw the challenge, I'll never win the million. Besides, and I hate to say it, I don't think my male pride would allow it. So," Kevin heaved a mighty sigh. "The way I see it, I can poison you, Mira—which might happen anyway, if I'm going to be helping in the kitchen. I'm a terrible cook. Or I can cross my fingers that we don't merge, and that Arcadia somehow manages to kick our butt next week."

♡

Kevin wasn't kidding about being useless in the kitchen, Mira discovered. When he burned the eggs the next morning, resulting in a mess that even Stanley refused to eat, it was clear that the roster was going to have to be adjusted.

"Consider yourself on garden duty, Kevin," Gabe announced, poking through the charred strips of bacon to find something edible. "Stanley and I are going to be helping Mira out in here from now on."

"When we're not plowing and planting," Stanley agreed. "We'll work out a schedule, get it fixed up. I can still do a day's work, but not on an empty stomach."

"Well, I will need some help," Mira said, "because I was thinking that I might try to bake a cake tomorrow. I'm no good at pie, so if we want something sweet, I'm going to have to try cake. And I kind of want a cake tomorrow anyway."

"Why?" Gabe asked, arrested in the act of buttering a biscuit. "What's tomorrow?"

"My birthday," she admitted. "Twenty-nine. And I know it's silly, but I want a cake."

"Baking your own birthday cake...that's a little sad, though," Gabe said. "You know how to make cake, Stanley?"

"Nope. Sure don't," he said regretfully.

"Me neither. And never mind," Gabe said when Kevin would have spoken. "We know you don't. All right, Mira, you have to bake your own cake. But what can we do for you that's special?"

"You don't have to do anything," she protested, uncomfortable at the fuss. "It's fine. I just wanted a cake, that's all."

"You don't ask a woman what she wants," Stanley instructed Gabe. "Not a woman like Mira, you don't. She's always going to tell you she's fine. You think of what you can do for her, and you make it happen, so she doesn't have to do a thing. That's the way it works."

"You sure know," Mira told him with a smile, putting a hand over his.

"I ought to," he said, turning his own palm up to squeeze hers briefly. "Trained by the best. Took her about thirty years, but she got there, in the end."

"All right," Gabe objected, "but what *do* we do?"

"We give her a day off, first thing," Stanley decided.

"Not the whole day," Mira said. "None of you knows how to cook on a wood stove well enough for that. But a few hours would be nice."

"Right," Stanley said. "And..." He looked at her speculatively. "A bath," he decided.

"You telling her she's dirty?" Kevin said, starting to laugh. "That's some Boyfriend School you've got going there for Gabe."

"You mean a *hot* bath?" Mira asked, ignoring Kevin. "How?"

"That washtub's pretty big," Stanley said. "That's how folks used to do it, you know, not so long ago. Saturday night, one after the other, in the washtub. Littlest kid got the last bath in that dirty water. My daddy told me about that."

Mira eyed the big washtub, hanging on the cabin wall, with longing. "A hot bath," she breathed. "Yeah. The only thing better would be shaving my legs. But still. Yeah. Happy Birthday to Me."

mira's birthday present

♡

"Don't worry about dumping the water afterwards," Gabe assured her the next afternoon. "The guys and I will take care of that." He set a bucket of steaming water down next to the washtub, together with a cup. "For rinsing your hair," he explained. "And I think this towel is clean."

"You thought of everything," she said, flushed with pleasure. She couldn't wait to squeeze herself into that tub and soak. "This is amazing."

He smiled. "I'll get out of here and leave you to it. Take your time. Go sit in the sun for a while afterwards, too. It's your birthday, after all. The guys will stay out of the way."

"The stove," she began.

"I'll keep it going," he promised. "Now get in there before you lose all the heat." He cast a last frowning look at Danny, filming from his corner. "There's a limit here," he warned the cameraman.

"I told you," Danny sighed. "We're not allowed to film anybody naked."

♡

"This is weird," Mira complained as Gabe shut the door reluctantly behind him. "Like some kind of awkward 1885 porn."

"Just ignore me," Danny said. "I'll be gone in a minute."

Mira did her best, but it still felt strange to take off the layers of clothes in front of him. First her apron, then her dress and corset, until she was finally untying the drawers and pulling them off from underneath the chemise, laying everything across a chair. She could see, out of the corner of her eye, the camera tracking her movements, then panning to her clean underclothes lying ready on the bench along with her towel and comb.

"OK," Danny said. "Just pull up the chemise. Just up to your thighs."

"My thighs on TV. Right," she sighed. "Exactly what I thought I *wouldn't* have to reveal on this show."

"Come on, Mira," he coaxed. "Ten seconds and you're in that tub. And...great," he said as she complied. "That's our money shot. And I'm out of here."

At last, he was gone and she was stepping into the blissfully warm water. She closed her eyes at the pleasure of it, even as she scrunched her legs up to fit them into the galvanized tub. Picking up the precious bar of castile soap, she laughed a little at the idea that this was the ultimate luxury in her new life. But it *was* a luxury, and she felt every keen lick of sensual enjoyment at the feeling of the warm water against her skin, the sheer bliss of getting really, truly clean. She used the white soap and the bathing sponge to wash her ears and neck, scrubbed her arms and legs and, finally, her feet until they glowed pink. Then scooped warm water with her hands, splashed it over herself to rinse off, and looked down at her body, studying it carefully for the first time in weeks.

Gazing at her stomach, she realized how much flatter it had become. And her thighs—they'd never had that curve to them, that was for sure. Her body was stronger and slimmer than it had been for years. Women spent all kinds of money for boot camps and spa vacations in an attempt to create this kind of transformation. And yet, ironically, this was the one time she hadn't been obsessing over it. There had just been too much to do. In the morning when she was hopping around, trying to keep warm while she pulled on clothes in the first gray light of dawn, trying her best to fix her hair, it was the last thing she was concerned with. And when she was finally pulling her clothes off in the light of her lantern, all she wanted to do was lie down and go to sleep.

It was more than that, though, she thought as she used the bucket and cup Gabe had left to wet her hair, worked up a lather with the soap and scrubbed at her head, then rinsed the suds out as thoroughly as she could with the rest of the water. What she'd enjoyed most had been the strength she'd felt—the ease with which she could now split a chunk of wood into stove-sized pieces, turn the handle to pull up the well water. And her strength of mind, too. It hadn't been easy these past couple days being the only woman here, but she'd gotten it all done. As hard and monotonous as the work was, she'd had such a sense of accomplishment that she had mastered it, that she was the last woman standing here on the homestead.

Hearing the rhythmic thud of the axe, the clatter of split wood falling, she smiled to herself. And the other thing she'd enjoyed was Gabe. The light in his eyes when he looked at her. All the little kindnesses he'd done her from the beginning, from filling the woodbox to carrying water, in addition to all his own work. The way he'd grated that huge pile of carrots this morning for the carrot cake she'd decided was her safest bet, joking when he'd grated his knuckle, kissing her when she'd bandaged it for him. No, having him around hadn't hurt at all.

Her tub wasn't hot anymore, but she lingered until it had cooled and she began to shiver before reluctantly climbing to her feet and reaching for the rough towel, rubbing herself vigorously and finally bending forward to wrap her hair in a turban.

She stepped onto the bare wood planks of the floor and pulled the clean chemise over her scrubbed body with a sigh of contentment, slipped her dirty boots on reluctantly but left them untied, then grabbed her comb and left the cabin.

It *was* Gabe chopping wood, she saw. She waved to him, then walked down next to the creek, sat on her favorite boulder and took off the grubby boots, then set about toweling dry and combing her hair, grateful once more for its shorter length. She should have cut it sooner, no matter what Scott had said. Well, she should have done a lot of things sooner. But at least she'd finally done them, one way or another.

She looked up at the sight of someone coming along the path. Gabe, she realized with a funny little lift of her heart. Carrying the bucket and a wooden box.

"Hi," he said with a smile as he came up beside her. He set the box and the heavy bucket, steam rising from its surface, on the ground next to her. Then sat down on the stump beside her rock. "Next part of your birthday present, coming up."

"More?" she asked with pleasure, belatedly sneaking a peek downward to make sure her chemise was covering her. She was so used now to wearing multiple layers of clothes that appearing before him in the thin cotton garment felt almost undressed.

"You said you wanted to shave your legs," he said. He lifted the folded straight razor from the box to show her. "Razor, hot water, shaving soap and mug. Just for you."

She looked at the razor with longing. "I don't know how to use it, though. I think I'd slice myself open."

"It's a good thing there's a doctor in the house, then, isn't it? And that I've had a little practice with this thing. Because you're right, it's pretty wicked, and I've just sharpened it."

She could feel the flush mounting up her chest, her throat as he smiled at her. He was offering to shave her legs? "So this is a doctor thing, then?" she asked tentatively. "Like…impersonal?"

"Nope. Not a doctor thing." His deep blue eyes burned into hers, and the firm, mobile mouth held no trace of a smile now. "It's a man thing. I want to make you feel good. And I want to touch you in as many places as I can manage. This one's absolutely personal."

"Oh," she breathed. The heat was flaming in her face, and in the rest of her too, licking right down into the center of her. "Then...yes. Please. Please shave my legs for me."

He smiled, then. Slowly. Lifted his right hand to his left shirt cuff, unbuttoned it and rolled the sleeve up his arm, exposing the skin, heavier than ever with corded muscle, the veins standing out in stark relief. Then did the other cuff, his movements deliberate. Finally, he lifted the shaving mug and brush from the box, dipped a bit of warm water into the mug, and began mixing the soap into a frothy lather. Still without speaking, he took hold of her left foot, laid it across his broad thigh, held it firmly in one big hand, shoving the chemise up over her thighs, and began stroking the soft bristles of the boar's-hair brush over her ankle, up her shin, over her knee, and beyond, halfway up her thigh.

Her breath was coming faster as the brush glided over her clean skin. He was completely focused on her, his grip firm on her ankle, his eyes intent on his task. Now he set the brush carefully back into the shaving mug and picked up the razor. He opened it, exposing the long, dangerous blade, and looked up, into her eyes.

"Hold still," he warned. Then set the blade to her skin, just above her foot, and stroked cleanly up to her knee, the hair falling away with the lather. A few more quick, skillful motions, and the rest of her shin, her knee, the front of her thigh were clean.

He set the razor back in the box to use the brush on the back of her calf. Shifted his position, reaching underneath, more carefully than ever, to shave the delicate skin at the sides and back of her ankle, around her knee. Dipped the cup in the bucket and poured warm water over her leg to rinse it, then reached for her towel to pat it dry.

He lifted her foot off his leg when he'd finished and set it back on the grass, then picked up the other foot, settled her leg firmly across his own and went through the same routine.

Mira closed her eyes, let herself drift with the sensations. The stroke of the soft brush over her skin, the pleasurable pressure of the razor, the tingle of all the tiny nerves as he cut away the hair, the warm water falling over her, the rough abrasion of the towel. And, most of all, the feeling of his warm, sure hands on her. Holding her foot in place, reaching up to the top of her thigh...

She opened her eyes reluctantly as he set the second foot down. Smiled slowly at him, saw the answering smile spread over his face.

"I won't offer to go any higher up," he said. "We'll save that for another time, when we're out of camera range."

"Where is he?" Mira asked with a start. She'd forgotten entirely about Danny, she realized. She'd seen him filming her walking down here, but she hadn't given him another thought since then.

"I followed your example, suggested this little episode might lose them their PG rating," Gabe said. And had followed it up with as intimidating a stare as he could manage. "Still, we'd better not push it. He could still be around someplace."

"No," she agreed breathlessly. "Good idea."

"What about your underarms, though?" he asked. "I'm guessing, if your legs are bothering you, that you wouldn't mind having those done."

"That *really* isn't PG," she said doubtfully.

He laughed softly. "As long as I'm careful where I hold you while I do it, I can keep it PG for now. When we're really alone, we'll get the rest of you. All the way to the bikini line.

And beyond, if you like. My skills are at your disposal. That's a promise."

He saw the color flood her face again. And could swear it made him even harder, if that were possible. He'd been aroused from the moment he pulled her foot onto his thigh, saw her head go back, her hair hanging down behind her, the smooth skin of her upper chest and the shadow between her breasts where the low-cut chemise dipped. He wasn't sure how he was going to get out of here without making love to her, but he couldn't risk that being caught on camera. Not that they'd ever show it, of course. But nobody but him should see her naked. And nobody was going to, if he could help it.

Now, he waited for her to make up her mind. Saw her catch that plump lower lip between small white teeth, then nod with decision.

"Please," she said. She raised her arm over her head, her hand reaching down to touch the opposite shoulder, and turned her head to look around her raised arm at him. "Is this OK?"

"Yeah," he said, heard his voice catch on the word. Cleared his throat. "Yeah." He swirled the brush again, painted her with the slick foam, then put a steadying hand on the delicate skin of her upper arm as he stroked the razor carefully over the contours of her underarm. He poured another cup of water over her, wiped it gently away with the towel, and watched as the moisture seeped into the fabric of her chemise. The thin white cotton clung to her breast, her side, and he saw the nipple pebbling under the cold, wet fabric.

He forced his eyes up from the sight. "Swing around this way," he said, doing his best to maintain. "And I'll do the other one."

At last, he was done. The entire front of her chemise was wet now, and she wasn't even looking embarrassed anymore as he used the towel, stroking it gently over her shoulders, under her arms. She was looking at him, mouth slightly open, breath audible. Her breasts were clearly visible, her erect nipples pressing against the wet fabric covering her, and he couldn't help himself. He reached out and lifted her off her rock, set her on his lap. His hand went to one of those firm, round breasts, settled over it, felt the nipple jutting into his palm as his mouth found hers.

He sucked that plump lower lip into his mouth, then released it again as his tongue licked into her to taste her. He held her breast with one hand, reached around her thigh with the other to pull her more tightly against him. Then concentrated on kissing her senseless.

♡

Mira couldn't decide which felt better. His mouth, his tongue on her, in her. Or his thumb moving over her nipple, each touch another lick of flame adding to the fire that was burning high now. She was holding onto his shoulders for dear life, melting into him, dissolving in the pleasure of it. And still he kissed, and stroked, and held her. As if he had all the time in the world.

"Gabe," she said into his mouth.

"Hmm?" He kissed the corner of her mouth, reached the tip of his tongue to touch her there. And God help her, even that felt fantastic.

"I want to…I need you to…touch me."

"We can't," he groaned. "We can't. Not here. We need to stop. We've done too much already." He lifted his mouth from hers, but didn't move her from his lap, didn't seem any more able to let go of her than she was able to leave him.

"We could be quiet, though," she pleaded. "Just do it…fast. And quiet. Up in my loft, maybe. They won't follow us up there. Please, Gabe. I really want to. I need to."

He smiled a bit at that. "When I make love to you," he promised, "it's not going to be quiet, and it's not going to be quick. It's going to take a long time, and you're going to be loud."

She dropped her gaze, looked down at her hands, ran her thumbs back and forth over the short nails, stared down at them as she spoke. "I don't think so. Because what Scott said...It's been a long time since it was good for me. And that might be... me. I'm not sure I'm very good at it anymore."

He covered both her hands with one of his own, stilled her restless thumbs, waited until she was looking at him again.

"That's OK," he told her gently. "Because I am."

He had left her, finally, of course. He'd had no choice. He'd walked her back to the cabin, let her go inside to dress. And had gone back and spent a good half hour chopping wood, the hard physical exercise the only cure available for what ailed him. Well, that and a dip in the frigid water of the swimming hole. If there'd been a cold shower available, he'd have tried that too.

Stanley had helped with dinner. He and Kevin had caught a good mess of trout during Mira's...bath. Together with the carrot cake, they'd managed a pretty credible birthday dinner for her, had sung "Happy Birthday," and kissed her, and told her she was special. And she had cried.

Now, the others had climbed into the loft, and she had picked up her lantern, lifted her skirts in preparation for climbing her own ladder.

"Good night," she told him softly. "Thanks for my birthday."

Gabe glanced up, confirmed that the others were out of sight. Stu was in the corner filming, but that was too damn bad. Mira was right. Who was really going to be upset that he'd kissed a girl out here? He took the lantern from her and set it back on the table. Put an arm around her waist, felt the unyielding shape of the corset instead of firm, warm flesh, and ached for the day he could hold all of her. He'd take what he could get now, though, since he had no choice. And that was a kiss.

He felt her soft mouth opening under his, accepting him, welcoming him, shoved the other hand into the hair at the back of her head, clean and soft since her bath, pulled her even harder against him, and deepened the kiss.

Her arms came up to hold onto his shoulders. Then one hand was stroking the back of his neck, and she was kissing him back with way too much passion for a woman who'd just told him that she wasn't good in bed. She was going to be good. And she was going to be his.

He pulled away from her, finally, breathing hard, heard the murmur from above, reminded himself that this was being recorded, and knew they had to stop right now. While they still could. He stepped back, saw her parted lips, her flushed cheeks and luminous eyes in the soft glow of the lamp. Then, with the last of his willpower, stood and watched her climb up the ladder. Watched her go to bed alone.

In his own loft, he pulled off his boots and socks, his shirt and pants, with a few jerky motions, hung everything ready for the morning. Eased himself under the blanket next to Stanley's still form, already deep into the sleep of physical exhaustion. He turned and looked across the scant few feet that separated their sleeping quarters from the other loft.

And there she was, just like every night, tormenting him. Her shape, silhouetted against the thin sheet in the lamplight, as she took off her clothes.

He had always felt guilty when he watched her like this, and thankful at the same time that Stanley was too much of a gentleman to look, and that Kevin couldn't care less. But tonight, knowing that she wanted him as much as he wanted her, he lay on the rustling, prickly mattress and drank it all in without remorse. The movements that, he could tell, meant she was unbuttoning her blouse, then the drape of it falling off her shoulders, her arms reaching to hang it on its nail. Unfastening her skirt now, the change in her silhouette as it fell to the floor and was hung up in its turn. Her arms moving, unhooking the corset, he knew. He shifted, the hay crackling beneath him, was grateful for the heavy breathing that meant Stanley remained asleep, as she lifted the heavy thing and hung it with the rest of her clothes.

Her chemise fell around her unconstrained with the corset gone, and she bent to slide off her drawers, put them on their nail. And then, he knew, she was wearing only the chemise.

He'd already seen her in it, he reminded himself. What he was looking at now wasn't anything he hadn't seen, and held, and touched. But the memory of the wet, transparent material clinging to her body didn't help one little bit. He could almost feel, still, the curve of her round bottom nestling into him, her firm breast under his hand, her moans into his mouth in response to his kiss, his touch, and he all but groaned aloud in his turn.

He had a wild, passing idea of climbing quietly down the ladder again, and up to her. And was forced to dismiss it. These damn mattresses. And the thought of the other men just a few feet away. Way too close. Way too public. He could be quiet, and he could keep her quiet if he had to. But neither of them could possibly be *that* quiet. Not this first time. Not if they were doing everything he wanted to do.

And meanwhile, he was remembering just how uncomfortable high school had been. The hours of kissing and touching in the car with Candy MacFarlane, parked on the street up from her parents' house. Tongues, and lips, and hands. And the ache he'd carried away from those marathon sessions. At least he'd had a damn bedroom, and a little privacy, to deal with the situation. What did he have here? The world's most persistent hard-on, that was what. And nothing in the world he could do about it.

by the creek

♡

"Man, it's hot in here," Gabe complained on Friday, wiping his forehead on his sleeve. "I think I'd rather be plowing."

"Tough," Mira said with a little toss of her head. "Time for you to find out how hard women's work is. You volunteered for laundry duty."

"You know why I volunteered. Time alone with you, whether it's hot or not. Well," he amended, "it's always hot."

She laughed, ludicrously cheerful considering that she was standing in the steamy kitchen sorting dirty clothes. Just because they were, for once, out of camera range. Danny couldn't film in here, complaining that the steam fogged up his lens, which meant that she and Gabe had privacy to talk, at least, something that had been sorely lacking since their little shaving party. Danny hadn't been happy about that, and had made sure ever since that either he or another cameraman was shadowing them at all times.

"Underwear first," she told Gabe now, lifting a pile of whites and dumping them a garment at a time into the kettle he was tending.

"I wish I didn't think that was as close as our underwear was going to get while we're out here," he said with a regretful sigh and a sideways grin as he saw her chemises entering the kettle.

She paused, arrested in the act of adding clothes. Then screwed up her courage and made the suggestion she'd been thinking about for days.

"Well, you know," she said, carefully not looking at him as she added a couple pieces of men's underwear, "there *is* one place I have privacy. Zara asked Danny right at the beginning, that first day when we went down to the swimming hole, remember? When you guys told us to go clean up?"

"I remember," he said. "What did she ask him? I'm starting to get a really good feeling about this."

She laughed. "Stir those, and keep stirring. And she *asked* if they were going to film us down there too. And he said that was off-limits, just like the other day with my bath. So maybe you could...sneak away, while I'm down there. And we could...do something. Or a few somethings."

"It's awfully risky, if they notice. And I don't have any condoms out here."

"OK, if you don't want to," she backtracked immediately. She'd been too forward. She should have waited for him to make the next move after all. "I just thought..."

"Wait, now. Hold on," he said in alarm. "I want to. Are you kidding? You know I want to. I just need to figure out how to make it work, make sure Danny doesn't catch on. Because I meant what I said before. I'm not going to let you get on film like that, even if they don't show it all. Because you know that'd be one hell of a storyline. And I am *not* having sex against the garden fence," he said sternly. "Not in front of Danny, at least, I'm not. You can put that right out of your mind."

"You won't let me forget that, will you?" she teased, light with relief. "We could keep some clothes on, maybe. Just in case. But I need it. I need it so much, Gabe. If you want to think about what we could do, what would work..." She stopped, feeling a lot hotter and more breathless than the steam in the kitchen could account for, that mood of recklessness coming over her again. "I'll tell you what, I'll go take my bath like usual today. And if you want to, you can come...surprise me."

♡

Gabe saw her leave for the creek that afternoon carrying her towel and comb, casting one last look behind her as she passed the corral. A look that, he thought with a tingle of anticipation, was meant for him alone.

He'd thought he might just spontaneously combust this morning, the heat in the cabin combining with the heat inside him to bring him to incineration point. He'd done the laundry with her, scrubbing every item on the washboard, working the mangle, laughing and talking. And, on another level, thinking about what she'd said. He'd watched her work, the sweat standing out on her forehead and upper lip, soaking through her cumbersome, unattractive clothes, and had never wanted anybody more.

He waited another five minutes, then gave a nod to Stanley and made his way to the creek, to a sheltered spot downstream of the swimming hole. He'd already changed into his last set of clean underwear, and he'd decided he was going to wash first himself. But he was going to do it fast, because he needed to be with her.

Five minutes more, and he was walking along the opposite bank, back upstream. Looking through the trunks of the cottonwoods lining the creek, searching for the spot.

And there she was. He stopped short, arrested at the sight of her, sitting naked on a boulder in the creek, shivering a little. Rubbing the soap between her hands, then setting the precious white bar down next to her, raising her hands to wash her hair, tipping her head back. And her breasts...He'd seen them before, he reminded himself. But not like this. Not wet, jutting out as she arched her back. Not naked, and gorgeous, and fully revealed to him.

As he watched, she stepped off her boulder, down into the deepest pool, stood facing him, still without seeming to notice him in the trees. And slowly lowered herself, ducked her head, rinsed her hair again and again.

Climb out, he prayed, feeling more like a Peeping Tom than he ever had in his life. Watching her through the sheet was one thing, but this...

But as she finally finished rinsing out her hair and stood in the shallows, picked up the soap again, and began to rub it over her body, her breasts, between her legs, he realized, his heart hammering, his breath coming short, that she knew. She knew he was here, that he was watching. And she wanted him to see.

As she reached a soapy hand between her legs, Mira was astonished at her own daring. She hadn't seen Gabe, but she knew beyond a doubt that he was watching her. She had known the moment he'd arrived. She could have acknowledged him. But instead, she was...performing for him.

She kept her hand moving, slick with soap, between her legs, enjoying the sensation as she explored. It had been so long, and it felt so good. And the knowledge that he was watching as she did it...that made it feel even better. She moved the other hand over one breast, then the other, languidly stroking, circling her nipples, trapping them between soapy fingers. Finally turned around, ran both hands over her bottom, spread her legs a little, and drew her hands down between them, oh so slowly. Bent forward a little to give him the best possible view, and did it again. If that didn't bring him out of hiding, she didn't know what would.

She turned again, saw that she'd guessed right. Because he was coming out from behind the trees, exactly where she had known he was, his eyes never moving from hers as he approached.

He stopped at the edge, five or six feet from where she stood below him. "Time to rinse off," he said, his voice sounding deeper than ever. "Because I'm coming over there."

She stepped into the deep pool to obey, rubbed her hands over her shivering body to remove the soap, watching as he bent to untie and pull off his boots and socks, then stood again, his hand on the top button of his shirt.

"No. I want to do it," she told him. "Come here and let me."

He smiled, rolled his pant legs up, picked up boots and socks and crossed downstream of her, at the stepping stones, and walked around to her where she had come to stand in the sunny, grassy patch at the edge of the creek, toweling her hair dry.

"I'll do that," he said as she picked up her comb. "But first," he sighed. "Just in case." He picked up the clean chemise she'd laid nearby, pulled it carefully over her head, settled it around her as she lifted her arms through. Then he took her comb from her hand.

"Sit down," he told her. She put her towel down on the large boulder, then settled herself on it, facing the creek, sensed him coming up to stand behind her. He began to work the comb through her hair, pulling out the tangles, his free hand against her neck, holding her hair.

"The first time I saw you," he said, "I thought what pretty hair you had. And now I like it even better. Because you look so free."

"Most men like it long, I thought."

"Not me. Well, I like it *this* long. Because I like to think about pulling your head back by it," he said, suiting the action to the words. He leaned over from behind her, put his other hand under her chin, and turned her head to kiss her. He pulled her lower lip into his mouth and closed his teeth over it, giving it a gentle nip, and the sensation, the possessiveness of the gesture brought her every nerve ending to shocked attention.

"Like that," he murmured.

"Oh," she breathed, unable to say any more. He let go of her hair, set the comb down on the boulder, and pulled her to stand facing him.

"I liked your show," he said, his hands coming down to hold her bottom, pull her against him. "I liked every bit of it. Did you enjoy doing that for me?"

She swallowed and nodded, looking up at him. "I did."

"Then get me out of these clothes," he told her. "I need to touch you, and I need your hands on me. Right now."

She smiled slowly. The thought that she had power over him, that she was making him as crazy as he was making her, was delicious. She reached for his suspenders, pulled them off his broad shoulders, undid his shirt buttons, tugged the shirt from his pants, and tossed it aside.

"Hmm," she wondered, her hands returning to his chest as if they were irresistibly drawn there. "Undershirt or pants first?"

She decided for herself. "Undershirt," she said, feeling the force of his heartbeat under her hands. "Because I love your chest. And I want to see it." She pulled the white cotton garment up over his stomach, up to his shoulders. Stood on tiptoe to pull it over his head, and threw it next to his shirt.

"Do you know how many times I've wanted to do this?" she asked, putting both palms against his bare skin, frowning as she felt him flinch.

"Your hands are freezing," he explained with a rueful smile, raising his own hands to cover hers. "Leave them there, though. I'll warm them up for you."

He would, she decided. His skin was burning up. And he was beautiful. The wide expanse of chest, the heavy shoulders and arms. That tattoo, running around the bulk of his bicep. The nipples, erect under her questing hands. She succumbed to impulse, pressed her mouth to his collarbone, bent and licked one of those brown nipples.

"Shit," he groaned. "Come on, Mira. Take my pants off. Or I'm going to do it myself."

"I was just warming you up," she protested, her hands moving all the same to his buttons, beginning to unfasten them. "I had a head start."

"Are you kidding? You don't think you got me about half-way there, just watching you?"

She didn't answer, just smiled, shoving his pants down over his lean hips, watching him step out of them and kick them aside, so he was standing before her in the cotton drawers.

He looked around for her skirt, laid it down on the ground next to them, grabbed his own shirt from where she'd tossed it, and spread it out above the skirt. "That's as good as I can do for a blanket," he told her. "Because I need to lay you down right now."

♡

He pulled her down, came down over her, groaned a little as he covered her. He propped himself on his elbows, took her mouth again in another long kiss, felt their lower bodies separated only by the two thin layers of cotton, and thought he might lose it right there.

He rolled to his side and looked down at her, lying there in her chemise, her wet hair spread out around her. And, finally, unbuttoned those three buttons at the top, the way he'd wanted to do every single day out here, watched as he slid his hand inside, cupped one of those generous, firm breasts.

"I've wanted to put my mouth here for so long." He raised his gaze to hers as he pulled the strap down to her elbow, trapping her arm. Her eyes drifted shut as his hand closed over her again. He lifted her to him, up to meet his mouth, and licked, and bit, and sucked at her there. He stayed there for a good long while, heard her sighs turn to moans, and then to little cries, then did the same on the other side, her arms pinned, her beautiful breasts at the mercy of his hands and mouth.

Finally, when she was squirming beneath him, crying out with tortured pleasure, he sent one hand down for the hem of the white garment, rucked around her thighs with her frantic movements. He ran a hand up her inner thigh, pushing it away from its neighbor. And settled that hand over her, touched her the way he'd been thinking about doing since the first day he'd met her. She was slick and wet with arousal, he discovered as he explored every fold and crevice. And unless he was mistaken, she was about two minutes away from orgasm.

"Gabe," she gasped, her head rolling back, her neck arching. "Let my...arms go. I want to touch you."

"No. You're going to come for me first. You're going to do it right now." He propped one elbow against the ground, his hand against her head, tangled in her hair. Bent his own head to that outstretched neck, sucked at her, bit her, held her there when her head wanted to thrash. Kept his other hand moving over her, faster and harder, now, finding the way she liked it. The way that was pushing her up, and up higher. Her legs were stiffening as she got closer, her upper body beginning to arch. And then he felt it, the spasms taking her, the high wail she couldn't keep from leaving her throat. The throat he held in his teeth, even as he held her fast with his hands.

She was still shaking when he pulled the straps of her chemise up her arms. "Now you can touch me," he told her. "Now that I've done what I had to do."

She stared up at him, still breathing hard, her eyes shining more green than gold in the sunlight. "Why did you do that? Hold me down?"

"Because I wanted to," he said honestly. "When I saw you doing your show, what I needed to do...I needed to hold your hands down like that and fuck you hard. And I couldn't do that. So I did this instead."

Those eyes got even bigger. "Nobody's ever said that to me."

"Well, I'm going to be saying it. Because it's what I want to do to you. But right now, I need you to touch me, or I'm going to die right here."

She smiled, pushed herself up on her elbows, and shifted off her makeshift blanket. "Then trade me places. Because now I'm going to kiss you, and touch you, and love you. And you aren't going to be able to do a thing about it."

♡

She repaid the favor, then. She started with his arms, put her hands around those biceps, felt the weight of them. Kissed him there, licking over the zigzags and arrows of his tattoo, feeling the muscle twitch under her mouth, his weight shifting beneath her as she moved her hands and mouth over him. Worked her way up to his shoulders, the slabs of muscle there. The smell of him, warm, and clean, and something that was...Gabe.

"You washed," she murmured against him, kissing his collarbones now.

"Didn't want to come to you dirty," he groaned. "Don't stop. Keep going."

She kept kissing down his chest, her hands moving on him. Until she got to those flat brown nipples again. She licked slowly over one, then the other. Took one into her mouth and sucked as she moved her hands slowly down his body. Down his chest, over the ridges of his toned abdomen. She found the buttons of the cotton drawers and eased them open. Heard the harsh intake of breath as she held him at last, huge and pulsing, in her hand. Began to rub her hand over him, felt his hips begin to move, his hands coming up into her hair where she lay against his chest, her mouth still working on him.

"I want to take you in my mouth," she whispered as she continued to stroke him.

"We can't," he groaned. "We can't. If Danny comes...we've taken too long. And you can't...show that."

"I know," she said. She moved her hand faster, felt the response in him. "But when we can, just as soon as we can, I'm going to do it. I'm going to take you in my mouth. All the way inside. I'm going to take all of you. You're going to hold my head, and show me how you like it, tell me exactly what to do. And I'm going to do exactly what you tell me to. And then when you're ready, you're going to come, and I'm going to take that too. And I'm going to love it."

As she spoke, she felt him pushing harder against her, his breathing growing louder. And with her final words, he exploded, into her hand, over her. She waited until he was finished, reached for the towel, wiped it over him.

"So how was that?" she asked him as he lay there, still gasping. "Payback? Did I manage to torture you a little?"

"Payback." He smiled up at her, his hands limp at his sides. "Oh, yeah. Absolutely."

"You know," she said, reaching for her drawers with obvious reluctance, standing to pull them on as he began to gather his own clothes. "I've been waiting for that orgasm since I first met you. That's how long that one's been building."

"Since you first met me?" he asked, startled.

"Well, at first I thought Alec was awfully cute too," she admitted.

"I knew it," he groaned. "Losing out to the pretty boy again."

"But ever since that day you showed me how to chop wood..."

He saw the color rise. "Ever since then, I've been...imagining."

"And here we are," he sighed, "still imagining. Although it's a lot more fun to do it together." He shrugged into his shirt, buttoned it quickly, tucked it into his pants, and pulled up the suspenders. "We'd better get back. Poor Stanley's probably run out of life story by now."

"What?" She stared at him. "What are you talking about?"

"He said he'd create a diversion, get Kevin talking about something too fascinating for Danny to want to miss out on. I shudder to think what's happening back there. Stanley may never forgive me."

"He knows?" she asked in appalled disbelief. "Gabe. How am I ever going to look him in the eye again?"

"He doesn't *know.* I just said I needed some time with you."

"During my bath," she said flatly. "Great."

"I have a feeling Stanley's had sex a time or two in his life. I don't think you've shocked him. Nothing you and I do together is wrong, or anything to be ashamed of. No matter what it is."

"No matter what it is?" she asked, raising her eyebrows. "What exactly do you have in mind?"

"I have lots of things in mind," he assured her. "Isn't your imagination working pretty hard by now? I know mine is. Seems like the longer we're out here, the more NC-17 my fantasies get. I have a pretty good list I've been working on. What about you? You said you'd been imagining."

"I have." She had her corset fastened now, was pulling her skirt on, dropping her head as she buttoned it, her hair falling around her face, hiding it from him. "I can't believe I'm saying this, but you seem to bring out my…wild side. So, yes. I have been."

"So what's the one you want to try first?" He grinned at her reassuringly, handed her her blouse. "Here," he decided, watching her fumble for the buttons. "Let me."

"Ummm…" she began, as his hands began fastening. "I can't say. Not like this, looking at you. I'm not that wild yet, I guess."

286

"You want me to go first?" He slid the last button into its hole with regret and reached down for her apron, pulled it over her head. "We'll start off easy, then. Oral sex."

He turned her, tied the strings in the back, then reached down to cup one round cheek in his hand, rub her there. "That's pretty much at the top of my list," he told her as he put both arms around her from behind, pulled her in tight against him. "I want you to do it to me, and if you want to do it the way you just told me...I'll take that. And oh, baby," he said fervently, "do I ever want to do it to you. For a long, long time. I want to tease you, draw it out, stop just short, over and over. Drive you up so high you're calling out, and grabbing me by the hair, and begging me. And then I'm going to make you come so hard you scream. You're going to be thinking it's actually going to kill you."

He'd pulled her skirt up now, had both hands up under there, and sure enough, she'd told the truth. Those drawers had a slit in them, open all the way. Oh, boy. This was going to make his life even more interesting. And meanwhile...

"You want to hear another one?" he asked. "Or are you ready to share?"

"Uh..." she moaned.

He smiled, kept his hand moving, felt her legs trembling against him. "Still not talking, huh? OK, I'll take the plunge. A lot of them involve the table in the cabin, since I've got kind of a limited menu here. I've had you from behind, bent all the way over it, your cheek right down against the wood, your hands holding onto the sides. Pushed you down on your back, wrapped your legs around me, and had you that way. I've even," he said, bending for her neck again, murmuring against her skin between bites at her, "fastened you down to it. Because that's just how nasty I am. I've had you tied by the wrists and ankles to the table legs with some of that clothesline. Got your hips at the edge, your legs pulled all the way apart. So you're all the way tied up for me, completely helpless. Mine to use, any way I want, for just as long as I want. That's one of my favorites."

"You're going to…give me splinters," she gasped.

"Hey. Quit messing with my fantasy," he frowned, rubbing a little harder in retaliation, feeling her delicious response to his words, his hands. "I'll sand it first, how's that. Or, oh, yeah. I like this. I'll put you across my lap, naked, while I pull those splinters out of your ass."

"Ah…" she got out. "Maybe…a little less…medical."

"Mira. Are you telling me you're a bad girl?" he asked, increasing the tempo. "Are you telling me you need a spanking?"

"Oh…Oh, Gabe. I'm going to…"

"Yes, you are. You're going to do it right now. Come on. Give it to me. You know I want it. Give it to me." His arms were holding her up now, his hand moving hard over her. And she was coming, just like that. Spasming against him, her breath coming in frantic gasps.

"Well, well," he said with satisfaction, releasing her skirt and letting it fall around her, but keeping his arms around her, holding her steady. "Who knew all that beautiful nastiness was hiding under there? I am such a lucky man."

"Oh, God," she moaned. "My knees are shaking. I didn't know you were going to do that. Or say…all that."

"Neither did I." He turned her in his arms to kiss her. "What can I say. It seemed like a good idea at the time."

"And now you're all hot and bothered again," she said ruefully, reaching a hand down and closing it around him. "Do you want me to…"

"No," he sighed with regret. "We really do need to get back. And yeah, I'm going to be aching tonight. So what else is new."

fighting for It

♡

Gabe might still be aching, but Mira was feeling good. Really good. And the glow of it lasted through the evening, stoked by Gabe's goodnight kiss, his murmured words at the foot of her ladder. She even fell asleep instantly for once, her body not only tired but satisfied as well. The hum was still there the next morning, when he gave her a smile over breakfast that had her all but fanning herself.

And then it was Saturday afternoon, and they were walking back to the Clearing again, and the glow was gone. Even Kevin was quiet today. They were all as apprehensive as she was, she guessed, about what lay ahead.

Two giant but thinly sliced tree stumps positioned on their sides in the middle of the Clearing, the outer, bark-covered edges turned towards the spectators' bench, and some smoke coming from both the wood stoves in the kitchen area, provided the only clues as they entered the big space.

"What do you think?" Kevin asked. "Homestead or Safety challenge?"

Stanley shrugged. "Could be anything."

"Welcome," Cliff announced once the remaining eight homesteaders were standing before him. "Let's get started right away. I know you're all anxious to get to this one. And in case you're wondering, yes, it's a homestead challenge." He nodded at the two production assistants who entered from the woods like some kind of medieval pages, each bearing a full-sized axe.

"Let me guess," Kevin said. "A fight to the death."

Cliff smiled a bit at that. "No, and not a wood-chopping contest either."

"Well, damn." Kevin again. "Our ringer's no use at all to us, then, in either case." He nodded at Gabe. "Behold the Axemaster."

"That's been noted," Cliff said. "Which is why this one's as much about accuracy as strength. You're going to be throwing them. Each man gets three tosses from ten yards out. Five points for every time you make the axe stick into your target, which, by the way, is a massive two feet wide. Simple enough?"

All the men nodded, not even Scott able to find an objection, seemingly.

"Then if Rachel and Mira will take a seat," Cliff said, "we'll get to it."

Quickly enough, the women were seated on the rough bench, and the men were standing near their starting line. First up were Stanley and Calvin, each testing the heft of the big implement.

Calvin looked across at his father. "Going to win this time if I can help it, Pop."

"You just try, boy," Stanley grinned back. "You just try."

"First toss," Cliff said. "Anytime you're ready."

Calvin brought the big handle behind his head with both hands, took a couple practice swings, and let fly. The heavy axe sailed through the air, blade over handle, swished past barely left of the stump, and stuck in the grass several yards beyond.

Stanley didn't comment, just swung his own axe one-handed, the weight of it trivial in his massive arm, and let it go. The blade hit the stump, but bounced off.

"Huh. Harder than it looks," he grunted.

Gabe and Alec, then. Alec's axe falling short of the stump, and Gabe's sailing just slightly right.

"Four down, and nobody's done it," Cliff commented unnecessarily. "It takes some practice."

Mira pressed her hands tightly together between her knees as Scott and Kevin stepped up. Kevin's throw was short. So far, the men were 0 for 5.

"We're going to sit here all afternoon," Rachel muttered. "Just waiting for somebody to throw the thing into the damn tree."

Mira didn't answer, her eyes on Scott. He'd played some basketball in high school, still played in a recreational league. The game suited his competitive nature, and he was good at it. She feared that might translate into success at this competition. And if there was one time she needed him to fail, it was now.

Scott stepped up to the starting line, his body language confident. Swung the axe behind his head with both hands and let it go, exactly like a free throw. It sailed through the air and landed in the center of the bark-covered stump, to the deadly sound of silence from both sides.

Scott stepped back, looked around defiantly. "That's one to Arcadia," he announced. "And two more to come."

Mira's throat grew drier with each throw in the second round. Arcadia was still leading by that same stubborn point going into Round Three, and when the contest ended, Arcadia had scored five times, two of their successes coming from Scott. And Paradise's total was four.

"I knew there was a reason I hated P.E.," Kevin said ruefully as his final throw hit the stump and fell to the side. He turned to Mira, gave her an exaggerated shrug. "Sorry. It's on you."

"So, that's Paradise with 20 points," Cliff reminded them, "and Arcadia with 25. It's up to the women now. Let's head over to the kitchen."

♡

"Sorry," Kevin said again to Stanley and Gabe as the men followed the women toward the covered structure, already well heated now by the fire in two wood stoves. "I actually did try."

"Yeah," Gabe said shortly. He didn't think he believed it. Kevin was athletic enough, and both Stanley and Gabe had made their final two tosses. But unless Gabe went home and discovered that Kevin had held the record for the javelin toss in high school, he'd never know the truth.

He settled himself with the other men on the observation benches, and saw with dismay what the challenge was. The lard, flour, and rolling pin on Mira's work table told the story, even if he hadn't gathered it from her stricken face. Her nemesis. Pie.

"How's Rachel at pie, do you know?" he asked Kevin quietly.

"No idea," Kevin said. "She never made one before we came out here that I know of. Not all that domestic, my beloved sister."

"She's fantastic at it," came Scott's vindictive tone from behind them. "Almost as good as I am at throwing an axe. You're going down, asshole."

Gabe whirled on him, felt Stanley's hand close on his arm in an iron grip. "Whoa," the older man breathed. "Back off. He's not worth it. Let Mira do her thing. She may surprise us."

"You've forgotten a little something, haven't you?" Kevin had turned to speak to Scott as well.

"What?" Scott asked belligerently.

"That little matter of voting rights?" Kevin reminded him. "If we'd won, who would've gone home, do you think? You imagine Gabe was going to vote his *girlfriend* off?"

Now it was Scott half-rising from his seat, his face purpling with anger, nobody seeming interested in holding him back, as Kevin continued. "Whereas if my sister turns out to bake a half-decent pie…Well, enjoy eating it tonight. Because it's going to be the last one you get out here."

"I'm sorry," Mira told the little group wretchedly at the end of an hour's labor. The outcome had been inevitable from the start, hardly needing Alma's expert eye to declare the winner. Rachel's piecrust seemed to roll itself into beautiful circles, her movements swift and competent, whereas Mira's seemed to have a mind of its own, pieces coming off and sticking to the rolling pin no matter how desperately she dusted it with flour.

"Take your pies home for dessert," Cliff said. "And Arcadia? It's finally your turn to talk tomorrow. And to vote."

If anything, the walk back to Paradise was even quieter than the trip to the Clearing had been.

"Want to do a little fishing with me, Kevin, once we take care of the animals?" Stanley asked as they neared the cabin. "Trout and pie for dinner'd be right nice. And you go on and get your bath, Mira," he instructed. "One thing I *can* do in the kitchen is fry trout. That corn looked like it was ripening up real good. Boil us up some of that, along with some green beans and your huckleberry pie, we'll be having a party."

Mira nodded numbly. She'd faced going home every week, she reminded herself. But while she was washing hastily in the creek, she felt despondent all the same. As hard as it was out here, as dirty and exhausted she felt most of the time, she didn't *want* to leave. Didn't want to leave Gabe, of course, but it was more than that. Something about being out here had got under her skin. And she was going to miss it.

She shook her head at herself, dressed quickly, and walked to the cabin, collected a basket to gather the vegetables for dinner. And met Gabe in the garden, doing a little extra watering on the tomatoes and waiting for her. Danny was in place already, getting some footage that she knew he was hoping would get more exciting now.

"Have a good bath?" Gabe asked, setting down the bucket at her approach.

"Not as good as yesterday," she answered, feeling her spirits lift a bit at the memory. "That seems like a long time ago, doesn't it?"

Gabe glanced at Danny. "Come on," he said. "Let's go pick corn." He pulled her quickly around behind the tall stalks, leaned down and kissed her quickly, then held her for a moment as Danny brought the camera around.

"I don't want you to leave tomorrow," he said against her hair. "If it's you—"

"Come on. You know it's me. There's no question."

"Maybe not, though," he insisted, stepping back from her and pacing a few steps along the row before turning back, his expression intent. "Look. Keeping you two makes strategic sense, and if Alec's anything, he's strategic. And I'll bet Rachel is too, though I don't know about Calvin."

"Nobody's *that* strategic," Mira said wryly. "I'm going. It's obvious. They've been dying to have Scott gone for weeks. That's going to outweigh anything else over there."

"Don't be so defeatist! Why can't you have a little faith? Why can't you even try?"

He really looked upset, she saw with a twinge of discomfort. "Gabe. I'm *going*. And that's OK. I'm sorry not to get another week or two, but it's really not that big a deal. And what could I possibly do about it now anyway?"

"It's not a big *deal?* That you're losing? That you're leaving with him?"

"Of course not," she said, smiling uncertainly. What was wrong with him? How could this be a surprise? "It's been obvious since the beginning that Scott and I would never win the million, and my half of that second-place money wouldn't exactly change my life. And I'm not leaving *with* him. Don't be ridiculous." She put a hand on his arm. "Come on. What's the matter?"

"Of course you're leaving with him. That's the point." He shook off her hand and, oblivious of the intently filming Danny, walked to the edge of the garden and stood, back turned to her, head down, hands in his pockets.

Mira stood, helpless to know what to do. The familiar tension twisted her insides at his annoyance. His...anger. She couldn't think how to make this right. Was he really this upset with her for losing? He'd been quiet on the walk home, but she hadn't realized that it was about her. She'd tried so hard. Why was that never enough?

He turned back at last, came back down the row to her.

"I'm sorry I lost. I'm just no good at pie," she said helplessly as he approached. "I tried my best, but..." She felt her chin trembling. "I couldn't do it. And I'm...sorry." The final word was almost a whisper as she fought the tears.

"Why are *you* sorry?" He frowned down at her. He still seemed annoyed, and her heart sank even further.

"I'm the one who should be apologizing," he went on angrily when she didn't answer. "I'm the one storming around here like a pr—like a jerk. You should be telling me to knock it off. Go on, tell me."

She smiled hesitantly, wiped the stupid tears, as always, with her apron. Why was he still mad? What was she supposed to do now? "I'm not going to say that."

"Why not? What's going to happen if you get mad at me?"

"You might..." She stopped, confused and shaken, not knowing what to make of his stormy expression. Did he *want* her to fight with him? "But," she said slowly, "you'd just get mad at *me*, then. Madder than you already are."

"So?" he demanded. "So you tell me off, and my male pride gets all wounded, and I snap back at you. Where's the disaster in that? Because then I'd walk away, like I just did, and come to my senses, if I know what's good for me. Realize that if I treat you badly, you'll be dumping *me* on the dance floor. And that I can't risk that, so I'd better walk right back here and apologize to you. Which, in case you can't tell, is what I'm doing right now. I've been acting like a jerk, because I'm worried about you. And a little bit jealous, too," he admitted.

Her heart was pounding with different emotions now. Relief, and pleasure, and confusion, still. He was jealous? Really? "I hate it when people get angry," she confessed. "Especially at me. I just hate it. I don't know what to do about it. I just want to make it be over." She was close to crying again, fought the tears back.

"Don't you see," he told her gently, pulling her close, laying one hand against her cheek, smoothing her hair back. "It's not your job to keep everybody happy. You're sure as hell not supposed to worry about keeping *me* happy. I'm supposed to be trying to be good enough for *you.*"

"Wow." She laughed shakily. "That would be a novel way to look at the world."

"Yep. You can get mad at me, especially when I get all stupid and possessive like that. You can tell me off, put me in my place. We can even have a fight from time to time." He grinned down at her, tightened his hold on her waist. "That's just going to make it so much more fun when we kiss and make up."

♡

"By the way," she said, after they'd done just that, for once oblivious of Danny. "You have no reason to be jealous, or to be worried. If I do leave with Scott tomorrow—we may be leaving at the same time, but I'm not going to be *with* him. Not ever again."

"I know that. Intellectually, at least. I'm not that much of a jealous idiot. But I don't like the way he looks at you," Gabe said. "He's been humiliated so many times out here. It's been his own fault every time, of course, but somebody like him doesn't see it that way."

"Yeah," she sighed. "I've realized that with him, it's always somebody else's fault. I thought he really liked me, but I realize now that what he liked was that I would take the blame. I'm good at that."

"You *were* good at that," Gabe corrected. "But whether or not you accept it, I don't want him throwing it at you. And I'm pretty sure he will."

"I'll stay away from him. He's not going to say anything in front of other people. Probably not, anyway," she added honestly. "As long as I'm not alone with him, I'll be fine. And anyway, I'm the one who should really be worried about leaving you alone out here," she said, trying to lighten the mood.

"Why's that?" he asked, standing back from her now, his arms around her waist, and looking down at her with a smile.

"I suspect Rachel has a little thing for you," she said sternly. "And I know how hard it is for you to keep your hands to yourself. You'd better be behaving yourself while I'm gone, or I *am* going to be dumping you on the dance floor. And remember, the camera doesn't lie. Danny's going to keep an eye on you for me, aren't you, Danny?" she asked over her shoulder.

"*Mira.* You're supposed to ignore me," he growled. "How many times do I have to tell you?"

Gabe laughed. "She looks all soft and sweet, Danny, but she's got a sassy side. Don't I know it."

The cameraman sighed with exasperation. "You are too. Supposed to ignore me, I mean. You guys are worse than Zara."

"Maybe that's because you're *always around,*" Mira complained, "so we've gotten to know you too well."

"Hey," Gabe protested. "Quit talking to Danny. This is *my* time. And you were just getting all jealous, and I was loving it."

"You were?"

"Definitely. You going to fight for me?"

"No. No fighting." She tightened her arms around his neck, looked into his eyes, and spoke from her brimming heart. "What I'm going to do is, I'm going to wrap my arms around you. I'm going to hold you so you feel it, so you remember it. And while I'm gone, I'm still going to be holding you, every minute of every day. And you're going to stop what you're doing, sometimes, to feel it. You're going to feel my arms around you, holding you. You're going to feel me loving you."

"Danny," Gabe said quietly.

The inevitable sigh. "What now?"

"Go away."

the tail of the dog

♡

Gabe stuffed his hands more deeply into the pockets of the wool jacket against the midnight chill and eyed the unfamiliar outlines of the cabin. He probably could have thought this out better. The full moon had lit his way reasonably well to the Clearing, and then along the path from which Arcadia had emerged so many times. Of course, he could always have turned around and asked Stu the way, but he preferred to forget that he was being followed by a camera. But whatever the case, what was he supposed to do now? He didn't even know which side of the loft the men were sleeping on.

Just as he was steeling himself for an exploratory trip that had every possibility of ending disastrously for Alec as well as himself, the cabin door opened, the figure stepping out into the moonlight more familiar to Gabe than his own reflection.

"Gabe?" Alec called softly. "You out there?"

Gabe stepped from the shelter of the trees and walked to meet his twin, performed the handshake they'd worked out when they were ten, the routine of fist-bumps and special grips both a little juvenile and the most comforting thing ever. Then put his arms around his brother for a quick hug.

"Who's got a Spidey Sense now?" he asked, keeping his voice low.

"I woke up and knew you were here," Alec agreed. "But let's go over by the creek where we can talk."

They walked through the night together. "OK," Alec said once they were seated on a couple of boulders. "What's up? This about the vote?"

"They going? That the plan?"

"You know it," Alec said with satisfaction, understanding the question perfectly. "It's obvious how you feel about him. Hell, when he said what he did at the dance, I wanted to deck him myself. So imagine living with him for five long weeks. It's like he's disintegrating. We're in *Lord of the Flies* territory over here. And if you're asking me to keep him on somehow," he finished, "I can't do it. And I wouldn't if I could. I'm counting the hours, and so is everybody else."

"We'll be merged after tomorrow, though," Gabe argued. "And then he'll hate me, not you. I'll deal with him. Plus," he went on in his most persuasive tone, "you still want to win this game, right?"

"You know I do."

"Well, that's our best bet in all respects. Go to the end with the two of them, and we win, no-brainer. And the same thing's true for Stanley and Calvin. Vote out Rachel and Kevin instead tomorrow, and you've removed one of the two obstacles between Calvin and a million bucks. All he and Stanley have to do is beat you and me in the Safety challenge, and he's won the whole thing."

He saw a more thoughtful expression come over Alec's face, and pressed his point. "And don't tell Calvin, but from yours and my point of view, it wouldn't even be that cut and dried. Stanley'd rather duke it out with you and me for the million than Scott and Mira *or* Rachel and Kevin. Even if he and Calvin win the challenge, Stanley's going to push for us to stay. That 'let the best man win' thing. Stanley isn't a real strategic player. Too straight-up of a guy for that."

300

Alec shook his head regretfully. "It sounds good when you say it, but I can't do it. I go to Calvin and tell him I want to vote Rachel? He's going to think I'm playing him, that I'm working with Rachel to vote him off, because he and Stanley are our biggest competition. Calvin *is* a strategic player. You and I'll find ourselves on the jury in no time flat if I do that. Because Scott's going to be voting you and me. You know he is."

"You can convince Calvin, though. You're good at that. You can talk anybody into damn near anything."

"Did you *hear* me? It's too risky, and I want to win!"

"Why?" Gabe demanded. "Because you need half a million more dollars? We wouldn't even be here if the producers hadn't recruited us. You never even wanted to do this. You didn't come here for the money, and you know it."

"I don't care," Alec said stubbornly. "I'm here now, I've put in the hard time, and I'm not shooting myself in the foot just because you're hot for some girl. She'll still be there in a couple weeks, after we've *won.* She can't exactly go anywhere. Anyway, I thought the whole idea was that we were supposed to be thinking deep thoughts out here. And *I've* actually done it. Got my next project all mapped out, thanks to a whole shitload of plowing and haying and wood-chopping time to work through it. You were right, thank you very much, great downtime. Now I'm ready to go back and get into it. Just as soon as we *win.* And meanwhile, what have you been doing? Not thinking, that's for sure. And not playing the game either. You're one of the most disciplined, competitive guys I know. If there was one thing I would've said I was sure of, it was that you'd want to win this thing even more than I do. And that you could do it. Who are you, and what have you done with my brother?"

"I've won already," Gabe insisted. "I've got what I came for."

Alec groaned. "Is this the sappy part where you tell me true love is the greatest treasure? Come *on.* You've known her, what, six, seven weeks? You're headed right over a cliff here, and you're supposed to be the cautious one!"

"If you mean I'm in love, the real deal, then you're right. I don't care how long it's been. Look at the people on Arcadia, even the ones who've left now. Compare them to people you've worked with for years, and tell me which ones you know better."

"You really mean it, don't you?" Alec asked wonderingly. "You're really ready to...what? Have you even *slept* with her?"

"Doesn't matter. And none of your business."

"Oh, man," Alec groaned. "You *haven't*. How do you know that it'll even be worth it?"

"You got a stove in your cabin?" Gabe asked.

"What? Of course we do."

"Does it get hot?"

"*Yes*, it gets hot. Why, you want to cook something? You've gone around the bend, you do realize that, right? You are now officially nuts."

Gabe ignored the comment. "How do you know it's hot? You ever touch it?"

"All right, all right," Alec muttered. "I get it."

"That's right. I don't have to make love with her to know I love her, that she's the only one for me. That's not how it works."

"Whoa, whoa, whoa," Alec said in alarm. "Slow down there, boy. This is Sir Galahad again, isn't it? OK, she was with the Prince of Darkness there, and you rescued her. Great. Good job. Doesn't mean you have to carry her off on your horse and take her to live at the castle."

"I think you're mixing your fairy tales," Gabe said with a little smile.

"Whatever," Alec said impatiently. "It's still too fast."

"No. It isn't. And I need you to do this for me. I need you to help me keep her safe."

"So *that's* what this is about," Alec said with relief. "That's ridiculous. You're letting your imagination get way ahead of you. Wherever they're keeping them, you know all the others are there too. So he says some nasty things to her. She's a big girl. She can handle it. This isn't actually the Wild West, you know, and you don't have to have her under your protective arm to keep her safe."

"I need to keep her here," Gabe said stubbornly. "I know I do, that's all. I need you to help me do it. You owe me, and I'm collecting on that. Right now."

"I *owe* you?"

"You sure do. All those years of you calling the shots? Know how many times I went along with you? Well, it's Payback Time. I'm not the tail of your dog anymore."

"What tail? What dog? We never even *had* a dog. You're seriously worrying me here, bro."

"All those Halloween costumes? The horse thing, seventh grade? The Slinky Dog? What was the common denominator there?"

"They were awesome? We won Best Costume? What?"

"They were always your idea, for one. And I went along with them."

"And I'm supposed to give up a million dollars, because I got to choose our Halloween costume. You. Are. Dreaming."

"And the other thing about them," Gabe went on inexorably. "Who was the head, and who was the tail? Who decided where we went, and who followed along? Me, that's who. I spent eighteen years being the tail of your damn dog. And I was happy to do it, most of the time. But I'm not the tail anymore. And I'm telling you that I'm right about this. It's important to me."

"It's a million dollars," Alec objected weakly.

Gabe said nothing, just continued to look at him.

Alec sighed and caved. "All right, Dog Head. I'll do my best."

the toxic person

♡

Mira gripped Gabe's hand more tightly as they took their seats the next afternoon. She looked over at Zara, seated with Hank on the jury, got a smile in return, a nod that set the older woman's long silver earrings jangling. Well, at least she didn't seem mad at Mira for voting her out. That would make the next couple weeks a lot easier. Gabe still seemed to think she might not be going today, but Mira couldn't believe that was possible. Keeping her and Scott might be a good strategic move, but the situation on Arcadia looked too tense to her. She'd seen that body language too many times in meetings. The person all the others turned away from, that nobody could look in the eye. The toxic person. The one who had to go.

"So, Arcadia," Cliff began. "Here's your chance to talk at last. And your chance to vote. Alec, did it seem like it would ever happen?"

"No," he said, dark brows drawing together. "Our teamwork hasn't been there on the men's side. And you can't win without that."

"Got a comment about that, Scott?"

"Are there arrogant guys on Arcadia?" Scott asked from his spot at the end of the row, at a little distance from Rachel. "You bet there are. People who don't want to listen when somebody else has a better idea, because only they know how to do everything." He shot a poisonous glare in the direction of Alec, sitting at the opposite end of the bench. "But you notice, when it was something where individual talent counted, and *all* of us could contribute, when one person wasn't deciding he had to call all the shots, we *did* win."

"Sounds like there've been some big personality clashes over there," Cliff said innocently. "Rachel, did winning improve the mood?"

"No," she said bluntly. "It's just made it more tense. I can't wait for today to be over."

"You think today's going to solve the problem, then?"

"Yes." Her glance at Scott couldn't have been more meaningful.

"Calvin," Cliff said. "Is that going to be the basis of your vote today? Harmony? Group dynamics?"

"It shouldn't be," Calvin said. "Because even though I know you're enjoying keeping us in suspense, we all know we're merging after this. It's got to be about strategy."

"Want to elaborate on that?"

"No," Calvin decided. "No, I don't. I'll let my vote do the talking."

"And with that," Cliff said, "it's time to vote."

The process was quick. Four people, walking one by one to the voting booth, writing a name on a strip of paper and holding it for the camera to record, then folding it, dropping it into a Wells Fargo strongbox with a hole cut into the top before returning to their seats. Nothing celebratory about it. The mood was grim, and the look on Gabe's face matched it.

Cliff moved to the voting area, and the usual pause ensued as he looked through the votes, arranged them for theatrical value.

"It's OK," Gabe said, looking down at Mira. "You're going to be all right."

305

"I know," she agreed, doing her best to smile reassuringly. "But I'm leaving. There's no other answer."

He shook his head. "I don't think so."

"Gabe," she said urgently. "It's *all right.* I'll see you in a couple weeks. When I vote for you to win a million dollars," she went on, trying to make him smile. "That'll be a good day. I can't wait."

They fell silent again as Cliff brought the box back to his podium, set it down and opened the lid.

"All right," he said. "I'll read the votes. The team voted out will follow Jay and the other jury members out of the Clearing," he explained unnecessarily, "and won't return until next week, when you'll be on the jury yourselves, watching the vote taking place that will determine our Final Four."

"First vote," he said, pulling out the first strip and pausing for dramatic impact. "Alec and Gabe."

"Scott's," Gabe muttered. "I hope."

"Second vote." An even longer pause this time. "Rachel and Kevin."

"You're kidding." That was Kevin, from his spot beyond Gabe.

Cliff looked up from the third strip. "Scott and Mira."

The hand holding Mira's was squeezing so tightly now, it was almost painful. A split vote? Mira wondered. How was that possible? Could Gabe be right?

"The fifth pair to leave," Cliff announced. Turned the strip around to face the group. "Scott and Mira."

Gabe turned a distraught face to Mira. "I'm sorry," he said miserably. "I thought it would work."

Mira pressed his hand, then dropped it to turn and give Stanley a quick hug.

"You take care, now," he murmured. She could see the tears standing in his eyes. "He gives you any trouble, you tell him he'll be answering to me."

"Thank you," she said. "For everything. I'll see you soon." She was choking up now too as she stood up, hugged Kevin briefly as well, then turned to Gabe.

He pulled her into him, squeezed tightly. "If you're worried," he said urgently, "tell somebody. And stay away from him."

"I will," she promised. She'd thought she'd prepared for this, but it was so much harder than she'd thought it would be. She reached out her hand, laid it along his unshaven cheek, and looked into his eyes. "I'm holding you," she whispered.

And then she turned to join Scott, waiting impatiently for her on the other side, his face a mask of frustrated anger.

"Well," Cliff said as Gabe watched Mira's straight back disappearing among the trees. "That's something that I frankly was expecting to happen a while ago."

He paused theatrically "And now, the moment you've been waiting for. The six of you will be walking back to Paradise. And don't worry, Arcadia. We've moved your clothes over while you've been here."

"I don't care about my clothes so much," Rachel said above the noise of the conversation that had begun at the announcement. "What about my pies, and the beans I've got soaking? Did you move those? I don't want to have to start over."

"I'm sure," Cliff said with a smile, "that those have been moved too. Six more days, guys. Then we'll see you all back here, and it'll be a whole new game."

"Sorry," Alec said, the minute he'd hustled to the front of the little group to catch up with his twin, striding ahead on the path to Paradise. "I tried. I really did. I talked to Calvin, did the only thing I could to keep him from thinking I was playing him. Told him you'd come over, and what you'd told me. That I'd promised you I'd help you. And I did my best to explain why it'd be a better strategic move to vote Rachel and Kevin out."

"You must not have tried hard enough," Gabe said grimly. "Because you're a persuasive guy. And that was a good argument."

"You're reckoning without Scott's truly spectacular level of unpopularity, though," Alec pointed out. "And I did more than that. I told Scott to vote Rachel off. Told him I wanted to go to the end with him. I thought that kind of blatant self-interest would be credible to ol' Scott. But as you saw, he didn't buy it. And it wouldn't have worked anyway, not without Calvin's vote. I almost thought I had it, there at the end. But as it was, the best we could've done was ended up in a tiebreaker between Rachel and Scott, and I can't imagine that Rachel wouldn't have won. But I *tried.*"

"That was *you?*" Rachel asked in astonishment. She and Kevin were right behind them, Gabe realized, and had overheard everything. "You stabbed me in the back? You tried to get me voted out? I can't believe you'd do that, after everything that's happened! After I won the challenge for us, finally, so we could get rid of him!"

"I couldn't help it," Alec protested. "It wasn't about you. You know how much I hate Scott's guts. I hate *more* than his guts. I hate his...capillaries. I hate his *tendons.* But I was under orders. I'm not supposed to be the head of the dog anymore. Mr. Big here's the head now. I'm just wagging along, being the tail."

"I have no idea what you're talking about," she said angrily. "Is this some kind of secret twin language?"

"Kind of like that. Apparently. So secret that even I didn't know about it till now. Sorry I voted for you. I really am."

"Sorry doesn't really cut it, though, does it?" Kevin asked thoughtfully as his sister fumed beside him. "You know you guys have a target on your back. Well, that target just got bigger, if that's possible."

"Yeah, but now we have a Safety challenge, right?" Alec said. "So there you go."

"Wow, you're cocky," Rachel marveled. "You're that sure you're the strongest person out here?"

"Nope. But I'm betting Dog Head here can pull us to victory."

telting the truth

♡

Mira stood in front of the bookshelf beside the giant fireplace in the big room that served as dining hall, lounge, and activity center for their little band of expelled homesteaders, looking for something exciting to read. It hadn't been much of a surprise when she'd climbed into the van and found that they were headed back to the hunting camp. Where else could they have stayed so well concealed? She knew how important it was to keep the identities of those voted off a secret until the show aired. After all, she'd signed a contract promising not to reveal anything about her own performance, how long she'd lasted out here.

She'd spent most of the five days she'd been here with Hank and Zara, partly because she enjoyed their company, and partly to stay away from Scott. She'd been for a hike with them earlier, in fact, but they were now back in their cabin for a "rest" that, Mira thought with amusement, probably wasn't very restful. This adventure seemed to have given their marriage a new lease on life, and she was happy for them.

The problem was, there just wasn't that much to do here. She'd taken her shower, changed into a skirt and sandals. That had taken all of half an hour. She could go into the kitchen where Alma was working with Lupe and Maria-Elena, but Alma tended to get grouchy when there were more than two extra people in her space. And although Mira had forged a tentative friendship with Melody during the blonde's brief week on the homestead, Chelsea still didn't have much use for her. Joining the two of them in their mani/pedi session, listening to their bored gossip about their lives in LA, wasn't that enticing.

She bent down to look at the books on the bottom shelf. Maybe a thriller, she thought. Something to sweep her up and take her away. She'd been unsettled, even jumpy since her arrival, and it was getting worse. Partly, she knew, because the change was so sudden and complete. She'd gone from being busy every minute of the day, and exhausted every night, to inertia and inactivity, nothing to do but wait.

Being this close to Scott, too, had been even harder than she'd expected. She'd managed to avoid him most of the time, but ten people at a table still meant sitting within a few feet of each other at every meal. Another two days, she reminded herself, and another pair of contestants would join them. She forced herself not to hope it would be Gabe and Alec.

She'd idly wondered, before being voted off, whether the ejected contestants were kept updated on the happenings on the homesteads, beyond their weekly appearance at the Clearing for the vote. Perhaps, she and Kevin had speculated, they even got to watch some of the footage. Well, she knew the answer now. She had no idea what was going on. Maybe that was why she'd become so restless, had even started having trouble sleeping. Or maybe it was just that she missed Gabe so much, that she ached to see him and hold him again. Was he missing her too? Not as much as she was, she was sure. He had a whole lot more to do than she did, and he had his brother with him again. Whereas she had…Scott.

As if she'd conjured him up by thinking about him, he appeared in the doorway, pausing at the sight of her. She grabbed a Tom Clancy novel she hadn't read before. All right, then.

Instead of relaxing in here on the couch, she'd lie on the bed in her cabin. Again.

"Running away?" he sneered as she waited for him to move out of the doorway so she could leave. "Can't face me, can you?"

"No," she said, trying to maintain her calm. "I'm not running. But I'm not interested in talking to you. Excuse me."

He didn't move, though. To get around him, she'd have to push past him, and she shrank from the idea of touching him.

"Too damn bad," he said. "Because I want to talk to *you*. I have a few things to say, and you owe it to me."

She didn't think she owed him anything, but she wasn't going to get out of this, so she braced herself and waited for what he'd say next, even as the tendrils of anxiety began unfolding in her chest.

"Let's forget that you came on the show with me, and started screwing somebody else as soon as I wasn't actually standing over you," he began. "You think Daddy's going to be proud of you? You think he'll be thrilled to have his not-so-darling daughter looking like a slut on national television?"

"I didn't have sex with anybody out there," she said, trying to keep her voice firm. "You, or anyone else." OK, she'd wanted to. And she'd done some fairly extreme making out. But Scott wouldn't know about that until he actually saw the show. By that time, he'd be long gone from her life. "And I broke up with you, remember?" she added, reminding herself too. "That makes it absolutely none of your business what I do."

"But that wasn't all you did," he went on as if she hadn't spoken. "You refused to follow my plan, even when I laid it out for you and reminded you of it every single week. You were over there with the group making the decisions, but did you work our alliances like I told you? Did you work on Melody and Martin, pull in Zara? Oh, no. That would've been too easy. No, you let all our best prospects go, left us out of options. That's all on you.

You're the reason we're here now, and not in line to win a million dollars. How strategic does that make you look? How *stupid* does it make you look?"

His voice had risen, and the cold tones he'd started with had turned to something much more heated. Mira glanced to her left, toward the kitchen door. She'd go out that way, she decided, get Alma to walk her back to her cabin. Scott wouldn't mess with Alma. She began to edge toward the door, Scott keeping pace with her.

"That alliance wouldn't have worked," she said. "Melody was always going to be out the first week. There was no other choice. Zara would never have gone along with anything else, and I don't think even Martin would have. I would have made enemies for no reason."

"You always think you know better, don't you?" he sneered. "So why are we here, if you're so *smart?* Tell me that!"

"Because your homestead hated you!" If he was going to abuse her, she was going to tell him the truth for once. "Because they were just waiting for a chance!"

"No," he spat. "Because you *lost.* Because you don't even know how to make a fucking *pie.*"

"And how many challenges did you lose for your home-stead?" she demanded, not even trying to get away from him anymore. "Every single one! That's the only reason we stayed as long as we did, and you know it. Because I did well, and they didn't want to lose me. Because I know how to get along with people! Arcadia didn't just want to vote you out, they wanted to *kill* you. If you'd been on fire like I was, nobody would even have put you out!"

"That's a lie," he ground out, his expression darkening even further. "Alec hated me because he can't stand the idea that any-one else might be better at something than he is. And he talked the others into voting us out."

"You say that," she said through trembling lips, "but it's *you* you're talking about." She knew she wasn't exactly making sense, but she didn't have time to formulate her argument better. All the frustration and anger was rushing out now. "*You're* the one who can't stand anyone being better! *You're* the one who lost the challenges! It wasn't Alec, and it wasn't me! It was *you!*"

She was almost to the kitchen door now. And she was done. She wasn't sure if it had felt good to say what she had, or horrible. But she'd said it, and now she was leaving. She turned to go, found herself yanked back again by Scott's hand, tight around her arm.

"Let go! You're hurting me!" She attempted to pull his hand off her, but he was standing over her now, almost spitting with anger, and suddenly, she was actually afraid.

"You've undermined me, and disrespected me, and tried to humiliate me since the day we got here," he said, his voice raw, his face twisted with hatred. "You've made me look like a fool in front of millions of people. But you know what you've really done? You've shown what a piece of trash you are. Even your own parents don't love you that much, do they? And you know why? Because you're not that loveable. You don't even know what it means to love someone, and to help them. It all has to be about you, every time, doesn't it? Because you're a selfish, whiny *loser.* 'Poor me,'" he mimicked savagely. "'Everybody feel sorry for Mira, because she's so, so pathetic.' And when that doesn't work, what do you do? You try to take down somebody bigger, just so you can feel better about yourself. Well, you're not going to get away with it, not this time. You took on the wrong guy. I've never turned the other cheek yet, and I'm not about to start now. You are going *down.*"

Mira tried to pull away from him, fought the horror his words, the look on his face had aroused in her. She scrabbled for the doorknob, but his grip on her arm was too tight, and he yanked her back.

"I'm going to tell everybody," he hissed at her. "I'm going to get on camera, and I'm going to tell the truth about you. You're never going to get another job. You're going to be a laughingstock all over the country by the time I'm through with you."

"No," she said, swallowing past the fear, the hurt, the anger, forcing the words out through the tightness in her throat. "No. That's going to be you. You're going to be the loser. You're going to be the laughingstock. And the beauty of it is, I don't even have to get on camera again for that to happen. Know why? Because it's already there for everyone to see. You losing challenge after challenge for your homestead. You refusing to listen to how to shoot a gun, and doing it wrong, every time. Getting dumped on your butt trying to scare off some little deer. You getting drunk and getting thrown out of the dance after I dumped you. And then, the crowning glory? Your homestead voting you off. All that's on camera, and a whole lot more too, that I don't even know about yet. But I sure will by the time the show airs, because they're going to show all of it. And every single bit of that's on *you*. It's nobody else's fault. It's all you."

She saw him raise his hand to her, tried to pull away, but couldn't move, trapped by the grip on her arm, the wall against her back. Could only see the hand coming toward her face, and wait for it to hit her.

Gabe poured another bucket of water down the row of tomatoes, tried to fight back the surge of unease. He'd been restless all week, no matter what Alec said, how reasonable his arguments sounded.

"No news is good news, right?" his twin had said the evening before on their way back from the creek. "If anything had happened, we would've heard. And what *could* happen? There are eight other people with her. *Eight.* What do you imagine he could do in front of everyone?"

"I know," Gabe said impatiently. "I know, I know. I keep telling myself all that. And it's not helping. I'm worried."

"Look, I know you're all hot for her," Alec said. "All right," he amended hastily when Gabe glared at him. "You're in love with her. Whatever. Same deal. But you need to chill."

Gabe had had trouble sleeping all the same. He always slept like a log out here, the hard physical labor more effective than any sleeping pill known to man. But last night, he'd woken again and again, the sleep he had managed broken by dreams he couldn't remember on waking. Just that he'd woken each time with a start, his heart pounding.

Now he went to the creek, refilled the buckets, carried them up again, trying to get a grip.

"I wonder what the challenge will be tomorrow," Kevin mused, leaning on his hoe for a moment among the zucchini. "Something in here, I'll bet. Some kind of garden thing that men and women can both do. Power weeding. Well, we've all had some practice with that."

Gabe didn't hear him. He stood stock-still, his buckets hanging from his hands, forgotten, and stared toward the house.

"Hey," Kevin said. "You OK?"

Gabe looked down, saw the goosebumps forming on his arms, felt the hair rising on the back of his neck. He set down his buckets and walked quickly to the gate.

"What is it?" Kevin asked. He'd come along with him, Gabe realized, was looking at him with alarm.

"Alec," Gabe got out. He started toward the cabin, broke into a run, outdistancing Kevin and Danny, who was hustling after them, his camera on his shoulder.

By the time he got to the cabin, Gabe was sprinting. He burst through the door, saw Rachel and Alec turning their heads towards him, their expressions startled.

"What?" Alec asked in alarm, potato in one hand, paring knife in the other. "What happened?"

"You OK?" Gabe asked on a gasp as Kevin came in behind him, Danny bringing up the rear.

"Of course I'm OK," Alec said, exasperated. "Well, I cut my finger a little. Want to look at my boo-boo?"

Gabe tried to calm his racing heart. "I was sure..." he began. "I *knew* you were in trouble." He stared at Alec in confusion, and his brother stared back at him, and each saw the truth in the dark-blue eyes looking into his own.

"Mira," they said together.

"What about Mira?" Kevin asked.

"Something's wrong," Gabe answered. "Danny, we need to get out of here. Call somebody to take us out, right now."

"Man, you can't leave," Danny protested. "It doesn't work that way. You know that."

"Call whoever it is *right the hell now*," Gabe ordered in his best hospital voice. "Get me a ride. Something's wrong back there, and I'm leaving."

"No, *we're* leaving," Alec corrected him. "Call, Danny."

"This is so against the rules," Danny muttered. "I'm not supposed to be doing this."

He asked a question over the two-way radio, turned back to Gabe. "Nothing's wrong," he told him. "Everything's fine."

"Give me that." Gabe grabbed the radio out of Danny's hand, pressed the button. "This is Gabe. There's an emergency. Get a truck here now."

He ran out to the clearing with Alec. Within no more than two minutes, the pickup bounced into the dirt yard from wherever it sat stashed during the day. Jay started to get out, was pulled back inside by Gabe, who had already opened the passenger door and climbed in with Alec close behind.

"Go," Gabe ordered. "Drive."

"Where?" Jay protested. "I can't just take you. I have to call and get authorization."

Gabe caught a glimpse of Danny hopping up into the truck bed. He made his decision, reached out and gave Jay a hard shove that pushed him out the open door, pulled the driver's door shut and was accelerating out of the yard before Jay had even got to his feet.

"Oh, man," Alec moaned. "We are so screwed. Grand theft auto. And we don't even know where they are."

"Open that back window and ask Danny," Gabe commanded, the truck bouncing over the heavily rutted dirt road.

Alec did it, somehow. "The camp," he reported, holding the bar by the door to keep himself in his seat, coughing against the dust coming through the opened rear window. Hanging on for the ride.

♡

By the time they pulled into the gravel drive, Gabe's anxiety was at fever pitch. He hit the brakes, shifted into first and turned the key, and was out the door of the pickup in moments, Alec right behind him, Danny leaping out of the back of the truck to follow them, filming the whole time.

Gabe didn't even notice him. He ran through the front door of the common room and saw them. Mira backed up against the wall, Scott's vicious backhand landing even as Gabe crossed the room, a moment too late.

Everything was hazy. Grabbing Scott by the back of the shirt, swinging him in an arc, shoving him backward. Scott's face, contorted with anger and shock. Alec saying something, pulling at his arm. Gabe wasn't even conscious of hitting Scott, only realized he'd done it when his fist landed on the side of the other man's head and Scott stumbled backward. Gabe followed him, pulled his arm back to hit him again. But before he could, Scott went down, taking Danny with him in a tangle of arms, legs, and camera.

Gabe was over Scott again, grabbing him by the front of the shirt this time, yanking him off Danny, when Alec got hold of him by both arms, pulled him back, shouting loudly enough to be heard over the roar in Gabe's head.

"Stop! Gabe! That's enough!"

Scott sank back down onto the floor, his hand to his head, looking dazed. Danny was fumbling for his radio again, speaking urgently into it. But it was hardly necessary. The trucks were already pulling into the yard, Cliff and John rushing through the door.

"What's going on?" Cliff asked sharply. "Gabe? What's happened?"

Scott was still on the ground, scrabbling away sideways like a crab, trying to put distance between himself and Gabe. Gabe shook his head, trying to clear it, reached a hand out for Danny, pulled him to his feet.

"Sorry about that," he said with a shaky laugh. "Just...Just taking out the trash."

Mira, he remembered. She was still against the wall, her hand to her face. Lupe, finally alerted by the commotion, had her arm around her, Maria-Elena and Alma standing helplessly nearby.

"Oh, baby." He reached out gently, noticed with detachment that his hand was trembling. He moved her hand from her cheek, saw the red blotches there, the bruising beginning from the blow.

"How does it feel?" he asked. "Any teeth loose?"

She shook her head, wincing at the movement. "No. Just hurts. My cheek and my head."

He took her to the table, sat her down in a chair. "Alma," he said, looking up. "Got an icepack in there?"

"You bet," she assured him, hustling back within a minute with a cold pack. Mira took it from her, pressed it to her cheek.

"I'm going to take Mira to her cabin," Gabe told Alec. "If anybody needs us, they can come see us there."

♡

Forty-five minutes later, a tall, fresh-faced sheriff's deputy who'd introduced himself as Ron Ohlsen was sitting on the little cabin's lone chair while Mira and Gabe sat on the bed facing him. Ron signed the summons, ripped it carefully loose from the copies, and handed it to Gabe. "Sorry, man. I doubt the D.A. will prosecute under the circumstances, but I have to cite you."

Gabe looked down at the piece of paper. "Battery, huh? Hell, if I'd known I was going to get cited for it anyway, I would've hit him a few more times."

"I hear you," Ron said sympathetically. "I would've done the same thing, somebody did my lady like that." He nodded to Mira. "How you doing? You sure you don't need us to get a doctor out here?"

"I've got medical attention." She smiled painfully, hugged Gabe's arm a little more tightly.

"I'm a doctor," Gabe explained, conscious for the first time of his dirty, disheveled 1880s clothes, the multi-day growth of black stubble on a face that didn't look all that civilized at the best of times. "All appearances to the contrary."

"Well, then," Ron said, "I guess you know best. And don't worry," he told Mira. "Mr...." He glanced down at his copy of the summons. "Mitchell's in the car now, getting used to the feeling of those cuffs. He'll get some time in a jail cell to think about whether it was worth it. Because he's an ex, right?"

"Right," she said. "Does that matter?"

"Yep. Makes it domestic battery, and means he's going to have to see a judge before he posts bond. Friday afternoon? Yeah, not going to happen today. He's likely to be in till Monday."

"What'll happen to him then?" she pressed.

"Still a misdemeanor, but he'll get a good fine. Probably no more jail time than that, if this was the first incident." He looked the question at her.

"Yes," she said. "The first one with me, anyway."

"And Cliff already told me that they'd put Scott up at a motel in town this next week," Gabe said. "He won't be coming back here."

"He'll get a restraining order for sure," Ron assured them. "All this was on film? Yeah, should be pretty cut and dried."

"Thanks," Mira sighed once Ron had left. Her cheek was really hurting now, and she felt as drained as if she'd been doing 1885 laundry all day. All she wanted to do was lie down and go to sleep. "That isn't enough to say, and I don't know how you knew I needed you right then, but thanks. Or did you get voted out?" she asked in sudden alarm.

"Nope," he said. "Door Number One. But here." He leaned down to the small ice chest Alma had given him, pulled out another icepack. "Time to put this back on."

"You mean you actually did know I was in trouble?" she asked, holding the cold pack to her cheek. "Like the twin thing? Does it work with other people too?"

"It never has before," he said slowly. "I thought it was Alec at first. But when it wasn't…I knew it was you. I have a feeling that means something, don't you?"

"I don't know." She took his hand with her free one, the simple contact as soothing as ever. "But I do know that I was awfully glad to see you. I was pretty scared for a minute there.

I'm not sure what else he would have done. Thank you for coming. Thank you so much. Don't you need to get back, though?"

He laughed. "Get back to what?"

She sat up straight, set the icepack down slowly. "Gabe. You and Alec didn't...you didn't quit the *game,* did you?"

"No," he said, still smiling.

She sighed with relief that was short-lived as he continued. "Not exactly, we didn't. But if you count carjacking a production truck, leaving the site, attacking one of the other contestants... Yeah, I'd say we've quit about as comprehensively as a person could. Well, maybe Martin did it a little more thoroughly, but it'd be a close call."

"You stole a *truck?*" She stared at him in horror. "Gabe, this is for a million dollars! You can't just *quit!* Isn't there something you can do? Talk to Cliff and apologize? Plead temporary insanity or something? You guys were going to *win!* You can't just walk away from that!"

"Yeah, I can. And I did. *We* did. That part's the twin thing, thank goodness. Alec's along for the ride. Literally," he said with another laugh. "Not too happy with me right now, maybe, but he came along for the ride all right. So they'd better have our cabin ready, because it's going to be occupied tonight. We're done."

"No," she said firmly. "No. You need to check first. Make sure you're really out. That there isn't some way to get back into it again."

"Mira." He took both her anxious hands in his own. "I'm out. And it's exactly where I want to be. At least it will be, if you'll lie down here with me and let me hold you for a few minutes. What's the point of saving the girl if you don't even get to kiss her?"

♡

"If you're really going to be here," Mira said drowsily a half-hour later, after waking from the doze she'd fallen into, lulled by the comfort of his arms, "do you think you could stay with me tonight? Actually…can you just stay, while we're here? Would you want to? Or do you want to be with Alec?"

He laughed, held her gently to him, gave her a careful kiss on the forehead. "Let's see now. I could spend the next week on a twin bed next to my brother, who's not exactly thrilled about being my Partner in Crime. Or I could sleep in here with the woman I've been wishing, and hoping, and praying to have sex with for a couple months now. Yeah, that's a tough one. I'll have to give that some careful thought. I'll get back to you, how's that?"

She smiled carefully around the pain of the bruises. "You do that. Let me know what you decide."

"But don't worry," he went on. "We're not doing anything tonight. Because I know how much that hurts."

"This is the problem with you being a doctor," she sighed. "Too much information."

a little late to breakfast

♡

Mira opened her eyes, saw the familiar wood ceiling of her cabin over her head. And felt the very unfamiliar warmth of the man beside her. She looked down at him, sleeping on his stomach, one arm shoved under the pillow, the other flung out across the bed, his head turned away from her. She eased out of bed quietly so as not to wake him up. He'd had a hard day yesterday. She'd let him sleep. For a little longer, anyway.

She winced a bit as she brushed her teeth, the movement aggravating the tender bruise that had come out in glorious red now. Her headache was gone, though. She moved her face experimentally. Not too bad. A whole lot better than it had been last night.

The others had all exclaimed over her at dinner, Melody and Chelsea seeming disgruntled at missing all the excitement of the day. Hank, Zara, and Lupe, though, had made a fuss over her that had made her feel a bit uncomfortable, but so cared for. Alma and Lupe, to her gratified astonishment, had made a rich tortilla soup just for her that didn't require chewing. She'd gone to bed early, had fallen asleep with Gabe holding her. And that had all been great. But this morning, she was hoping for a whole lot more.

She climbed carefully back into bed and looked down at him. He'd shifted around while she'd been gone, the white sheet slipping down almost to his waist, leaving his broad, muscular back on full view nearly all the way down to the navy blue boxer briefs that, to her enjoyment, had been all he'd worn to bed. His head was turned towards her on the pillow now, mouth slightly parted in sleep, his hair and face clean, but the black stubble remaining.

"Oh, please," she'd exclaimed impulsively when he'd pulled the razor and shaving cream from his toilet kit after his shower. "Leave it for a while."

"I've got a good three days' growth of beard here," he objected, running an exploratory hand over his face and grimacing. "Too hard to get a close shave out there. And you don't want that, do you?"

"I do," she insisted. "It looks good. Really hot, if you want to know."

"But it'll scratch," he pointed out. "Especially..." He looked at her, a slow smile beginning. "On the tender parts."

"I want that, though," she said, amazed at her boldness. "I want to feel it. It's...exciting."

The dark blue eyes remained intently on her a moment longer, before he put the razor away with deliberation. "I have a suggestion for you," he said.

"What?" she asked, a little breathless.

"Get well soon."

♡

Now, she looked again at his broad back, the muscles more defined than ever after two months of chopping wood and sawing down trees. He'd complained yesterday, after he'd finally got his shower and changed into modern clothes, that his shirts were too tight across the chest and shoulders. He might have to buy a new wardrobe, but she loved it.

She gave in to temptation, lifted herself up to sit on her knees beside him, and ran her hands lightly over those shoulders.

Put her thumbs in the valley of his spine, opened her hands over the ridge of muscle lining that valley on either side, slid them all the way down to his narrow waist, and sighed at the solid bulk of him under her palms.

He opened one eye to look at her, his mouth curving in a smile. "Either I'm finally in bed with the woman I love," he decided, "or I'm having the world's best dream."

"Door Number One," she assured him with a happy smile of her own.

"Then," he said, sitting up and swinging his legs over the side of the bed, "give me a sec."

He came back from the bathroom, put an appraising hand under her chin. "Bruising's coming out pretty good there," he said. "How does it feel?"

"It hurts if I touch it," she admitted. "Not too bad otherwise."

"Head still hurt?"

"Nope." She looked up at him hopefully.

"Anything still hurt?"

"A little achy, that's all."

"Would a massage help?"

"A *massage?*" She couldn't have been more surprised.

"Yeah. Here's something you didn't know about me. A fun fact for you. I'm a certified massage therapist. At least, I used to be."

She eyed him suspiciously. "I thought you were a landscaper."

"I am a man of many talents. And much early poverty. Come on," he said, pressing her down gently. "Are you OK on your stomach, if you put the good cheek down?"

"Yeah," she said, trying it out, her voice muffled against the pillow. "OK."

"Then stay there. Let me make you feel good."

She heard him getting up again, then felt the dip in the mattress as he came back, smelled the familiar honey-almond scent of her body lotion.

"Lift up," he instructed. She pushed herself up on her hands, felt him pulling her short nightgown up, easing it gently over her head, and tossing it aside.

"Put your arms down like this." He moved them so her hands were lying by her sides, palms up. She felt the air on her skin, then, as he pulled the sheet and blanket all the way back, sighed at the weight of him settling astride her thighs.

"Too cold?" he asked.

"No." It was another sigh, because cold was the last thing she felt.

His lubricated hands stroked slowly from the base of her spine to her neck. And he was right. He really *did* know how to give a massage. He seemed to sense exactly where she was tight, where she ached, because his hands unerringly found the spot, worked it.

"How can you tell?" she asked drowsily as his hands continued to move over her.

"What?"

"Where it hurts."

"I don't know," he said. "It's like my hands know. I can usually tell where people are hurting anyway, see it somehow. And when I touch somebody...yeah. Then I can really tell. That's what makes me a good doctor. Haven't you noticed that I know how to touch people? I was kind of hoping I'd impressed you already, a time or two."

"Mmm. Maybe you have. Maybe once or twice. I forget, though. Maybe you can remind me."

"Maybe I can." She could almost feel his smile as his hands continued to move. "You just lie there and enjoy it. And let's see if I can remind you."

When she was all but purring, he shifted his position. "I'm going to take off your underwear now," he told her. "Purely for therapeutic purposes."

He was lifting her hips, pulling the cotton bikinis down her legs and over her feet, settling her back down again. Massaging the muscles of her buttocks, her thighs, moving down to her calves. His hands on her feet then, gentle against the sensitive arches, rubbing more strongly over the ball of her foot, her heel. Pulling on each toe in turn, and she was drowning in bliss.

"I thought," she murmured, "this was going to be one of those guy back rubs. You know, where they rub your back, and then they rub your..."

"Don't worry," he promised. "We'll get to that. I've got all morning to rub you. Time to turn over for me."

He settled her on her back, began to work on her shoulders, her arms. She could almost have thought he was detached, except that what she was seeing inside those boxer briefs was very much attached. And very much aroused. She reached out the arm he wasn't working on, ran her hand down the length of him, felt the instant response, the way he seemed to leap into her palm. And the rigidity in his muscles, his hands stopping their movement.

"I haven't done your thighs yet," he objected. "Stop it. No touching till I say."

"Mmm. Bossy," she sighed.

He smiled. "You know it."

By the time he had her legs apart, his strong hands working her thigh muscles, she was ready to scream. She shifted again, felt his hands, slick with lotion, kneading and stroking. His thumbs gliding up her inner thighs, stopping just short. Again, a little bit higher this time. And still not quite where she needed him to be. She squirmed, looked at him, saw the concentration on his face. Then caught him casting a sly glance at her, and knew.

"You're teasing me," she groaned. "You're doing it on purpose."

"Just trying to build anticipation," he said, letting the smile loose now.

"OK," she said crossly. "I'm anticipating. And you're a great masseur. I'm really, really impressed. And if you don't touch me, or kiss me, or *something* in the next ten seconds, you're...you're going to be sleeping with your brother tonight."

"Now who's bossy?" He brought his hands up a third time, the thumbs moving up slowly. So slowly. Almost there.

She grabbed his shoulders. *"Touch me."*

"No," he told her. "No. I'm going to kiss you."

And he did. Over and over again. His tongue, his mouth on her, in her, over her. His hands gripping her thighs, moving them farther apart, holding her. Her hips trying to rise off the bed, unable to move against the restraint of his mouth, his hands. Her hands clutching the sheet beneath her, grabbing and twisting the white cotton. And as he went on, a little harder now, a little faster, her palms beginning to beat against the mattress like wings. Trying to fly.

His mouth was on her, and it was exactly the right spot, the only spot, and he had one palm under her, lifting her into him, the fingers of the other inside her, thrusting into her. It was hard, and it was urgent, and it was almost too much to take. And she was soaring. Her hands were beating, beating. Until they rose into the air, stretched taut to either side of her. And she flew.

♡

"Gabe," she gasped. "Gabe. I...I..." She was pulling at him. "Up here. Up with me. I need you inside me."

"Condom," he groaned. Grabbed for it, somehow got his underwear off, got the thing on. Looked down at her, stretched out beneath him, the orgasmic flush on her chest matching the red on her inner thighs, where his beard had scraped. She was right, not shaving had been the right choice. Because seeing that...God help him, it *was* exciting.

He grabbed a pillow, lifted her hips and pushed it beneath her. Looked at her, lifted for him, and grabbed another, so she was stretched over the height of them, offered to him. Raised himself on his hands, looked down to watch as he entered her. Felt her stretching to take all of him, closed his eyes as the sensation threatened to overwhelm him. He dropped to his elbows, reached for her hands, threaded his fingers through hers, and began to push into her, keeping it slow, hearing the little moan she let out at every thrust. Kept on, felt the softness and the strength of her, the way her excitement was rising again to match his own.

"I've got you here," he told her, his breathing shallow with effort. "Open your eyes and see."

Her lids fluttered open, her beautiful eyes shining nearly gold in the early morning light, her pupils dilated. Her soft mouth open, panting.

"This is me," he said as he moved, long and slow. "This is how I feel inside you."

"Gabe," she whispered.

"That's right. I've got all of you now. You're all mine." He was starting to move faster now, driving deep, the angle increasing the penetration, and she was gasping with it. He released one hand, reached down, lifted himself a bit off her, and began to rub in time with his thrusts. Felt her respond to the increase in the stimulation, saw her tensing again.

"Come for me," he told her, breathing hard with the force of it. "Come on, baby. You're so beautiful. Show me you're mine. Come for me." He increased the tempo of his hand, his hips, his other palm flat against the bed now. And felt her beginning again, the beautiful contractions drawing him tighter and tighter, higher and higher, until they overtook him and he was coming too, long and hard, the groan it pulled from him mingling with her wail, like the cry of an ocean bird, filling the morning air.

♡

They were a little late to breakfast. Chelsea and Alec were still missing too, Gabe noticed.

"Pancakes are gone," Alma told them from her spot at the end of the table, where she was finishing a cup of coffee and chatting with the others.

"It's OK," Gabe said. "You mind if I fix us some eggs and toast? Sound good to you?" he remembered to ask Mira.

"Sure," she said with surprise, pausing in the act of pouring them each a cup of coffee. "I didn't realize you could cook."

"As long as I don't have to do it on a wood stove, I can cook just fine. I've been taking care of myself for a while now, you know. I can cook, and do laundry, and clean the toilet, and all sorts of wonderful things."

"Want to come over to my house, then?" Zara asked. "I've got a few jobs you could take care of."

Gabe laughed. The truth was, anything would have made him laugh this morning. He was feeling good. The only blot on his happiness was the sight of Mira's bruised face. He'd have to get her to put that icepack back on after breakfast, he thought as he headed into the kitchen to see what he could rustle up.

He was just turning bacon and pouring scrambled-egg mixture into the hot frying pan when Alec appeared in the doorway, then came across to join him at the big six-burner range.

"How about adding a few more?" his brother asked hopefully.

"Forget it." Gabe gave the eggs a flip with a spatula. "I'm almost done here, and Mira's hungry. Make your own."

"You know I'm a lousy cook," Alec complained.

"Then you should have got up earlier, shouldn't you?"

Alec sighed with resignation. "I'd ask Chelsea to cook, but she said all she wants is coffee and a slice of toast. Figures." He watched as his twin turned the fire off under the eggs and lined a plate with paper towels for the bacon, began to butter toast. "So was the stove hot?" he asked innocently.

Gabe glanced up at him in surprise, registered the smirk, and caught on. "None of your business, and you know it," he growled.

"Too bad I know you so well, then. Because that stove was on *fire*."

"If you already know," Gabe said irritably, "why do you ask?"

Alec laughed. "Just messing with you, that's all."

"And I take it you've been heating up the stove a bit yourself," Gabe said. "Judging by appearances this morning. Who was it who promised me he'd keep it in his pants for the duration?"

Alec snorted. "That's rich, coming from you. And the duration's over. It was over the minute you shoved Jay out of that truck. Now it's about my consolation prize, and Chelsea's too. She's *bored* out here. Just helping a lady out."

"I'd tell you to be careful, not to get in too deep, but you never do, do you?"

"Yeah, right," Alec scoffed. "I don't think I'm the one in danger of losing my heart. And hey, I *am* being careful. Did you see the look on Melody's face this morning, when you got in here?"

"She didn't look too happy," Gabe said. "Barely said hello to us. What did you do?"

"I didn't do anything. That's the point. That was me being careful. We could all have had even more fun if I'd put in just a little more effort. They'd have gone for it, bet you anything. But," Alec sighed, "I'm being conservative, so as not to embarrass Mr. Purity."

"And that's me?"

"Yes," Alec agreed. "That would be you."

"One of these days," Gabe warned, "you're going to crash and burn. You do know that, don't you?"

"Well, until that happy day..." Alec stretched. "I guess I'll see if I can manage to cook a couple eggs without any industrial accidents. Since apparently not even a million-dollar sacrifice merits a little help from my loving brother."

picnic

♡

"Good place to stop for lunch?" Gabe asked Mira almost a week later.

They'd reached the top of the ridge, the view of rolling hills spreading out before them like some kind of idyllic painting. They'd gone for a hike, just like, Mira thought with amusement, they'd done almost every day. Sometimes picking huckleberries, sometimes just walking and talking. Well, you couldn't spend the *whole* day in bed, and they were both used to being active now.

"How about over here?" Gabe walked over to a shady spot under a big old oak.

"Yeah, right," she said. "We'll just pull into this diner. I'll stop for a minute, though."

"Hey," he protested. "You don't think I'm capable of providing lunch?"

"Really?" she asked, ridiculously pleased. "I didn't know you'd brought food. How did you manage that?"

"Had a little talk with Alma last night," he said smugly, dropping to one knee to pull a rolled blanket from his pack. "But first..." With her help, he spread the blanket out on the grass. "Madame, your table is ready."

"Is it really a picnic?"

"You said a walk and a picnic would be a good date," he reminded her. "Well, not to mention that it's the only kind of date I can actually manage right now. So that's what I've got for you. With adult beverages, even." He reached back in for a bottle of white wine, a corkscrew, and two plastic glasses. "I can't guarantee that it's top of the line," he cautioned. "Hazards of not being allowed off school grounds. I don't think John's a big wine shopper in the normal way of things."

He dealt with the metal wrapping and the cork with his usual economy of motion. "Also not as cold as it was an hour ago, but such as it is..." He handed her a glass. "Here you go."

She took an appreciative sip and sighed in contentment, spent some time just being there, and looking.

"Hold this a moment for me," she decided after a few quiet minutes, handing her glass back to him. "If we're going to be here for a while, I'm going to take my shoes off. I think that's one of the things I missed most, being barefoot. Worrying about those splinters."

"That's right. The splinters," he said thoughtfully. "Seems to me I had a plan for getting those out of you."

"Your plan sounded a little painful," she protested. She finished pulling off her shoes and socks, crawled across to him. "But I'll get you barefoot too, how's that?"

"You have permission to take off as many of my clothes as you like, anytime you like," he assured her as she untied his shoelaces, pulled off first one shoe, than the other, set them next to the blanket, and went for his socks. "Keep going, if you want."

"It's funny about that," she said slowly, sitting up on her knees between his legs, putting her hands on his thighs and looking down at him where he lay sprawled on his elbows beneath her. "We've had sex quite a few times now."

"Yes," he agreed solemnly. "I remember."

"And it's been good, right?"

"No. It's been *great,*" he corrected. "For me, anyway. And if you have any suggestions, feel free. Always happy to improve."

"Well..." she began, then stopped.

He sat up a little straighter, set both glasses of wine carefully down on the grass next to the blanket. "You really *do* have a suggestion. Go on." His eyes were beginning to burn now, the intensity of his dark-blue gaze, as always, awakening her every nerve ending. "Let's hear it. I can't wait."

"Wasn't it kind of amazing that first time? When we were outside, by the creek," she elaborated. "A little worried that Danny would come. And we had to keep some clothes on. Especially when you held me, that time, and you...told me things. Or was that just me?"

"No," he assured her. "That wasn't just you. You told me a few things too, if you remember. And I enjoyed hearing them. Almost as much as I'd enjoy having you do them."

She smiled slowly. Wriggled up a little further between his legs and reached for his belt. "I'm going to do them," she promised.

He reached for her wrists, held her fast. "On two conditions."

"Oh, yeah?" She tossed her head a little at that. "Pretty cocky, aren't you? Giving me conditions for this?"

"*Very* cocky. As you know. First, unless your underwear today has a slit in it, you're going to take it off right now. Keeping that pretty dress on is one thing. But I need access."

She shivered. Reached under her dress and pulled down the purple cotton panties, wishing they were something more exotic. If he had any complaints, he didn't share them, watching as she lifted one knee, then the other, pulled them over her feet, and tossed them next to her wine glass.

"What's the next condition?" she asked him, already feeling the throb and pulse of arousal, just from the look in his eyes, the knowledge that she was naked under her dress.

336

"Take off your bra. Because I'm going to be going there too."

She didn't answer, just reached for the front clasp and unfastened it. Shrugged out of one cap sleeve at a time, then replaced them on her shoulders before dropping the cotton racerback next to her panties. "Anything else?"

"Reach in my right front pocket," he said. "I've got something for you there."

"It's not in your pocket," she said saucily. "And I'm planning to reach for it. You don't have to worry about that."

"Getting pretty sassy again, aren't you? I warned you that smart mouth was going to get you in trouble. And that's just about to happen. Reach on in there, now."

She reached where he told her, got a little distracted by the bulge she encountered during her search, but finally managed to pull out the little packet.

"Hey," she said, setting it aside. "I clearly wasn't the only one with this idea."

"I was a Boy Scout, remember?" His voice seemed to have deepened somehow. "Be Prepared."

"Yeah, well." She gave him a shove in the chest with both hands that put him on his back. "Prepare yourself for this, then. Because you've just run out of conditions."

♡

Oh, yeah, Gabe thought as her fingers worked the belt buckle. He'd take this. She knelt over him, the gaping neckline of her dress revealing her gorgeous breasts, and he reached for them, ran his hands over her, felt her still at the sensation.

"You're distracting me," she complained breathlessly. But she still managed to undo the buttons on his Levi's, pull down his boxer briefs to free him.

"It's not a race," he promised, giving her nipples a tweak that had her gasping. "Distraction is allowed."

She shoved his T-shirt up over his chest, leaned over him to kiss him there, ran her hands over his shoulders, down his arms, her touch, as always, igniting him. And then she was moving lower, forcing his hands to slip from her breasts, until she was poised over him, her hand gripping him, stroking him.

"Remember what I told you?" she asked softly.

"Uh…" He wasn't sure he could think anymore. All his brain cells seemed to have migrated south.

"You're supposed to tell me," she reminded him. "What you want me to do. Everything you want. Because that's what I'm going to do for you. Whatever you want."

He'd told her once, he remembered dazedly as she obeyed every gasped command, that he was going to drive her up slowly, until she was grabbing his hair, begging him. He'd done it, too. And now she was doing it to him. His hands were wrapped in her hair, and then he'd stopped giving her instructions, because he couldn't talk anymore. If she didn't stop right now, he wasn't going to be able to do anything else. And he needed to do something else.

"Mira. Stop," he ground out. "Stop."

She came up on her hands, looked at him. And he almost lost it right there at the sight of her soft mouth, the lust and longing in her eyes.

"The condom," he remembered. "Put it on me."

She reached for it, unrolled it onto him. He put his hands around her waist, dragged her towards him.

"Ride me," he told her. "Now." She settled herself over him, and he felt her stretching, taking more of him, until she was fully impaled, and he was already halfway there.

He'd had enough of the dress, he decided. He grabbed a handful of cotton in each hand, pulled the thing over her head, tossed it aside. And then she was naked, and she was on top of him, and her breasts were in his hands for him to use. To hold, and fondle, and take into his mouth, exactly as he pleased. And oh, the sensation as she slid over him, the sight of her wriggling, finding the spot that worked for her, rubbing herself against him, beginning to pant.

"You like that?" he asked. Her hands were on the ground now as she took him even more deeply, pushed herself fully onto him, rose again.

She couldn't answer, he saw, and he felt the power of it surge through him. He reached a hand down for her, found the spot, began to rub it himself, send her higher.

"Ah..." She was getting louder as he went on, her movements slowing. "I can't...I can't keep..."

"You can't move, can you?" He kept his hand going, saw what it was doing to her. "You need me on you? You need me to fuck you?"

"Yes," she moaned. "Please, Gabe. Please." Her face was twisted with passion and effort, straining towards fulfillment, her hair in wild disarray around her.

He pulled her off him, pushed her onto the blanket next to him, face down. "Get on your knees," he told her. "Put your elbows down."

He rolled over her, the constraint of the clothes he still wore only increasing his excitement. The sight of her naked bottom rising towards him, her legs apart, her head resting on her hands, telling him he had to have that. And that this was going to get rough.

Then one hand was on the ground, the other rubbing her hard from in front, and he was taking her with a ferocity he'd never experienced. Aware, in one part of himself, that she was climaxing, feeling the pull of it around him, hearing her cries as if from far away. But he was someplace else. Someplace that was all darkness, all need, all possession. Driving into her as she lay sprawled, pushed down beneath him now. *Mine,* he found himself repeating with each savage thrust. *Mine.*

And when the wave rose, higher and higher, took him in its grip, tumbled him over, he was the one who thought, for one wild, impossible moment, that it was going to kill him.

♡

"Some picnic," she got out, struggling to her hands and knees, feeling wobbly and uncoordinated, once he had rolled off her to lie on his back, breathing hard.

"That wasn't exactly in the plan," he agreed after a moment. "Come here." He pulled her to him, wrapped his arms around her, lifted his head to kiss her. "You OK?"

"Mmm." She nuzzled the salt of his neck, felt the pulse galloping there as he began to put himself to rights. "But I'm hungry." She laughed against his skin, felt the answering chuckle rising from deep within him. "And I want some more wine."

"You might like doing it with clothes on," he said once they were seated, decorously dressed again, eating Alma's chicken sandwiches and drinking wine that went instantly, gloriously, to their heads. "But I like you naked best. Nothing's going to change that."

"I noticed that you preferred that," she agreed, reaching out a bare foot to rub it against his. "And I like it when you take my clothes off."

"Remind me to do it more often, then."

"OK," she said agreeably. "Do it more often."

He laughed. "I'll be doing it as often as possible from now on, believe me. And that's a conversation we should have too."

"What? How often you should take off my clothes? Every day, please. Or more. I'm easy."

"You are," he said, leaning over for another kiss. "Lucky for me. But no. I meant, how I'm going to keep you around to do it in the first place. How tied are you to staying in Seattle?"

Her heart began pounding for a different reason now. "Uh…
What are you asking me?"

"Whether you'd consider moving," he said promptly. "I'll do
long-distance if we have to. And I know it hasn't been long. I'm
sure right now, but I don't want to push you if you're not ready
to make that kind of change in your life."

She felt the familiar rush of disappointment. Well, what had
she expected? That he was going to propose to her after knowing
her for two months? That would be way too impulsive for both of
them. They needed time together back in the real world to make
sure it was right. And she knew all the same, all the way to the
bottom of her heart, that she was already sure. That for her, it was
right, and it always would be.

"I'd consider moving," she said cautiously. "I need a new job
anyway, since I already quit on camera. Something new to do that
doesn't involve airplanes and hotels."

"Maybe we could both move," he suggested. "I've been
thinking, while I've been out here." He began to laugh. "Well,
some. I've been a little distracted, a lot of the time."

"What's distracted you?" she asked with a smile.

"You," he said with another kiss. "And you know it. But in
between imagining you naked," he went on, "and a few other
things I may have mentioned, I've been thinking about going
back. About how I want it to be when I do. I know I want you
to be there, but there's more too. Something about pretending to
be a homesteader, imagining these people risking everything to
make a life out here, has made it easier to think about the risk I
really want to take. To open up my own practice, do it my way.
And to do it someplace else. The main reason I live where I do is
to be near my family, especially Alec. But I'm wondering, does
it have to be right in the Bay Area? Could it be someplace less
crowded and busy?"

"Well, it had better be someplace with people who hurt themselves a lot doing sports, and can afford to do something about it," she said. "That might narrow your choice a bit."

"See," he said, "that's why I need you, to help me do the analysis. And we need to find someplace that'll work for both of us. Can we take some time and do that, do you think?"

"In case you haven't noticed," she pointed out, "I'll have all the time in the world. I'm going to be at liberty the moment I tell my boss I'm not coming back. And you're right. I'd like to live someplace where there are...birds. And sky. I mean," she elaborated with a little laugh, "there are always birds. Pigeons, anyway. And obviously there's always sky. But someplace where you can see the mountains, do you think?"

"That's exactly what I think," he agreed. "Someplace where we can both see the mountains."

"But I won't live with you," she found herself adding, "if that's what you're asking. I can't play house with you on some kind of trial basis, trying to fit into your life, trying to figure out how to be what you want so you'll want me too. I just can't do it. It would hurt so much."

"Oh, Mira." He began to reach for her, seemed to realize for the first time that he was still holding his sandwich, and set it hastily down, then pulled her into him and held her close.

She laughed a little shakily, sat back and picked up her glass again. "Sorry. Blame the wine. I didn't realize it was going to come out quite like that. I was just going to say, I'll move. I'll help you do your research, and I'll find a place not too far away from wherever you end up. I have to live someplace, after all." She swallowed against the bleakness of it.

"Don't be sorry," he protested. "I want to know. I've always wanted to know, but you've never seemed to want to say. But I want you to tell me. Because we all have scars, you know. That's just being human. It's OK to show me your scars, and let me help you heal them, just like you'll be helping me heal mine. It'll always be OK."

She looked at him searchingly, felt the emotion tightening her chest, her throat at the look in his eyes, the understanding she saw there. It really was, she realized. It really was OK to show him.

"You mean," he prompted gently, "that's how it was for you. With your parents, growing up."

"Yeah," she said, staring down at the blanket, studying the plaid pattern, blue stripes on a cream background, as if she were memorizing it. She picked at a ragged edge, wanting so much to tell him, to explain it to him, but unable to meet his eyes. "When everybody has this fancy new life, you know, and you're just a...a leftover from the old life, and there isn't anyplace you belong, no matter what you do, how hard you try. Anyplace you fit, where they...*want* you. Where if you were gone, they'd miss you. That they'd say," she said, her voice breaking a little despite her best efforts, "where's Mira? It's just not Christmas without Mira. It doesn't feel right without her here. Without her at home with us. So I've decided something too," she said fiercely, looking up at him, keeping her voice as even as she could, despite the treacherous tears that insisted on rising, threatened to spill. "I'm not going to be that person anymore. I'm not going to be wishing. I'm not going to hang around, trying to keep you happy, hoping that if I try hard enough, if I can somehow please you enough, you'll love me enough to want me forever, like some sad, desperate stray dog who's trying to be good so I won't be sent back to the pound. I'll live near you. And I'll love you. But I won't live with you."

critical moments

♡

Gabe scraped the razor over his throat and chin with the inadequate aid of the small age-spotted mirror hanging over the cabin's bathroom sink. And thought about Mira, everything she'd revealed to him yesterday, the raw vulnerability she'd exposed.

It was as if she had opened her chest, showed him her beating heart. He'd held her, kissed her, told her he loved her. Had wished he could go back and erase her past. Had wanted nothing more than to promise her a shiny new future. How could anyone who'd been given the gift of Mira toss it away like that? he wondered, angry all over again for her. He just couldn't wrap his head around it.

He finished shaving, put the razor and shaving cream neatly back into the medicine cabinet. Held onto the chipped porcelain sink for a moment, looked at himself in the mirror. At the man who was going to be doing his best from now on to deserve her trust, her loving heart.

"Your turn," he said, coming out into the bedroom again. "Although you look perfect to me now."

She smiled ruefully, got up from the bed where she'd been reading, already wearing the yellow dress she'd had on the first time he'd seen her, hanging a bit loosely on her now. Her hair pulled back on one side, the waves falling to her shoulders.

"That shows what you know," she said. "I'm not going back on camera without makeup. Not for the grand finale and my first time in the jury box. And not sitting next to Chelsea and Melody, I'm sure not." She came to him, reached up for a kiss that had him pulling her against him, forcing her up on tiptoe.

She dropped to her heels again, ran a soft hand over his smooth cheek. "I think I miss the stubble," she decided. "It's a good look for you."

He laughed. "It's a little bit caveman, though. And I've probably presented that side of myself enough on the show, not to mention to you. I do have a professional image to maintain, you know. It'd probably be a good idea to look a civilized, twenty-first century man at least once, instead of some kind of half-barbarian on testosterone overload."

"I predict," she said, her hand on his bare chest now, "that your...*image* isn't going to suffer one little bit from being on this show. And that every woman within a hundred miles is going to have an unfortunate sports injury that requires your immediate attention once this thing airs."

"Alec's the good-looking one," he reminded her, watching her from behind as she walked into the bathroom to begin the all-important makeup process. One of his favorite views. Well, that and the front view.

"Maybe so," he heard just before she closed the door. "But he's not the sexy one."

By the time she came out again, he'd pulled on the white button-down shirt she'd ironed for him, tucked it into his Levi's.

"We're ridiculously early," he told her. "You're not nearly high-maintenance enough. And we've both gotten way too used to getting up at five. We've still got an hour before breakfast. Plenty of time to climb back into bed and have some more sex to relax us first."

"Dream on," she said, showing him the sassy side he liked so much. "I'm not redoing all this makeup. Come on. Let's go see if we can get a cup of coffee."

♥

He was standing in the common room, examining the old tools and firearms hung on the wall, when he heard the sound of the door opening behind him.

"Hooray," he began to say, turning. "Breakfast." But it wasn't Alma kicking the door shut behind him. It wasn't Alma who had Gabe frozen to the spot, finding out what it meant to have your blood run cold.

It was Scott. Nothing of the smooth lawyer left about him now. His navy blue T-shirt and jeans wrinkled, hanging on him, looking as though he'd slept in them. His expression fixed, eyes burning with fury and hatred. No rationality left. And with a semiautomatic in his wavering hand.

He came across the room fast, stopped a cautious fifteen feet away and steadied the weapon with both hands so it pointed directly at Gabe's chest. Gabe stared down the barrel, the hole in the ugly black thing looming huge as he imagined in sickening detail what a bullet would do to him. What it would do to Mira.

Stay in the kitchen. It wasn't a thought. It was a prayer. *Please, Mira. Stay there.* His mind was racing. How long did it take to start a pot of coffee?

"Scott," he said, his voice sounding bizarrely calm in his ears, a contrast to his thundering heart. "What are you doing here?" *Keep him talking.* That was his only hope. Alma had to come in soon. Any moment, she'd open the door, give Gabe the couple of seconds' distraction he needed to rush the other man. Without that, the expanse of floor between them was too broad. Scott was too close to miss him, too far for him to grab.

Scott sneered at him, seeming to read his mind as he kept well back, out of Gabe's reach. "What do you think, asshole? I'm here to kill you. You and that bitch. I spent three nights in a jail cell like some kind of criminal. *Three nights,* just because she set me up, pushed me until I finally slapped her one lousy time. Three nights with the two of you laughing about me, thinking you'd beat me, thinking you'd won. But who's won now? Who's laughing now?" He laughed himself, the sound high-pitched and wrong. "Me, that's who. Because you're both dead."

Gabe caught the movement of the kitchen door to his left, just behind Scott. Kept his gaze fixed on the other man. *Oh, no. Please, God.*

"Scott. Listen. You don't want to kill us," he said loudly. *Run,* he prayed. *Run.* He saw the door pause in its opening in his peripheral vision, didn't dare to believe that she'd heard. "Nobody's laughing at you. You can turn around right now and we'll forget all about this. You don't want to do this."

Scott laughed again. "Oh, yeah. I do. I really do. Where is she? Where's that two-faced bitch?"

"Staying with Zara," Gabe improvised madly. "We had a fight, and she left me. She's sleeping over there." *Keep him talking,* he thought again. *Give Mira time to run for help.*

"Yeah, right," Scott scoffed. He staggered a little, and Gabe realized he was drunk. Had probably been up all night drinking, alone in his motel room, nursing his grievances. Why hadn't he anticipated this? Gabe thought in despair. Why hadn't he realized how far gone Scott was?

Scott was talking again now, and Gabe forced himself to listen, to concentrate. "She's not worth protecting, haven't you figured that out? She's nothing but a whore. And you know what's really great? You don't even have to pay her. She's so pathetically grateful for a little attention, all you have to do is talk nice to her and she'll fuck you. It's so easy."

Gabe forced himself not to react, kept his voice level with the greatest effort of his life. "You're right. She's not worth it. You can turn around, walk away right now and go on with your life. But if you shoot us, you're going to spend it in prison. It's not worth it. No woman's worth it."

"It's worth it to win," Scott insisted. "It's always worth it to win. And I've got news for you, asshole. I'm winning. Who's scared now? Who's losing now?"

"Me," Gabe admitted immediately. "You've won. I'm terrified. You've done it." Which was no more than the truth. His heart was galloping wildly, and he could feel the cold sweat of adrenaline under his arms, between his shoulder blades as his mind considered and rejected alternatives. He couldn't protect Mira if Scott shot him. His only chance was to keep him talking. "You've won," he said again. "You win. I lose."

"That's right, asshole. I win. And after I kill you, I'll find her. I wanted to kill her while you watched, but what the hell." Scott laughed again. "What the hell. You can't always get what you want. And I still get to listen to her beg. I'll get her on her knees, begging me for her life before I shoot her in the head. That'll be sweet. You can think about that while you die."

Gabe saw the intention in his face, the tightening in his arms, and dropped just before the gun went off, hit the ground and rolled, coming up fast and launching himself at Scott from across the room. Knowing it wouldn't work. That he was too far away. That even Scott couldn't miss again.

And, even as he did it, saw the door crash open behind Scott, saw the figure rushing forward like an avenging fury, swinging a piece of two-by-four like a baseball bat, screaming as she ran. Saw Scott whirling, the gun going off just as the solid piece of lumber connected with the side of his head. Saw him dropping like a stone, the heavy black weapon falling from his hand and hitting the floor with a *clunk*.

Gabe ran to the gun, scooped it up from the floor, ejected the magazine and racked the slide to collect the final round, stuffed loose round and magazine into his pocket, set the weapon on the table. Then turned to Mira where she stood over Scott's sprawled body, holding the two-by-four with hands that were visibly shaking now. Eyes wide, a red stain spreading rapidly from her left shoulder, soaking the yellow dress. And starting to laugh.

"Sorry," she told him on another shaky laugh, her voice high and unsteady with shock and pain. "Just...just taking out the trash."

a million dollars

♡

" W ay to create an anticlimax," Kevin complained, seated at last on the bench beside Mira. "This is supposed to be *my* moment."

Mira laughed. The painkillers made her a little fuzzy, made everything seem a little bit funnier, made her that much happier. "Sorry I got shot and messed up your grand finale."

The vote had had to be postponed, of course. Until the Sheriff's Department, the ambulances had shown up. Until Scott had been taken away, a reluctant examination by Gabe having confirmed that, to Mira's immense relief, she hadn't actually killed him. Until Gabe had ridden in the second ambulance with Mira, talked to the doctor at the hospital in Moscow as she sat there, the furrow along her shoulder bandaged, her head swimming with Vicodin and the aftermath of adrenaline.

And, of course, until the endless interviews with Ron, another deputy, and the Sheriff himself were over, and charges had been filed against Scott.

"Good news is," Ron told Gabe after they'd each been interviewed separately, again and again, and were sitting in the little room together, Gabe holding Mira's hand, "the D.A.'ll be dropping your case for sure now."

"Whoopee," Gabe said grimly. "Hell of a price to pay."

"Lucky he was such a lousy shot," Ron continued. "And that you've got somebody willing to go to bat for you." He smiled at Gabe. "So to speak. I'd say she's a keeper. I'd go home and ask my wife if she'd do that for me, but I'm afraid of what she'd say."

♡

But now that long day was over, it was another sunny August morning, and they were trying again. Assembled in the Clearing, and about to vote.

"Only eleven members of our jury now," Cliff said. "Well, it can't be a tie, anyway. And let me just remind you, you're voting *for* a team today. For the team you think deserves to win a million dollars."

"Me," Kevin whispered next to Mira. She smiled, but she knew who her vote was going to. And who was going to win.

One by one, the erstwhile contestants stood and walked to the voting booth. Mira held Gabe's hand, and ran a tally in her mind.

Chelsea. Stanley and Calvin, she guessed. She imagined that Rachel and Chelsea hadn't been the best of friends out here.

Melody. Stanley and Calvin again. Blame Kevin's sharp tongue for that, or credit Stanley's kind heart.

Arlene. Rachel and Kevin, probably, a bond formed in the kitchen. Unless Martin and Arlene had decided together, and Mira was willing to bet that Arlene had made an independent choice.

Martin. Stanley and Calvin for sure. One too many Martin-teases for that to go any other way.

Lupe. Rachel and Kevin, she'd bet, another kitchen vote, although she could be wrong.

Maria-Elena. Stanley and Calvin, the big man's comforting warmth winning him that one too.

Hank. Hard to say. He and Zara *would* have made a decision together. Rachel and Kevin had made the bigger journey, and Zara would have admired that.

Zara. Too close to call, but if Mira were forced to predict, she'd guess Rachel and Kevin.

Mira. She wrote down "Stanley and Calvin" without a second's hesitation. Yes, Kevin had surprised even himself out here, and she wished him nothing but the best. But she loved Stanley, and she had a sneaking suspicion that a fair amount of his prize would find its way to his beloved church. Who knew, maybe her vote would be buying new choir robes. She'd like to think of that.

Alec. Stanley and Calvin, she was sure.

Gabe. Stanley and Calvin. Neither of the brothers would have broken their word. There was too much of the PK in them for that. Even for Alec, as much as he liked to play the bad boy.

♡

And when the votes were finally counted, in fact, there were no surprises. Four votes appeared in quick succession for Rachel and Kevin, and Mira could feel Kevin tensing beside her. She'd been right, then. Hank and Zara had admired the siblings' effort out here, their ability to step out of their comfort zone and work so hard at something so unfamiliar. But Mira knew that those were the only four votes they would receive.

"And the winners of *America Alive 1885,* and a million dollars," Cliff announced, unfolding the final ballot and holding it up to the camera. "Stanley and Calvin."

"Well, damn," Kevin said. Then stood and, to Mira's relief, shook Stanley's hand.

♡

"Here's the question I have," Cliff said twenty minutes later, after the winners had been congratulated, the vote dissected, and Mira's analysis, to her immense gratification, proven absolutely correct. "Did Gabe and Alec really walk away from a million dollars? Let's have a show of hands. If it'd been Rachel and Kevin, Gabe and Alec at the end, who votes Gabe and Alec?"

Seven hands went up.

"Well, that's pretty convincing," Cliff said. "And if it'd been Stanley and Calvin against Gabe and Alec?"

He paused to count. "Six. Close, but still a win. Alec, how does that feel? To know that you probably turned down half a million dollars for your brother? You notice I'm not asking Gabe how he feels. I have a fairly good idea of what his answer would be."

"It's a twin thing," Alec smiled. "You wouldn't understand."

"Fair enough," Cliff conceded. "But I'll just say here, since all the voting's over, that you don't exactly need the money, do you?" He reached down, pulled up a copy of *Inc.* magazine, held it up so the contestants, and the camera, could see. "This face look familiar? In fact," he told a stunned group, "Alec's one of those dot-com millionaires we hear so much about. You just sold your latest venture to Google, for, what was the figure?"

"Sorry," Alec grinned. "Confidential."

"Did that ease the pain of turning your back on the money a little?" Cliff pressed.

"Well, the money part, sure," Alec conceded. "But the losing part? Nope. Ol' Dog Head still owes me for that. And he's going to keep owing me for a long, long time."

"Next question," Cliff went on. "This one's for Mira. You've been burned out here. Been hit in the face. Been shot at twice. Been *shot.* Are you the unluckiest *America Alive* contestant ever, or what?"

She smiled at him serenely, not sure if her continued blissful mood was the Vicodin, or escaping death, or just the pure pleasure of sitting with Gabe, holding his hand, and knowing that he was safe here with her. That she'd saved him. That she loved him, and he loved her, and Scott was locked up where he couldn't get to either of them.

"No," she said. "No, I'd say just the opposite. That I'm the luckiest woman in the world."

"That's a pretty good testimonial, Gabe," Cliff commented. "How do you feel about that?"

"Undeserving," Gabe said with an unsteady laugh. "Humbled. And like the luckiest *man* in the world. I came out here for a million dollars. And instead, I found a woman I now know beyond the shadow of a doubt I'd give my life for. And you know what's really incredible? I know she'd give hers for me too. Because she almost did." His hand tightened around Mira's.

"What do you think, Stanley?" he went on, turning to the big man beside him. "You know a thing or two about love. What do you think a man should do when he finds somebody who won't just put up with him, but who'll put her life on the line for him?"

"I'd say," Stanley said, his deep voice rumbling with satisfaction, "that you'd better hustle up and put a ring on that."

"What a good idea." Gabe got up, turned to Mira. "You OK to stand up for a minute?" he asked her, the tender expression on his face an arrow to her heart.

"Yeah," she whispered. She was aware of the cameras zooming in on them, the other contestants turning to look at them. But she could only see Gabe.

He helped her to her feet, turned her to face him.

"I love you," he said simply. "I think I started falling in love with you the first moment I saw you. When you turned around and smiled at me because you saw something beautiful, and you wanted to share it with me. And all that beauty you saw was reflected in your face, because it was coming up from your beautiful heart. I love you," he went on, "and I want you with me forever, as long as I live. Because…" He smiled down at her, and she saw the tears glinting in his blue eyes, "my life just wouldn't be the same without Mira. Because it wouldn't be Christmas without Mira."

He reached into his pocket, pulled out the worn velvet box and flipped it open. "This was my grandmother's. She gave it to me before she died, and she told me, when I found somebody I loved as much as she loved my grandfather, that I should give it to her. But that I should wait until it was the right one."

His voice became a little less level as he went on. "And I asked her, 'How will I know? How will I know she's the right one?' And she said, 'You're going to know. When it's right, you'll be sure.' We can replace the diamond with something bigger. And I know it hasn't been long, that we still have a lot to talk about, a lot to figure out. But..." He took a deep breath, dropped to one knee, right there in the dirt of the Clearing. "She was right. I'm sure. So I asked my dad to send this to me last week. Because I knew then that I wanted to ask you to marry me. And here I am, in front of everybody, putting my heart in your hands. I'm asking you to wear my ring, and be my wife." He laughed up at her, just a little shakily. "What do you think? Will you marry me?"

"Oh, Gabe." She reached for an apron that, she realized, for once wasn't there. "Yes. And no." She saw the startled look on his face and laughed through her tears. "Yes, I'll marry you. Because I love you too, more than I can say. More than I'll ever be able to say. And I'm sure too. I'm so sure. But I don't want to change anything about this ring. If it was good enough for your grandmother, if she was happy wearing it, it's good enough for me."

She watched the smile blooming now as he took her left hand gently in his, slid the ring onto it, rose to take her in his arms. She smiled back at him, then closed her eyes and held him tight. The way she'd be holding him forever, every minute of every day. So he could stop what he was doing, sometimes, to feel it. So he could feel her loving him.

He kissed her, and she kissed him back, again and again, while Stanley beamed his approval. And the rest of the contestants, and Cliff too, began to applaud. And Danny filmed the whole thing.

epilogue

♡

Ten months later
"You realize," she murmured, still in his arms, "that you've just broken the hearts of millions of women."

By the time the show had got halfway through its season, Gabe had begun to receive dozens, then hundreds of messages every week, forwarded by the network. Emails, and letters, and...pictures. *Lots* of pictures. The network had been ecstatic, of course. Female viewership of the show was up. *Way* up. He and Mira had turned down an offer from *People* for their wedding photos, and Gabe actually *had* received an offer of a spot as a TV doctor that he had declined without a bit of regret.

"You getting this, Danny?" he demanded now. "Want me to kiss the bride one more time for you?"

"Gabe..." He got the usual exasperated sigh. They had agreed to have their ceremony filmed today, on the condition that Danny do the filming. He'd captured every other bit of their courtship, after all. Well, *almost* every bit.

"I know, I know," Gabe said with a grin. "I'm supposed to ignore you. And I'm supposed to pay attention to my wife. My wife," he repeated slowly. He looked up at his dad, standing patiently before them, an understanding smile on his face, the battered Bible that was part of him held firmly in both big hands. Closed, now, its job done.

Gabe turned to Mira again, bent to kiss her one more time before beginning the walk up the aisle. "What was that about hearts?" he asked her. "I got all distracted there. Must be being a husband. It's a pretty new feeling."

She smiled up at him, her eyes misty with a love that humbled him in its intensity, its generosity and courage. "I said," she repeated, "that you've broken a lot of hearts today."

"There's only one heart that matters to me from now on," he promised. "That's the only one I care about." The one that had been offered so freely and fully into his keeping. The one he had just vowed to love and to cherish, to have and to hold, from this day forward, as long as they both did live. The one he'd live for, from now on. The one he'd die for.

Hers.

The End

Sign up for my New Release mailing list at
www.rosalindjames.com/mail-list to be notified
of special pricing on new books, sales, and more.

Find out what's new at the **ROSALIND JAMES WEBSITE.**
http://www.rosalindjames.com/

"Like" my **Facebook** page at facebook.com/rosalindjamesbooks
or follow me on **Twitter** at twitter.com/RosalindJames5
to learn about giveaways, events, and more.
Want to tell me what you liked, or what I got wrong? I'd love
to hear! You can email me at **Rosalind@rosalindjames.com**

by rosalind james

Cover design by Robin Ludwig Design Inc.,
http://www.gobookcoverdesign.com/

Turn the page for a preview of the next book in the series!
Read on for an excerpt from
Nothing Personal
(The Kincaids, Book Two)

prologue

♡

Desiree was cold. She was so cold.

Her head hurt really bad, too, like something sharp was pounding into it. She tried to raise her hand to touch it, but the pain sliced through her chest, hot and hard, at the movement.

"Mommy," she whimpered. "Hurts. Mommy."

She could hear noises, long, low groans, but it was dark, and she couldn't see. Then she heard the voice, not mad anymore. Scared.

"Lacey? You OK? Lace?"

Desiree was scared too, so scared she couldn't have moved even if it hadn't hurt so bad. She was crying now, the tears trickling, warm and wet, down her icy cheeks. And she kept moaning. She couldn't help it. The same word, over and over.

"Mommy. Mommy."

♡

She woke up clammy with sweat, not sure if she'd said it aloud or not. The tears were there, hot, salty rivulets exactly like the ones in the dream, and the cold was the same too.

Because she'd kicked off her comforter, that was why, and the temperature had dropped, the previous day's sunshine merely the false promise of late October.

The sadness dragged at her, black and heavy, trying to take her down, under the waves. But she couldn't afford that, especially not right now.

She reached a hand out for the switch of the bedside lamp, sat up in the pool of light cast by the pretty frosted art glass shade. Swung her feet to the soft surface of the area rug beside her bed and stood, shivering a little in the chilly bedroom. Pulled off her wet undershirt and dropped it into the wicker hamper, found another one in the top drawer of the mahogany bureau, settled it into place, and immediately felt better, less chilled. She sat down again and took a long drink of water from the glass on the bedside table, then switched the lamp off and scooted to the other side of the bed, the clean, never-used side. Pulled the sheet and down comforter up, making herself a cozy nest against the cold and dark.

The dream, sure sign of anxiety, still hovered around the edges of her mind, threatening the sleep she needed if she were going to be at her best the next day. And that wasn't going to work, so she set about replacing the dark images with a meticulous catalogue of every feature of her cottage. The chandelier in the living room, the rug with its floral pattern in shades of dusty rose and soft green, the small hand-painted wooden table that sat beside her couch.

By the time she got to the robin's-egg blue of her stove, she was fading. The last thing she saw before sleep took her was the antique glass doorknob of her bedroom, the rubbed, dark bronze fittings around it. Leading into this room, where she was warm. Where she was safe.

coffee break

♡

"Shoot."

Alec heard the soft exclamation, the clatter of multiple small objects hitting stone, and turned. Well, he turned the rest of the way, anyway. Because he'd already been half-watching her, had seen the moment when the important-man-in-a-hurry had bumped into her as she reached the doorway to the lobby, causing her to lose her hold on her purse in her haste to secure her coffee and laptop case.

Now, she crouched as best she could in the slim skirt and narrow heels, scrambling to retrieve the bag's contents, spilling out over the polished granite floor of the high-rise office building.

Alec stepped out of line and bent to grab a rolling lipstick, a tumbling apple. Handed them to her along with a little notebook, a couple of pens, the energy bar and the tiny container of Tic-Tacs. He let her pick up the travel toothbrush, the metal case with the pinup girl on it. He was pretty sure that was for tampons, because his sister had the same one, and that she'd rather get it herself.

"Thanks," she said, looking up with a smile that turned a little frozen when she met his eyes. That was puzzling. She looked down again, finished stuffing items back into her purse, picked up her cup of coffee from the floor where she'd set it, and straightened.

He stood along with her. She was taller than he'd realized, her slimness causing him to misjudge her height from a distance. Only three or four inches shorter than his six-two in her heels, and they weren't that high. He'd already checked them out, along with the rest of her. Gorgeous honey-colored skin, great bone structure, clearly visible with her hair pulled back into a businesslike twist. Classy all the way around, in a deep brown suit with a pencil skirt and belted jacket that showed off her figure, and that he'd been appreciating. A deep yellow top underneath the jacket that contrasted with her auburn hair. And, he realized as he kept looking into them, a pair of truly spectacular eyes.

Tiger eyes. Brown flecked with gold, a deeper brown edging the rim. Tilting up at the outer corners, and he didn't think it was just the eyeliner. And he was staring.

"Thanks," she said again with a brief smile.

"Got your lunch, anyway," he offered. It was lame, he knew, but he had to say something, because he didn't want to let her get away.

"Yeah." She smiled a bit at that. "Didn't spill my coffee, that's the main thing."

Her voice was low, soft. Sweet. A little husky. Her voice said *sex.* Long slow kisses and cool white wine. And, much later, tangled sheets and breath returning to a heaving chest. That feeling you had when you were lying beside the woman who had just taken you all the way around the world.

Yeah, that's what her voice was saying. But those tiger eyes weren't saying anything of the kind. They were wary, watchful. The full, soft lips, painted a conservative rose, were curved in a cool smile.

Her voice said *touch me.* And her eyes said *don't you dare.* It was all very confusing. And the hair was standing up at the back of his neck. Something about her...Something...

"You've lost your place," she pointed out. "Go get your coffee. Thanks again." She turned and left the shop without looking back.

He considered following her, gave it up after a split second's hesitation, and went to get back in line. He had a meeting coming up, and the shot of caffeine would help, though he didn't really need it. He was fired up, and he was ready.

Because he wasn't some nerdy programmer, tongue-tied at the sight of a beautiful, confident woman. He was Alec Kincaid, poised at the start of yet another spectacularly successful venture, Master of the Universe.

And his touch was gold.

it's not personal, it's business

♡

"So there you have it," Alec said three hours later, sweeping the conference table with a glance that made brief contact with each of the venture capital firm's board members. He offered his best dazzling smile, proven one hundred percent effective to date in three out of three road shows exactly like this one. "That's Hal. The best virtual assistant software ever, the one that's going to reset the bar. Just a little something that'll change the world as we know it."

"You're asking for ten million." That was Ron Jacobs, EnVisitech Capital's managing partner. "That's over 120 percent more second-round funding than last time."

"Because it's 200 percent more project than the last one," Alec answered smoothly. Objection One, right off the bat, just as he'd anticipated. "And if you look back at Page 17, we're projecting a five-year ROI that's more than 250 percent higher than the projections I showed you three years ago. And that one paid off pretty well, as I recall."

"It did," Ron agreed, as the rest of the board looked back through their presentation packets, or gazed at Alec with unreadable expressions. "But there were some bumps in the road."

Alec made a dismissive gesture. "There are always bumps. Show me a startup without any bumps, and I'll show you...Well," he laughed, "I can't even show you one, can I? Because they don't exist. But we'll sail right over those bumps. We've done it before, and we'll do it again."

Ron exchanged a glance with the man to his left, a finance wizard named Calvin Tang whom Alec had never cared for much. Buttoned up, like all finance guys. Focusing too much on the bottom line, and losing sight of the top line, of the limitless revenue potential that would pay the bills, and make all of them rich. Alec forced himself into patience, never his strong suit, and waited.

"We'd like a little more documentation. A little more... insurance. Regular assurance that AI Solutions is on track, and is going to stay that way," Ron said after a pause.

"Whatever you like," Alec promised easily. "We've got a new Ops guy just about to come on board who's got some pretty fantastic credentials, and we're ready to roll. You'll see all the reports you could wish for."

"We've got an alternative arrangement in mind," Ron said, and the look in his eye left Alec in no doubt, despite the mildness of his words, that he meant business. Ron wasn't a yeller, but he hadn't got where he was by being soft.

"Rae Harlin," he said now.

"Ray Harlin?" Alec said blankly. "Who's he?"

Ron smiled a little. "You've never heard of Rae Harlin? Not exactly keeping up with your industry journals, are you? Quite the up-and-comer, Rae, with all due respect to your candidate."

"On the technical side, I'd say I'm pretty current," Alec said, keeping his cool with some effort. "Operations, I'll grant you, I'm not up on all the latest." And he'd been out of the loop for a while, but that wasn't the kind of thing you reminded people about. Not when you were asking them for millions of dollars, you didn't.

"Exactly," Ron said. "Hence the insurance." He rose from his richly padded black leather chair with athletic ease, reminding Alec that Ron, despite the gray hair, still played handball three times a week.

The older man stepped around the deeply polished mahogany table, walked across the large conference room with its panoramic view over the San Francisco skyline, and opened an interior door, leaning inside for a few words. Then stood back and held the door for a woman who walked past him and seated herself composedly, raising her gaze politely to Ron and waiting for him to continue.

Alec was never at a loss, but he was at a loss now. It was the woman from the coffee shop. What was she doing here?

"Meet the fourth member of your executive team," Ron said. "Rae Harlin, your new CFO."

"Oh, *hell* no." That was Joe, on Alec's left. The words were muttered, but Alec heard them. He'd been listening to Joe mutter since their freshman year of college. When he was writing code, Joe's patience was limitless. And when he wasn't, he could get a little…intense. He wasn't happy now, and neither was Alec.

"I have a candidate," Alec insisted. "A good one. You can see his resume on Page 34." He recited from memory, as always. "I prefer—*we* prefer to choose our own team." His glance to left and right took in not only Joe, but Brandon Matthews, in charge of sales and marketing for their fourth new venture. Fourth time lucky, Alec could feel it. Just like the third time, and the two before that.

"You can choose your own team, if you like," Ron agreed. His tone was affable, his eyes weren't. "And look for funding someplace else."

"We've done well with you, Alec," he went on when Alec would have retorted. "This isn't personal, it's business. At this level of risk, we want accountability. And we want adult supervision."

"Adult supervision," Alec repeated.

"That's right," Ron said. "We know you're good on the tech side, and so is your team. But it's not a frat house, and it's not somebody's garage. It's serious money, and serious business. We want to back your venture, but it's up to you. Accountability that satisfies us, or find yourself other funding."

"And, Alec," he said, pulling the younger man aside when, at last, the meeting was over. After Alec had pulled the mask back on, smiled and shaken hands across the table with Rae Harlin—who'd still barely spoken a word, just fixed those tiger eyes on him in a level, assessing gaze that he found oddly disconcerting—and promised her he'd call her later in the day to set up a time to meet. When she'd left the room with the rest of Ron's group and Alec's two partners, and Alec was preparing to do the same.

"I'm saying this to you alone," Ron said now. "But I'm saying it seriously. This part *is* personal. Keep it zipped. This industry's about to hit a wave of sexual harassment litigation that's going to make the last couple decades look like a company picnic. Companies have got to start toeing the line, or it's going to come back to bite them. That's one reason I insisted—and make no mistake, *I'm* the one who insisted—on Rae. You've always kept the work under wraps, though she'll be keeping a good eye on data security too. But privately, or not so privately, you—you personally—have earned yourself one hell of a reputation. Don't let it screw you up, or screw us up, or you'll regret it."

"I've never harassed a woman in my life." Alec forced the words out through lips that had stiffened. What I do in my personal time is nobody's business but my own."

"Then," Ron said, "we have nothing to worry about, have we?"

♡

acknowledgments

Many people assisted in the research for this book. However, any errors or omissions are my own. My sincere thanks to (in alphabetical order):

Carpentry: Jake Druffel, Mike McRae (Jake, thanks for actually going out and throwing an axe for me! You are awesome!)

Farm life/Palouse history/Natural history: Alma Druffel, Bernie Druffel, Jake Druffel, John Druffel, Charlotte Iiams, Erika Iiams, Elizabeth Sullivan

Firearms: Rick Dalessio; Keita Moriwaki, SFPD; Bob Pryor; Jennifer A. Roybal, Certified Firearms Instructor

Fighting: Jake Druffel (Maybe start knowing less about this one, OK?)

Legal issues: The Hon. Barbara Buchanan

Reality show strategy and structure: Bob Pryor (Sorry, Bob: I stick to my guns that astronauts are not sexy!)

Wildlife: Rick Dalessio

As always, my heartfelt thanks to my awesome critique group: Barbara Buchanan, Carol Chappell, Anne Forell, and Bob Pryor.

And, of course, to my husband, Rick Nolting, who sat across the kitchen table and talked out the idea of this book with me, and whose support, encouragement, and love are what started me writing and have pulled me through every doubt and fear since.

Cover design by Robin Ludwig Design Inc.,
http://www.gobookcoverdesign.com/

www.ingramcontent.com/pod-product-compliance
Lightning Source LLC
Chambersburg PA
CBHW051320250626
47155CB00007B/2390